To Sheila who can be held responsible for this and other books being written

The Swaying Sixties

R.T. Cain

R T Cain '08

authorHOUSE®

AuthorHouse™ UK Ltd.
500 Avebury Boulevard
Central Milton Keynes, MK9 2BE
www.authorhouse.co.uk
Phone: 08001974150

© *2007 R.T. Cain. All rights reserved.*

No part of this book may be reproduced, stored in a retrieval system, or transmitted by any means without the written permission of the author.

First published by AuthorHouse 12/31/2007

ISBN: 978-1-4343-5285-9 (sc)

Printed in the United States of America
Bloomington, Indiana

This book is printed on acid-free paper.

Table of Contents

Foreword	vii
"Now you've had it in black and white!."	1
"Everything all right Jenny?."	19
"Can you stand on your hands?."	29
"No you mean Billy Dawes is her 'cockeyed' Granddad."	47
"Well….I'm sure he's filling them with confidence."	55
"O.K. then……..Let battle commence."	67
"Sounds too good to be cockeyed true to me."	83
"I hope that score won't count as a record Vic."	93
"I feel sure we are unanimous."	101
"Hey steady on Alf….Play the game."	111
"How do you mean Peggy…You were selected?."	123
"All above board……..Documents to prove it."	131
"You deserve a medal Norman."	141
"Don't be daft Ricky….I'd love to."	153
"The double seats are always the first to go."	161
"Oh……Are you sure it was me?."	179
"That's nothing to be ashamed of."	187
"Is there anything the Trust could do for you Bert?."	195
"I'm too much of a lady to repeat his actual instructions."	203
"And we thought this was just another ordinary day."	217
"Look there's no need for panic…"	223
"The drinks are on the house….Steady now!!!!."	231
"I must have been soft asking you Lenny."	235
"Worry not my son…..Worry not."	243

"If I'd hadn't seen it with my own eyes.... I wouldn't have believed it."	247
"Just find a cubicle....Doctor will see you in a minute."	253
"ME?.....There's nothing wrong with me Arnie...."	265
"Don't worry Mavis....I won't let you forget."	269
"I think someone has been pulling your leg."	275
"There are more urgent priorities than a van Lad."	279
"I think I'd rather have my leg off."	285
"Good afternoon Reverend....How nice to see you."	293
"It's great to see old Billy back in circulation again."	305
"Why me?........WHY ME!!!!?."	313
"Come on give us a kiss and lend us a shilling."	317
"What was the problem?....Not enough milk?"	325
"Carry on please.....Everything is under control."	333
"Natural has got to be best."	343
"I'm not here to cause any sort of trouble."	347
"Not a dirty dish to be seen and spotless."	355
"O.K.....Time I pulled my finger out."	363
"Quite a character old Mabel Brooks."	369
"Everything arranged for the Christening Ricky?."	375
"Thank you Gentlemen....That appears to be unanimous."	381
"It's a pity they didn't knock me back in 1944.."	389
"Bert McCabe.....You're one in a million."	393
"And that's for forty years after you die."	405
"I'm sure that was just a slip of the tongue."	417
"We always insist on things being done in the traditional way."	425
"Thank you............Thank you...."	433

Foreword

Probably because I was born in 1940 I was able to enjoy my most formative and productive years during the 1960's.

I sincerely feel, without the slightest doubt, the 1960's was the most exciting, enjoyable and memorable decade the entire Twentieth Century had to offer.

Ask any person what they know about the 1960's, either from their own personal experiences or by what they may have read, heard or been told. I can almost guarantee the chances are that somewhere along the line they will make some affectionate reference to "The Swinging Sixties".

Generally speaking we tend to reflect upon the whole era as being synonymous with revolutionary Political and Social changes in our Country especially in individual attitudes towards freedom within newly formed bounds of acceptability and decency. This led to new levels of overt personal expressionism, both in conduct, music and, perhaps most strikingly, in the mode of dress. The influence of popular music had an unexpectedly profound, vibrant and vital place in the new structure of day to day life and living. Perhaps some may think of the Mini, not just the car but also the skirt, which was more of a pelmet than an item of clothing.

Not many would challenge the legitimate claim that this era deserves it's cheeky reputation and catchy, memorable, name. There is no doubt the happenings at that time have had a intense and permanent influence upon our Modern Society particularly in the general attitude of many younger people.

Yet the overwhelming majority of those fortunate enough to live through this decade were, like myself, blissfully unaware of all these dramatic changes taking place. Most of us continued to pursue our own traditionally accepted standards in attitudes towards our morals and conduct. We still found our own very wide ranging forms of entertainment completely ignorant of any of the pressures being slowly but surely exerted mainly by a small, soon to be very wealthy, group of entrepreneurs initially based in the, the then newly identified, trendier parts of London and eventually in some of our other major Cities.

The bulk of our populace tended to remain secure and contented within our strong community based social structure with it's incumbent limitations on individual expression, choice and acceptable codes of conduct.

Now, in the Twenty First Century, we all enjoy higher standards of living with greater individual prosperity and social freedom. Yet, in the process, have we evolved into a commercially driven, selfish and less empathetic Society where community life, as such, no longer commands a prominent place in the order of our day to day lives?.

Maybe, like me, you may mourn the passing of those happy, less trend driven, days long before habitual drug abuse, outrageous criminal conduct and gratuitous street violence became a constant cause for concern and stress and, for many, sheer misery. People in the sixties expected much less from life. They were more content with what they actually had. They were not familiar with the legitimate modern illness, ironically diagnosed as, 'Stress'.

What I want you to do now is simply sit back, make yourself comfortable, and relax. Please allow me to transport you back to the 1960's to experience everyday life in a typical small Town situated on the old Lancashire/Yorkshire County Boundaries up in the North West of England.

You must be the Judge but after experiencing a very intimate insight into the day to day lives of a close knit group of ordinary Folk living in the Sixties over a period of a year or so you may also consider the decade should be renamed, "The Swaying Sixties". Perhaps you may even join me in feeling an intense personal yearning, from time to time, when the various Characters bring tears of genuine, old fashioned, laughter to your eyes because of their natural, unspoilt, humour or on other occasions through their enchanting charm and pathos.

"Now you've had it in black and white!"

Situated in a desirable location close to the Town Centre of the small Lancashire Mill Town of Lapley Vale the Lapley Vale Bowling and Social Club is well known to anyone who enjoys even the slightest local knowledge of the area.

Although, when viewed from the outside, the ageing, single storey Clubhouse appears to be quite drab and run down, even by the 1960's standards, and admittedly, is even less inviting when seen from the inside, Lapley Vale Bowling and Social Club enjoys one exceptional and outstanding feature. Their Crown Bowling Green is the finest for many miles around. In the biased opinion of many of the local people, especially Members of the Club, the Green is the best, of it's kind, in the whole of South East Lancashire.

There is little doubt that the Bowling Green is a remarkably good one. This deserved distinction is almost entirely due to the dedication and skill of an eccentric character named Woody Green. The devoted Woody has willingly given his sweat and knowledge to the preservation of the excellence of the quality of the grass and surroundings of his beloved Bowling Green for as long as anyone can remember. In addition to his fame as a Green Keeper Woody is also respected as one of the finest exponents of the art of Crown Green Bowling in the vicinity. It is difficult to estimate Woody's age. He is probably in his mid to late fifties. A staunch bachelor he lives alone in his own small terraced house which is situated across the road from, and within sight of, the

Clubhouse. His entire daily life revolves around a manicured square of grass. In the evenings, without fail, he drinks beer with a group of his closest friends in the Clubhouse. Woody is not well paid for his services but anyone who knows him could tell you that Woody would willingly done his job for nothing. This is a pure example of a labour of love.

With just over a month to go before the opening games of the Crown Green Bowling Summer Season of 1961 the Club and it's Members are facing, what could only be described as, grave financial difficulties. The Chairman, Ralph Jones, a retired, small time, Building Contractor, has been forced to call an emergency meeting of the Club Committee. In his middle sixties Ralph is not a very rich man. In the opinion of some people this is possibly as a result of his fondness for strong drink and Crown Green Bowling. However, Ralph is a lifelong supporter of the Lapley Vale Bowling and Social Club and is held with due regard, able to command the necessary respect as the Club's Chairman. Having held his office for more than five years Ralph is well aware that a gradual erosion of the Club's finances has been occurring for some time.

The Emergency Meeting has been called for 3.30pm and the punctual Members of the Committee have duly assembled in the Snooker Room inside the Clubhouse well before the appointed time. The full time Club Steward, Alf Morgan, always prepared the Snooker Room for Committee Meetings by placing a large sheet of plywood over the top of the snooker table, which gave it a passing resemblance to a very large desk. The Members of the Committee are obliged to sit around the "desk" on bar stools because of the height of the table. Alf has been the Steward at the Club for a number of years. In his late fifties, Alf had taken up, what he considered to be, another labour of love, when he retired to return to his home Town after a long career in H.M Royal Navy. He is honest and trusted. He works very hard in the interests of the Club and consequently enjoys respect and popularity from the Members of the Club and the Committee alike. He is always present at Meetings because he holds a non-voting advisory status on the Committee.

The Secretary and Treasurer is Vic Callow, a rather insignificant, some people thought boring, man in his late sixties. As a retired Bank Clerk Vic had been the obvious choice for the positions he proudly holds. Vic is articulate in the extreme. He consciously attempts to hide his natural local accent by using big, impressive, words. He also quotes poetry and philosophises quite regularly. Unfortunately he frequently quotes out of context and rather badly but is able to get away with it in his usual company because most of them do not have a clue what he is talking about in the first place. Vic is also completely devoted to the Club and it's Members spending most of his time attending to the Club's business and affairs. Because of his position Vic is only too well aware of the difficulties facing the Club's current finances. Possibly due to his submissive past, as a fairly insignificant and lowly ranked person within the Banking Profession, Vic is well schooled in the art of self preservation and unashamedly sucks up to Ralph, the Chairman, at every opportunity.

The other three elected Members of the Committee are each characters in their own rights. Eddie Brown is a retired Mill Worker in his mid sixties. A polite and very well mannered man at all times Eddie is a respected and trusted representative for the Members who voted him onto the Committee. Although he was born in the West Indies, Eddie has lived and worked in Lapley Vale for many years. Whenever possible Eddie avoids personal confrontation and arguments. He normally votes with the majority and invariably gives his support and loyalty to Ralph, the Chairman.

There is always one person on every Committee who will try their hardest to be obstructive to the other Members as a matter of principle. Bernie Price fills this role adequately. Bernie, a retired Textile Worker also in his sixties, is well known as an outspoken and even loudmouthed character. As a minor Trade Union Official in his working days he feels obliged to be confrontational whenever possible. Bernie is always ready to criticise anything and anyone but rarely says or does anything on his own initiative.

Last but by no means least the final Member of the Committee is Billy 'Cockeye' Dawes. Billy is around the seventy mark and has been retired from his lifelong employment as a Council Workman for a number of years. He is known to everyone as 'Cockeye' because of his frequent use of the word. Having been forbidden to curse or swear by his wife Billy developed the habit of substituting the word 'Cockeyed' whenever he meant to curse or swear. Judging by his common use of the word in almost every sentence he uttered perhaps his wife knew exactly what she was doing. Although Billy is a likeable man who is prepared to work hard for the Club he is limited and rarely meets with much success. He is especially disliked by Bernie Price who considers Billy to be an idiot on his better days.

So the scene is now set. Although Lapley Vale is a mere three hundred miles to the north of London on the map of England, Carnaby Street and all the other trimmings of the famous "Swinging Sixties" scene might well be on the Moon as far the vast majority of the good Folks of Lapley Vale are concerned. As a matter of fact this comment could adequately describe most of the Great British People especially those living outside the Capital of London however, let me get on with the story. Please read on:

* * *

Ralph is seated at the head of the table. He raps the wooden surface with his knuckles to bring the Meeting to order as soon as Vic eloquently concludes relating the depressing factual contents of his Financial Report to the attention of the responsive but stunned Committee. There is no disguising the gloomy ambience throughout the room. Ralph attempts to lift spirits by speaking with a forced, yet encouraging, tone in his voice.

"Well...Thank you Mr Secretary...and...Er of course Mr Treasurer as well because you're...Er both...Er...Yes."

Vic acknowledges his Chairman with a polite smile.

"For…Er…Completing the sad and depressing but nevertheless… Er…Necessary formalities…Yes…Very well presented Vic…Er…As usual."

Vic blushes slightly as he glances around the table, smiling weakly as Ralph continues.

"I'm sure that none of us here present can be left in any doubt whatsoever as to the very sorry plight of our beloved Club."

Everyone sadly nods their agreement.

"Far from breaking even…As we might have wished and hoped…. We seem to be steadily dropping further and even deeper into the shi… Er…Mire…I fear we must face this as a fact Gentlemen…However… Chins up…Never say die…Let us try to be positive…Eh?…Surely there must be a way out of this mess…Our beloved Club has been in existence for more than 50 odd years and I dare say that we've seen some bad times before in the past but we're still here…EH?…And where there's life there's hope…Eh? What say you Gentlemen of the Committee?."

True to form Bernie sits back on his stool clearly radiating his overall contempt as he speaks.

"And that's probably more by good luck than good management if you ask my opinion…Talk about organising Piss-ups in bloody Breweries."

He throws his head back in disgust before he lurches forward to venomously add.

"Let me tell you this…"

Ralph interrupts him firmly.

"O.K. Bernie…O.K…Let's not get overheated and allow things to get out of hand…Eh?…Correct me if I'm wrong but I seem to recall asking you to be positive…Eh?…Now Please let's all keep calm and examine all the possibilities."

Bernie growls as he shrugs his shoulders before sitting back on his stool. Eddie Brown nods his agreement with the Chairman's remarks as he decides to speak.

"Here… Here… Yes…Of course you're quite right Mr Chairman…… Nothing will be gained by conducting a slanging match…We must pull ourselves together and haul ourselves back onto a firm piece of ground."

Bernie sneers as he interrupts.

"Yes...O.K...Well alright…...Where do we start? Eh…..That's the burning question...Eh?.. Where...I said… Where do we begin?."

Bernie turns his gaze on Billy Dawes, who looks defensive in anticipation of an imminent personal attack. Bernie adopts a mocking tone.

"I suppose Billy here will be helping us out will he?...What wonderful cash raising ideas have you got for us today Billy?...Another Sportsman's Night is it?."

Bernie pauses momentarily as Billy drops his head in a submissive manner. It is obvious that the others are far from impressed by Bernie's attitude and performance but this does not deter him.

"What a balls up...What a monumental 'Tits up' night that was... Eh?...I wonder if we'll ever be able to get our Members to come in here ever again...Ever...After that bloody fiasco..."

Billy is obliged to defend himself but in all fairness he does experience some difficulty trying to sound convincing.

"Just a cockeyed minute there Mister...I don't hear you coming up with many brilliant ideas...Anyways...Who said it was a cockeyed fiasco?"

Bernie almost falls off his stool in his eagerness to respond. He spits his words out with venom directed at the hapless Billy.

"Listen Billy!...That Sportsman's Night was nothing less than a 22 carat fiasco...Listen...You Bloody Stump!.......You're supposed to have Celebrities attending a 'Do' like that…....Or at the very least...A Celebrity...What a bloody fiasco!."

To everyone's relief Ralph intervenes.

"Now hang on Bernie...Billy did his best...He was let down badly... But I'm not sure the evening was a total loss."

Bernie can hardly believe his ears. Sounding even more annoyed as his voice gradually rises in volume.

"Let down!...LET BLOODY DOWN!...I don't believe he ever intended to invite any well known Celebrities."

Bernie glances around looking for signs of support but there are none. Once again, this does not deter him.

"That Bloke...That Bloke Billy...You know?.....The Bloke you brought with you...The one you brought with you to get pissed at our expense?."

Bernie glares at the now cowering Billy.

"I very much doubt if many of us know very much about Accrington Stanley especially since they are no longer in the bloody Football League at all...EH?...Never mind that he was suppose to have been one of their top scorers in 1930 something...Come on Billy the whole thing was nothing short of an Ocean Going Fiasco!........Just a bloody good excuse for you and some of your lesser known Cronies to indulge yourselves in a free piss-up!."

Eddie can hardly hide his contempt for the manner in which Bernie is conducting himself. He feels obliged to rally to Billy's support. Attempting to be fair he adopts a rather defensive approach.

"Yes...Well O.K. Bernie...I think we all have to accept that a lot of the Members who attended our Sportsman's Night were quite disappointed but at the very least Billy is not afraid to give things a try and we can't expect miracles to happen all at once...Anyways...Let's not forget there was that dog...That caused a lot of interest...Mick the Miller was it?."

Bernie almost falls off his stool laughing at the final remark made by Eddie. Alf, smiling, tries to be helpful.

"Unfortunately Eddie I don't think too many people were very impressed there...You see....."

Bernie rudely interrupts Alf in mid sentence.

"Mick the Miller?...MICK THE MILLER?...My arse!."

Bernie glances around the table again realising that Eddie has played right into his hands. He adopts a calm but nevertheless mocking tone as he continues.

"For one thing Mick the Miller is probably dead and also...And I want you to listen very carefully to what I am about to say Billy.... Because this is most important."

Bernie is now glaring at, the defenceless, Billy as he rises up on his stool to venomously spit out his words.

"Paying attention Billy?...You Bloody Great Puddin'......Mick the Miller is or was a GREYHOUND!...That bloody thing looked like a cross between an Alsatian and a tin of Heinz 57 varieties!...But...One thing for sure Billy.... It definitely wasn't a greyhound and was therefore was not the famous Mick the Miller."

Bernie sits back laughing in a mocking fashion. Billy looks and sounds totally deflated.

"Well fair enough then Bernie...I've got to accept that the wool was pulled over my eyes there...You've got to believe what people tell you sometimes...I have to admit that I know absolutely nothing about greyhound racing...I never did…..So how was I to know that Mick the Miller was suppose to be a cockeyed Greyhound?."

Bernie stops laughing as he launches himself into another attack.

"Christ Almighty Billy...Mr Chairman please!.. This man is a complete Muffin...What a Pillock!.

He directs his next remarks straight at the cowering, pathetic Billy.

"I just hope you didn't show him on the Expenses Sheet...Because if you did there'll be trou....."

Alf intervenes curtly, yet calmly.

"Don't worry about that Mr Chairman...I saw that bloke off and his dog very rapidly...A well known Conman from the other side of Rochdale...I believe he's prepared to go to any lengths if he thinks there might be free booze in it...I clocked him as soon as Billy mentioned who the dog was supposed to be.. Actually the Bloke was having a bloody good laugh when I was throwing him out...There was no real harm done and no hard feelings...He didn't even get to finish his first pint."

Ralph has been quietly attentive although he feels disappointed that the Meeting is apparently going nowhere, fast. He exercises his authority as Chairman by speaking calmly but at the same time firmly.

"Gentlemen....Gentlemen please...Recriminations are not going to get us anywhere...We all make mistakes...Everyone is mortal...Please... Can I appeal to all once again...Try to be more positive....Please."

He glances around to ensure that he has regained the dignity of the proceedings. He is relieved to see that Eddie appears to have something else to say.

"Eddie...Good man...Anything else you would like to add before we're forced to move on to the next item on our Agenda?"

As usual Eddie is conciliatory. As expected he consciously attempts to avoid upsetting anybody.

"Well...No thank you Mr Chairman...I have to admit that on reflection the Sportsman's Night was a bit of a disaster but I..."

Bernie interrupts rudely as he obviously thinks he has won a victory. Glaring at Billy again he snarls.

"There you are Billy...Perhaps you'll accept what I've been saying all along....It was a bloody disaster! and now you've had it in black and white."

With the exception of Billy, all the others cannot help themselves from sniggering. This is a well timed tension breaker but, as usual, Bernie never knows when to quit. Sensing a modicum of support he is ready to continue his personal attack on Billy.

"Yes...Thank you Eddie...But let's be clear it was a bloody fiasco never mind a bloody disaster!"

He rises up on his stool again to enable him to lean towards Billy. He attempts to exercise his unearned authority.

"I very much fear that Mr Billy Dawes is nothing less than a gold plated ocean going PILLOCK! And...I think that should be recorded in the minutes of this Meeting."

Although he is plainly upset by Bernie's tirade of abuse Billy elects to remain silent. Ralph, merely shakes his head as he dismisses Bernie's suggestion with a wave of his hand. He is about to speak as he notices Vic raising his right arm, attracting his attention. Ralph seizes upon the opportunity to bring him into the current discourse.

"YES VIC!... Yes the Chair recognises Vic...Order please."

Vic clears his throat. He appears a little nervous as he smiles, weakly, before he speaks.

"I thank you Mr Chairman...As I have already indicated in my detailed report at the commencement of these proceedings... WE... The respected and venerable Lapley Vale Bowling and Social Club are staring fiscal ruin in the face...Unless urgent steps are taken to rectify the situation we are on the brink of imminent and devastating disaster."

Although everyone is having difficulty following exactly what Vic is saying, Billy is the only one humble enough to be prepared to ask.

"Excuse me for asking Vic...but...What do you mean? I haven't understood one cockeyed word you've said up to now."

Vic glances around the table with a slightly superior expression flashing across his unimpressive features. He gets enjoyment from his ability to confuse his colleagues with his oral dexterity. He makes sure he has full attention before he continues.

"In short....Gentlemen...We have to find ways to encourage our Members to grace us with both their presence and their money more frequently to enable us to enhance our turnover."

Vic turns to face Billy, whose mouth has dropped open.

"If we don't start taking more money through our till we are going to be in the SHIT!...Right up to our necks."

Billy nods and smiles because he now realises what Vic has been talking about. Bernie snarls as he turns on Vic.

"Why the hell didn't you say so in the first place?...You like the sound of your own voice you do."

Bernie sits back shaking his head in disgust as, unperturbed, Vic ignores his comments to continue.

"Thank you...Right...Now that WE ALL!...ALL understand the full extent of the implications...Please can we do as the Chairman has implored us to do by discussing some useful suggestions and put a stop to all this infantile and childish bickering?...Eh...Please?...... Gentlemen."

Ralph is pleased with Vic's contribution.

"Yes quite right too...Thank you Victor...Now come on lads...Now's the time to come up with some sensible suggestions I'm sure there is a way out of the mess...Please!...Eddie!...What about you?."

Eddie responds immediately with enthusiasm.

"Yes...What about some kind of a competition?...Eh? Competitions always generate a lot of interest."

Bernie throws his pencil on the table as he retorts cynically.

"What did you have in mind Eddie?...A Miss Arthritis Contest? or perhaps the Zimmer Frame Olympics?"

Bernie is conscious of the fact that he is about to be pounced upon by the Chairman so he quickly turns defensive.

"Christ...Most of our Members are past it or getting very close to it and that's a fact we need to face for a start."

Although everyone dislikes Bernie's observations they reluctantly accept the credibility of his comments.

Vic is looking through the pile of papers laid out on the table in front of him. He is determined to make some kind of progress if he can.

"Yes...Here it is...We have been invited by the Brewery to enter a team in the Spring and Summer Darts League. I haven't given it much thought since the letter arrived because of other things on my mind but what do you think?....Is this an area where we can procreate interest?."

Alf lurches forward as if electrically shocked. His tone indicates a high level of enthusiasm.

"Hey!...Now then Vic...I think you might have hit on a good idea there...We've got a Dart Board out the back...It's in bloody good nick... Almost new...Never really been used much."

Alf immediately realises that he has innocently highlighted their basic, underlying problem by his own comments. His keenness immediately wanes. Billy has not lost interest though.

"Well excuse me for saying so and no disrespect Mr Chairman but I think that's the best cockeyed suggestion I've heard so far today....If we have a Darts Team it means that we will get visiting teams coming here and they'll be supping our cockeyed ale...Well done Vic I think we're on a cockeyed winner here."

Bernie shakes his head as he sarcastically asks Billy.

"And won't our team have to play any away games then? they won't be supping our Ale on those nights will they?."

The expression on his face indicates that Billy had not considered this point, once again, aptly raised by Bernie. Ralph is eager to maintain some signs of progress and is most anxious not to stem the flow.

"O.K. good points made and raised...Let's not dismiss the topic out of hand...We need to think about this...I suppose the first thing we need to do is hold some trials to gauge if there is a level of interest sufficient enough for us to raise a team...If we pass the word around I expect to receive a positive response...Even if most of our regulars don't actually play they may have sons and the like who might jump at the chance of being in a team...I definitely think we've stumbled onto something here...What do you think?...Vic?.."

Vic is delighted that his offering has been so well received. He sounds most responsive.

"Well Mr Chairman as Billy so eloquently illustrated.. It's the best suggestion to date...I can prepare a couple of notices and have them displayed and exhibited...We can only try. Give people a week or so to enter their names on the lists and we can arrange to hold the trials on..."

He turns to Alf, whilst eagerly thumbing through his Diary.

"Right...Tell me Alf...Which is our slackest night?."

Alf does not have to dwell on Vic's question for too long because he realises that, once again, he is about to put a dampener on the proceedings. He is unable to conceal his heart felt disappointment and sadness.

"Unfortunately Vic...Mr Chairman...Gentlemen...The way things have been going lately it's hard for me to single out which is the worst of all our slack nights...but...Tuesday.. Yes Tuesday is probably the worst night of the lot...Yes...When I think about it there isn't really anything much on the Telly that night and if we could attract an extra half dozen or so into the Club it can only be a vast improvement."

Everyone sits back looking rather pleased with themselves due to the most welcome signs of progress being made.

Ralph is able to smile with feeling now. He looks and sounds more confident as he merrily poses the motion raised.

"Thank you Gentlemen all...Motion proposed by Eddie and seconded by Billy."

Smiling broadly Ralph poses to allow Vic to prepare himself, in his role as Secretary, to take down in writing the record of matters arising. Vic eagerly raises his pen in his right hand before he beckons the chirpy Ralph to press on.

"Thank you Mr Secretary...Invitations to Members and their families...To pay heed and give attention to the trial taking place with a view to the selection of a Darts Team to represent our beloved Club in the forthcoming Spring and Summer Leagues sponsored by the Brewery...To take place in the Clubroom a week this Tuesday night... All those in favour?...."

They all raise their right hands with enthusiasm. Ralph tries to control his obvious delight as he exclaims loudly.

"Motion carried unanimously...Thank you Gentlemen of the Committee....Let's hope we have just placed our leading foot on the long road to our eventual salvation....Let's hope and pray so anyways... Right then....Are there any more suggestions?."

The Chairman is about to bring the Meeting to a close, a popular move because they traditionally enjoy a couple of free drinks on the Club at the conclusion of Committee Meetings. Smiles are wiped out because Bernie speaks as he raises his hand.

"Look...I'm sorry to say this Mr Chairman but I don't think Doris does anything to help with the image of our Club."

Although they are all slightly miffed, Bernie does have the attention of his colleagues. Ralph looks puzzled as he enquires.

"Doris?...Doris?...Do you mean Doris who helps Alf behind the bar at weekends sometimes and when we have a Bowling Match on the Green...Do you mean that Doris Bernie?."

The focus returns to Bernie who responds quite curtly.

"I'm afraid we all know who I am referring to Mr Chair.. I'm sure you'll be interested to hear that she's now earned the less than affectionate nickname of "Doris Karlof" with most Members who encounter her at the bar...Jesus Christ!...She's so bad tempered and ratty that people tend to think she's being nice to them if she doesn't give them a bollocking for asking to be served with refreshment...Doesn't need a reason...Well...I mean to say...It's hardly encouraging custom is it?."

Perhaps with some reluctance the other Members have to accept that, once again, Bernie has made a valid point. They all turn their attention towards Ralph.

"Yes...I think we must agree that you've got a point there Bernie but let's not be hasty.... I think we should hear Alf's views on this."

There is a mumbled agreement as Alf, looking a little embarrassed, tries hard to be diplomatic.

"Mr Chairman I have noted the remarks made by Bernie and I have to confess to being in sympathy with his observations but... This a simple matter of economics...Doris is employed by the Club as the Cleaner, as you are aware, she reports for duty every morning without fail and I'm sure you all agree she does a splendid job keeping the place Shipshape and Bristol Fashioned. Now she has recently taken it upon herself to assist me behind the bar on the odd occasions when we get busy...Sometimes I think she possesses a sixth sense or something... She just suddenly appears when there's a sign of queues at the bar..... Anyway the point of all this and what I must draw to your attention is the fact that she doesn't receive any extra payment for her barmaiding activities...So...Bearing that in mind I think we might meet up with some problems if we decide to sack her...Plus let's not forget she is a first class cleaner and also makes a very nice cup of tea as well...It's not an easy situation to deal with Mr Chairman the only thing I can say is that things have been so slack behind that bar lately that she's not been needed but come the Bowling Season and I have to admit I do appreciate an extra pair of hands behind the tiller sometimes even if it's just to help with the washing up."

The men are stunned to silence as they consider the clear observations made by Alf. They also appear to indicate that the points made are quite relevant. Ralph, coughs, then replies.

"Yes...Points very well made and well taken...If I may say so...We don't want to smite our noses off just to spite our faces do we?...At the same time of course I also have to admit that Bernie also has a point... It would go a long way towards solving some of our problems if we were able to generate enough trade to enable us to employ a proper barmaid."

There are grunts and nods of agreement. It is obvious that there can be no quick solution to their particular problem in the current, difficult, climate. Vic desperately attempts to
recapture the positive vibes recently being enjoyed.

"Mr Chairman...If our Darts idea takes off...Perhaps we could... At a subsequent future Meeting...Decide to give some thought and consideration to the possibility of us entering a Team in the Brewery Snooker Leagues as well...I accept that this can be construed as speculation in the extreme but...Well...It's early days yet and who knows?...Still first things first as my old Dad used to say Bless Him."

Vic's contribution brings the return of a mild air of hope and expectation. Ralph is keen to end on a happier note. He shuffles the papers on the table in front of him as he is about to bring the Meeting to a swift close.

"Points well made Gentlemen...Thank you all."

He leans over to speak directly to Bernie.

"We certainly don't want to shit in our own nest do we?."

Before Bernie can respond Ralph swings his attention to Vic in a very businesslike fashion. "I hope you won't be including that little matter about Doris in your recorded minutes of this Meeting Mr Secretary." Vic grins, positively shaking his head. Ralph goes no. "Well

I can't speak for anyone else but I...Myself.... Personally...Am spitting feathers here...Are there any other matters on the Agenda Vic?." Vic is about indicate nothing because he realises that Ralph is keen to adjourn to the bar but he suddenly realises that there is another pressing matter. He sounds apologetic. "No...Oh sorry...Sorry...There is one further matter Mr Chairman...Woody...Woody has made himself available." Vic stands up to enable him to extend his view into the main area of the Clubroom as he calls out in a loud voice. "Woody!...Woody!...Are you there?." An instant reply flies back from Woody. "I've been here all the bloody time." Woody appears in the Snooker Room wearing a very old pair of overalls, a tatty jacket and a weather beaten cap. He sounds a cross between annoyed and bored.

"And that's not as if I haven't got better things to do with my time than to stand around here like a spare prick at a wedding while you lot gas on and on and..."

Vic is hoping that Ralph will chastise Woody for his rude attitude but realising that Ralph is obviously not going to do so Vic decides to ensure that Woody does not escape scot-free. He is calm as he speaks with an official ring to his tone.

"Yes...All well and good Woody...Point made and taken...Still the humble man must learn to give way in the face of urgent matters of State."

Vic glances around the room with a self-satisfied expression across his feature but no-one seems very impressed so he coughs rather falsely before he continues.

"Yes...Anyways I understand that you have a small request for consideration by the Committee Woody...Would you please get on with it now?.....Thank you."

Woody scowls at Vic as he drags his cap off in preparation to address the Chairman. Everyone is giving Woody their full and undivided attention. Woody speaks.

"Weed killer!."

They all gaze at Woody waiting for more but very soon they realise that they have received the full content of Woody's communication, albeit fully contained within just two words. Ralph, looks a little bemused. He coughs politely before enquiring.

"Yes Woody...Weed Killer?....What about it?."

Woody's tone denotes more than a touch of frustration as he replies very sharply.

"I have to have some bloody weed killer if you expect me to keep our Green the tops in the whole District...He!"

Woody points and glares at Vic, who immediately cringes.

"He...The tight arsed keeper of the purse strings here informed me that I cannot purchase the necessary chemicals required for treatment of the grass without first getting the consent of Committee...Now all together I need to spend about twenty quid...That will provide me with enough to last the whole bloody Season....Christ I don't know just what you expect from me I have always prepared my own special fertiliser made from an old and secret formula...Which incidentally is known only...ONLY!...To me and without going in to too many details involves the use of chicken shit which reacts with selected chemicals supplied to me by Harry Jeeps the Pharmacist...AND!...Let me tell you this...If you don't know what you're doing you can very easily make a right royal balls of the whole procedure...BUT!...Whereas I have no problem acquiring free chicken shit unfortunately even I have to exchange coin of the realm over the counter for the chemicals and without them I cannot make my own fertiliser."

There is a noticeable feeling of relief that the request is a modest one. Ralph quickly glances around the table before he sits back to speak in a friendly, understanding manner.

"Of course Woody....Yes of course....I'm only sorry that you've been put to such trouble but in fairness to the Honourable Secretary and Treasurer...In the person of our very own Vic...I don't know if you are fully aware or not Woody but the Club is currently going through a very sticky patch...Financially that is and I'm sure you appreciate that Vic was only doing his duty... Like it or not we are not riding on the crest of a wave at the present time."

All smile weakly as they return their attention to Woody. He is far from impressed. He speaks with a mocking tone.

"More like lying at the bottom of a stagnant pool under a bloody big stone if you ask me...Look...I don't like asking for money like this but surely you don't expect me to foot the bloody bill for it myself do you?."

Noticeable gasps can be heard before Ralph responds.

"Certainly not Woody...Good Heavens No!...I don't have to remind you just how much your labours on the Green are appreciated by myself and everyone...Look...We can find your money from somewhere...See Vic afterwards and he'll fix something up for you...I'm sorry you've been put through this ordeal."

Woody nods and returns his cap to his head obviously appeased. Ralph rubs his hands together glancing around the table as he does so. He turns to Vic, who appears to be a little sulky.

"Anything else Victor?."

Vic shakes his head and is about to reply but Ralph does not give him the chance.

"Right...Great...O.K. Alf...If you'd be so kind as to pull us a few pints of best bitter please...Now before anyone panics it's Chairman's treat...I'm paying on this occasion...And pull one for Woody as well please Alf."

The Members of the Committee and Alf need no further encouragement whatsoever. They are all standing against the bar in the Clubroom before Alf has time to reach the pumps.

* * *

"Everything all right Jenny?."

Eric McCabe's journey through life seems to be progressing very smoothly so far. From a personal point of view everything is fine and well within his expectations. Despite the acceptable handicap of being the only child of Bert, the Local Police Sergeant, and his wife Alice he is a contented fellow. He has never been interested in academic studies although he has always been considered to be a bright and intelligent lad. Eric, better known to all his friends as "Ricky", enjoys doing the sort of work he knew he is inclined towards and is naturally good at. He is 19 years old and his contented state has been brought on by his good fortune when he lands a job which involves and stimulates his genuine interest in flowers, plants and many other kinds of growing things. He has been taken on as an apprentice by Dicky Mitchell, the Local Nurseryman, when he left school and, mainly due to his family connections, he is also understudying Woody Green, the Green keeper at the Lapley Vale Bowling and Social Club. Although his time with Woody is unpaid Eric considered it is an honour and a privilege to be chosen to work with the man who is held in the highest esteem throughout the entire surrounding Area as an outstanding Green keeper.

Eric is not afraid of hard work and as a result of his good attitude and application Dicky Mitchell is more than accommodating with his approach to Eric's training at the Bowling Green. For example, if Woody particularly wants Eric to be with him during the morning

Dicky will normally allow Eric to make up his time by working with him in the evening. Dicky is an ardent admirer of the skills of Woody Green. He sincerely considers his apprentice being chosen as the 'Heir Apparent' to Woody's cherished Bowling Green Empire is of great benefit and bonus, not only for the Lad but also for himself.

Eric is a likeable Lad, tall, good looking and in normal circumstances, reasonably quiet, although this could be tested when he is enjoying the company of his close Pals, Sam Best and Peter Franks. Eric deserved his reputation for being polite and respectful by all those who are acquainted with him. In keeping with local tradition and practice he enjoys a few pints of beer at the appropriate times although, it has to be said, he is not in the same league of drinkers as his Father and the likes of Woody and most of their other Friends and Associates.

It is mid morning and Eric is on High Street, Lapley Vale carrying out a mission. He is entering The Lapley Vale Pharmacy. Dressed in a clean pair of overalls, heavy boots and a decent sports jacket Eric notices that the Chemist and Proprietor Harry Jeeps, who always wore a really white jacket, is standing behind the counter at the rear of the shop. His young female assistant, Jenny Dawes, the granddaughter of the famous Billy 'Cockeye' Dawes is alongside him. Eric does not know Jenny, a very pretty seventeen years old girl, who has worked for Harry Jeeps since she left school. Jenny is wearing a neat white overall which tends to flatter her firm, well proportioned, young body. Jenny always seems to have a pleasant welcoming smile for all of her customers.

As Eric approaches the counter the ringing of a telephone can be heard. Harry, quickly, disappears through a door at the rear of the counter leading into his Office and Dispensary.

Harry's sudden departure appears to unsettle Eric. He appears to be a little anxious as the smiling Jenny looks up into his face with the expectation that he was about to ask for something. Eric greets Jenny in an awkward fashion.

"Oh!...Er......Good Morning...Er......Miss..."

Jenny seems to smile even more sweetly as he adds.

"Yes...Er...Can I have a packet of plasters please?."

Jenny nods as she turns to pick up a small box of assorted plasters from the shelf behind her. She places it on the counter in front of Eric and politely enquires.

"Something like these is it?."

Eric lifts up the box to examine it as Jenny points out to him.

"There's twelve in each packet...All different sizes and really good value for two shillings."

Eric nods as he places his hands inside his overalls to reach the money which is kept in his trouser pocket. As Eric searches for his cash Jenny places the packet in a bag saying.

"Thank you...Will there be anything else Sir?."

Eric manages to expose his money and is searching through his loose change. He shakes his head as he speaks.

"Er no...No thank you...Will Mr Jeeps be very long?."

Eric nervously nods towards the door through which Harry had disappeared. He coughs politely before he explains.

"I really need to see Mr Jeeps himself you see."

Jenny still smiling gives Eric a knowing look before she reaches under the counter to produce a packet of "Durex" contraceptives. She places them in front of Eric with a coy but sympathetic expression on her face. Eric picks up the packet to take a closer look as Jenny leans forward slightly. Lowering the tone of her voice she says.

"Look it's quite all right...You'd better pay for these before you buy something else you don't want and run out of money....Really... It's fine...I'm quite used to providing gentlemen with their personal requisites."

Jenny smiles reassuringly as Eric realises what he he is holding in his hands. He throws the packet down on the counter as if it is on fire. Eric gasps, looking horrified, as Jenny now appears to be having difficulty comprehending the situation. She finds herself carefully demanding.

"Well....Do you want them or not?."

Eric is so embarrassed he can hardly speak. When he manages to do so his tone reveals an element of sheer panic.

"No!....Actually No!...I don't...I'm afraid I've no idea what you're going on about...Woody Green sent me to see Mr Jeeps on his behalf... He said that Mr Jeeps has some chemicals for him or should I say for his grass....Woody said to be sure I saw Mr Jeeps himself...Personally... I'm sorry."

Jenny is now the embarrassed one. She is blushing as Eric holds up the bag containing the plasters.

"We use a lot of these in our game because we often pick up little cuts and grazes when we're working on the Green and we ran out of them last week."

As if to prove his point Eric points to a small plaster on one of his fingers on his left hand.

Jenny swiftly removes the 'Durex' off the counter and puts them back where she got them from. She is unsure what she should say in the circumstances. Her cheeks are now almost a burning colour of red as she manages to splutter.

"Oh my God...Look...I'm awfully sorry...But...But I was only trying to be helpful...Some men are very shy about buying those things from a girl...I'm very sorry...I don't know what to say...I just don't."

Eric feels much better now. He is confident enough to try to re-assure her. Smiling weakly he attempts to relieve the tension.

"Look it's no problem...It's O.K. honestly...I wouldn't know what to do with them anyways."

He attempts to laugh but Jenny's stares at him in a way which clearly indicates to him that she does not really wish to discuss the problem with him. Eric feels his face going red again so he opts to abandon his mission for the time being.

"Anyways...I must press on."

He moves away slightly as he adds.

"I can always call in to see Mr Jeeps later...I...Er."

As he speaks the door behind Jenny opens. Harry reappears smiling broadly as he nods a greeting to Eric.

"Did I hear my name being mentioned?....Hello Young Ricky... Have you called in for Woody's special package?."

Eric nods vigorously to Harry and then to Jenny.

"It's all ready for him....Just a tick...Hang on a minute please Ricky...I'll fetch it from the back for you."

Harry disappears from view again. Eric glances towards Jenny but she is pretending to be very busy checking and dusting the rows of stock behind her. Harry returns promptly with a wrapped and sealed brown paper parcel. Passing it over to Eric he makes a point of warning the Lad.

"There you go....Please be very careful with that Lad... Don't get any of it on your hands.....Or spill it on yourself...I suppose Woody told you to be careful eh?."

Harry is smiling as Eric take possession of the parcel. Harry turns to Jenny but she immediately turns away from him. He senses that there is an atmosphere of some kind but is unaware of what it is or what has caused it. He makes a point of making eye contact with Jenny and then with Eric as he carefully asks.

"Look....Is there something wrong?."

Eric replies with some enthusiasm.

"No...Oh no everything's fine Mr Jeeps...Thank you...Is there anything to pay?."

Harry is shaking his head before Eric finishes asking.

"Don't you worry about that Son...I'll sort it out with Woody....We usually settle up over a pint or two in the Club."

Harry is still curious to know what has been going on. He takes a good look at Jenny again before he turns to stare straight into Eric's eyes. He cannot disguise his curiosity.

"Are you sure there's nothing Ricky?...That's it is it?."

Eric turns on his heels, even manages to smile.

"No that's it...That's fine thanks."

He walks the length of the shop to reach the front entrance before he turns, nodding to Harry.

"Thank you very much Mr Jeeps."

Opening the door and stepping through he suddenly ducks back into the shop to call out.

"And thank you Miss."

Jenny's head drops as the door closes behind Eric. Harry still puzzled, stares at Jenny. He sounds more understanding than inquisitive.

"Everything all right Jenny?."

Jenny tosses her head back and rapidly straightens herself up as she pulls herself together.

"Yes....Yes...No problems Mr Jeeps...None at all."

Harry cannot put his finger on anything but he has a strong feeling that something has happened. He thinks for a few moments before he decides to return to his work in the dispensary As the door closes behind him Jenny puts her head in her hands and then places her elbows on the counter. She looks up and blows her breath out between her clenched teeth. Jenny is suffering from an acute attack of embarrassment.

* * *

Woody Green and Alf Morgan are sitting on one of the benches on the veranda at the rear of the Clubhouse, overlooking the Bowling Green. Both are drinking tea from large striped mugs. They both hear the sound of Eric walking through the Clubhouse behind them. Alf shouts through to him.

"Out here Ricky...Get our tea Lad....The kettle's on the hob...Just pour the hot water on the makings in your mug."

Eric arrives on the veranda as Alf finishes speaking. The Lad immediately turns on his heels to disappear from their view as quickly as he had appeared. A few moments later Eric re-appears carrying a steaming mug of hot tea. Woody has just lit his pipe and is extinguishing a match as he enquires in a polite and friendly fashion.

"Did you find the time to collect that little package for me from Harry Jeeps Ricky?."

Eric is blowing on his tea but pauses to reply in a casual way.

"Yea...It's there in the kitchen...No problems."

Eric thinks and suddenly corrects himself.

"Well that's not all together true."

Woody and Alf are giving him their full attention.

"Aye...I was almost sold a packet of 'Durex'...You know...'French Letters'...Whilst I was in the shop."

Eric unconvincingly sniggers. Woody and Alf look rather curious as they glance at each other before returning their full attention to Eric. Eric realises that he needs to explain.

"It was more of a misunderstanding than a problem I suppose."

Eric emits a silly sort of laugh but is aware that his friends want more information. Eric would rather drop the subject.

"Anyways...Harry Jeeps handed the package over and said that you and him would settle up...You know?...For the stuff later on...Er...In the bar."

Eric takes a long drink of tea. The two men's eyes remain fixed upon him. He is about to take another mouthful as Alf asks in a sneering, inquisitive tone.

"What the bloody hell are you going on about young Ricky?...And what...May I ask?....Would a youth such as yourself be wanting with a packet of French Letters?...Eh?."

Although he wishes he had never mentioned the 'Durex' he has an uncomfortable feeling that they will not be satisfied without a full explanation. He tries to keep cool and sound casual and credible.

"Well....There was this young girl behind the counter in Harry Jeep's shop...A very pretty little thing...For some reason best known to herself thought I had gone in there after a packet of French letters... Especially after I asked her for the plasters and then asked to speak to Mr Jeeps himself…..Er...In person like."

Eric is aware from his Companions blank expressions that he is not making a very good job of giving his explanation. He tries even harder to clear things up.

"You see!."

He pulls out the packet of plasters to exhibit.

"I bought these plasters from the girl whilst I was waiting for Mr Jeeps to finish talking on the telephone in his Office...Er...Out of sight...At the back of the Er..."

Woody has had enough. He loses his patience.

"For Christ's Sake Ricky!...What the bloody hell fire are you twittering on about."

Eric is stunned. He stares at Woody as he is pressed.

"What the hell have the plasters got to do with the French letters?...Eh?."

Eric is clearly squirming. Woody manages to give Alf a playful nudge before he continues.

"Did you think you needed the plasters to fasten the French letters on the end of your 'Nudger' Ricky?."

Woody and Alf both roar with laughter. Now Eric is beginning to lose his patience. He resents being teased so he tries one last effort to explain his comments. He is finding it more and more difficult to control himself.

"NO!...I'm not bloody daft am I?...Eh?...Listen!...I didn't want any bloody French letters in the first place."

The more he becomes frustrated the louder his voice gets.

"Look!...Hell fire!...It was a simple misunderstanding. O.K.?...The girl must have thought I was too shy to ask for the French letters from her...Right?...She was merely trying to be helpful...O.K.?...Anyways that's all there was to it...Christ!.. I'm bloody sorry I even mentioned it to you pair now...Hell's teeth!."

Eric is upset and hurt. He feels he has done enough explaining. Alf is enjoying the fun and decides to continue the teasing...He deliberately acts stupid.

"And does your Father know about you and all these French letters you've been buying Ricky...Eh?."

Eric has reached breaking point. He flies into a rage as he sees Woody and Alf laughing so much that they are having to hold their sides. He is about to speak but he cannot. He stamps off towards the Clubhouse. Before entering he looks over his shoulder to spit out.

"BOLLOCKS!!!."

This only causes the others to laugh even more.

"BOLLOCKS!!!!BOLLOCKS!!!"

Alf barely manages to control himself enough to make a final comment. Turning to Woody, but obviously intended for poor Eric's consumption, he remarks.

"Chip off the old block there Woody...Eh?...In more ways than I'd care to mention in mixed company...Eh?."

Eric shows his contempt by slamming the door behind him as the two older men experience uncontrolled merriment.

* * *

"Can you stand on your hands?."

It is Thursday evening and apart from a small group of men at the bar and two elderly men playing, a painfully slow, game of dominoes at one of the otherwise empty tables the Clubroom was almost desolate.

Alf is in his usual position behind the bar. Ralph and Vic are standing at the bar taking a drink with Charlie Walsh, a retired Local Factory Manager. Charlie has been a very cautious drinker since he narrowly escaped disaster with the Police when he attempted to drive home in his car after a long and drunken drinking session. He had learned his lesson that night. He was so grateful that he had not been locked up that, ever since, he has been extremely careful with the amount of alcohol he consumes when he is in possession of his motor vehicle. Woody Green is seated on his stool at the opposite end of the bar by himself. He has a near full pint on the bar in front of him and he is obviously enjoying a smoke as he sucks on his briar pipe. Although Woody enjoys selected company he is the sort of man who is also quite content with his own company.

Vic is holding court and has a hint of enthusiasm in his tone and manner.

"I must say that I'm enormously gratified by the initial response to our Dart Notice....There are twelve names on the list for the trial and as we are merely required to muster a squad of eight players to enable us to participate in the Brewery League it does seem to be rather promising....Fingers Crossed Eh?...We may get even more before Tuesday...Who knows?."

They are all pleased to hear this news. Alf asks.

"Excellent news Vic but do we know if any of them can actually play the game?...I've never really played very much myself....Throwing harpoons was more in my line."

Alf grins and winks because he does not expect any of his friends to believe him. Ralph speaks before Vic can reply.

"And do we know if they're keen enough to turn up for all the fixtures?...Home and Away?....If we do commit ourselves Vic that will become a vital and valid point you know?."

Vic throws his head back to ponder for a moment or two before he responds.

"Pertinent questions Gentlemen...I find myself unable to adequately respond to either query until after we have held our trials next Tuesday evening...Your points are well made though."

Ralph, in particular, is enjoying the conversation about the darts because it is providing to be a little ray of hope for the Club's future. He poses another question to Vic.

"Who have we put in charge of the trials?...I hope you weren't thinking of me Vic...I know bugger all about darts I don't think I've ever actually played in a proper game."

Ralph is hoping for an inspirational reply from Vic but Charlie responds first.

"It's been a long time since I played but I used to represent the Works in their team on a regular basis a few years ago....I still know all the rules and regulations and what may be more to the point I can recognise a good player if I see one and I'd be more than willing to help out in any small way I can in view of the present circumstances."

Vic's face lights up as he seizes the opportunity.

"Stout fellow Charlie...One volunteer is worth two in the bush... Eh?....What?...I'll be present to give you any assistance you may require Charlie...The taking down of relevant notes and the like...Well done

Charlie you've just landed a job for yourself and you've also taken quite a weight off my mind."

Charlie is not sure that he really meant to volunteer so easily but he feels ready to accept the challenge. Ralph is delighted that things seem to be going from good to even better.

"Well that seems to have wrapped up that little item for the time being....Well done Charlie...Are you sure you don't mind?...We've no idea how the whole thing will turn out on the night you know?....Isn't that right Vic?."

Vic shakes his head and then wipes his brow in an attempt at humour. Charlie manages to smile. He sounds quite genuine.

"Pleased to be of any assistance Ralph...Gives me another excuse for getting out of the house for the night...Not that I have to have an excuse but it helps if you've got a specific reason or purpose...The wife watches me like a bloody hawk these days."

They all enjoy a chuckle as Charlie adds.

"As long as the darts won't interfere with my Bowling activities I'm quite happy to take anything on."

Alf is keen to reassure Charlie.

"Don't worry about that Charlie...That will not be a problem because the dart matches will obviously take place in the evenings won't they?...Just one thing...If Charlie manages to win on the Bowling Green during the afternoon he might have a problem seeing the board after he celebrates in his traditional fashion."

Alf smiles and winks at Charlie as he gestures by raising his hand up to his mouth a few times. Charlie takes the point without offence but is then a little defensive.

"And tell me this Alf...How many times was I beaten last season?... Eh?...Not once at home and not that often away.....My motto has always been 'To the Victor the spoils'."

Ralph supports Charlie.

"Quite right too Charlie...What's your other motto?...'Any excuse for a piss-up' isn't it?."

The small but happy throng are disturbed by the sound of the front entrance door being opened. Into the Clubroom in all her glory enters Mary Pickard, infamously known to all as 'Worthington Mary'.

As usual Mary is over-dressed and the worse for drink. She is a well preserved, one time quite attractive, woman in her early to mid fifties. As usual Mary is in the company of a Gentleman who is normally expected to spoil her by plying her with drink in return for her well used favours. Dan Smith is the 'Lucky' man on this occasion. Dan, the Local Scrap Metal Dealer, is about the same age as Mary, he appears to be slightly embarrassed and his face looks very flushed as he supports Mary, who is a little unsteady on her feet, preventing her from falling over an empty table as she makes her way to the bar.

Alf has already reached for a bottle of 'Worthington Pale Ale' off the shelf behind him. He smiles and nods to Mary in a warm and friendly manner. Mary is attempting to maintain a dignified stance but is unable to hide the fact that she is not about to partake of her first drink of the day. Alf nods to Dan as he cheerfully greets them both.

"Evening Mary...Dan...Your usual tipple is it Mary?.....And what can I get for you Dan?."

Mary smiles broadly and replies with a drawl.

"Alf...Alfred...Alfie...My Darling...I know why I always insist upon coming in here...It's the service...What do you say Dan?...First Class every time from Alf.....Eh?."

Dan half smiles and nods as he rummages through his pockets for money. He pulls out a handful of loose change as he responds to Alf's enquiry.

"Thanks Alf and a pint of bitter for yours truly if you please."

He turns to greet the others at the bar. There are mumbled greetings from Ralph and his Company. Woody is staring at Mary with a disapproving expression on his gnarled features.

Mary is taking a long look around the Clubroom. She winks and gives Woody a cheeky smile but he chooses to ignore her as he takes a drink from his glass. Mary suddenly turns to grasp the bar rail with both hands. She looks and sounds rather girlish as she enquires.

"Any of those delicious pies you sell Alf my darling?"

Alf, sadly, shakes his head before he replies.

"Sorry Mary Love...We only bother to order them on special occasions at the moment...Caused by a lack of steady demand at the present time...Plus we're also trying our best to cut down on any wastage whenever we can…....I'm sorry to disappoint you Dear....I haven't even got any decent crisps just now."

Mary pouts like a child to exaggerate the level of her disappointment as Dan carefully steers her onto a chair at the nearest table. He detects the beginnings of a sulk emanating from Mary so he decides to act cautiously.

"Bloody hell Mary...You're not hungry are you?."

Mary immediately responds with a very sharp retort.

"Yes Dan my darling I bloody well am...What with one thing and another I seem to have overlooked dinner this evening."

With a wicked wink and a firm, yet playful, nudge in his ribs Mary decides to teases the slightly over anxious Dan.

"I certainly can't concentrate on the job in hand if my little tummy is empty and making growling sounds can I Danny Boy?....Might spoil our fun later if you know what I mean?."

Dan realises that Mary is deliberately pressurising him because he knows her so well. He does look and sound rather touchy and frustrated.

"And just what do you expect me to do about that Mary?...You heard Alf saying there are no pies...Why don't you have another nice drink?...You'll survive...Come on drink up."

Mary is aware that she possesses the power to twist Dan around her little finger as and when she feels the need to do so. She changes to her, silly, girlish voice again.

"Do you know what I could really murder right now Danny darling...Some of those delicious fish and chips...You know the ones I adore from Billy the Chip's shop?...I wonder if anyone loves Mary enough to go out and fetch some back for her?."

Dan is not pleased with the way things are going but he also realises that he will have to appease Mary if the whole evening is not to turn into a total disaster.

"Bloody hell Mary...I've only just got this pint and anyways I don't think Alf would be best pleased if I brought bags of fish and chips in here...That's considered to be very bad form you know?."

Mary is far from appeased. She throws her head back in a very haughty fashion, continuing in her childish mode.

"Well of course if you don't think I'm worth putting yourself out for Dan you can bloody well forget it...O.K.?."

She turns away from Dan to look straight at Woody. He, once again, chooses to completely ignore her although he cannot avoid being aware of what has been going on between herself and Dan for the previous few minutes. He sucks hard on his pipe and places a comforting hand around his half empty pint glass.

Dan unashamedly accepts defeat as he realises that Mary will sulk for England unless she gets her own way and a bag to put it in. He is annoyed but knows what he must do for his

overall interests in the eventual outcome of their evening.

"All right! All right!...Bloody hell fire...Mind my pint will you?...I hope I won't be very long...Watch for me at the door Mary...You'll have to eat them outside...I'll give you the nod as soon as I get back and then you will have to come outside to fill up your bloody little tum tum... O.K.?.".

Mary smiles very sweetly before she playfully sticks the end of her tongue out at Dan. He is growling to himself as he storms out of the room without a word to any of the others.

Mary takes a drink from her glass as the door slams behind Dan. She stands up to walk over to where Woody is seated at the bar on his stool. She glances across towards Ralph and the others before she starts swinging her hips and her handbag. With a false teasing manner she stares at the less than impressed Woody. She talks to Woody in her most sexy way.

"Hello Woody you little devil you...Have you been waiting here for me for very long darling?...There.....There....It'll be all right now.... Little Mary's here for you now."

Woody actually looks at her for the first time as he removes the pipe from his mouth. Without the slightest sign of any emotion he snarls at her in a controlled but positive way.

"Look...Piss Off Mary...Just piss off and leave me alone will you?... There's a good girl."

Rather than being put off by this rejection Mary

laughs loudly and throws her arms around his neck to hug him. Ralph, Alf, Vic and Charlie are enjoying the floor show. Charlie nudges Ralph as he purposefully shouts over to the couple.

"Now then Woody...Give us a shout if you need a hand to cope with her won't you?...I believe she can be quite a handful our Mary... Will you be all right old chap?."

The others are laughing as Woody roughly pulls Mary's arms from around his neck. He gently pushes her away from him but Mary realises that she is playing to an audience. She leans back on the bar in a provocative way, wiggles her hips and speaks in an even sexier voice to the obviously annoyed Woody.

"Oh come on Woody darling...You're not that old...I'd love to give you a really nice treat...Know what I mean you old sex pot?...Come on Woody there's still life in the old dog yet I can tell...Eh?...I bet you can bring the colour back to a girl's cheeks...What?...Come on Woody I'm all yours."

Woody is still in control of his composure as he puts his glass down on the bar. He places his pipe in an ashtray. He looks straight into Mary's eyes to speak to her very clearly.

"Mary...Now listen carefully please...Can you stand on your hands?."

Mary suddenly becomes quite puzzled. She stares into Woody's face appealing for more clarification from him.

"Stand on my hands?....Whatever do you mean darling?. Do you mean like we used to in the school yard when we were little girls Woody?...Is that what you mean darling?."

Woody's facial features immediately change. He now has the look of an outright winner as he declares very calmly.

"Yes that's exactly what I mean Mary because it's the only way I would be able to take advantage of this little treat of yours...I think that's what you called it...You'd need to stand on your hands in front of me so that I could drop it in... O.K.?...Get the message?...Eh?...Eh?."

Mary gazes at Woody for a moment. Then it dawns on her exactly what he means. She claps her hands together and roars with laughter. By this time Ralph, Alf, Vic and Charlie are all helpless with tears running down their cheeks.

Mary laughs so much that she needs to feel her way back to the table to snatch a drink as she collects her handbag en route to the ladies toilet.

* * *

The clock above the bar is showing the time to be 10.45pm as the entrance door swings open with enough noise to draw everyone's attention to it. Three young men walk in looking hopefully at Alf behind the bar. Alf makes a point of looking at the clock as he speaks with a hint of sarcasm in his tone.

"Oh Aye they've put the towels on at the Flying Horse have they lads?."

Before anyone could respond Ralph steps forward to greet them in a friendly manner.

"Now then Alf...Let's not be inhospitable now...Come on lads there's always a welcome in here for serious beer drinkers like you young chaps."

They lurch forward towards the bar looking relieved and thankful. Ralph nudges Vic as he whispers.

"And we desperately need any and all of the passing trade we can manage to get...Know what I mean?."

Vic and Charlie enjoy a chuckle as Alf begins to pull three frothing pints of bitter through the pumps.

* * *

The time has moved on to 11.15pm. Woody, who has actually been upset by Mary's antics has decided to have an early night. Vic has left with Woody. The young men from the 'Flying Horse' are still seated at one of the tables laughing and chatting. Mary, looking a cross between drunk and bored, is still seated at the table where Dan has left her. Two empty 'Worthington Pale Ale' bottles next to her full glass and Dan's, now almost flat, pint of Bitter give a clear indication of the length of time Mary has been left waiting for her supper.

Mary has a faraway look about her as she sings quietly to herself. She happens to glance towards the front door just as Dan pokes his head inside. He vigorously gestures to her to come over to him with his right hand and arm. Mary arises to stagger over to join him. As she reaches the doorway Dan pulls her through into the Car Park and in doing so reveals a glimpse of a bulky portion of fish and chips wrapped in newspaper which he is holding his left hand.

* * *

About ten minutes later, Bert McCabe, the local Chief of Police dressed in full uniform, drives his Ford Popular saloon car across the Car Park. Bert, Eric's father and Honorary Member of the Club, is a well known and frequent visitor.

As Bert swings his vehicle into a position where he can park in front of the Clubhouse he notices some movement, in the darkness, at the side of the building near to the main entrance door. Bert immediately stops to reverse his car. He switches on full beam headlights to illuminate the whole area at the side of the Club where he has seen the movement. The lights reveal Dan and Mary. Bert peers through the windscreen to witness Mary standing with her shoulders and part of her back leaning against a windowsill. Dan is clutching her around her backside with his head bent over Mary's chest. Bert can clearly see that Dan is in the act of making love. Mary is eating fish and chips from newspaper wrappings as he is doing so. Bert chuckles to himself as he reverses the Ford Popular away from the touching scene to park in front of the entrance into the Clubhouse. Dan and Mary do not appear to have been disturbed by the intrusion, in fact they are both so focussed, Dan on his love making and Mary on her supper, that neither of them really noticed. As Bert switches off his lights and engine to alight from his car he pauses to shake his head, before he actually laughs out aloud.

Bert is still sniggering and shaking his head in a gesture of disbelief as the enters the Clubroom. Before Bert has time to take a look at them the three young men from the 'Flying Horse' immediately spring to their feet to dash past Bert on their way out. In their indecent haste one of them accidentally knocks their table causing a small amount of beer to spill from each of the three full pints of Bitter they have just purchased.

Bert looks slightly bemused as he nods to Alf behind the bar. He then notices Ralph and Charlie standing at the corner of the bar so he springs smartly up to attention to present them with a very overdone salute. As he walks up to the bar he speaks with a teasing tone in his voice.

"What's all this then?...Now then...Eh?."

He turns to look towards the door and then his attention is drawn to the recently vacated table with the three almost full pints abandoned on it.

"Something I said was it?."

Ralph is not the slightest bit concerned that the local Police Sergeant has walked in on them well after the time permitted hours had finished. Smiling he greets Bert in a friendly welcoming fashion.

"Evening Bert...What will you have to drink with me then?...Your usual tipple is it?."

Bert smiles in a cheeky fashion as he concentrates his full attention on the vacated table and the three pints of Bitter. He changes his tone to sound rather 'Matter of Fact'.

"Hold onto your money for the time being Ralph...I think I'd better confiscate this Bitter first...Shame to waste Alfred's finest draught beer."

Bert carefully transfers the three pint glasses from the table to the bar. He then removes his uniform cap before he pulls up a stool.

Sergeant Bert McCabe is a larger than life character. Even in a Town like Lapley Vale, which sported more than an average share of notable characters, Bert is outstanding. He has been in charge of Lapley Vale Police Station for a number of years. Now approaching his retirement age Bert's unique style of policing, although not quite to the book, is accepted as most appropriate by the vast majority of the local populous. People do not go out of their way to upset or annoy Bert but it is fair to say, generally speaking, most of the good folk of Lapley Vale support and respect him and many are genuinely fond of him.

Quite tall with a strong and powerful frame Bert no longer looks as striking and impressive in full uniform because, in keeping with anyone else, even he cannot escape from his age beginning to show. His natural full head of hair is dyed jet black in a rather obvious way. His vibrant, striking hair fails to match the lines and wrinkles on his ageing features. Bert has to wear prescription spectacles at all times due to his failing eyesight. Despite this current critical description it is still possible to see that Bert has been a fine figure of a man in his younger days. Allowing for his age and life style he is still in surprisingly reasonable shape.

Bert downs one of the confiscated pints in one long draft. He wipes his mouth with the back of his hand before he smiles broadly to settle down for a chat.

"I've just witnessed a very moving scene outside in the Car Park not many feet away from where we are now sitting... I am able to inform you that an act of passionate love making is taking place at this very moment in time up the side of these very premises."

Bert pauses to pick up another of the pints of beer from the bar. The others are very curious as he lifts the glass to his lips. He downs more than half of the contents as they await an further explanation.

He smacks his lips to show his enjoyment of the beer to continue in a philosophical sounding way.

"I think I can say without fear of contradiction that Dan Smith, better known as 'Dan Dan the Scrap Metal Man' is unfortunately not doing a lot of good for Mrs Pickard better known and loved by us all as 'Worthington Mary'."

Ralph, Charlie and Alf all smile as they immediately put two and two together to guess what Bert has witnessed. After taking another swig, emptying the second pint glass, Bert grins broadly before he carries on.

"I reckon the only way he will see the earth move for our Mary...Or notice any movement whatsoever...Will happen if she burns her fingers on her chips....Not that Dan seemed to be too bothered...They were both enjoying themselves in their own separate ways...I've a feeling that the only ways in which Mary has not been shafted is whilst actually flying or possibly when she was standing up in a canoe."

They all laugh as Bert moves the third pint in front of him. Although they are not absolutely sure what Bert has been a witness to they are all aware of Mary and her antics. Alf shakes his head to speak in a sincere, affectionate fashion.

"She's quite a girls is our Mary...If she'd taken out a block of shares in 'Worthington Pale Ale' when she first took up drinking I dare say she would be a very rich woman today."

Ralph breaks into the conversation.

"What you might correctly refer to as a self-made millionaire."

They all nod and laugh as Charlie adds.

"No doubt about that Ralph...By Christ she can put it away all right..."

Bert takes over.

"And Worthies aren't the only bloody thing that Mary can put away I can tell you...Eh?...Eh?...You have to admit it though...She is quite a girl our Mary."

Since his close encounter with the law Charlie has remained naturally apprehensive with Bert and his men but that does not stop him continuing the present line of conversation as he speaks directly to Bert.

"No arguments there Bert you should have seen her in here earlier on…She certainly made a positive play for Old Woody…Didn't she Boys?…Mind you she didn't get much change out of him."

Everyone nods and laughs. This time it is Bert's turn to be unsure just what he was laughing about. Ralph speaks.

"I think if we're being fair though she was trying to get blood out of the proverbial stone…I've never known Woody to show much interest in trouser worm activities.."

Bert stops half way down his third pint to intervene.

"Hold on a minute there Ralph…Don't under estimate Old Woody…He used to have a bit of stuff on the side you know?. Up to quite recently as well…Kitty…Yes that's her name… Kitty…Surely you remember her?…Eh?…Kitty Kitty with the enormous big…..Blue eyes?…"

Everyone laughs loudly as Bert continues to hold the full and undivided attention of the other three men.

"We all appreciate that Woody has always enjoyed a reputation for keeping himself to himself and it is true that he has never ever threatened to take the plunge into the holy state of matrimony or anything of the like but take my word for it Gentlemen…Woody has certainly had his moments."

They do not appear to be completely convinced. Bert places his glass on the bar leaning forward, making his points loud and clear.

"Woody used to visit Kitty on a regular basis…She had been made a Widow at a young age and lived down the same street as Woody…All alone by herself…Woody himself once informed me that he used to enjoy casseroling her on cold Sunday afternoons during the wintertime."

Bert pauses as the other are shocked and also puzzled.

"Casseroled…That's the word he used…I had to look it up in the big dictionary we have a the Police Station…..Oh aye. There it was.… To casserole….Done slowly for several hours.. Eh?…Eh?…Not a bad pastime Eh?…Eh?."

They all realise that Bert is exercising his well known and accepted sense of humour.

Ralph is still curious to know more about the mysterious side of Woody Green. He tends to agree with Bert.

"Yes…You're on the ball there Bert…That's just the sort of expression Old Woody would use…I've always suspected that he's a bit of a dark horse…What happen to Kitty then Bert?…Is she still around?."

Bert sadly shakes his head causing Ralph immediate concern. He cannot wait for Bert's answer.

"What?…Passed away has she Bert?."

Bert has a sombre expression as he replies.

"Even worse than that Ralph…She packed up all her belongings and went to live with her only daughter in…North Wales!."

There are tutting noises and shaking of heads to indicate a genuine level of sympathy. For some inexplicable reason North Wales is not considered to be a desirable place to live by the Locals in the Lapley Vale area.

Ralph notices that Bert has drained all three pint glasses. He nods to Alf.

"Give our Guest another of those delicious pints you manage to pull through your pumps please Alf…What about you Charlie?….You can force another down I'm sure."

Recalling that he is without his car Charlie nods enthusiastically, draining his glass.

"And don't forget to pull one for your good self as well Alf."

A beaming smile breaks out across Bert's face as Alf passes him a frothing fresh pint. Bert comes out with one of his famous expressions.

"How kind…How very kind Ralph."

Bert swiftly takes the top of his new drink before he changes the subject.

"What's all this I hear about a Darts Team Ralph?."

Ralph is unable to cover a hint of concern.

"I don't know what you've heard Bert but we're holding trials here next Tuesday night with a view to entering a Team in the Brewery Dart's League...I'm sure you're aware of the Club's dire financial state at the present time.....This darts thing is one of the Committees attempts to generate more custom and hopefully lift our money troubles out of the shit where they have been languishing for a while now...Things look very bleak but we're giving it our best shot...Never say die."

Bert is shocked to hear Ralph's statement.

"Bloody hell fire Ralph...I had no idea things were so bad...I can't even imagine this Town without this Club...It cannot be allowed to happen...Eh?.....Eh?...Not bloody likely...Is there anything a poor old badly paid Policeman can do to help Ralph?."

Ralph pauses for a moment and then seems inspired.

"Didn't you used to be a Dart's man Bert?."

Bert stops midway through taking a draft from his glass. He pretends to be offended as he sits up in an erect pose to reply in a deliberate and cocky way.

"A Dart's man?...A Dart's man?...Eh?...Eh?... Eye of Eagle McCabe... That's what I was known as."

The others appear to be very impressed. Bert quickly decides to sound a little more apprehensive.

"Mind you the years have taken their toll...That was all yonks ago now....Before I was forced to wear these things to see where I'm going."

Bert pauses to tap his spectacles.

"As a result of these I haven't thrown a dart in anger for ages...Mind you they do say it a bit like riding a bike or riding Worthington Mary if it comes to that...They say you never forget how...Even if you can't perform to the same dizzy heights of excellence...Eh?...Eh?.....What do you say Alf?."

Alf nods and smiles but Ralph intervenes before he can reply.

"You could very well be the man we've been looking for Bert."

Bert squirms a little, now becoming even more apprehensive. Ralph sounds keen.

"Charlie has already agreed to cast his eye over the trialists and if you could also give us the benefit of your vast experience by watching the hopeful players I'm sure we will end up with a Dart's Team which might eventually be the equal of our
 exceptionally fine Bowling Team...You won't have to do any playing Bert...Charlie here will appreciate your presence...You know?... Two heads are better than one.....Eh?....You really would be helping us in a time of need."

Charlie is nodding eagerly. Bert drains his glass again. He is fighting off his natural reluctance to make firm commitments. Bert is pondering as Charlie picks up his empty glass to pass it behind the bar to Alf, who immediately starts to refill it. This action brings an immediate response from Bert.

"How kind....How very kind Charles...Well...I'm not sure that I could commit myself to playing in your actual team Ralph...Due to the enormous pressures of my duties and what have you but...But I can certainly assist with the management and training side of things...Yes... That's O.K....Next Tuesday night did you say?...Eh?...Eh?."

The other three are all nodding hopefully.

"Yes...Fair enough...O.K. count me in...I'm prepared to make the effort on your behalf...What I consider to be a most worthwhile cause... As far as I am aware I have nothing arranged for Tuesday next...Yes... What time are you going to bully off"

Bert's deliberate use of a technical term has the desired effect. They are impressed. Alf responds with enthusiasm.

"The notice says 8.30pm but I don't suppose we'll get down to any serious dart throwing as a prelude to the selection procedure much before say...9pm...Charlie and Vic will be here...Will that suit you Bert?."

Bert pulls out his pocket note book from the top pocket on his tunic. He makes an entry in the book saying.

"Provided that we maintain a fair wind and the natives don't suddenly become restless...Eh?...Eh?....I will be here."

The others cheer loudly as they all return their full attention to their drinking.

* * *

Everyone is about ready to call a halt to the proceedings for the night. Alf is busy tidying up behind the bar when he suddenly remembers a message he has been asked to pass on to Ralph in his capacity as The Chairman.

"Oh shit!...Sorry Ralph but with one thing and another I almost forgot to tell you that the Young Man who calls in here every Thursday evening to collect the Football Coupons left behind the bar for him... You know the Collector from Littlewood's...Nice young Lad...His Dad plays for the Second Team at the 'Black Horse'.....Not a brilliant bowler but keen...Well.....The point is Ralph I don't think we can rely on him calling for very much longer...There were only a few to collect tonight again and he regrets that unless things look up it won't be worth his while making a special journey here...He wasn't being nasty and I think the lad had a fair point of order to make in the circumstances."

Ralph shakes his head sadly.

"Another sign of the times as if we needed one Alf...I don't think too many people can still afford their little flutter anymore...Even though this little arrangement with the Collector saves them the cost of postage and the poundage on the postal order...Still as you say the Lad has a point...Remind me if you will to mention this to Vic...He can put one of his notices up warning that the facility will be withdrawn unless more Members are prepared to support it.....You never know it might just re-kindle that desire to have a go...Give me a coupon for next week please Alf."

Bert sadly shakes his head as he comments.

"I reckon I've about as much chance of becoming the next Miss World as I have of winning on the Pools...Mind you...It does give you a tiny glimmer of hope and one thing for certain Gentlemen...You certainly can't win if you don't have a go...So let me have one for next week as well please Alf."

Alf passes Bert the coupon trying to encourage them a little.

"You've got a point there Bert but you never know…..The Lad was saying that there have been a number of quite reasonable pay outs to some lucky Folk around this vicinity and quite recently at that."

Bert perks up immediately. He is curious.

"Did he mention who they were Alf?...I'd like to visit them to offer my congratulations...Eh?...Eh?."

Alf laughs as he explains.

"No...He didn't say anything about that...I don't think they actually know themselves but of course the Lad has the right connections for hearing all the gossip and rumours...I bet you couldn't keep a Pools win quiet around this neck of the woods for very long even if you'd taken the precaution to put a cross against no publicity."

Ralph smiles ironically.

"You'd be able to tell if it was me...Because I'd be running up and down the streets shouting 'Eureka' at the top of my voice for days... Are we all set Gentlemen?...I think we should take Alf's advice and abandon the ship for now...O.K.?."

* * *

"No you mean Billy Dawes is her 'cockeyed' Granddad."

Eric McCabe and his two closest friends, Sam and Peter, are enjoying one of their regular evenings out together. The 'Ritz' is the only Cinema in Lapley Vale and because of the popularity it enjoys with the younger people of the Town the Management have been able to lay down very strict rules of general conduct and behaviour which are rigorously enforced. Being banned from the Ritz by the Manager for any period of time would have a serious affect on anyone's social calendar. The Lads have been looking forward to the Film tonight. Entitled "The Curse of the Mummy" the show is a must for all those who get an enjoyable thrill from exposure to horror.

There are only a few persons watching the Film in the downstairs, Stalls, area of the Cinema. Apart from Eric and his two friends, who were seated in the centre block on the back row close to the central aisle, there are only about a dozen persons in the whole of the Stalls. Jenny Dawes, the girl from Harry Jeeps the Chemists, and her best friend Kay Brown are seated about six rows from the back on the block of seats to the right of the Lads. Eric has noticed the girls because they are quite isolated in the seats they have chosen.

The only other person seated near to the girls is a local character called Terry Price. Terry is about the same age as Eric and his Friends and they are all known to each other from their schooldays. No-one is particularly friendly with Terry because he is a loner with an odd sense of humour. Terry is generally considered to be strange and an 'Odd Ball' type. Terry is seated alone four rows behind the girls closer to the back in the same block of seats.

The Film is reaching a very tense part where the 'Mummy' dressed in ragged white bandages is wandering around looking for someone to kill or frighten to death. The sound track is a repeated steady throb of a single terrifying note. Jenny and Kay have their eyes fixed on the big screen. They are giving their total, undivided, attention to the Film as they nervously clutch each other's hands.

Sam nudges Eric and Peter to draw their attention to the furtive actions being carried out by Terry Price. Although the Cinema is in half-light they have been inside long enough for their eyes to have adjusted to the gloom. They are able to see fairly clearly. Terry is sneakily extending a telescopic dark coloured pole. He is aware that the Lads are watching him so he winks and signals to them to keep looking. The pole extends to a length of about eight feet. He balances it across his knees and the arms of the vacant seats on either side of him. Making sure Eric, Sam and Peter are still watching him Terry pulls out a white glove from his jacket pocket. He carefully fastens this glove over one end of the pole. Having done this he takes a furtive and cautious look all around him.

Jenny and Kay are still absolutely transfixed on the antics of the stumbling 'Mummy' on the screen. Terry very carefully manoeuvres the pole across the four rows in front of him, towards where the girls are seated. In the gloomy light the only thing visible, at first glance at least, is the white glove which actually appears to be floating. Turning to check that the Lads are still giving him their full attention he carefully raises the pole causing the glove to gently tap Jenny and then Kay on their shoulders. In their anxious state both girls immediately turn to see the floating white hand which has just touched them.

Instantly both girls spring to their feet screaming hysterically. Terry is almost doubled over laughing, and to be fair the Lads are definitely able to see the funny side of Terry's antics as they chuckle loudly. Within seconds Gordon, the Doorman resplendent in his smart double breasted uniform overcoat, is dashing through from the Foyer. Peering down the central aisle he is very concerned. Because of the commotion the girls are making the Projectionist freezes the Film and the House lights slowly start to come on.

The lights are not fully illuminated by the time Gordon reaches Jenny and Kay. He has difficulty making out if they are laughing or crying. He then notices Terry who has fallen off his seat and is on his knees laughing so much that tears are running down his cheeks. The assembled pole with the white glove attachment can now be clearly seen. The Manager appears in the central aisle. Wearing a dinner suit and bow tie he cannot be mistaken as he strides towards Gordon and the two shocked girls. Before the Manager reaches them Gordon very smartly, if roughly, grabs Terry by the scruff of his neck. Spinning him around into the aisle Gordon then takes hold of the seat of Terry's trousers and unceremoniously frogmarches the still laughing Terry towards the Exit. Gordon is far from amused as it becomes obvious that he knows and recognises Terry. Passing the astonished looking Manager, Gordon snarls at Terry.

"Not you again!...Out you go my Lad!...OUT!... You're nothing but a bloody nuisance you are."

There is little point in Terry struggling because Gordon is very strong in the arm if, perhaps, a little weak in the head. As Terry makes his undignified exit the girls seem sufficiently recovered from their shock to now be seeing the funny side of the incident. The Manager mumbles something to Jenny and Kay before he signals to the Projectionist with his hand. The girls, with their arms linked together take their seat with a giggle as the House lights dim, once again, and the Film continues.

Eric, Sam and Peter, although still chuckling to themselves are being careful not to attract too much attention in case they are in line for similar treatment from Gordon on his return from dispatching Terry. As the Manager slowly withdraws from the Stalls, Peter nudges Eric leaning across to get Sam's attention. He is careful to speak in a lowered tone.

"If either of you two were Gentlemen you'd nip over to ask those young ladies if they are requiring any toilet paper."

All three burst out laughing but have to stifle this almost immediately as, a still fuming, Gordon reappears at the back of the Stalls.

Gordon waits a few moments, glaring around the whole Stalls area. Satisfied that all is now well he turns on his heels to vanish from sight through the Exit. Peter nudges Eric and leans across to get Sam's attention as he whispers.

"Serves them right if you ask me young girls like that coming to the Pictures on their own...They should have someone looking after them...Like me for instance."

Peter smiles as he flexes his biceps. They all want to laugh again but they are suddenly bathed in the beam from a torch. They turn to make out 'Florence of the Lamp' the ageing Usherette standing behind them with her torch focussed directly on the three of them. They instantly pull themselves together as Florence snarls.

"Keep that noise down there if you please....Be quiet now...The fuss is over and done with now...Some people have come here to enjoy the Film...So button it...All of you O.K.?."

The three Lads slump down in their seats without the slightest hint of them giving any sort of argument. Jenny and Kay turn to witness the fuss now being caused by Florence and as they show their faces Eric suddenly recognises Jenny as the very same girl he had recently encountered in Harry Jeep's Chemist Shop. Eric smiles and is about to wave but the girls

quickly turn away. Florence finally switches her torch out as she spits out a final warning.

"Now behave...You won't be told again!."

The Lads slump even lower in their seats as the Cinema swiftly returns to peaceful normality.

* * *

Eric, Sam and Peter leave the Rex and are walking along Huddersfield Road towards Billy Chip's 'The Golden Chip' Fish and Chip shop a few yards further down the road. They are laughing and joking as they catch sight of Jenny and Kay. They are seated on a bench at the bus stop sharing a bag of chips. They are well illuminated by the, startlingly extravagant, brightness of the lights coming from the Chip Shop.

After coppering up their available cash the Lads manage to scrape enough together to purchase a large bag of chips each.

In keeping with most young men of their age Eric, Sam and Peter are more food destroyers than eaters. All three have more of less eaten their supper as they walked the short distance from Billy's shop to the 'bus stop. Sam has demolished his food first. He addresses the two girls who are still sitting on the bench awaiting the arrival of their bus. He speaks to them in a polite, non-threatening and friendly manner.

"Enjoy the Film did you girls?...Not too frightening for you I hope."

The Lads burst out laughing which causes the girls to join in with them. Kay is aware that they had witnessed the incident in the Cinema. She retaliates without being too aggressive.

"We could have managed quite nicely without the antics of that 'Nutter' Terry Price...He needs to be put away him."

The Lads nod in agreement and laugh as Kay adds.

"Oh Aye...We can all have a good laugh now......But......Seeing that white hand....In the dark...Coming from nowhere."

She glances at Jenny for support. Jenny's eyes are wide open. She nods her head vigorously to endorse and emphasise her full agreement. Kay makes a gesture with her hand.

"Just floating there in mid air...Well...It wouldn't be very ladylike to tell you what I nearly did to myself....Eh?...I bet you could wager a close guess......Eh?."

All five of them roar with laughter as the bus approaches to pull up at the bus stop. Jenny quickly screws up the newspaper wrapping from their chips, throwing them into a nearby litter bin. Kay is waving to the bus driver to make double sure he will not miss them. Jenny climbs on the bus first. Kay, now feeling quite cocky, follows her onto the platform. She turns to call out to the Lads.

"Nighty Night then Boys...Tell that 'Nutter' Price we won't forget...We'll be getting our own back sooner or later...Night. Night."

Jenny has to pull Kay into the bus because the driver has started pulling away from the kerb. She waves and the Lads wave back, all with rather silly grins on their faces.

The Lads take over the possession of the bench.

Peter throws his papers in the litter bin as he comments.

"Nice pair of Hens there...I certainly wouldn't say no to either one of them...Not bad at all."

Sam glares into Peter's face and speaks with more than a hint of sarcasm in his tone.

"Peter...Let's be honest about this...You wouldn't say No to a tall dog with sore eyes...Would you?."

Eric smiles as Peter takes a playful swipe at Sam. As they settle down for a moment Eric, perhaps rather hastily, decides to tell them all about his prior meeting with Jenny.

"I had a funny experience with that girl...You know the pretty little one that works in Harry Jeep's Chemist Shop?.. She only tried to sell me a packet of 'French Letters'."

Sam and Peter gasp with genuine shock as Eric continues to hold their full attention by adding in a 'Matter of Fact' fashion.

"All I wanted was a packet of plasters and a package of special chemicals for Old Woody."

There is a short silence whilst Sam and Peter analyse the implications of Eric's revelation. Eventually Sam leans forward to make an announcement with genuine conviction.

"Bloody Hell Ricky...You know what this means don't you?...Eh?."

Eric stares at Sam. He is puzzled and eager to hear what his friend has to say.

"She bloody well fancies you!...Oh Aye...There's no doubt about that Ricky...A definite sign if I ever heard of one."

Peter nods his head in agreement but Eric is very dismissive.

"Get off!...Don't talk so bloody daft...I don't even know the girl... First time I've ever noticed her...Fancies Me?...Huh!...You do have a tendency to talk through your arse at times Sammy."

Peter enthusiastically supports Sam.

"NO!...No...I think Sam is right there Ricky!... Bloody hell she couldn't drop a bigger hint than that could she?. Eh?...Come on Ricky be fair she must have fancied you like mad."

Sam nods and grunts his wholehearted agreement. Eric is starting to lose his cool. He is still smarting from the treatment he had received from Woody and Alf on the same subject. He is struggling to control his temper as he makes an attempt to drop the subject. He does sound rather irritable.

"LOOK!...FOR CHRIST'S SAKE!...IT was a simple misunderstanding...JESUS CHRIST!...I'm bloody sorry that I even mentioned it now...To anyone!...You're much better off around here if you keep your gob shut...Especially when you find yourself surrounded by dirty minded swine like you lot.....And a couple of others I don't care to mention....Hell Fire!."

Sam and Peter know better than most that Eric should not be provoked too far. Sam carefully attempts to compromise.

"You have it your way Ricky.....But...A nod is as good as a wink in my books."

Before Eric can round on Sam Peter calmly intervenes.

"She lives with her Nan and Granddad around the corner from our house...In Sugden Street...Jenny...Aye that's right... Jenny...Jenny Dawes...She a very quiet type as far as I'm aware but you can never really tell."

Eric glares at Peter so he immediately re-adopts the straight forward informative role.

"I've never seen her with a boyfriend or anything like that...She's usually with that girl she was with tonight... I'm not sure but I think she's called Kay."

Eric has calmed down enough to show an interest.

"Jenny Dawes?...Is her Granddad...?"

Before Eric can finish his question Peter nods and smiles with a confident answer.

"Yes that's correct Ricky My Lad...Her Granddad is Old Billy Dawes...As far as I'm aware she's always lived with her Nan and Billy...I've never knowingly seen her Mum...or her Dad.....She's been with her Nan ever since she was a baby."

Eric breaks into a broad smile as he enquires.

"Are you telling me that that gorgeous girl is Billy Dawes's granddaughter?...Really?...You mean Billy Dawes is her COCKEYED! Granddad...Let's have it right Pete he will definitely be her cockeyed Granddad no doubt about that."

All three Lads laugh loudly and the tension has disappeared. Sam eventually shakes his head and adds a warning note into their conversation.

"That'll do for me then...I don't think Old Billy Cockeye would appreciate the likes of us sniffing around his Granddaughter...We'd end up getting a good smack...Or should I say...A cockeyed good smack?...Or a good cockeyed smack... Eh?...What?."

They are still chuckling as they stand up. Sam stretches himself before he announces.

"Well...Come on Boys...Let's get walking...I bet you're regretting the fact that we spent our bus fares on the chips now...Eh?...Come on...It's not a new experience for any of us being skint...Is It?...EH?."

The three contented young men happily wander off down the road making their ways home.

* * *

> "Well….I'm sure he's filling them with confidence."

At long last Tuesday evening has arrived. It is the appointed time for the Darts Trial. Much may be riding on the outcome of the proceedings and nerve ends are jangling amongst the Committee and, perhaps more than anyone else, Alf the Steward.

The Trials are well under way. Although the Clubroom is far from full the attraction of the Darts has made a significant improvement on the numbers normally seen in the premises on a Tuesday evening.

True to his word, Charlie Walsh is standing by the dart board alongside the blackboard type scoreboard. Charlie is wearing his old army tin helmet and an even older pair of motor cycle goggles. There are two men playing against each other and about a dozen more are watching them with genuine, keen, interest. Vic Callow is positioned at a table which is not too close to the action but is near enough to enable him to gain a full view of the on-going proceedings. Vic has an open note book laid on the table before him. He appears to be giving his full concentration to the game as it is taking place. Eddie Brown is at the same table looking less interested. They are all drinking freely and are obviously enjoying the evening.

Eddie glances around to see that the clock over the bar indicates the time is 9.20pm. Alf is very busy behind the bar and seems to be delighted with the way things are going. He is being assisted by the unpaid, occasional, barmaid Doris, the subject of numerous complaints and discussions. Doris, in her late sixties has a forbidding and unfriendly aura about her. Woody Green is seated on his usual stool, close to the bar. One of his closest friends, Norman Smith, is perched on the stool alongside him.

Norman, in his fifties, less than four feet in height is a true Dwarf. Woody has adapted Norman's stool by adding two steps to the side of it. Without these additions Norman would find it impossible to climb to the top of the stool without assistance. As Norman sits on top of his seat his little legs stick out in front of him. Norman tries not to be over sensitive about his stature. He likes to be treated just like anyone else and is a respected and popular Member of the Club.

Standing between Woody and Norman is Jack 'Peggy' Hackett. Peggy is a rather small, rounded, man in his sixties. He has acquired his nickname because his right leg was amputated when he was wounded during the War and he has always chosen to wear a wooden peg leg with a rubber ferrule, very similar to those worn by legendary pirates.

These three do not appear to be paying the slightest notice to the Darts. There seems to be a heated discussion taking place. Woody speaks very clearly and quite deliberately as he stares into a rather down cast features of Peggy.

"Now listen Peggy....Are you listening?...Right.... No-one... Especially me...Is saying that it's your fault that some crack shot German marksman got lucky with a shot in 1944 which cost you your leg when you....AND INCIDENTALLY!...Quite a few others including myself for instance...Were over in France putting paid to the unwarranted advances of Hitler and his Third Reich...O.K.?....Now... Have I made that point perfectly clear to you Peggy?."

A sullen and sulky looking Peggy does not reply but Norman is nodding his head to indicate that Woody is coming through loud and clear. Woody continues.

"What I am saying is that under no circumstances can you continue to play on MY Bowling Green unless you start wearing the proper artificial National Health leg provided for you many years ago and which you chose to keep under your stairs at home."

Peggy is about to speak but Woody raises his voice.

"IF!...IF!...Due to rain...The grass is wet...Right. O.K.?.....Now are you still listening?...Or becomes soft because it has been raining...YOU CANNOT GO ON WITH YOUR PEG!."

Woody sits back feeling confident that he had been able to make his point with clarity. Peggy is offended. Eventually he manages to speak.

"Well that's bloody charming that is...That's what I would call blatant and cruel discrimination directed towards an Old Soldier..."

Woody is losing his temper. He leaps off his stool to stand feet to foot with Peggy. Glaring into Peggy's face he is now almost yelling.

"BOLLOCKS!....BOLLOCKS PEGGY!...Have you got any idea just how long it took me to repair the holes you left in the green the last time you were playing when it pissed down with rain?...Eh?...Come on...Have you?."

Woody pauses to glare into Peggy's guilty looking face. He is struggling to control himself.

"NO!...You bloody well haven't...I bet you've never even give it a thought...Christ Peggy I spend a lot of my valuable energy and time making our green the best for miles around and I'm afraid I do take exception to you PEPPERING it with your peg leg."

Peggy attempts to protest but finds himself unable to get a word in as Woody continues.

"Bloody hell fire Peggy...If you care to cast your mind back to that particular day you might well recall that it took two of us to pull you out when your peg eventually sunk into the ground leaving you stuck."

Peggy spits back his reply determined to have his say.

"And if you recall Woody I still beat the Bastard I was playing despite a considerable handicap induced by circumstances beyond my control."

Woody feels like screaming but contents himself by simply glaring at Peggy as he tries to calmly return to his stool. Eddie has overheard most of the conversation between the two men as he patiently waits to be served at the bar. He and Norman are staring at Peggy as they recollect the incident. Peggy knows that Woody has right on his side but he desperately tries to think of a suitable retort as Woody settles on his stool again. Woody is conscious that he has upset Peggy and he tries to calm things down and be conciliatory. He pulls his unlit pipe out of his mouth to speak in a soft, reasonable, tone.

"Christ Peggy it's nothing against you personally it's just that I've got to think about my turf and…Well…All I'm asking you to do is please wear your proper false leg with the boot on it and we'll avoid any of these problems arising in the first place…O.K. Mate?."

Peggy is aware that he has lost the argument. He answers Woody quite calmly but rather sharply.

"Look I don't deny that there's something in what you're saying Woody…..But…It's not as comfortable to wear as my old peg is…It's all right for you…You don't have to suffer."

Woody's eyes flash with rage as he shoots to his feet again.

"I DON'T HAVE TO SUFFER!…It's not only you that has to bloody suffer Peggy!…The whole bloody team has to suffer!……The future of the best Bowling Team in the League will have to suffer if you carry on digging the grass up every time we get a shower of rain."

Woody can see from Peggy's expression that he is hurting the old man. He backs off as much as he can without losing the points he has already made to good effect.

"Look Peggy…We've known each other most of our lives…Christ you know that it's nothing personal but surely you can see my point of view…I don't want to hurt your feelings but I've got to protect the green…I'm sorry Peggy but that's the way of it and I will vigorously defend my opinions and conclusions."

True to form Eddie attempts to mediate. He speaks calmly and sympathetically to Peggy.

"I'm sure that what Woody is saying is quite correct Peggy…There was a lot of comment passed last season and to be fair you did start to wear your proper false leg at one stage... Now isn't that correct Old Pal?."

Peggy responds with feeling.

"Yes I did wear it once Eddie and let me tell you this...It gave me jip!...Bloody jip it gave me!...And what was even worse it didn't do much for my concentration and game either and to be FAIR I came very close to losing that game...I'm very proud of my unbeaten home record."

Norman decides to add his comments to the discussion before either Eddie or Woody can respond.

"I'm sorry to say this Peggy but aren't you being a little stubborn over this matter?...You always wear the false leg at all the away matches don't you?..."

Peggy answers very sharply.

"Only to stop those bloody moaners Norm...Christ some of those other Green keepers are even worse whingers than Woody and...If you recall...I lost my game at the Constitutional Club...Remember?...Cost us the whole match that did...Had I been wearing my peg I would have taken that Puddin' I was playing apart and there's no danger there.... You don't seem to appreciate that I cannot concentrate on my game when my leg is giving me jip."

Even though he is trying to mediate Eddie pulls Peggy up quite positively.

"Hang on a minute Peggy.....I can't remember the last time we ever beat the Constitutional Club on their own green... As a matter of fact it's usually touch and go when we've played them here...I'm sorry Peggy but I don't think you can blame your leg for that...The whole point... Which you seem to be avoiding or failing to grasp is that Woody is asking you as a friend to wear your proper leg in an effort to avoid him having to ask the Committee to ban you from playing on the green."

Peggy gasps. He is horrified.

"Ban me?...Ban me from playing?...You can't be serious...Ban me?..."

Eddie senses a break through.

"Oh yes Peggy my old friend...I am being very serious...If Woody.... As Head Green keeper...Places a complaint before the Committee I can assure you that they will be forced into making a very sad decision as far as you're concerned... I think you realise that there would only be one outcome."

Peggy thinks he has found new ground to launch his attack from.

"Head Green keeper?...What do you mean?...Head Green keeper?... There's only Woody so how can he be called the Head Green keeper?."

Norman intervenes smartly.

"As a matter of fact you are quite wrong again Peggy...Woody has recently acquired an assistant...Isn't that correct Woody?.

Woody nods.

"And in any case if there was only him he would still be officially entitled to be addressed as the Head Green keeper...Stands to reason does that."

At last Peggy can see the tide rising against him. Eddie attempts to make Peggy's inevitable loss of the whole argument a little more palatable.

"You know it all makes sense Peggy...Please don't even think about putting the decision of the Committee to the test...There's no doubt about the outcome there....Is there?"

Peggy is shaking his head. He looks and feels very dejected. Eddie slides his arm around his shoulders to add.

"Let's not be silly about this Peggy...Woody has requested you as a Friend..A fellow Team Member and as an old Soldier to be reasonable so...Please get used to wearing your official National Health Leg with a boot on it at both home and away fixtures next season...That's all you're being asked to do Not too unreasonable when you think about it eh?... Is it now?."

Peggy concedes with lingering reluctance.

"O.K. you win Woody...I don't want to be accused of being.... Unreasonable!....So I have to accept that you have a valid point....And I'm on a good hiding to nothing."

They all sigh a sigh of relief as Woody extends his hand in a gesture of friendship. Peggy grasps it warmly and they shake hands with pleasure. Peggy still wants to be defensive.

"Mind you I shall hold you all responsible if this causes me to lose my magic touch around the Greens."

Anxious to put end to the matter Eddie says.

"Don't be daft Peggy...A player of your standing..."

He nudges Norman and winks wickedly.

"Standing?...Eh?...Get it Norm...Standing?."

They all laugh as Eddie closes with a smile.

"Anyways Peggy...Most of the visiting players who come here couldn't beat you even if you were wearing two wooden legs...Eh?."

Eddie turns to catch a glimpse of Vic. He is far from impressed at the length of time it is taking Eddie to replenish their drinks. Eddie pulls himself together and taps the empty pint glasses on the top of the bar in an effort to attract either Alf or Doris's attention. Doris spins around to glare at him.

"Excuse me...Er Doris...Could you please...Er could you please pull me two pints of best bitter in these please Love?....Thank you."

Scowling, Doris grabs one of the glasses and places it under the nearest pump. She starts to slowly pull the beer into the glass as she snarls at Eddie in a very unfriendly way.

"And I hope these will be your last...You lot seem to think that Alf and I have nothing better to do than to stand here pulling pints all night...You'd guzzle ale until the cows came home if you were given half a chance...Why don't you slow down a bit?...You might find that you will enjoy it more if you take your time supping it."

Eddie tries very hard not to be angry or to show that her remarks have upset him.

"Sorry Doris Love....Steady on now please...That's only the second pint I've had all evening so far."

Doris bangs the first filled glass on the bar as she yanks the other off the bar and under the pump, snorting.

"Never mind all that...You lot will never learn because you never bother to listen."

Eddie stares at his friends seeking sympathy for the treatment he is so unjustifiably receiving. They merely shake their heads and smile ironically. They are suddenly aware of the presence of Bert McCabe. Bert is wearing a colourful sports jacket over the top of his uniform shirt, tie and trousers. Eddie smiles broadly and calls out to Doris.

"And another pint of the best for the good Sergeant if you please Doris."

Doris bangs the second glass down in front of Eddie. She starts filling a fresh pint glass without making any comment. Bert breaks into his usual smile as he pats Eddie on the back.

"How kind...How very kind Edward My Boy."

Doris does not get the chance to bang Bert's pint on the bar because he takes it from her en route. Raising the glass high he shouts.

"Cheers Boys....Here's hoping."

Bert takes a long drink as Doris glares at him. Doris hands Eddie some change as Woody leans forward to address her in a very polite manner.

"Thank you Doris...At the risk of you blowing a gasket may I also have three pints of the finest bitter for myself...Mr Smith and Mr Hackett?...If you'd be so kind...Thanks awfully nice."

Doris is now glaring at Woody as she whisks one of the empty glass over to the pump. Woody turns to Bert shaking his head and gesturing towards Doris. Bert makes a point of leaning over the bar to speak to her.

"Evening Doris...Still attending the charm lesson at night school I see...Eh?...Eh?."

All the men chuckle as Bert adds.

"Come on Doris...Lighten up a bit...Try to be nice for a change.... Smile...Give your face a treat."

Her facial expression does not change at all as she pulls the pints for Woody. She places the full glasses in front of Woody and take his money. Looking down her nose in a deliberate way she replies with a nasty ring in her voice.

"With respect Sergeant McCabe...Kiss my arse!."

Doris throws her head back in a defiant way as Bert winks to Woody before he replies.

"If you were to wash and talc your arse Doris...I might...Might mind you...Be tempted to kick it and that's my best and final offer."

Doris throws her head back again this time in a gesture of disgust.

Bert looks around the room before he enquires.

"How's the Darts going then Eddie?...Overcome by the vast talent on parade are you?."

As he is addressing Eddie, Bert notices Charlie standing alongside the Dart Board wearing his tin helmet and motor cycle goggles. Gasping in disbelief for a moment he roars with laughter before he adds.

"Christ they're not that bad surely...Bloody hell fire...I think I've seen it all now.....What is the man up to at all?.....Bloody hell fire!."

They reach the table where the thirsty Vic is seated and after carefully placing their pints down Eddie responds. Eddie cannot hide his own amusement at Charlie's appearance.

"The first couple on were a bit rusty to put it mildly Bert...One of the darts hit the wire and flew off...It didn't even go close to Charlie but he immediately demanded protection...Said he was not prepared to take any unnecessary risks...He then nipped back home to reappear about ten minutes later wearing the helmet and goggles."

Bert shakes his head as he takes a chair. Nudging Vic as he is keenly lifting his drink he comments.

"Well I'm sure he's filling them with confidence...Eh?...Eh?."

Bert and Eddie are soon empty and return to the bar Bert keeps glancing over at Charlie and laughing to himself. As they reach the bar Bert nudges Norman, nodding in the general direction of Charlie. Unfortunately Bert's nudge is rather heavy in the circumstances and Little Norman almost disappears off the top of his stool. Bert manages to catch Norman before he actually falls. Bert immediately apologises to the shaken Norman.

"Bloody hell Norm...Sorry Mate....Are you alright? Sure now?...I just can't get over Charlie with the helmet and goggles...Still I am sorry Norm...I don't suppose Darts is your sort of game is it?."

Norman sits up very straight before he calmly offers his reply.

"That's where you might be wrong Bert...Take it from me I can play a bit and from what I've seen over there tonight so far I can throw a bloody sight better than any of those hopefuls"

Bert smiles politely but is obviously not totally convinced. Norman detects his doubt and re-iterates his claim with some feeling.

"Just because I'm small doesn't mean that I can't be a sportsman you know?...I mean what I've just said Bert."

Bert is smiling in a conciliatory way not wishing to hurt Norman's feelings. This makes Norman more annoyed.

"Look Bert...I'll tell you what I'll do...Now...I'm prepared to take on the best player...Selected by yourself Vic and Charlie at the end of the trials....O.K.?...I'll just have to prove it to you....To you all."

It is quite apparent that Norman is serious. Woody has been enthusiastically nodding his head as Norman was speaking. Eddie is very anxious not to upset Norman anymore.

"No offence Norm...If you're serious I'm sure we can arrange a match for you...If that's what you really want...I'll have a word with Vic right away."

They all watch as Eddie whispers in Vic's ear. Vic obviously asks Eddie to repeat what he had just said before he turns to face the men at the bar. They are all smiling and nodding keenly. Vic turns away to have a mumbled conversation with Eddie and they two men end with an obvious agreement.

Eddie returns to his friends at the bar looking very pleased with himself. He addresses Norman directly.

"Having conferred with the Honourable Secretary come Treasurer Norman I am delighted to inform you that you're on!... There's just one game to go and then Vic will be pleased to make a suitable announcement before we have the highlight of the whole evenings proceedings...O.K.?."

Norman and Woody appear to be delighted. Bert and Eddie smile looking amused and expectant.

* * *

"O.K. then……..Let battle commence."

The time has moved on to 10.45pm. There are still a considerable number of men in the vicinity of the Dart Board. They are all engrossed with the proceedings. The tables around the Clubroom have also filled up with other men, not directly concerned with the Darts. They are creating a very pleasant and vibrant atmosphere. The Clubroom has not witnessed such a large gathering at an evening session for many a good year.

Woody is still seated at his usual place at the bar quietly chatting with Bert, Eddie, Norman and Alf. Alf picks the glasses up and starts to refill them as Vic and Charlie re-join them.

They all anxiously turn their full attention to Vic. Purposefully referring to his open note book Vic is well aware that everyone is waiting to hear what he has to say. He speaks directly to Norman with a pronounced authoritative tone.

"Well Norm….I think we've just about managed to sort things out for this challenge of yours…You are sure that you still wish to carry on with it aren't you?."

Norman seems offended at Victor's question.

"Certainly I am!...Why?...Did someone think I was joking or something?."

Vic backs off immediately very anxious not to upset their little friend.

"Oh no Norm...Nothing like that Old Pal...I was merely confirming that your challenge is still valid with relation to tonight's proceedings."

Norman is still annoyed because he resents anyone who does not take him seriously. He swings around on the top of his stool enabling him to look into Vic's eyes as he speaks.

"Victor....I'm not in the habit of issuing idle threats and what is more I'm quite prepared to lay a little wager with you...Or with anyone else for that matter.....That I shall beat your best player...Now have I made myself clear?."

Victor senses that he has created an unnecessary situation through his ill chosen comment. He is keen to smooth things down as quickly as possible.

"Please Norman...Please forgive me if I have inadvertently ruffled your feathers...There is no need to make a bet with me because I believe you...I accept that you have made a valid challenge and I will swiftly finalise the necessary arrangements for this contest to take place without further delay with the assistance of Charlie...Who incidentally has done a really marvellous job for us all tonight...And what is more has managed to come through it all so far without collecting a wound or even a scar of any type or description...Isn't that right Charlie?."

Charlie nods and holds up his helmet and goggles to the amusement of all the others.

Eddie looks and sounds quite excited.

"Who is the chosen one Vic?...Which one of the assembled hoard have you and Charlie selected to meet Norman's challenge?."

Charlie answers with enthusiasm before Vic can speak.

"I'll tell you this Eddie...It's a very close run thing...I'm astonished and delighted to report that quite a number of very promising players have graced us with their presence here tonight...A very high standard in my estimation."

Vic nods his agreement and is about to speak as Charlie carries on.

"We should have no problems raising a good team for the League… I really am gob smacked at the level of the response we have received… Exceeded my expectations by a mile."

Alf keenly adds his comments before Vic can manage to get a word in edgeways.

"And if tonight's taking are anything to go by this Darts Team is just what the Doctor ordered for our Club…I've had to put three new barrels on since we opened tonight…I haven't been moving three barrels in a bloody week recently…All good Beer drinkers…Not just excellent darts players but what is more pressing and urgent for us at the present time is…And I'm delighted to report…. They all appear to be able to sup in the First Division as well."

Alf's remarks are greeted with various sounds of obvious approval and general pleasure as they pause to survey extent of the activity throbbing all around the Clubhouse.

Woody straightens his cap and sits up to attention on his stool. He immediately attracts everyone's attention as he speaks in an impressive but 'put on' false voice.

"As Mr Smith's Manager."

He nods and winks to Norman who responds to him.

"I wish to suggest that consideration be given to the appointment of an independent referee for this contest…I put forward the name of Sergeant Bert McCabe…That's if you don't mind Bert?."

Bert lifts his empty glass off the bar and waving it around to demonstrate the lack of beer in it he replies.

"NO!…No not at all…Be my pleasure I'm sure."

Bert drains his glass before he holds it up against the light to look though the bottom of it.

"Bloody thirsty work mind…Refereeing..EH?…EH?."

Vic gives a resigned nod to Alf who immediately places Bert's glass under a pump and starts to fill it. Alf is grinning broadly as Vic actually manages to get a word in at long last.

"Yes that's right Alf…One for the Referee and one for Charlie and myself please…Oh and please have one for yourself."

Bert eagerly takes possession of his full pint first. Vic speaks to Woody and Norman as he waits for the remainder of his order to be filled.

"Yes...As Charlie pointed out it was a very close decision but young Leo Banks just managed to pip his Mate Taffy Evans in the final selection and I'm delighted to inform you that he has accepted your challenge...So whenever you're ready we can make a start...So...Let's get this show on the road."

Bert makes a point of acknowledging his pint from Vic before they make any moves towards the playing area.

"How kind...How very kind Victor."

Bert almost empties his glass in one swig. They move off rather sharply before he needs another re-fill.

Woody is rubbing his hands together looking very businesslike.

"O.K. Norm...Ready when you are...The show is about to get on the road...Yes sir."

Looking determined Norman scrambles off his stool and they all make their moves.

Realising that he has a ready made audience Vic adopts an official stance by his table to make an announcement.

"Gentlemen...Gentlemen please...Here we go then.... Now Mr Leo Banks....As tonight's Victor Ludorum."

There is a buzz accompanied by puzzled expressions before he enjoys explaining.

"Top Man...Winner...Best Player."

Leo nods rather coyly in response to a ripple of applause

"Leo...Permit me to introduce you to your challenger.. O.K. Norm...Norman."

Norman suddenly appears from behind Woody's legs. As he steps forward Leo and Taffy stare at him in disbelief. Taffy nudges Leo and whispers loudly and cheekily.

"Christ Leo...You've heard of Rumplestiltskin haven't you?."

Leo nods and smiles.

"This must be his first cousin once removed..... Crumpled foreskin."

Leo, Taffy and their group roar with laughter but it is obvious that Norman and his friends are not amused. Bert comes to Norman's rescue.

"Now then...We'll have less of that for starters... Cheeky buggers.... Let's get on with the game shall we?...Now as the official referee I want to lay down the parameters of this legal contest...What do you want to do Norm?...One straight game or the best of three legs?."

Before there can be any response from Norman Woody steps forward to speak.

"As Mr Smith's Manager I would suggest the best of three legs... Firstly Mr Bank's has been playing all evening and Mr Smith may be a little rusty so I ask for the best of three as the fairest solution...Do you and your Manager agree Leo?."

Leo nods as Taffy speaks up.

"Yes thank you Mr Woody....As Mr Bank's Manager we accept the terms as laid down.....Best of three legs it shall be."

Leo is getting bored with all the pal larva.

"Managers and parameters?...What the bloody hell are you all going on about...I didn't ask for a Manager but as the leader of my fan club I suppose Taffy is the clear choice...Can we get on with the bloody game please?."

Bert elects to stamp his authority on the proceedings forthwith. He admonishes Leo and Taffy.

"Look...Listen to me you two...As the Officially appointed Referee I will decide if you need a Manager or not and it stands to reason that if Norm has Woody as his Manager then Taffy must be considered to be your Manager...So belt up the pair of you...Just remember...My word is final and must be obeyed at all times without question...Do I make myself clear?...To all concerned?...Eh?...Eh?."

Everyone nods and agrees although Leo insists on making a final comment.

"Yes...O.K....Although I personally consider all this crap to be totally unnecessary...If it makes you lot happy...So be it...Can we get on with the bloody game now please?."

Woody steps forward once again to speak.

"As Norm's Manager I will draw his darts from the board after Charlie has recorded his score...O.K?...Understood? Saving time for everyone concerned...O.K.?"

Leo is getting irritable.

"Yes...Fine please yourself...I'll be drawing my own darts out...If you don't mind that is."

There is a general nodding of heads and mutterings of agreement amongst all those around Norman and Woody. Leo checks that Bert is nodding and smiles as Woody shouts out.

"O.K. then...Let battle commence!."

Woody steps forward dragging Norman's bar stool behind him. He makes his way to the firing line, known as the Oche, as he politely enquires.

"What do you want to do Leo?...Nearest to the Bull or the toss of a coin for the Off?."

Leo shakes his head as he carefully adjust the flights on his three darts. He responds in a polite and friendly way.

"No...No I'll give the honour to Norm...After all is said and done he is the challenger...Best of three legs it is then...First to 301 finishing on a double."

Everyone moves about attempting to gain the best vantage point to view the match from. Charlie, still not taking any chances replaces his helmet and goggles before he picks up his piece of chalk and adopts his position alongside the scoreboard at the side of the dart board. Bert, Vic, Eddie and Taffy sit at the official table. Woody carefully places Norman's stool behind the ochre and makes certain that it stands level and firm. To the astonishment of the majority of those present Norman then climbs to the top of his stool where he carefully takes up his stance for throwing. Holding two darts in his left hand he flexes his right arm to extend the remaining dart in his right hand. Leo appears to be stunned as he witnesses the performance. He eventually feels compelled to speak.

"What the bloody hell is going on here?."

Leo gestures towards Norman's stool with a bemused expression on his face as he half-heartedly enquires.

"He's not thinking of using that to throw from is he?....Please tell me that this is a wind up."

Woody answers in a matter of fact manner.

"Certainly...And why not?...Norman has a slight disadvantage from an altitude point of view and...."

Taffy stands up to object loudly.

"Jesus Christ....This is now getting to be bloody ridiculous...There was no mention of any stool being used... Surely you're not standing for this are you Leo?....What about it Mr Referee?...This is turning into a farce."

Bert pauses and ponders whilst the whole assembled throng awaits his response to Taffy's outburst. Bert clears his throat before he announces in a curt fashion.

"I am allowing the stool."

Leo, Taffy and their friends gasp and groan in disbelief. Bert adds a rider to demonstrate his neutrality.

"And just to make sure everything is fair and above board...Leo may also stand on the stool when he throws...If he so wishes...Eh?...Eh?."

Leo is speechless. He glares at Bert in astonishment then turns to glance at Norman, patiently standing on top of the stool waiting to play, finally he looks at Taffy in an appealing way. Taffy just shakes his head. Leo decides to carry on but his frustration is reflected as he shouts.

"Right!....Fine!...O.K....What a bloody performance Hell Fire!...Come on let's get on with it for Christ's sake."

He turns to direct his next remarks directly to Bert who seems to be feeling quite pleased with himself.

"And for your information Mr Referee...I will not be requiring the stool when I throw...Thank you...Now can we please get on with the bloody game...PLEASE!."

Norman nods to the official table. He waits for and gets silence from the crowd. He takes aim and is just about to throw his first dart when he suddenly decides to speak to Leo.

"Now I did make mention that I was prepared to place a wager on the outcome of this contest...What do you say Leo?."

Leo is still suffering from delayed shock as there are instant mumblings all around the room. Leo shakes his head as he replies with a sense of resignation.

"Anything you like Pal....Anything you like."

Norman seems delighted with this response.

"A pound be acceptable Leo?."

Norman smiles broadly as a rapidly becoming even more bewildered Leo accepts.

"Yes...Yes a quid...Agreed."

Norman waits for expected silence once again after he regains his throwing position. Looking over to Charlie he politely enquires.

"Right all settled...Can I set this contest in motion please?....Are you ready Mr Marker?."

Charlie nods and wets the end of the chalk on the tip of his tongue. Norman looks across at the official table.

"Are you ready Mr Referee?."

As Bert nods in an official way Leo loses his patience as he snaps.

"GET BLOODY STARTED FOR CHRIST'S SAKE! We'll be here all bloody night at this rate...Come on Norm let's see what you can do....PLEASE!."

After taking aim and carefully leaning forward on his precarious perch Norman fires his first dart. It lands in the treble one, scoring only three. Leo smiles, winks at Taffy. As Norman's second dart lands in the treble twenty the smile is wiped off Leo's face immediately. Norman cautiously moves his position on the top of the stool before he fires his final dart which also hits the treble twenty. Charlie checks that there are no further missiles to come before he checks the board to make a formal announcement.

"Mr Smith scores One hundred and twenty three."

There is a ripple of applause as Charlie makes the deduction from the 301 marked at the top of the scoreboard under Norman's name. Norman scrambles off the stool as Woody removes his darts from the board.

Leo takes a deep breath as he stands behind the ochre to take his turn. He extends his right hand and as he flexes his arm he is a study in concentration. The dart lands in the single twenty segment. His second and third also score single twenty. Although close all three darts narrowly miss the small treble score area of the segment.

Charlie quickly announces.

"Mr Banks has opened with a score of sixty."

Leo is retrieving his darts from the board as Woody replaces Norman' stool behind the ochre. In a flash Norman is standing on top of it ready to throw. Without any apparent effort Norman hits one treble and two single twenties scoring one hundred. A concerned looking Leo sends the first and second dart of his next visit to the ochre once again into the single twenty segment. Already becoming rather desperate he switches his aim to dispatch his third dart at the treble nineteen at the bottom of the dart board. He narrowly misses and scores a single three instead. There is an audible gasp from the onlookers as Charlie checks and then announces.

"Forty three scored Leo...Norman you are required to score seventy-eight to take the first of the three legs."

Norman nods to Charlie. There are gasps and exclamations from the crowd as his first dart lands in the treble eighteen portion scoring fifty four, leaving him twenty four to get. Double twelve is his next target in order to win the first leg of the match. Norman pauses, looking quite pleased with himself. He settles, soon regaining total concentration. He then dispatches his second dart. It lands firmly in the centre of the double twelve segment on the board. This is greeted by instant applause and cries of adulation from most of those watching the game.

Charlie tries not to express his delight as he says.

"Game to Mr Smith...When you're quite ready please Gentlemen...Order please!...Second leg....Mr Banks will throw first... GENTLEMEN!....Best of order if you please."

Leo is now experiencing a rather sick feeling in his stomach. He glances over to the official table where his friend Taffy is seated. Taffy realises that Leo requires moral support so he gets to his feet to walk over to his Pal. He attempts to boost Leo's flagging confidence by whispering to him.

"Just a flash in the pan Leo....Beginner's luck.... You've got him by the balls now...Don't panic his luck won't last show him what you're made of Buddy."

Leo's spirits rise immediately as his first dart lands in the treble twenty. His others both score 20 each and the relief is obvious in his face as Charlie makes his official announcement.

"One hundred scored...Leo starts the second leg with a score of one hundred...I thank you."

There is a ripple of applause as a now smiling Leo recovers his three darts from the board. Woody and Norman are swiftly into their tasks. Norman is poised ready to throw without any delay. Norman's first dart lands next to the treble twenty in the treble one, scoring only three. Leo has to stifled his joy as he starts to believe that things are turning his way. Norman concentrates after changing his position on his stool to send his second dart into the treble nineteen. Norman pauses for a moment after he reverts to his original position and stance. His third dart hits the treble twenty. His efforts are greeted with instant applause as Leo and Taffy both looked stunned. Determined, Leo scores a very good one hundred with his next three darts. Norman emulates his previous throws by hitting treble eighteen, nineteen and twenty with his next effort. Charlie appears to have some difficulty adding the total score but he eventually shouts out.

"One hundred and seventy one scored!."

Leo is standing behind the ochre waiting for Charlie to deduct Norman's score on the scoreboard. There are gasps and muttering as Charlie deduces that Norman only require ten to win again. Charlie nods and turns to announce to Leo.

"Leo...You require one hundred and one to win the Leg....Game on....Order Gentlemen please."

Leo is fighting to keep his nerve as he waits for complete silence before he takes careful aim. His first dart lands in the treble nineteen, exactly where he wanted it. This shot is appreciated by gasps and applause from the crowd. He appears to be doing some mental arithmetic working out that he still requires forty four to win the Leg. His second very good dart hits the double twenty and he immediately turns his full concentration onto the double two segment on the board. He dispatches his dart and is about to leap for joy until he notices that the dart lands just the wrong side of the wire and scores nothing. There are groans of sympathy all around the Clubroom. Charlie announces curtly.

"Hard luck Leo....Ninety seven scored...Leaving you requiring four...Order Please!...Norman you require ten to win the second Leg and the Match...Gentlemen Please!....Order."

There is total silence as Norman throws his first dart. It lands above the wire on the double five segment. There are some groans as Norman drops his arms to his side and takes a deep breath. He adjusts his stance and is carefully taking aim with his second dart as Taffy quietly moves away from Leo's side edging towards the rear of the ochre. As everyone's attention is focussed on Norman taking aim Taffy sneakily shoots his foot out to kick the bottom of the leg on Norman's stool just as Norman is firing his dart. Norman almost crashes to the floor but Woody manages to grab hold of him. The dart lands in the double two right at the bottom of the board. There is uproar as Taffy attempts to indicate that his foot caught the stool by pure accident and he is sorry. Bert McCabe is incensed. As the Official Match Referee he feels duty bound to take action.

Anyone who knows Bert is aware that he has a little ritual to go through before he engages in any sort of physical combat. His pre-violence mode is executed when he takes off his spectacles and then removes his top and bottom set of false teeth. He places the glasses in his top pocket and the teeth in his handkerchief.

Bert shoves his handkerchief across the table to Vic and Eddie with a nod. He then strides across towards Taffy who is anxious to make himself scarce. As Taffy tries to escape his exit is quietly blocked by onlookers. Bert grabs the cringing Taffy by the scruff of his neck. With consummate ease he spins the helpless Taffy around before frogmarching him across the Clubroom. As Bert and Taffy arrive at the door Alf is already

there waiting to swing it open. The two men disappear out into the darkness of the car park.

Out of view from inside the Clubroom a high pitched squeal is heard moments before a purposeful appearing Bert returns into the room alone.

All eyes are upon Bert as he returns to his seat at the table. He carefully unwraps his false teeth from the handkerchief. In a flash Bert returns his teeth to his mouth. He makes a couple of trial bites to ensure that they are seated correctly before he takes a long drink from his glass of bitter. He glares around the room. Norman is still standing on top of his stool behind the ochre with his third dart in his right hand. Leo has turned white with fear. Bert glares at him for a second and then addresses Vic and Eddie sounding most annoyed.

"The cheeky hard faced little swine....I just cannot understand or believe the antics of some of today's youth.... Bloody Hell Fire!...Totally out of order!!!.....Eh?......Eh?."

There is not the slightest sign of disagreement from any person present. There are tuttings and murmurs of approval for the suitable action taken. Bert drains his glass before he stands up to call across to Norman.

"If you wish to claim the Match Norman I am quite prepared to accept your plea...After all is said and done that little 'Gobshite' Taffy was Leo's official second and Manager."

Norman glances at Leo, who is not making any sort of protest, before he turns to wink at Woody. He is very calm.

"Not necessary Bert thank you...I think I require six to finish this Match is that correct Mr Marker?."

Charlie nods eagerly as he double checks the scoreboard.

"Yes...That's correct Norman...Four scored leaving you requiring six...Order please...Gentlemen!."

Norman turns to Leo, speaking quite rationally.

"Just to show that there's no ill feelings Leo I would like to complete the Match...If I am to be the winner I wish to win fair and square... O.K.?."

A deflated looking Leo nods his bowed head as the delighted Bert calls out.

"Nice one Norman....Right...Best of Order! please Gentlemen!... Over to you Charlie...Norman to throw."

In absolute silence Norman takes careful aim and throws his final dart. The dart lands squarely in the centre of the double three segment. The whole room erupts with sheer delight. A jubilant Woody sweeps Norman off the top of the stool to carry him on his shoulders back to the bar. Eddie brings Norman's special stool back to the normal position it occupies alongside Woody's at the bar.

Everyone is buzzing with excitement as they discuss the amazing spectacle they have just witnessed. Norman raises his pint in the air. He is delighted with the reception his actions have received. He is about to take a drink when he notices Leo sneaking off towards the way out. He calls out.

"Hey...Leo...Where do you think you're going?... Come on...I think the least I can do is buy you a pint out of my winnings....Come on Leo...No hard feelings....Come on...Don't spoil my night you're welcome to join me."

A sheepish looking Leo nods and then smiles before he dashes back to shake hands with the victorious Norman and gladly shares in his celebrations.

The general euphoria continues as Peggy Hacket appears alongside Woody at the bar. He nudges Woody to declare.

"If I hadn't seen it with my own eyes I would never have believed it...Bloody Hell!...What a performance....What a Darts Player."

Woody enquires.

"What do you mean by that Peggy?."

Peggy is cautious, anxious not to offend.

"Well you know Woody...Little Norman...With the darts. I mean to say...Who would have thought that?...."

Woody interrupts Peggy mid sentence.

"Let me tell you something Peggy...If Norman had laid flat on his back as he threw his darts he would have given Leo a even worse hammering."

Peggy smiles but is bemused. Woody explains.

"Don't you remember all the trouble Norm had with his back?... He's only been able to get out and about again quite recently."

Peggy nods and smiles as he thinks for a moment. He half-nods because he does not really appreciate the significance of Woody's comments. Woody gets closer to Peggy to give him a fuller explanation.

"The poor bugger had to wear one of those plaster jackets for months on end....Sent him home from the Cottage Hospital trussed up like a chicken...Poor bastard just lay on his back in his bed at home with only his dear old Mother looking after him...Nearly sent him round the bend it did...Well...To cut a long story short I took an old Dart Board around to him...I fixed it up on the wall facing him as he lay in his bed...Once he took to it he realised that he was a natural...His poor old Mum spent half of her time pulling the darts out of the board for him...I must admit I was amazed at how good he was myself...

So… Anyways…Perhaps people will take more notice of what he says in future…Eh?."

* * *

"Sounds too good to be cockeyed true to me."

The great day has arrived at long last. Today the opening game of the new Crown Green Bowling Season is taking place. The Green at Lapley Vale Bowling and Social Club has never looked better at the start of a long Spring and Summer Competition. Bathed in the bright midday sunshine the small grassed square looks very close to being immaculate.

Woody is raking over the gravel chippings in the gutter directly below the veranda. The whole square of the manicured turf is surrounded by a shallow gully or gutter about two feet wide filled almost to the top with loose gravel. This essential barrier around the perimeter adequately prevents any of the wooden bowls from travelling too far if they are over played and cross the edge of the grassed part of the Green.

Alf emerges from the Clubhouse onto the veranda carrying two large mugs of steaming tea. He calls out to Woody.

"Tea up Woody Lad.....Come on Lad you've earned this and no mistake."

Woody nods, raising his arm in acknowledgement. He steps back to proudly admire his handiwork before he saunters over to the veranda to join Alf on one of the benches. Alf rapidly passes Woody his hot mug and Woody carefully blows on the tea before taking a welcomed sip. Alf is in a very good frame of mind. The opening of the Bowling Season together with the formation of their Darts Team has given the Club funds a new and very necessary lease of life. He smiles as he speaks.

"I don't think I have ever seen the Green looking better in all my years of experience hereabouts...Well done my Old Friend....Well done indeed."

Both men feast they eyes on a long satisfying look all around the whole Bowling Green area. Alf's facial expression changes and the culmination of many weeks of strain and worry become apparent as he speaks.

"I can tell you this Woody I'm bloody glad to greet the arrival of the new Season...Let's hope that it can help to save our bacon Eh?...We've definitely been doing better lately but we're still not out of the woods... It's a constant worry... Old Vic was telling me last night in the bar that the Accountant has sent for him...Urgently...He has to take all the books and the outstanding bills and what have you around to his Office today.....He was saying that he expects to receive a summons soon for not paying the rest of the Rates...Not this years...Last bloody years... Poor Vic...He fears the worst...Unless something turns up very soon I shudder to think what will happen to us all...I think he's struggling to raise the money to pay our wages each week."

Both men sip their tea and sadly reflect on their painful plight. Woody shakes his head and then attempts to be positive.

"Not to worry Alf...I wasn't about to ask for a rise anyways....You never know....What is that old saying?...Every cloud has a silver lining or a bird in the hand is worth two in the back of a taxi or something?... Cheer up Pal...Things can only get better."

Alf is trying hard to cheer up but he suddenly remembers something else on the deficit side. He is about to revert to the exposure of his persistent misery.

"Oh Aye...And pigs might fly as well."

Before he can tell him, Woody interrupts, still trying his best to cheer Alf up.

"And if they do Alf can you make sure you steer them away from our Bowling Green...I take a lot of time and care to measure exact amounts of the fertiliser I apply to the grass... One load of unwanted pig shite would be too much of a good thing."

Alf smiles and nods but he is having great difficulty snapping out of his current depression. He sadly shakes his head.

"As if all that's not enough to put up with...And I'm sorry but this is going to affect you as well I'm afraid my Old Mate...Billy Hancock took my old Austin Somerset into his garage the other day....You know...To see what could be done to make it roadworthy and safe...But...I very much fear that Austin will be going to that big garage up there in the sky."

Woody is aware that Alf is very fond of his old car. He shakes his head sympathetically as Alf continues.

"Not really worth spending the money on repairing him Billy said...Throwing good money after bad...I trust old Billy the Garage and I know he has my best interests at heart...He wouldn't give me duff gen...The engine...The transmission...The gearbox... All shot at."

Woody shakes his head again as Alf is getting close to tears.

"Apparently the only things he found to be in good working order were the wing mirrors and the bloody ash trays.... It's bloody marvellous isn't it?...There's no way I can afford a replacement at this moment in time...It looks as if we will have to make other arrangements when we travel to away matches this year...Sorry Woody but that's the top and bottom of it...Sorry Mate...I wish I could be slightly optimistic but I've got to face the hard facts and there's no escaping it."

Woody realises how much the loss of Austin will mean to Alf and he knows it will be a loss to himself as well. Apart from the convenience when the Team are playing away from home, Alf is always prepared to provide Woody or anyone else in need with a lift for any reason. Woody is keen to snap Alf out of the deep depression he is sinking into to. He tries to make light of the situation whilst keeping a element of sympathy and understanding.

"Never mind Alf I'm sure we'll manage somehow...We always do don't we?...With the best will in the world we would have to admit that the old car has seen better days...I remember twigging just how old it really is when you showed me the log book that day and I noticed it was written in Latin...Eh?."

He nudges his old friend and notices a glimmer of a smile which encourages him to persevere.

"Let's face it Alf...Towards the end of last Season it a touch and go whether it would've been quicker to walk......Eh?"

He gives Alf another nudge and is delighted to see that his Pal is on the brink of a revival. Alf grins and shakes his head but even as he speaks he recalls yet another problem looming on the horizon.

"I suppose you're right as usual Woody but we'll miss that old jalopy...But listen Mate....I haven't told you the rest of it yet have I?.....Doris...Doris has regretfully informed me that she will no longer be able to clean for us...That's another job I'll have to take on myself."

Woody has never pretended to like Doris but he is interested in this latest bit of news.

"I don't care what anybody says about her Woody she's always been a bloody good cleaner and what is even more relevant and to the point she was cheap...And irrespective of the attitude of some of our Members we must not forget the value of her voluntary work behind the bar from time to time."

Woody glares at Alf searching for credibility. He snaps out his comments.

"How the bloody hell could anyone forget Doris behind that bloody bar Alf?...Christ...Talk about the proverbial Bear with the sore arse."

He tutts and shakes his head as Alf has to concede that Doris had never been the most popular person in the Club. He decides not to carry on any further discussion about her lack of popularity. He presses on with his tales of woe.

"Anyways all things taken together...She's packed in.. As a matter of fact she's had a little bit of good fortune...Come into some money unexpectedly from somewhere or another...A couple of thousand pounds by all accounts and rumours...She's off to Canada to visit her Daughter and to see her Grandchildren.....She's never actually seen them in the flesh...She says it's the best thing that's ever happened to her and she's like a dog with two dicks I couldn't believe my own eyes when she was telling me all about it…She kept smiling…. I could hardly recognise her she was so happy…So I'm very pleased for her although I definitely will miss her."

Woody appreciates the loss to Alf but will not allow himself to be a hypocrite.

"I'm very sorry for you Alf and I mean that…But… I can't say I will miss her sour puss behind that bar…Sorry Alf but I won't….And… Incidentally…Neither will many others… Having said that I am happy to hear that she's got want she wants and I hope she enjoys her good fortune."

Alf is not sure if he can return to the aura of contentment experienced earlier in the morning when he first looked out at the Green and welcomed the new Bowling Season. On reflection he decides that thanks to Woody he has managed to get a load of misery off his chest and at the end of the day things must go on irrespective. He sounds quite resigned.

"I suppose I will manage the cleaning until things start to look up a bit…I very much fear that the Committee will have to roll their sleeves up and give me a lift behind that bar as and when the need arises."

Alf manages a smile as he perks up slightly.

"Think about it Woody…If we have to use Billy Dawes behind the bar we'll be the only place in Lancashire selling….. Cockeyed…..Pints of bitter."

They both roar with laughter as they are suddenly aware of the fact that they have been joined on the veranda by Ralph, who is not only the Club Chairman but is also the Captain of the Bowling Team. He is with Eddie Brown and appearing into view via the kitchen door is Billy Dawes. Alf nudges Woody to say with a stifled chuckle.

"Christ Woody…Talk of the Devil…..Eh?."

All three men are carrying their little leather bags containing their personal sets of bowls and they all appear to be very pleased with themselves.

Crown Green Bowlers only use two Bowls as opposed to Flat Green Bowlers who use four each. When playing in a match a Standard Jack, that's the little one they all aim for, has to be used. No-one is permitted to use their own Jack in any form of competition. Many people consider Crown Green Bowling to be much more demanding than the, perhaps better known, Flat or Panel Bowling. In playing Crown Bowls the player not only has to cope with the bias or offset weight in his Bowl, better known as Woods in Lancashire and the North, but also with the fact that

the centre, or *'Crown'*, of the Green is higher than the sides. Hence the name Crown Green Bowling. The Greens are laid with a crown in the centre which very gradually slopes down to the edges and gutters. Another marked difference is Crown Green Bowlers are permitted to place their Jacks anywhere on the available surface of the Green. They are not restricted to the narrow marked out strips or panels as is the case for all those involved in Flat Green Bowling.

Ralph cannot hide his excitement as he greets Woody and Alf.

"Good Day Gentlemen…Alright are you Boys?…Here we go again then…The start of yet another New Season…I must say the Green looks to be in first class condition again Woody."

There are nods and grunts of agreement from all of those present causing Woody to coyly nod his appreciation for the remarks and observations made. Ralph rubs his hands together as he continues.

"I don't think this lot visiting us today will present us with much of a problem…We should see them off without too much ceremony eh?."

Billy joins in to voice his opinions.

"If we can't beat the Team that finished at the bottom of the cockeyed League last Season we might as well burn our cockeyed woods here and now…What do you say Eddie?."

Eddie responds but they are oddly aware that he seems to be less enthusiastic as he would normally be at the commencement of a new campaign.

"Yes…I suppose you're right there Billy but you never know…New Season….New start and the 'Powers that be' haven't done us any favours with the handicapping this year… It's not going to be easy giving away thirty points to some of the other Teams and that's exactly what we're having to do today…The Liberal Club play off scratch…Stands to reason we can't afford to give any silly points away…It'll make sure we don't sit back on our laurels as the reigning Champions that's for sure."

In most of the Crown Green Bowling Leagues in the North of England a Team consists of eight players on each side. Each plays a single game against one of his opponents. Each of the eight individual games is won when one of the players is first to reach a score of twenty one points. However to facilitate a genuine contest taking place the Inter Club Fixture is won by the Team which scores the highest total number of points. For instance if a Team wins all their matches twenty one to ten then the Final Result would be 168 points to 80. Obviously this rarely happens because each Team is made up of players of varying skills and experience so the Governing Body examines the previous Season's results and in an effort to make all the Matches as competitive as possible they handicap the better Teams by making them score, in the case of Lapley Vale for instance thirty points, before they can count their points scored towards the final total. Another way to achieve this partial parity could be the deduction the penalty points awarded by the handicappers from the total number of points scored in order to give the weaker Teams a glimmer of a chance of winning even when they actually score less total points than their opponents. The onus is on the stronger Team to overcome their handicap to become the winners of the Match. In the example previously explained a grand total of 168 points scored against 80 would become 138 to 80 if the winning team had a handicap of thirty points to be deducted. If Lapley Vale played another Team who had the same handicap as themselves then they would both start from scratch.

Ralph readily agrees with Eddie's observations but attempts to put things into their right perspective.

"But that's the whole purpose of handicapping isn't it?....Be fair now it does tend to make more of a game of it against every Team we play...I was pleased to see that our arch rivals at the Constitutional Club have been given a handicap of thirty the same as us...That's fair... At least we'll start off on equal terms with them when we meet."

Billy looks annoyed as he interrupts.

"Fair?....Nothings cockeyed fair about it if you ask my opinion.... Why should we give other Teams thirty cockeyed points?...I don't agree with handicapping and never did...My motto has always been…..'Let the best cockeyed Team win!'."

Eddie shakes his head in a gesture of disagreement.

"Oh come on now Billy...It definitely makes more of a game of it against a lesser Team if you have to make up thirty points to get on level terms with them...It keeps everyone on their toes and also gives the less talented and experienced Teams a chance to make a name for themselves by possibly beating better Teams...If there was no handicapping the only Team in this League we would have any difficulty in beating would be the Constitutional Club...Am I Correct?...And they're in the same boat as us because they can't afford to slip up against any of the weaker Teams either...What it amounts to Billy is handicapping brings the element of competiveness into all of our playing."

Billy does not agree but decides there is little point in arguing because handicapping is a fact of life.

They are all aware that Eddie is not his usual self but are unable to identify any obvious cause. Eddie also detects that his friends are growing more curious about him. Before anyone can make the necessary enquiries to establish the reason, Eddie's face suddenly breaks into a broad, toothy, grin. With more than a hint of excitement, possibly sheer delight, in his tone he eventually elects to reveal all.

"Incidentally I'm afraid you're going to have to manage without my services on the Green at least for a few of the Matches this Season."

Stunned curiosity results. All need to know more.

"Because...I'm going on a Cruise to the West Indies. I can hardly believe it...Two tickets arrived in the post at our house in a letter...

Right out of the blue...An all expenses paid First Class Voyage on a Luxury Liner...I can hardly wait...For years I've yearned to return to the land of my birth for a holiday but in my heart of hearts I never really believed that I would ever make it....But my Missus and I are definitely going there's no doubt about it at all...Really...It's all in hand."

Anyone knowing Eddie could verify that he frequently talked about going back to visit the West Indies before he died but no-one, including Eddie himself, actually believed that he would ever do so. He had always worked very hard to raise his family but he has never been a wealthy man. His friends receive the news with shared delight. Ralph warmly shakes his hand as both Alf and Billy happily pat him on his back. Obviously, there is no disguising the elation being experienced by Eddie. Ralph is confident that he speaks for all of Eddie's friends.

"Good for you Eddie....I'm sure it will be the trip of a lifetime...I think I know how much it will mean to both Mrs Brown and yourself... I think I speak for us all when I say how delighted we are to be told of your wonderful news."

Eddie is beaming with delight as he responds.

"Thanks Ralph...Yes she's on cloud nine...We didn't believe it at first...We thought it might be some sort of cruel prank...But it's not!... It's all verified as correct...All above board....It's just like having a dream come true."

Although genuinely excited by the news Alf is keen to hear a little more about the circumstances surrounding this sudden change in fortunes for Eddie. He cautiously enquires.

"How has all this come about then Eddie?...Have you won in a Competition or something?."

Eddie replies, shrugging his shoulders, laughing,

"No...No nothing like that Alf...I'd have a job because I never go in for those kind of things...That's why I thought it was somebody's idea of a joke at first...But I can assure you it is not...I don't know all the ins and outs yet but as I understand it the whole trip has been arranged and paid for by some Trust....The name of which I'd never even heard of...But there's no mistake the Missus and I are going...

And not only has everything been laid on and paid for but we've also been given Traveller's Cheques which amount to more than we will ever need to cover all our personal expenses...More than generous I can tell you.. Absolutely astonishing isn't it?.....I can't get it out of my mind for more than a few minutes at a time ever since I was told it really was genuine...Having said that I hope it won't affect my normal high level of concentration which in turn may cause me to lose my usual ability to thrash any opponents daring to challenge us on our own Green today."

Billy is also amazed and delighted for his friend but he expresses his doubts as only Billy can.

"Most players couldn't beat you on here if you were playing in a cockeyed coma Eddie....It's great news but I have to say it does sounds too cockeyed good to be cockeyed true...I hope I'm wrong."

Eddie nods and smiles, placing his arm around his old friend's shoulders. He attempts to explain.

"Billy...I felt exactly as you do at first but my son Dean has been in touch with the Shipping Company at Liverpool and the tickets and everything else have been arranged and paid for...Like I said...By this Trust and there's absolutely no doubt about it at all.....The tickets are made out in our names with the correct details and addresses and everything...They told Dean that they had been expecting us to contact them because they aren't at liberty to explain or even tell us anything other than the name of the Trust and they obviously suspected that we would be surprised to say the very least...They weren't wrong...I'll tell you what Boys...It's nothing short of a bloody miracle."

Everyone shares Eddie's joy as they all hug and pat him on the back again, making Eddie an ecstatically happy man.

* * *

"I hope that score won't count as a record Vic."

The scheduled Bowling Match versus Shaw Liberal Club is well under way. Four matches are currently being played on the Green. Amongst them Billy Dawes is playing against Arnie
Brooks. Arnie is the Captain of the visiting Team. Eddie Brown is up against Frank 'Punchy' Davies, an ex-boxer and well known local character. They are all old friends of many years standing.

All of the benches around the Green are occupied by spectators and other players from each Team. Some are recording the scores in the current matches being played on the Green on official scorecards as each end is completed. These scorer sit together. Their representative player shouts or signals to them with the score after the result of each end has been agreed. The players sign these cards at the conclusion of their game before they are collected by the two Independent Referees, appointed by the 'Powers that be'. The Referees also arbitrate when there is any dispute. This may entail them going onto the Green with their various types of precision measuring equipment to enable them to accurately establish the distance of each Wood from the Jack after which they will decide, with any doubt, which Woods are closest and consequently which of the players is entitled to score either one or both of the available points.

Vic Callow is scoring for Billy and Sid Sparrow, the Chairman of the Liberal Club, is sitting next to him scoring for Arnie. A very good crowd has gathered, some are standing and others are seated on the benches by the tables on the veranda. Alf is very busy serving vast quantities of beer through a large hatch which gives convenient access to the bar without entering inside the Clubhouse. Vic glances at Sid's scorecard before looking at his own. He sounds quite pleased with himself as he confidently addresses Sid.

"Looks like old Billy Cockeye is proving a bit too good for Arnie today Sid."

Sid smiles and nods.

"Yes...And I'm afraid that's been the story all afternoon Vic...Even allowing for your big handicap I'm sorry to report that we are still taking a hell of a hammering from your Chaps...I feared the worst when Old Woody beat Charlie twenty one points to three...I thought I had a reasonable game against Ralph but I only managed to notch up ten points by the time he'd finished me off...You made short work of Alfie Harrison Vic but I was pleased to see our most improved player... Old Tricky Dickie Scott got into double figure against Old Peggy... Incidentally... I see he's taken to wearing his proper leg today."

Vic nods and smirks as he replies.

"Oh Aye....Poor Old Peggy....It's a long story so I won't bore you with the detail just now Sid."

Vic is mindful not to be immodest but he does allow himself to gloat a little bit.

"Mind you Sid...There's not too many Teams around this District who can match us on our own Green...We've been very lucky this year... Same Team as last year...Not lost one first Team Player throughout the long cruel Winter Months...And we've got some very promising Reserves coming along as well...One or two young fellows...I think that's very encouraging for all our futures Sid...Don't you?."

Sid nods his agreement, adding.

"Yes...But when it comes down to it I think you'd have to admit that Woody makes the big difference...Not just with his Bowling...He must be the finest Green keeper in this County... This Green is a credit to you all but especially Old Woody."

Vic smiles, agreeing enthusiastically.

"You can say that again Sid...It's a true labour of love for Old Woody...He lives for this Club."

The two men are interrupted from their pleasant conversation by the raised voice of Billy calling to them from across the other side of the Green. Billy has both his arms lifted over his head indicating that he has just scored a maximum two points. A dejected looking Arnie is standing alongside him. Vic raises his hand to acknowledge that he has received the message. Billy relaxes his arms. He sounds rather brisk.

"Come on Vic...You got it at last did you?.....Two for me...Try to pay attention to the cockeyed game will you?."

Arnie points down with both his hands. Sid had already marked him two points down. He waves to Arnie as Vic shouts back to them both.

"Yes got it two to you Billy....The score is now Nineteen playing four...Off the mat."

The mat is a small rounded piece of rubber which is placed under the players supporting foot. His full weight comes down onto the grass at the actual moment he dispatches his Wood across the Green in the direction of the Jack. The winner of the previous end not only gains the advantage of sending the Jack but he also chooses the position of the mat on the grass where the next end of four Woods will be sent from. Had Arnie managed to score the point or points on the previous end he would have had the honour and advantage of placing the mat and sending the Jack. In those circumstances the game score would have been called as four plays nineteen off the mat. However....Billy casually tosses the mat onto the grass. He picks up his first Wood with the Jack. Holding the Jack in his right hand he show it to Arnie, as he declares, quite, loudly.

"Finger peg Arnie...O.K.?."

Arnie nods anxiously straining to get the best possible sighting of the track the Jack follows across the Green. On this occasion, from one corner, across the crown, to the other.

'Finger peg' indicates that the Jack, which is weighted with a bias exactly the same as the Woods, is being sent with it's biased side nearest to Billy's little finger on his right hand. Had Billy chosen to send the Jack with the bias on the other side he would have declared 'Thumb peg'. It is a rule that the Player sending the Jack must inform his Opponent accordingly before the Jack leaves his hand. Both men concentrate closely on the line the Jack follows across the manicured grass. The Jack comes to a stop and Billy places his Wood in his right hand before swiftly dispatching it across the Green towards the stationary Jack. As he carries out this action Billy breaks wind, from the rear, very loudly. Arnie, who is standing very close behind him trying to watch his line, jumps back immediately. Billy appears to be a little embarrassed as he apologises.

"Sorry about that Arnie."

Arnie pulls a face and waves his hand under his nose in a gesture of disgust. He sounds bitter as he responds.

"Christ Billy...Surely you're not getting nervous at this late stage of the Game...Bloody hell you haven't given me a bloody look in today."

Bernie Price, the loudmouthed tormentor of Billy during Committee meetings, is standing on the veranda holding a full pint in his hand. He has everyone laughing after he shouts.

"Don't rip that cloth Billy keep the whole piece."

Not to be outdone Peggy Hackett then calls out.

"Wrap that one up Billy I'll take it home for the cat's dinner."

Billy is anxious to keep his concentration on the game. He watches his Wood glide up alongside the Jack before he turns to fully apologise to Arnie.

"Sorry Arnie...It's the Wife...She will insist on giving me a plate of those cockeyed baked beans before I take part in cockeyed Bowling Matches."

Arnie ignores Billy to send his first Wood. It stops woefully short of the Jack and Billy's first Wood. Billy nods and swiftly moves onto the mat as, getting more frustrated, Arnie steps off it. Billy takes aim, starting to bend his back when another ripping retort blasts out from

Billy's trouser region. He anxiously rubs his stomach, looking rather sheepish.

"Oops...Sorry again Arnie...What can I say...It's all down to those cockeyed beans...Sorry."

Billy then sends his second Wood which comes to rest touching one side of the Jack, a perfect shot, expertly delivered and extremely difficult for any opponent to beat. Downcast and defeated Arnie is about to accept the inevitable. He sends his second Wood which stops shorter than his first. They walk over to check on the obvious outcome of the end. Vic shouts over to them.

"If that's two for you Billy...That's Game Over."

Arnie signals two down to Sid even before he reaches his Woods. He kicks his Woods towards Billy's and the Jack and sportingly extends his right hand. As they shake hands Billy cockily confirms the score with Vic.

"Two it is Victor...I thank you."

They collect their Woods, the Jack and the mat. They start to walk towards the bench where Vic and Sid are sitting. Billy is smiling proudly, Arnie looks and feels well beaten. Arnie speaks to Vic in a sarcastic, even peevish, manner.

"I hope that score won't count as a record Vic.... Because it was definitely wind assisted."

They all smile as Arnie addresses his next remarks directly to Sid.

"It was like trying to Bowl through a big brown cloud following old 'Billy the POO' here onto that mat today Sid... Still I have to admit I was well and truly thrashed...I wish I'd had the presence of mind to fart in his face on the odd and rare occasions when I actually held the Jack...No hard feeling Billy."

Billy and Arnie leave heading towards the Clubroom for two well deserved pints just as Ralph joins Vic and Sid. Ralph definitely appears to be rather pleased with himself.

"I don't think our handicap will really be of much assistance to your final scores today Sid...I'm afraid a small
    miracle will be needed now."

Sid is resigned to defeat.

"You're quite right Ralph...There won't be any miracles happening around here today I'm afraid......We're not ahead in any of the last three games and it looks as if Eddie Brown is giving Old Punchy a right royal seeing to...Still there you have it...To the Victors the spoils...No hard feeling from me...None at all....Mind you it would have been quite a turn up for the books if we had been in with a shout against you lot you are the current Champions after all is said and done...Eh?."

Ralph and Vic are quietly contented to witness Sid being so humble in defeat. Sid suddenly changes the subject, possibly hoping to wipe the smirks from their faces.

"Anyways...How are things going Ralph?...A little dickie bird informed me that the whole future of your Club might be hanging in the balance at the present time...I do hope this talk is an exaggeration of the real facts as they stand Ralph."

Ralph glances at Vic, who sadly and quickly looks down at ground. Ralph tries hard not to sound too down hearted.

"I'm afraid the little dickie bird wasn't too far off the mark Sid...We have definitely seen better times from a financial point of view there's no denying that...But...Where's there's life there's hope Eh?....Never say die."

Vic attempts to be supportive with one of his little quotations. Initially he sounds quite plausible.

"You know what I always say Gentlemen?."

He clears his throat to pronounce clearly.

"A bird with a broken wing can still sing....But you cannot pluck feathers off a frog."

He stands back looking smugly satisfied as both Ralph and Sid blankly stare at him. Neither has the faintest idea what Vic is on about and they will not be bothering to enquire.

As the three men make their ways towards the Clubroom Vic suddenly turns to Ralph, to speak urgently to him,

"By the way Ralph can we arrange a Committee Meeting for tomorrow afternoon please?...I've got an appointment to see Tom Morgan the Club's Accountant at eleven o'clock tomorrow."

Ralph immediately realises the significance and the hidden gravity behind Vic's statement. He had been attempting to dismiss the worry from his mind, at least for the time being, but he is mature enough to know that those relevant pressing matters will not simply go away. They have to be addressed.

"I understand Vic.....Yes I'm afraid we have to face up to our responsibilities from time to time...No problem about warning the Members of the Committee they're all here this afternoon...Bloody hell Vic....Let's not panic eh?...Let's wait and see what transpires....Fingers crossed....Eh?."

They make their way through a crowded veranda. Ralph is politely nodding to all the happy drinkers as he speaks.

"A few more days like this won't do us any harm Vic...Eh?..... Leave all those necessary arrangements with me Vic you've got more than enough on your plate at the moment...Don't worry I'll make sure everyone is made aware of the Meeting and I'll have everything crossed when you have your encounter with Tom Morgan in the morning Vic. He's not one for beating about the bush Tom Morgan...Calls a spade a bloody shovel."

He sadly shakes his head before making a positive effort to cheer himself up as they make their way into the Clubroom.

"Come then Chaps...We appear to be the only Blokes hereabouts without pints in our hands...Let's wet our whistles with some of the finest draught bitter money can buy...Nothing like a nice pint to lift the spirits I always say....Eh?"

There is no argument from either of his companions as they lick their lips before making a beeline for the bar

* * *

"I feel sure we are unanimous."

The full Committee are seated around the suitably covered Snooker Table in the Clubhouse at Lapley Vale Bowling and Social Club. They are silent, Ralph is sitting at the head of the table. Alf, Eddie, Bernie and Billy are sitting on stools along the sides. Vic's usual place at Ralph's right hand is vacant. They all appear to be most concerned and apprehensive.

Vic suddenly appears looking excited and flushed. As he takes his seat Ralph breaks the silence.

"Bloody hell Vic....We were just starting to get a bit worried about you...We imagined that the shock of your meeting with the Accountant this morning had proved to be too much for you...Yes...Anyways...Well we're all here Vic...So…...Er.. The floor is yours."

Vic does not respond immediately. He lifts his old battered briefcase onto the table as he settles onto his stool. He gazes all around the table verifying that all are present and correct. All eyes are focussed on him as he slowly opens his briefcase. He pauses for a moment, taking a very deep breath, before he speaks. Most detect that Vic has got something up his sleeve because of his odd demeanour.

"Apologies Mr Chairman...Gentlemen...Please just bear with me for a moment or two...You are right about the shock I have just received at Tom Morgan's Office but please do not panic because it was not the type of shock I was expecting...Oh No... I find it very difficult to believe what I am about to relate to you myself...Please allow me another few moments to gather my thoughts."

The tension is too much for Bernie. His patience is ebbing away. This is clearly reflected in his tone.

"Well don't bloody rush Victor will you?...Christ... We've all been sitting here fearing the worst and you waltz in with what I can only describe as a bloody silly expression on your face....Prolonging the agony....Come on!....Let's hear the worst!...The suspense is killing me... Come on!."

Bernie glances around the table gauging the reaction to his outburst but the others are all staring at Victor in stunned anticipation. Vic realises that he is causing unnecessary tension. He coughs politely and speaks very purposefully.

"I entered the Accountant's Office this morning feeling very similar to a lamb going to the slaughter...I confess I was expecting the worst... But then....I found to my complete amazement that I was being given the Royal Treatment...I was whisked into the Bosses Office...You know?...Tom Morgan himself. The first thing he did was to ask me if I would care for a nice cup of tea or coffee...I was gob smacked...I wondered what was going on...I thought they may have mistaken me for someone else by their attitude."

Bernie is near cracking point. His temper is close to snapping.

"For Christ's sake Vic!...."

Ralph raises his hand to put an end to the unwelcome interruption. He justifiably administers a mild scolding.

"Look Bernie...We are all as anxious and interested as you are..... But...Please let Victor continue will you?... Vic you have the floor once more."

Bernie mutters something nasty under his breath as he folds his arms across his chest and glares. Vic nods to Ralph before he continues.

"Instead of being nailed to the wall as I had expected Tom Morgan handed me a neat new balance sheet detailing our accounts...I quickly read it but I could not believe my eyes... I had to pinch myself to prove I was not dreaming...Far from being in a vicious shade of red I could see that all our outstanding bills had been paid and we stand with a very healthy balance in hand."

They all stare at Vic in disbelief. Victor starts to chuckle. His whole face lights up with sheer delight.

"You're right...I couldn't believe it either...Anyways Tom Morgan realised what a shock he had given me and went on to give me a full explanation for this current state of affairs."

He pauses for a second. His colleagues all lean forward in keen anticipation of the promised explanation.

"The simple truth is there has been a considerable injection of capital into our funds."

They are puzzled. Although all equally curious, it is Eddie who actually asks first.

"How do you mean Vic...An injection of Capital?... I can't understand what you're telling us...How can this be possible?...Debts don't just vanish...Where on earth did this injection come from?...It all sounds too good to be true to me but I'm prepared to be proved wrong."

There are nods and grunts before Vic regains their full undivided attention once again.

"The reason I was late for this vitally important Emergency Committee Meeting is because I refused to leave Tom Morgan's Office until I had received a full and clear Explanation from him."

Ralph notices that Bernie is about to interrupt again so he abruptly raises his arm in a threatening gesture causing Bernie to back off immediately. Vic nods his appreciation to Ralph before he goes on.

"It would appear that we are the recipients and dare I say the fortunate beneficiaries of a large cash donation from a Trust Fund... Sufficient to pay off all our debts and pending bills and still leave enough to provide us with a very stable financial base for the future."

They are fascinated by the information but need time to absorb the full implications. Suppressing his delight and relief at the unexpected news Ralph remains desperate for more information for his own peace of mind.

"A Trust Fund?....What sort of Trust Fund?...I'm sorry if I'm about to put a dampener on the proceedings Vic but I don't recall us ever being associated with any Trust Fund....Are you absolutely satisfied beyond a reasonable doubt that everything Tom Morgan has told you is above board?."

Ralph and the others all stare hopefully into Vic face praying that their dreams have actually come true. Vic can no longer contain his own excitement and pleasure. He rises to his feet in his eagerness to convince them. He exclaims.

"YES!......YES!...YES!...Absobloodylutely one hundred percent certain!...There is no doubt about it...Even though I put a considerable amount of pressure on Tom I'm afraid I have to report that I'm still no wiser as to the exact identity of our Saviours...He did supply me with the name of the Trust but he was adamant that he could not and would not disclose any further details by order of the Trust."

He opens his briefcase to extract his tatty looking note book. It would have been possible to cut the air with a knife as he carefully opened the book to read out a name in a slow, calm and deliberate fashion.

"The Kenneth Gordon Trust."

Everyone gazes all around the table hoping to detect a glimmer of recognition from anyone amongst their number. There is no reaction at all. Slightly un-nerved, Victor continues.

"Tom Morgan was unable to give me any further details about it... Except to say that the Bank Manager in Oldham had been authorised to sign cheques on behalf of the Trust and that even he had been sworn to secrecy and was forbidden to divulge any information which might lead to the source of the money being traced...But...BUT!...You can take it from me Gentlemen the monies have been received on our behalf and there has not...I repeat...THERE HAS NOT!....Been a mistake of any shape or form."

Eddie suddenly sits forward on his stool with an inspired expression on his face. He sounds excited as he speaks.

"Wait a minute!...The tickets....Er...The tickets and so forth for our trip to the West Indies...There was mention of a Trust...I didn't really catch the name of it but they definitely said that it was the Trust who were responsible for everything and also that they wished to remain anonymous...I wonder....I wonder if it can be the same Trust?." implications brought about by their unexpected but welcome stroke of good fortune. After a short time their doubtful expressions all change into broad smiles. An elated Ralph shakes his head and does not even try to hide his unbridled delight.

"For once in my life Gentlemen I find myself lost for words.... It would appear from what has transpired that a miracle has actually happened...And...I for one am finding it very difficult to take in immediately...But."

Alf suddenly rises to his feet to gleefully interrupt.

"All I can say is three cheers for the mysterious Trust...I personally don't give a shite who...Or even what the bloody hell it is."

He stops to address Vic with a hopeful tone in his voice, which appears to be rising in volume as the whole impact of the news sinks in.

"Does this mean that I can look for a new Cleaner and...AND...A real Barmaid to help me behind the Bar?...Eh?.....Does it Victor?."

They are all thinking about their wonderful and welcome change in fortune, contemplating their own ideas about the affects of their solvency. Vic tries to bring everyone back to Earth as he answers Alf.

"No problems there Alf....But let's not go berserk all at once...I think it is incumbent upon us...The duly elected Committee...To ensure that the best possible use is made of this stroke of good fortune...And now that we find ourselves..... Unexpectedly...Back on an even keel...We must ensure that we set a steady course in the future...And I sincerely hope we have learned a lesson or two from recent events."

There is a general acceptance of this comment all around the table which enables Vic to carry on forcefully.

"We...The Committee...MUST!...Ensure that we... NEVER!... EVER!...Drop into the depths of despair that we have just escaped from......NEVER!....EVER!...Again...I think I can add without fear of contradiction that without this undoubted miracle we would now be very likely engaged in the painful process of winding up the affairs of our beloved Club...So....Whilst we can quite rightly rejoice let us learn from our past mistakes and always keep as our prime consideration in the future the maintenance of our financial stability."

This statement is met by spontaneous applause from everyone present, even Victor is surprised and delighted by his own strength of conviction. Ralph feels he is speaking for them all.

"Here...Here....Quite correct Victor...And very well said into the bargain....It is absolutely essential that we keep our feet well and truly planted firmly on the ground."

Billy has been silent throughout the revealing of the most welcome and shattering news. He is slow on the uptake but the magnitude of exactly what has happened dawns upon him. He shakes his head in a happy fashion before he exclaims.

"It's a miracle....No other word for it Boys... It's a cockeyed miracle."

They all burst out into laughter, strongly influenced with great feelings of relief. Ralph allows a few enjoyable moments to pass before he returns the Meeting to order in a very businesslike manner.

"Right....Back to business....Alf....You can take steps to fill the vacancy left by the untimely departure of Doris."

The mention of her name causes faces to be pulled and a little squirming to take place but he ignores this.

"I feel sure that I speak for all the Members of this Committee as well as the majority of our rank and file Members when I extend my grateful thanks to Alf for coping so well throughout...What can only be described as...A full blown state of emergency."

These comments are greeted with instant applause and mutters of 'Here' Here'. Alf shyly acknowledges the tribute as Ralph politely enquires.

"Will this present you with any foreseeable

problems Alf?....Filling this vacancy I mean...For a part time cleaner that is?."

Alf is bubbling with sheer delight. He cannot hide a sense of excitement in his tone.

"No...No none at all Mr Chairman...I take it that I am in a position to offer the successful candidate a reasonable hourly rate?...As a matter of fact I have had a couple of discreet enquires since Doris left...Mind you...With the circumstances as they were I was forced to be rather vague with my responses....How about a nice Barmaid whilst I'm at it?."

Everyone's attention automatically swings to Victor who responds in a 'Why not' gesture with his hands and a delighted nod of his head, indicating his full authority had been given. Billy cannot stop himself from speaking.

"I should cockeyed think so as well...And as far as Barmaiding goes anyone you might think of would be a cockeyed improvement on Doris...Hellfire!...I for one won't miss her...No not one cockeyed bit."

Vic laughs as he intervenes.

"As we are now in a position where we can contemplate engaging Staff without fear of instant liquidation I would like to see a nice, bright, attractive young woman behind that bar...Alongside Alf as and when required and...Of course each and every weekend from now on."

A strangely quiet Bernie cannot resist making a coarse but amusing remark.

"Speaking for myself Mr Chairman I don't care who Alf appoints just as long as she has big tits and wears those kinky boots."

Roars of laughter greet Bernie's intervention. He is so pleased with himself that he nudges and winks at Billy on one side and then Eddie on the other. Ralph joins in the merriment but quickly restores order with a loud bang on his gavel. He glances at Vic's half hearted smile before he speaks.

"Alright Bernie...O.K....I think we can all guess what your particular preferences might be but I must ask you all to be sensible and...Above all...Remember just who we are.....Eh?.....I suggest we leave these appointments in the most capable hands of our loyal and trusted colleague Alf."

Again there are mutters of 'Here' 'Here' and general noises of approval. Alf smiles in a satisfied fashion as he replies.

"Thank you Mr Chairman...Thank you for those few kind words... Please allow me to assure you that I will make suitable appointments for both of these posts...Thank you."

He looks at Vic and then Ralph before he adds.

"Well...I don't know if there is any further business to discuss at this rather extraordinary Meeting but...Speaking for myself...I think it might be a suitable time for us all to adjourn and retire to the bar where we can all enjoy a nice pint each...On the house of course!."

This suggestion is greeted with cheers and applause. Everyone's attention focuses on Ralph. He nods.

"Thank you Alf...I don't think any of us here present today would have guessed in their wildest dreams that this Meeting would be brought to close with a proposal for drinks on the house...But...Heavens be praised...We will respond in the affirmative to that excellent offer.!"

There are more cheers as Ralph raises his arm to attract everyone's attention before he adds.

"I'm sure that in the fullness of time we will need to examine our overall expenditure and general financial position in more detail and depth when Vic...Our Treasurer... And of course our Hon Secretary as well...Sorry Vic...Has sorted everything out but in the meantime let me endorse Alfred's proposal and I think I can say without fear of contradiction that we are unanimous on that motion...Just a word of caution Gentlemen...I don't think we need to advertise our stroke of good fortune to anyone outside the precincts of this Room.....Eh?..... Well at least for the time being...Understood?...Agreed?."

All grunt and nod their acceptance of Ralph's closing remark as they stand up to rapidly make their ways to the bar. Alf is first in position behind the pumps as Ralph shouts over to Eddie and Bernie who are making an urgent visit to the Gentlemen's Toilets en route.

"Give Woody a shout will you?...He's should be out the back somewhere...I think we can make a exception to the rule and tell him what has happened...Just to put the poor Bugger out of his misery...Just wait until he realises that his beloved Club has been saved from extinction...Saved from the very brink of disaster."

The atmosphere within the Clubhouse is loaded with undiluted happiness.

* * *

"Hey steady on Alf....Play the game."

Woody has arranged for Eric McCabe to join him for a morning session on the Bowling Green. Eric needed little or no encouragement because of his keenness to learn from the Master. His actual employer, Dicky Mitchell, the owner of Lapley Vale Nurseries, as usual, had been most understanding to any such request from Eric to adjust his normal working hours with him.

Charlie Walsh had been kind enough to give Alf a lift in his car to a more confident monthly visit at the Brewery but he has to rely upon Public Transport to find his way back. Unfortunately Alf's old Austin car is still at Billy Hancock's Garage. Unfortunately he does not anticipate much good news emanating from that particular quarter.

The newly appointed Cleaner, a delightful Widow with a pleasant, endearing, nature probably in her late fifties but very well preserved and presentable named Mavis Nicholson has, in a relatively short time, already made a good impression on everyone at the Club. Mavis is a good natured and willing woman who is fitting in like a duck taking to water. She enjoys carrying out all the tasks allotted to her. What is even more pleasing to Alf, Woody and Eric, is the fact that she makes a nice brew of tea and she has now started to bring in home made cakes and scones for their eager consumption during tea breaks. It has even become noticeable that Woody has actually started to make an effort to improve his general appearance since her arrival and has, so far, endeavoured to be sociable and polite to her at all times, even curtailing his swearing to some extent.

Woody and Eric are working inside the wooden pavilion. Eric is busy cleaning the big lawnmower as Woody moves away from his work bench to open a large metal cupboard with his bunch of keys. Woody removes a package, the one collected from the Chemists by Eric, from the cupboard. He carefully places it on top of the work bench, pausing to talk to Eric.

"Now here we go young Ricky...It's time I started to let you into some of my little secrets...There's an awful lot I need to teach you My Lad before you'll be capable of producing grass of the quality you see outside there on our beloved Green...So stand by for a very important lesson...O.K.?."

Eric springs to his feet immediately giving one hundred per cent attention. Woody carefully cuts the string to open the brown paper package. There are three separate packages inside. Eric is buzzing with excitement as Woody explains

"Now you don't need to know the details of what the actual chemicals are Ricky...I'm not that sure myself and anyways Harry Jeeps is the expert in that field...What you and I are going to do this morning is add these chemicals to some special water I keep in a butt around the back of here...Have you seen it?...A big barrel with a heavy wooden lid on it."

Eric nods and anxiously awaits the next step.

"When we have successfully completed this task you and I are going to water the whole Green evenly...Now all I can reveal to you Ricky is that this mixture will not only fertilise the grass but will also give it the desired colour and texture."

Eric nods again as Woody carefully carries the chemicals towards the door. He nods towards the far corner of the workshop as he instructs his young assistant.

"Fetch yon old spade handle will you Ricky...You're going to be needing the use of that My Lad."

Eric complies with Woody's instruction before he follows him out to the rear of the Pavilion. They stop alongside the large water butt. Eric notices that the heavy wooden lid has quite a large stone placed on top of it. Woody is taking special care carrying the chemicals. He jerks a nod to Eric.

"O.K. Lad....Open her up will you?."

Eric quickly lifts and removes the heavy stone, placing it on the ground. He then lifts the wooden lid. As he raises it a foul smelling vapour instantly escapes from inside the butt. Eric yelps, leaping back. He holds his nose with both hands. Horrified, he turns to Woody, demanding an explanation.

"Jesus Christ Woody!....What the hell is that dreadful stink?....What is it?...Phew....That really is absolutely bloody dreadful...Christ I think I'm going to pass out here....Bloody hell.....What is it?."

Woody does not noticeably react. However, he removes a rather dirty looking old handkerchief from his jacket pocket to briskly wipe under his nose. He is trying very hard to act in a normal, casual, manner although, it has to be said, he is far from completely convincing.

"Come on Lad...Bloody hell...It's not that bad."

Eric can hardly believe his ears. He is unable to understand why Woody has not reacted to the smell. Astonished he still demands some sort of explanations.

"Not that bad?....Not that BLOODY BAD!...It smells as if at least a dozen skunks have farted in there...Bloody hell Woody I can almost taste it...It's dreadful...Awful."

Woody merely smiles, shaking his head. He opens one of the smaller packets of chemicals to empty it into the butt. He attempts to reassure his shaken assistant.

"Well Ricky...The only thing I will say is I've smelt far worse than that...Although not recently...These are some of the things you have to live with if you want to be the best...Now.. Come on get that handle in there....I need you to paddle it around whilst I'm adding some of this other stuff."

Leaning back as far as he can without falling over backwards Eric dips the handle into the foul liquid and starts to stir. Woody carefully adds most of the contents of the other two packets one at a time. He continues to instruct Eric.

"That's it...Right...Keep stirring Lad...Make sure that these secret ingredients are well and truly dissolved in the solution of water and ripened chicken shit....That's it."

The stench becomes even worse as a fine vapour is visibly rising off the surface of the contents of the butt. Woody watches closely as Eric continues to stir, feeling more and more nauseous as he does so. Woody continues to encourage him.

"There now...That's not too bad is it?."

Eric's face is contorted as he glares at Woody.

"O.K. Ricky...Stop stirring now...That's right... O.K....Put the lid back on for a few minutes now...Give it time to settle and blend...Now this is an opportune moment for you and I to adjourn so that we may both partake of a nice mug of hot steaming tea...Eh?...What do you say Lad?."

Eric is still recovering from shock as he very cautiously replaces the wooden lid on the butt. His tone reflects the level of his disgust as he curtly remarks.

"A nice mug of tea?...I think you'd better go on without me Woody....I've an awful feeling I'm about to see my breakfast for the second time today...Bloody hell fire...I have never...NEVER!...Smelt anything as bad as that before...No NEVER!."

Woody smiles, even allowing himself to openly chuckle a little as he responds to the pitiful Lad.

"Well please yourself I'm sure...But I'm off to have my tea with you or without you...She makes a grand brew of tea does that Mavis... Come on Softarse don't be such a Bloody Wimp."

Woody giggles to himself as he steers Eric to the front of the Pavilion. Mavis appears on the Veranda. She smiles, waving to them as she calls out.

"Oh…There you are!…I was about to send out a search party to find you two….Tea's up…Come and get it."

Mavis sniffs the air and gasps.

"Good Heavens!."

She sniffs the air once again very briefly before she swiftly places a small lace handkerchief under her nose.

"Poo!.....What's that terrible smell?…Poo…It must be coming from that Tannery…Poo…They don't seem to have much regard for any of the Folks living in the vicinity do they?…. Poo…I think that's awful especially when people like you are working outside in it…Still never mind…Come inside and have a nice cuppa because you've certainly earned it this morning."

Woody winks, nudging Eric as they make their way to the Clubhouse. He calls out to Mavis sounding quite cocky.

"Oh we get used to nasty smells like this in our game Mavis….It doesn't really bother us…Does it Ricky?."

Eric glares at, the still winking, Woody before he manages to blurt out.

"What?…Eh?…Oh no…Not the likes of us Mavis. No…Hardly noticed it myself….What smell is that then?…Ha!"

He throws his head back indicating gay abandon but he is very careful not to sniff too vigorously.

" No…I hardly noticed it myself."

It is now Woody's turn to glare at Eric before he breaks out with a broad grin all across his gnarled features.

Mavis ushers the men into the kitchen. She is clearly delighted to be able to fuss and spoil her new friends. She manages to sound quite businesslike.

"Well come on then the kettle's boiled and everything is ready….I don't know what's happened to Alf I thought he would have been back from the Brewery by now…The poor Chap really does miss that old banger of a car he used to drive around in….Still we can't really wait for him can we?."

The men admire the sight of their kitchen under the new Management. Mavis has scrubbed and cleaned every nook and cranny and the whole room smells hygienic and welcoming. She has even placed a neat floral tablecloth on the table. She gestures to them to sit down as she produces a large dinner plate ladened with freshly baked and still warm scones.

"I've made some more of those scones you seem to like so much Woody...There always better if they're eaten while they're still warm from the oven."

Woody's face lights up as he quickly takes his place at the table. Mavis smiles.

"I've always loved cooking and baking but I haven't had much cause to do much since my Fred passed away...I can't be bothered doing it for myself but it's a real pleasure to bake for people who appreciate their food...Now come on tuck in."

Both men are ready, willing and able as they stare expectantly at the plate of scones. Mavis places a butter dish next to the scones, she then shoves a side plate and a knife in front of them. Woody's mouth has already started to water as he greedily grabs the biggest scone, putting it on his plate. Eric is about to copy his actions until he suddenly glares down at his hands. He almost knocks his chair over in his haste to move to the sink where Mavis is carefully pouring boiling hot water into a large porcelain tea pot. She moves slightly to allow Eric access. She glimpses at the sight of Woody already keenly biting into the scone which he has liberally covered with butter. Satisfaction and delight are apparent in her tone as she remarks.

"That's right Woody Love...Just help yourself that's it....Get stuck in...Come on Ricky Love...You too...Wash your hands properly there's no need to rush...There's plenty for everyone...Use that clean hand towel to dry yourself."

Eric gives his hands a good rinse under running water as he turns to comment, in a falsely superior fashion.

"Thank you Mavis...I think I'll give my hands another little rinse first...You can never tell...You know?.. That nasty stuff...You know from the...Er Tannery?...Some of it might have landed on them whilst I was out there."

Woody is well into his second bite when he suddenly stops to stare at his hands. He reluctantly replaces his half eaten scone on his plate. He stands up rapidly making his way across the room to the sink. He continues to glare down at his hands as he rudely shoves Eric out of his way with a flick of his hip. He snarls at the Lad.

"Come on Young 'un...Don't be hogging all the water...You'll rub all the skin off if you overdo it...Come on!"

Eric gives Woody a look of distain which is returned with a deliberate grimace. He then cautiously sniffs at his less than clean hands before plunging them into water. He then commences a thorough cleansing procedure using large quanties of soap and running tap water. Eric has a smirk across his face as he stands back wiping his hands on a fresh clean towel. He takes his seat at the table and quickly places the largest remaining scone on his plate, reaching for the butter and jam. Just at this moment Alf's voice is heard coming from the Clubroom as he is smartly walking through.

"Bloody hell!!!...It looks as if I've missed the bloody boat good and proper here today."

As he enters the kitchen he speaks, with a definite hint of an appeal in his tone, directly to Mavis.

"These pair are not noted for the amount of food they leave behind them you know....They don't so much eat as destroy large quantities of food."

A smile of relief adorns his features as he realises that there are plenty of scones left on the plate. Mavis places a side plate in front of him as Alf sits down. She then starts pouring steaming hot tea into Alf's private mug. Alf politely smiles at his two friends who are far too busy eating their scones to even nod back. Mavis places his mug on the table as she hands him a clean knife. Alf shrugs his shoulders before he remarks, with feeling.

"Bloody buses...You could grow very old waiting at bus stops around these parts you know?."

He takes a swig from his mug and places a scone on his side plate. Suddenly his whole face lights up. A cheeky grin breaks out as he speaks to Eric.

"Here you go now Ricky Lad....You're a bright sort of young fellow....When I was standing around waiting for public transport this morning a thought crossed my mind....Perhaps you will be able to help with this...Right...Can you tell me this?....What is the difference between a double decked bus and a giraffe?....Eh?...That's a nice little poser for you Ricky."

Eric thinks very hard for a few moments before he shakes his head. Alf looks delighted at this response as he leans forward to declare with undisguised delight.

"O.K...Give in?...Right...Well there are two F's in giraffe and F'in buses...Eh?...Get it?...Something for you to ponder upon my Lad."

Woody laughs along with Alf. Eric struggles trying to work it out. Mavis pretends she has not heard what Alf said but she has to turn away in order to stifled a definite giggle to protect her reputation as a Lady.

Woody demolishes his second scone and licks the butter and jam off his fingers. He sits back gently rubbing his stomach as he declares.

"I can guarantee you one thing Alfred Old Pal......You will not find many leavings on my plate when the cooking is as good as this...And I don't mind who hears me say it neither."

Both Alf and Eric grunt their agreement, unable to speak because their mouths are full. Mavis blushes as she she acknowledges the compliment made.

"That's very kind of you to say that Woody...Thank you...I'm going to let you try my special 'Meat and Tatter' pie tomorrow so I hope you will all bring those appetites with you.. Does everyone fancy trying it?... Eric?....Alf?...My late Husband used to love it...I'll bring some mushy peas in as well....I like it myself but I can never be bothered to make one just for my own consumption."

Both Alf and Eric almost choke as they nod their heads and saying in unison.

"Yes please Mavis."

Alf wipes his mouth before he adds with sincerity.

"That really will be a treat for Woody and I Mavis we don't often get the chance to sample real home cooking...I'm looking forward to it already...Are you sure it's not too much trouble Mavis Love?."

Mavis shakes her head happily as she reassures them, with confidence.

"Trouble?...No trouble at all Alf...It will be my pleasure I'm sure...I wonder if you two eat the right kinds of food...I'd be willing to place a bet that you'll put up with any sort of old rubbish...Chip shops and even worse...A working man needs good wholesome food inside of him if he expects to carry out his duties to the best of his abilities at all times..... Believe me it will be a great pleasure for me to treat you Boys as a gesture of my appreciation for the way you've all made me feel so at home in such a short time...So there you are...All sorted out for tomorrow then."

Mavis smiles contentedly as Woody and Alf reflect upon the real difference Mavis is making to their everyday lives. Woody gets to his feet remembering that they still have plenty of work to do. He replies to Mavis, exposing sincere gratitude.

"I can't remember the last time my belly felt so well treated Mavis...Those scones were absolutely delicious and no mistake...Thank you very much...You're a little treasure you are...Thank you...I can hardly wait for tomorrow to come now."

Eric decides to latch onto Woody's remark in an attempt to be amusing. He laughs as he speaks.

"Yes...That's very true...You really are a little treasure Mavis....I've heard quite a few people asking Alf where he dug you up from!...Eh?...EH?..."

Eric holds his sides, chuckling. Mavis does not appear to be upset but Eric is suddenly aware that Woody and Alf are not laughing. They are both staring at him with distain. The young man immediately feels uncomfortable. Alf reprimands him.

"Hey...Buggerlugs....Nobody loves a smartyarse you know?... Some of us are not as fortune as others you know?...We aren't all lucky enough to still have our Mums looking after us.. So don't be so bloody cheeky."

Eric is very embarrassed. He immediately tries to cover his blushes, desperately attempting to apologise.

"Hey...I was only joking Alf...You don't think I meant that....Hey... Look I'm very sorry Mavis...I was only trying to make a joke...I didn't mean that...."

Mavis smiles, as placing her arm around his broad shoulders to delicately interrupt him.

"Bless me Ricky...Don't you worry your head for one minute... There was obviously no offence meant and there was certainly none taken...I think these two are being a little over

protective this morning...I'm not that easily upset you know?."

She smiles, nodding to Alf and Woody who gradually nod and grin at a very relieved Eric. Woody rubs his hands together in a businesslike manner before calling out to Eric.

"Right come on Lad....Tea break well and truly over...Let the Dog see the Rabbit...Work to be done…...Chop...Chop. I just hope you're not planning to come out with any further witty remarks that may place our 'Meat and Tatter' pie in any further jeopardy."

Eric's head drops as he arises from his chair.

Woody and Eric are making their way back to the Bowling Green when Mavis suddenly remembers something she wished to tell Eric. She dashes out onto the veranda.

"Incidentally Ricky one of my oldest and dearest friends was enquiring about you with me last night....Mrs Dawes.. You know Billy's wife...She is one of my neighbours."

Alf immediately seizes onto this comment. He winks at Woody as he speaks.

"Well...I'm not altogether surprised at that Mavis Love...We were confidently expecting things to take a turn in that particular area... There's no smoke without fire...Eh?."

Woody obviously does not want to tease Eric any more but Alf is gleefully enjoying himself.

"You see Mavis...What it is...Our Little Ricky here has only been sniffing around her Granddaughter...She must be checking up to see if he's a fit and proper person to be seen in her company...I bet that's what it was probably all about Mavis."

Eric stops in his tracks, looking offended at first but then becoming, clearly, annoyed. Shocked by Alf's remarks, he sounds genuinely hurt.

"Hey steady on Alf....Play the game...Please... What are you saying?...I...I'm supposed to be sniffing around her Granddaughter?...Eh?...That's bloody rich that is....Perhaps it may have slipped your memory but it was her who tried to sell me that packet of fren...."

Woody swiftly interrupts in a commanding manner deliberately cutting Eric off before can finish the sentence.

"That'll do now!....Don't be drawn Ricky you soft bugger...Can't you tell when someone is pulling your leg... He's only winding you up...Pack it in Alf...The Lad's had enough for one day...Leave him alone now."

Eric gestures his disgust with an arm movement, throwing his head back, hoping to demonstrate total control over his emotions. Alf laughs as he impishly points his finger at the Lad. Woody really turns on Alf this time. He tugs on Eric's arm, forcing him to walk away from both Alf and Mavis.

"Behave yourself will you Alf!...Christ Mate give it a bloody rest please!...Go and sort your beer out...It'd better be on best form from now on...Eh?.....Seeing as we've actually paid the Brewery for it before we sup it for a pleasant change...Come on Ricky we've got work to attend to."

Mavis feels responsible for causing the upset. She desperately tries to rectify the situation by explanations.

"As a matter of fact she didn't even mention their Jenny...I thought Nan Dawes knew you Ricky...She knows your Dad very well...Mind you I think most people in Lapley Vale know your Father in one way or another....But...Listen...Listen to me now!...There's no need for anyone to get upset or anything because I certainly didn't say anything nasty to her about you Ricky...As a matter of fact I told her what a nice young man I thought you are...And besides...Their Jenny is a credit to Nan and Billy...She's a very polite and well mannered girl and very pretty with it."

Even Alf considers that the subject should now be closed. Woody slaps Eric on the back as they walk towards the Pavilion. Woody sympathetically attempts to cheer him up.

"Come on 'Lover Boy'...It's long past time we got back to our work....Perhaps that horrible stink from the.... Er...Tannery....Eh?... EH?...Has gone away by now."

A sudden look of horror flashes across the Lad's features as he reluctantly follows behind his leader. Both men soon disappear out of sight behind the wooden Pavilion.

* * *

"How do you mean Peggy… You were selected?."

Possibly due of the absence of the tension which had prevailed throughout the past few months being lifted by the sudden and welcome upturn in the Club's finances, the ambiance in the Bar in Lapley Vale Bowling and Social Club Clubhouse has definitely taken on a new lease of relaxed contentment.

Quarter to ten on a mid week evening and the attendance is keeping Alf alert and busy behind the bar.

Woody is seated in his usual place enjoying the company and a drink with Little Norman Smith and Eddie Brown. There are a number of younger men playing and watching a snooker game with several others playing and enjoying a game of darts. As well as these there are about another dozen customers gathered around various tables merely enjoying a chant with a drink. The whole place is indulging itself in a very pleasant atmosphere.

Alf finishes serving two young men with a fairly substantial order of beer and crisps. He wipes his brow as he turns his attention to Woody and friends. Alf looks contented.

"It just goes to show you doesn't it?....Business is on the up and up...We are definitely back on the drinking map again....Who could guess now that it's only a few weeks ago we were sadly contemplating whether or not the Club would actually survive much longer...It's bloody marvellous...Isn't it?."

All men smile, nodding their unanimous agreement as they happily survey the activity all around the Rooms. Just at this very moment Arthur Rose, one of the oldest and longest serving Members, unfortunately almost profoundly deaf, approaches the bar with an empty glass in his hand. Alf reacts immediately stepping forward to take the glass from Arthur. Holding it under the bitter beer pump he shouts a greeting.

"EVENING ARTHUR!...YOUR USUAL IS IT?."

Smiling, Arthur nods as he grasps hold of the bar. He looks straight into Alf's eyes, speaking excitedly.

"No need for you to shout when you're speaking to me anymore Alf my old friend."

Alf and the others are puzzled. Arthur continues.

"I've just been fitted with the last word in hearing aids at the Cottage Hospital this afternoon...Imported from America...Fits inside the ear hole...Invisible to the human eye and one hundred per cent efficient...Eh?.....What?...So no more shouting at me if you please Alf."

Arthur has everyone's attention whilst Alf fills his glass to the top. Arthur sounds jubilant as he adds.

"There you go....Invisible eh?.....I'm lucky enough to be one of the first persons to be fitted with one of these in the whole of this Country...They only become available recently...It'll be changing the quality of my life in future I can tell you....You can bet on that."

Alf carefully places the full glass in front of Arthur. He is genuinely delighted for the Old Man.

"Bloody hell Arthur...Good for you...I bet they set the NHS back a few bob...Eh?...How much do they cost?...Did they tell you?...Do you know how much they are to buy?."

Arthur is nodding and smiling at Alf. He pulls his pocket watch out of his waistcoat pocket, glances at it and replies chirpily.

"Ten minutes to ten Alf...What's wrong with your own clock....To tired to look at it are you?."

All present have to be careful not to burst out laughing as Arthur places his money on the bar and walks away. When Arthur reaches the table where his friends are seated they all relieve themselves with a good laugh. Norman comments.

"Bloody hell fire...It's cruel isn't it...The poor old bugger...I bet it won't be long before he goes back to his old and trusted hearing aid again."

Laughing lustily, Woody adds.

"And if I know Arthur he'll make a special trip to the Cottage Hospital to tell them exactly what he thinks of the latest piece of American technology very soon and you can bet on that for certain... EH?."

They all enjoy the fun. Woody changes the subject.

"I dare say this latest bit of good news about the Club's finances has come as a great relief to you as much as anyone eh Alf?."

Alf replies with feeling.

"Christ Woody you can say that again...I was getting to feel like The Fugitive...You know the one on the telly programme?...Keeping my head down whenever anyone showed up brandishing a bill for payment... I honestly don't know how much longer we could've survived...I'd received a final warning about payments from the Brewery...They were adamant that if we didn't pay at least some of the outstanding balance due they were going to refuse to send out any more beer to us."

This information induced a chilled and shocked reaction from the others. Alf's expression suddenly changes, lifting their spirits high once again.

"Anyways that all past history now....Thank God and anyone else who might be responsible for our deliverance from the brink of disaster."

Alf nods to a customer waiting at the bar as he cheerfully breaks out into a song.

"Happy days are hear again…All the skies above are clear again."

His friends immediately react by pulling their faces and gesturing their displeasure in other ways. Eddie shouts across the bar to him.

"Don't think about giving up your now more secure day job Alf... I hate to tell you this but you'll never make a career for yourself in the world of singing and entertainment."

They are still laughing a 'Peggy' Hackett joins them at the bar. He launches himself into conversation with Woody without even saying 'Hello'.

"I've had a funny visitor at our house today.. A bloke it was... From a firm in Manchester that specialises in artificial limbs of all sorts and varieties...Not National Health Service you understand....Oh no...Private...Top quality...I nearly gave him the bum's rush when he introduced himself...I thought the bugger was after getting his hands on my money...Not that I've got any to spare...But...But it would appear that I have been selected to try out their latest model...He had one with him...They have to be adjusted to cater for individual needs but I tried it on...Bloody marvellous it was...Bloody marvellous As far as I can remember almost as good as the real thing...What an improvement on that tin rubbishy piece of crap they supplied me with from the National Health."

Norman interrupts Peggy politely.

"How do you mean Peggy?...You were selected?."

Peggy shrugs his shoulders.

"I'm buggered if I know Norm...All I can tell you is what this bloke actually told me...There's no charge to be made as far as I'm concerned because all expenses have been paid by...Er...A Trust....Or something of a like nature."

This explanation almost causes Eddie to choke on his beer. Peggy continues.

"It's not a wind up or anything like that...I don't know all the ins and outs of it but I can tell you for sure that everything has been bought and paid for...He took my new leg away with him for some final adjustments and promised me he would be back with it early next week...And I can also tell you this Gentlemen...I can hardly wait...I feel sure my new super leg will be making my old leg and even my Peg completely redundant."

Peggy pauses to look straight into Woody's eyes. He taps his old peg leg with a coin to add, rather sarcastically.

"And that'll please some moaning Old Gets around these parts in particular won't it Woody?...Eh?....What?."

Woody refuses to be drawn by his remark. He calmly and carefully lights his pipe. Blowing out the match he casually comments.

"All I can say Peggy is I'm pleased for you and I really mean that... But I will also add that I for one will not be sorry to see the ass end of that bloody peg of yours on my Green....But the main thing...The main thing is if it suits you it will definitely suit everyone else and I am very pleased to hear of your excellent news Peggy....Honestly."

Eddie manages to recover his composure following his close encounter with choking on his own beer to speak with shocked astonishment clearly present in his attitude and tone.

"Here we go again!....A Trust!...It's that Trust again...Bloody hell.... This has got to be more than a coincidence surely!....It would appear to me that this Trust...Whatever or whoever it is...Is smiling down upon quite few of us Gentlemen... And to some bloody tune as well if you want my opinion...Bloody hell fire."

He shouts across the bar to Alf who had moved away to serve another customer.

"Alf!...Alf!...Did you hear what Peggy has just been telling us about his new superdooper leg?."

Alf walks across to them. He looks and sounds rather philosophical.

"I did Eddie...Every bloody word Mate...It's another bloody miracle that's what it is alright...I beginning to wish I knew a little bit more about this Trust but...What the Hell!....Do we actually care who or what it is?...The one thing coming out of all this for certain is the mysterious Trust is bringing a lot of happiness down our way...Long may it continue to do so...That's what I say."

Alf's comments and observations are met with complete approval and total agreement by all those involved. He is about to move away again when he suddenly remembers some news.

"Oh!...By the way....I almost forgot to tell you there could be someone else in Lapley Vale who has had a bit of good luck sent his way...You know the young chap who calls in here to collect Football Coupons for Littlewoods Pools?...Well he was in here earlier this evening...As usual....And he was telling me that he has heard a very strong rumour that someone local... Or at least in this area has recently touched out on a very nice win on the Treble Chance...Not the Jackpot but he has been led to believe that it was a sizable amount and very well worth having.. Nice for some lucky bastard eh?...He has no idea who it may be but he's fairly certain that the news is genuine and not just a rumour...For some reason the Good Lord up above appears to be smiling down on our beloved Town of Lapley Vale...Eh?."

Everyone smiles and nods as Alf starts re-filling their glasses. Each of them, in their own way, is attempting to come to terms with and absorb the consequences of this recent, wonderful, beneficial, upturn in a number of lucky individuals fortunes and future prospects. Norman is the first to break the short silence.

"I've often wondered what I would do if I came into a load of money like that...Have you?...I've no idea how it would affect me..... What about you Woody have you ever thought what you would do if money was no object?."

Woody thinks for a second or two and then delivers his considered opinion.

"Chance would be a fine thing Norm...But...Well I don't think it would change my life very much...It all depends upon what you want out of life...If you're happy and contented as you are a windfall like that might not bring the instant joy and happiness you expect... What I'm saying is this type of sudden richness is no guarantee of an improvement in your every day life or your future contentment."

Eddie appears to be surprised by Woody's remarks.

"It doesn't stop you or the rest of us filling in our coupons every week though…Does it?."

Woody nods his agreement. He attempts to justify his comments.

"Admitted Eddie…I think we all need a little flicker of hope in our lives but the Pools are only a bit of harmless fun for most of us…I enjoy listening to the results on the radio on a Saturday evening…It doesn't cost a fortune and as I for one don't bother with the Horses or the Dogs I enjoy my little flutter on Littlewoods and will continue to do so for the foreseeable future."

All are now day dreaming of what might be. Eddie suddenly smiles to declare positively.

"Well I suppose it would be nice but even if I did have a win I've already got everything I've always wanted…The chance to visit my Homeland once again before I die…I mean to say…Who the bloody hell could of guessed that it would be possible for me to have my dreams come true?…And in such a mysterious manner as well…Eh?."

Woody aptly sums up their conversation.

"You never know what might be waiting for you just around the next corner…Life is a funny thing…You have ups and then you have downs…You must learn to take the rough with the smooth….Never expect too much and you'll never be too disappointed."

Norman agrees with Woody.

"You've hit the nail on the head there Woody… Mind you…It's very nice to hear about so many of our friends and acquaintances who are definitely on the up at this particular moment in time…We should just sit back and make the best of it whilst we can…..Incidentally you would be able to tell if Alf won a fortune…He would be running up and down High Street shouting and jumping for joy for several days… Be a bit of a giveaway that would I suppose."

All have plenty of food for thought as they raise their glasses to happily drink their beer.

* * *

"All above board……..Documents to prove it."

The following morning Alf is busy re-filling all the shelves behind the bar with full bottles. He is in high spirits due to the obvious increase in the Club's turnover during the past few weeks and he is quietly singing to himself as he carries out his necessary duties. Woody enters the Room via the door giving access to and from the kitchen. Alf hears him and glances up to see Woody sitting on his usual stool. As he completes the re-stocking of the shelves he rises to his feet, removing his apron as he does so. Alf looks up at the clock and nods to Woody.

"Thanks Pal...I'll try not to keep you away from your work for too long Woody...But...Er...I asked you to come in because I wanted to ask a little favour of you as it happens...I wouldn't trouble you if it wasn't necessary and an emergency... So to speak...Anyways I think you know that without me telling you....Eh?."

Woody seems to be concentrating on the lighting of his pipe as Alf continues.

"I've had a message from Billy Hancock at the Garage...You know?... Says he needs to see me urgently...I hope it's not another bloody bill....I did ask him to dispose of Austin for me...I was hoping that that would be the end of it and there wouldn't be a bill from him for doing a job like that for me...It was hard enough for me to have an old friend put down but as you know too well Austin had come to the end of his time as a useful mode of transport...The cost of the parts would've been twice the value of the bloody car at the end of the day and there was no guarantee that Austin's life would be extended for any considerable length of time...And that was just the bloody parts...There would be labour charges on top of that...It was a difficult decision to make but I feel I did take the right course of action in the long run."

Woody has built up a full head of smoke from his pipe. He removes it from his mouth to speak.

"I shouldn't think it'll be a bill Alf...I image the vehicle would have some sort of scrap value...Perhaps he wants to give you a few quid...After all you did tell me the other day that the ashtrays and wing mirrors on Austin were in excellent condition...Keep your fingers crossed Alf you never know we could be enjoying a couple of drinks from the revenue collected from Austin's ashes tonight."

Both men pause to think for a second or two. They both dismiss this unlikely possibility with a wave of their hands. Alf shakes his head.

"You must be joking Mate...I'm definitely not expecting anything like that I can assure you....Perhaps I'm needed to sign some forms or the like...I just don't know."

Alf laughs weakly as Woody re-lights his pipe again. Blowing out his match he sits back to enjoy his smoke. Woody then speaks in a fairly positive fashion.

"There's only one way to find out Alfie my old Mate...Get yourself up to the Garage and see Billy."

Alf latches on to Woody's suggestion like a shot. He was looking for some way to ask Woody his favour and he above all others is well aware that Woody does not take kindly to any unforced interruptions to his work on the Green.

"Well that's exactly why I asked you to come in for a word you see Woody...I've finished setting everything up for the usual dinner time session...You see I'm not certain when I will be back.....I've got to walk up to the Garage and back so I've arranged with Billy Cockeye to come in at twelve o'clock to cover the bar for me...If it's necessary that is and...And well...I was wondering if you'd be kind enough to let him in...I don't want to leave the front doors unlocked and although I realise that you're very busy out the back there...I know you will be able to hear Billy if he shouts over the wall...I hope you don't mind Mate... I think I've covered all the angles on this before I just bugger off... So to speak...Old Billy Cockeye will be on time...He's very reliable...I took the liberty of telling him to give you a shout if I'm still out when he arrives....I hope you don't mind Woody but I don't want to mess Billy Hancock about...He's always been very fair with me and Austin over the years...I hope it won't interfere too much with whatever you're doing."

To Alf's relief Woody gives him a re-assuring smile.

"No problem at all Alf...I understand...Are you sure that Billy Cockeye is capable of looking after your bar for you?....He can be a bit of a Tithead sometimes."

Alf smiles and nods as he pulls his jacket on.

"Oh Aye....He's probably the pick of the bunch to be perfectly honest with you....Still...I'll be bloody glad when I manage to fix up the new barmaid....Oh incidentally...I didn't tell you did I?...Bert McCabe has recommended a young woman from Salisbury Street... Denise somebody...Experienced and in need of a little extra cash to manage...I've arranged for her to pop in this evening so we can have a little chat."

Woody is pleased to be kept informed of any developments concerning his beloved Club.

"If Bert is recommending her you can be sure that she's alright Alf....Bert has his bad points the same as us all but at the end of the day Bert is a genuine supporter of this Club and he wouldn't do anything to interfere with our enjoyment of our facilities as they stand and have stood for many years."

Alf is nodding his agreement when he suddenly breaks into a broad grin, Woody wonders what is coming next.

"Agreed on that point Woody and besides Bert tells me that she passes the elbow test with flying colours."

Alf laughs and shakes his head. Woody does not know what his friend is talking about.

"The elbow test?...What the bloody hell is the elbow test?."

Woody's enquiry makes Alf giggle even more.

"Oh...You've never heard of the famous elbow test? Well...What happen is this....You ask the lady applicant to grasp her hands together behind her head...Like this...Then you ask her to walk up to the nearest available wall...Like this....And.... If her elbows touch the wall before her tits then she's failed the test."

Woody almost falls off his stool as he takes it all in. They both roar with laughter. Woody changes the subject.

"I believe Billy Cockeye has had the offer of a permanent job recently."

Alf is astonished.

"Yes...Old Arnie...You know Old Arnie who plays for the Liberal Club Bowling Team...Tall Chap with a big hooter."

Alf is trying hard to recognise Arnie. Woody attempts to enhance his memory cells with encouragement.

"You remember...The Bloke who played against Billy in the first game of this Season...When Billy kept farting?."

Alf suddenly remembers Arnie, with relief, he nods as Woody continues.

"Yes that's right...Anyways...Arnie is punting it about that after their match Billy was approached with an offer of full time employment as a test pilot for Guinness."

Alf has now realised that Woody is returning his attempt at humour because the tears are now running down Woody's cheeks. He is experiencing great difficulty trying to speak.

"Poor Old Arnie...Billy almost blew him off the bloody Green... Then had the nerve to blame his Missus for giving him...Cockeyed... Beans...For his dinner."

Both men are now almost helpless with laughter. Woody has to jump off his stool because his sides are splitting. Alf is on his way towards the front door, still laughing. Woody rubs his hands together in a businesslike manner. He calls out.

"Off you go My Bonny Buddy...Bugger off...The premises are in good hands...Off you go to see Billy the Garage...And...And don't be worrying...Everything is under control...I guarantee that this Club will still be standing here when......And if...You ever return...Bugger off Alf...Good Luck."

Alf disappears through the front doors, Woody follows to lock the doors behind him.

Later the same morning Woody is standing in the middle of the Bowling Green, gently pronging the grass with a small fork. He jumps at the sharp sound of a car horn. He listens again and detects that the sound is emanating from the Car Park at the front of the Clubhouse. The car horn continues to sound intermittently. Woody heads through the Clubhouse where the noise is louder. It is now beginning to annoy him. Woody peers out through the front windows to see a brand new Ford Cortina car parked in the middle of the otherwise empty Car Park.

As Woody takes a closer look his attention focuses on Alf. He is seated behind the steering wheel, exhibiting a smile which extends from ear to ear across his beaming face. Alf is gesturing to Woody in an over-emphasised, very excited, way. Woody fumbles with the keys before he manages to open the front doors. Flabbergasted, he makes his way across the Car Park until he finds himself standing alongside the highly polished and gleaming driver's door. Alf is experiencing great difficulty containing his exuberance. He is having a hard time just speaking as the level of his excitement rises, almost out of control.

"Cancel what I've been telling you about making other arrangements for us to travel to away matches this Season Woody...We are going to be travelling first class from now on."

Woody steps back to take a closer look at the impressively beautiful, brand new, vehicle. He is bemused.

"What the bloody hell are you going on about Alf? What's going on...Christ Alf you look like the cat that got the early bird...You're not making sense....What's going on?."

Alf leaps out of the car, spreading his arms out wide. He is throbbing, almost ready to burst, with sheer joy.

"I can hardly believe this myself Woody...When I arrived at Billy the Garage's he just handed me an envelope... When I opened it I found it contained the keys and the documents for this brand new motor car...He took me to where it was parked and told me to drive off in it...I thought he was taking the piss at first but then he explained that everything was above board... All the documents...Including a vehicle Excise Licence and full comprehensive insurance cover for twelve months were made out in my name...He kept on telling me it was all mine...All paid for."

Alf leans inside the cab to reach for a brown envelope lying on the passenger seat. He thrusts it at Woody.

"Look for yourself Pal...No kidding...All above board....Documents to prove it...You are now in the presence of the extremely proud owner of the very latest De-Luxe Model in the Ford Cortina Range of Saloon Motor Vehicles."

Woody is amazed. After momentarily glancing at the contents of the brown envelope he shares in the sheer delight being exhibited by Alf. Alf places his hands on top of Woody's shoulders, Woody grasps hold of Alf's. They then start to jump up and down with unbridled joy. Alf is anxious to maintain his total submission to the full attack of infectious bliss.

"Come on...Climb in Buddy...I'll take you for a little spin...It's great...Smooth as a snakes belly...Come on."

He drags Woody towards the passenger side of the vehicle. Woody resists him.

"Hang on a second Alf...First things first Buddy what about the bloody Club...Billy Cockeye hasn't arrived as yet."

Alf's smile wanes a little. He looks at the car then stares up at the Clubhouse. Forcibly pulling himself together, he inhales, taking a very deep breath of air.

"You're quite right Woody....Let's not forget our main responsibilities...We can go out for a spin later...We can.. Yes we can go out for a bloody good spin whenever we feel like it....Bloody hell fire

Woody what a turn up for the books Eh?...I can hardly believe that this is actually happening to me."

Both men stand back to admire the sleek lines and smart shape of the impressive vehicle. Alf then nudges Woody. There is a sinister note clearly discernable within his tone.

"And wait for it Woody....Guess where the money to pay for all this bloody lot came from?."

Woody ponders but Alf blurts out the answer.

"The Trust....You know?...The mysterious bloody Trust?....The same one that saved our beloved Club from almost certain extinction... And also fixed up things for Eddie and Peggy Eh?...You know which Trust I mean?...Eh?...Of course you do!...It was slowly dawning on me even before Billy Hancock told me what little he knew about this anonymous benefactor."

Woody is transfixed, struggling to absorb the great news. Shaking his head, a wry smile flickers across his lips. He seems to be incapable of making any response. Alf's voice now trembles with undiluted, genuine, emotion.

"It's another miracle....Another bloody wonderful miracle...I never for one moment ever thought that anything as fantastic as this would ever happen to me Woody."

Alf nudges Woody as he points up towards the sky.

"I'm telling you this Buddy...Someone up there loves us...Eh?... What?...There appears to be no end to our happy surprises...Eh?."

Unable to speak any further both men hug each other with total abandon. They start jumping up and down again cheering loudly until they suddenly hear the sound of Billy Cockeye's voice ringing out from behind them as he makes his way, walking across the Car Park, towards the Clubhouse.

"Pack that in you two...People around here will think you're a couple of cockeyed Willy Woofters."

Billy stops. He pauses, enabling him to take a good look all around the surrounding, overlooking, area.

"You never know who might be taking a cockeyed look out of their cockeyed window...So stop it...Pack it in."

Still smiling ecstatically they immediately release their holds on each other. Alf re-assures Billy.

"Don't you worry about us Billy...I think you'll find that Woody and I are well known around these parts as 'Crumpet only' men... Anyways...Who cares...Still...Listen…..It's very good of you to turn up as promised Billy...Always as good as your word eh?.....But as you can see I don't think I actually need to call upon your services now...Thanks all the same...I've managed to conduct all my business affairs in quick time and all systems are now ready to go."

Billy smiles.

"No sweat Alfie My Boy....I was ready for a cockeyed pint anyways.... I've been on the receiving end of Nan's tongue all cockeyed morning.... I blame Bert McCabe for getting me into a drunken state last night... He's a cockeyed menace at times She won't be told...Insists on giving me the cockeyed lectures."

Billy has been viewing the car whilst speaking.

"Hell fire Boys....Who's is this?...Have we got a cockeyed V.I.P. visiting us or what?....Or possibly Royalty by the appearance of this cockeyed limousine....It's a real beauty isn't it?."

Although he is still bubbling over with excitement and joy Alf tries to look and sound casual as he replies.

"Like my new Motor Car do you Billy?."

Billy takes a closer look at the car and glances towards Woody, who quickly turns away from him. Billy suspects he may be having his leg pulled. He sounds quite patronising.

"I bet you wish it was yours Alf."

Alf is having a real battle fighting back his natural impulses which are urging him to leap up and down shouting for joy. He really struggles to remain reasonably calm.

"Well O.K. Billy...I have to admit I do find it rather difficult to believe myself but...BUT...The fact remains.. I...Alfred Morgan...Am the proud owner of this magnificent... Brand spanking new...Luxury motor vehicle."

Billy is shocked. He stares at Woody who is now smiling as he slowly nods his head. Alf's voice rises as he adds.

"All above board....Documents to prove it."

Billy is still uncertain as to whether or not his two Old Friends are telling him the truth or trying to tease him. The obvious state of excitement in both Alf and Woody soon convinces Billy of the truth and at the same moment he actually manages to put two and two together. He sounds astonished.

"Don't tell me....Not that cockeyed Trust again?....Hell fire Boys.... When will these cockeyed miracles end....Well done Alf...You won't forget your Old Pals when you're giving lifts to every cockeyed Tom Dick and cockeyed Harry in Lapley Vale will you?."

Billy shakes Alf's hand warmly with sincerity. Turning, he is about to hug Woody until he quickly manages to pull himself together. He is now as thrilled as Alf and Woody. Never one to miss an opening, Billy steps back to emphasise the obvious importance of the moment.

"If this doesn't call for a cockeyed pint on the house I'd very much like to know any occasion that would Boys... EH?...EH?....Come on Alfie...Get the cockeyed Ale in."

* * *

"You deserve a medal Norman."

The hour is approaching ten o'clock on a convivial Friday evening in the Lapley Vale Bowling and Social Club.

There are groups of Members playing darts, snooker and dominoes. Almost every one of the tables is occupied, mostly by men but there are a few ladies present. Alf is delighted to be kept busy behind the bar where he is now being assisted by his new Barmaid, Denise. Denise is a pretty woman probably in her mid to late thirties. She has very blonde hair with a slim, shapely, body. The first noticeable thing about Denise is her make-up. She enhances her overall pleasing appearance with heavy make-up which together with her low cut blouse and very short mini skirt has already made her an instant centre of attraction. In addition to her physical attributes Denise also has a very friendly nature with a keen and broad sense of humour. She is already very popular. This is not in any small way due to the obvious fact that she had passed Alf's elbow test with flying colours and many inches to spare. Denise looks and acts the part very well and is expected to increase the attendance even more when her description is circulated amongst some currently lapsed Members.

Woody is seated in his usual place with Little Norman Smith alongside him. Eddie Brown has the stool next to Norman. Seated at the table just behind them is Ralph, the Chairman, Vic Callow the Hon. Secretary/Treasurer, Sergeant Bert McCabe off duty and Charlie Walsh. All are drinking very steadily from pint glasses. They appear to be happy and in good spirits. Ralph leans back on his chair to enable him to address his remarks directly to Woody.

"It does my old heart good to see this Club thriving like this again... Eh?...What do you say Woody?...We've haven't seen this many people in here on a Friday night for many a long year or more...EH?."

All aware of the significance of Ralph's remarks most instantly nod and others express other clear gestures of pleasurable agreement. Woody is more than keen to respond.

"You can say that again Mr Chairman....Things certainly seem to be on the up and up...Especially since Alf found Denise for us...Eh?... She's a little belter and no mistake...What an added attraction she's proving to be."

They all look at Denise who smiles very sweetly as she pulls beer into another pint pot. Woody nods and smiles back to her.

"She really is a Bonny Lass as they say...She's got that vital spark gained only through experience behind bars for many years or more. I believe we've got a definite odds on winner in Denise...Mark my words...Can't fail."

Grinning, as only he can, Bert joins in the discussion with his usual injection of humour.

"She's a little spanner...That's what she is...A little spanner."

No-one has the slightest idea what Bert is taking about. Ralph checks around to see everyone present is equally as bewildered as himself before politely asking for an explanation.

"A little spanner?....How comes a spanner?...A spanner?.....What do you mean Bert?...A little spanner?."

Bert glares at Ralph and the others expressing mock surprise that they are not aware of his meaning. After a short pause he replies in a rather condescending fashion.

"I mean exactly what I said....She's a little spanner...Think about it....I can only speak for myself but I may well be speaking for many others...I have correctly described Denise as a little spanner for one simple reason...She causes my nuts tighten every time I take a look at her."

Bert's explanations is met by raucous loud laughter. Denise, unable to hear what was said, suspects they are talking about her. Bert shouts across the bar to her.

"You just carry on Darling....You're doing a good job there...You're causing some of these old men to have dirty thoughts but you mustn't worry yourself too much...They're quite harmless....It's all in their minds."

Woody, still laughing, adds.

"You're probably right there Bert I think I'll give Doctor Berry's Surgery a visit tomorrow to see if I can have them moved down a little bit."

With all the men laughing Denise smiles giving Woody a cheeky wink as she wiggles her hips. She continues to serve the customers with an air of confidence and efficiency.

Charlie Walsh comes into the conversation.

"Talking about looking well...You know that young Grandson of mine?...You know the youngest one?...Brian?...Our Susan's boy?."

His friends all think very hard until, almost in unison, they grunt and nod positively.

"Right well...I told you he had joined the Army... Signed up for twelve years...Well he's home for his first spot of leave...Before they post him off abroad somewhere...And I have to say...Even though he's my own flesh and blood...The Lad really does look very smart in his new uniform...Makes me and his Nan very proud...He did say he'd try to pop in later for a quick pint but you know what these young soldiers are like...Eh?."

Eddie agrees enthusiastically.

"We certainly should do Charlie...Quite of few of us in here did our little stints for King and Country...Yes... Of course not all of us were given the chance to sign up on a voluntary basis...We were called up...You went in if you wanted to or not....Nobody even asked...Letter arrived...In you went."

Nods and sounds of agreement greet these remarks.

"Still it didn't do any of us any lasting harm did it?...I think the Services provide a wonderful career prospect for the young men of today...Good luck to him Charlie...You've every right to feel justifiably proud of the Lad."

Norman suddenly spins around on the top of his stool to vigorously contribute his observations.

"Especially when there's no bloody wars going on it must be great... I agree with Eddie wholeheartedly."

Norman's demeanour then changes in a flash. He sounds rather defensive and a little pathetic.

"Unfortunately they couldn't find a place for me in the Army the Navy or the bloody Air Force even when there was a full scale World War taking place."

Victor interrupts sympathetically.

"Hardly your fault that Norman....Someone had to stay behind to keep those home fires burning...If we're being honest some of us might just as well have stayed at home for all the actual use we were to the Allied Fighting Forces...Take me for an example despite the fact that I had never seen the sea or a real ship they put me in the Royal Navy... Me...A confirmed Landlubber...In the Navy!...I really hated it at first but after a while I got used to it...I was only being violently seasick once a day eventually...After a few years there was even a slight danger that I was beginning to enjoy the life...Then all the hostilities suddenly ended...And...Let me openly admit it to you all...I was extremely relieved to be demobbed...I suppose it was an experience but I was very glad to see the end of it all and I can tell you without fear of contradiction I got myself back home with the utmost of haste and I've never been anywhere near a ship or the sea since."

All those present appear to reminisce for a few moments until Ralph stimulates the conversation by addressing Bert McCabe, who seems slightly disinterested.

"You were in the Royal Navy weren't you Bert?."

Bert takes a swig from his glass before he elects to lighten the substance of the subject under discussion.

"No...Not quite Ralph...I was in the Royal Stand backs...Yes that was my Unit...We were famous for being last onto the field of battle and the first off."

Because they are aware that Bert is not being serious they all chuckle and smile. Bert's face lights up.

"Oh Aye....I was on the beach at Dunkirk when the first shot was fired....When the second shot was fired I was safely back at home having resigned from the Army with immediate effect....Eh?....Eh?."

Bert nudges Charlie in the ribs and they all enjoy a good laugh. Woody intervenes on a more serious note.

"Come off it Bert....You were in the Royal Marines I know that for a fact...A Commando...You can't fool me...I can recognise all those medal ribbons you proudly wear on your police tunic when you're on duty...Royal Stand backs my arse!...They didn't take any duffers in the Royal Marine Commandos."

Although slightly embarrassed Bert is also quietly pleased that Woody has taken it upon himself to make such flattering remarks about him. Bert responds.

"O.K. Woody...You're quite correct...When I think back I must've been bloody crackers...It got rather hairy in our Outfit from time to time to say the least...Still as someone has already pointed out...It hasn't done any of us any lasting or damaging long term harm...Eh?...Eh?."

As Bert is afraid that serious conversation is impeding devoted beer drinking. He sets about lightening the general line of their discussion once again.

"You know Old Arthur Rose?...The Chap with that miraculous new hearing aid?...Eh?....Eh."

Everyone laughs immediately.

"Well...Old Arthur was telling me about the time when he volunteered for service in the First World War...He said he was drawn in by those famous posters....Your Country Needs You...So Arthur finds himself having a full medical examination with all these other Blokes at the Town Hall in Rochdale...All of them are bollock naked.... Oh Aye...In their pelts barefooted right up to the neck and all standing in a row....The Medical Officer moves along the line and stops in front of Arthur.....He stands back a little before pointing at Arthur's wedding tackle.. According to Arthur he then remarks...By Jove Rose you are very small made...Are you not?....So Arthur tells me that quick as a flash he replied...Well Sir we're only going to fight those Germans aren't we?."

Bert's little tale has the desired affect. They all burst out laughing. Vic indicates his intention to purchase beer with a nod to Alf, struggling not to laugh too loudly.

"Oh come off it Bert...Come...Come...Surely that is not true.... That must be one of your jokes."

Bert smiles at Vic in a teasing manner as he places his empty glass on the bar in front of him. Charlie takes over the lead. Initially he actually sounds quite sincere.

"I was demobbed before the end of the hostilities of course...Oh Yes...When the Allied Forces surrounded Berlin which as you are aware swiftly brought proceedings to a halt in 1945 the Major in charge of my Mob called me into his Office... Oh Yes....He offered me one of his fags and then said to me.... You can go home now Walsh...You've killed enough Germans...Leave one or two for all these other Lads to finish off."

Charlie's remarks are treated with amused contempt but all those present are now enjoying some good clean fun. It becomes Woody's turn to add his contribution.

"I was best known in the Army for my athletic abilities...Track events mostly."

Woody slips off his stool to pump his arms up and down whilst running on the spot, thrusting his head forward, demonstrating what he was referring to. His friends seem to be impressed. Woody sees that he has their full attention.

"Oh Aye....It was my fast running mainly...Mind you the Army had another name for it...Oh Aye...They called it desertion."

There are roars of laughter as Alf completes Victor's order for beers all around his friends. Woody takes a sip from his freshly pulled pint, remarking to Alf.

"I know you're under a bit of pressure behind there Alfred but please try to keep up with your Regulars pace of consumption...They can turn very nasty if...For any reason...The flow of their favourite brewery juice is interrupted for any length of time."

Alf thinks about giving Woody a sharp and pertinent reply but opts to appear sarcastically servile.

"Oh one hundred thousand apologies...As you know your word is my command....Oh mighty mouth!."

Everyone in the company is really enjoying their drinking and chatting. Denise is busy serving a group of customers at the far end of the bar. Suddenly the attention of all those in the vicinity is attracted to the noise made by Joe Summers, the well known local troublemaker, banging his empty glass on the top of the bar counter. Obviously Joe has had a lot to drink. He looks to be reaching his nastiest level. He snarls to Alf, who is also engaged serving drinks.

"Come on Alf for Christ's sake!...What does a person have to do in here to get some bloody service?."

All are annoyed at Joe's rude and uncalled for conduct but Bert McCabe seems incensed. He glares at Ralph.

"Who let that Bastard in here?."

Bert removes his glasses and rummages around in his trouser pockets for his handkerchief. Ralph instantly recognises the McCabe's ritual pre-violence routine. He nervously grabs Bert by the arm.

"Now...Now then Bert...Let's not be too hasty."

Bert finds his handkerchief and is about to remove his false teeth. He is now growling.

"There's only one way to deal with him...Stand back whilst I demonstrate."

Vic joins Ralph in his attempts to prevent Bert from introducing instant violence. In a desperate effort to pacify the situation Norman

Smith stands on top of his stool to speak to Joe in a calm and reasonable manner.

"Hey up Joe….Now steady down Lad…Everyone will be served eventually….You just have to wait your turn."

Norman smiles nervously as Joe glares at him in a threatening, aggressive, way. He sounds even nastier.

"And who asked you for your opinion?... Mind your own business.... You little prick!."

Joe grips onto the bar as he sways back a little to get a better look at Norman. Laughing, with distain, he spits out another vicious insult.

"Keep your nose out Shortarse…Christ if your ass was any closer to the floor you'd have to fix a wheel on it.. Just Piss Off!....And mind your own business if you know what's good for you."

This comment obviously upsets Norman. Eddie who is seated between Norman and Joe makes an effort to calm things down

"There's no need for that kind of talk in here Joe. Just behave yourself please....Or...Or go home."

Joe's face contorts with bitter anger as he turns his attention onto Eddie.

"And who rattled your cage….SAMBO!."

Joe's outrageous conduct is now affecting everyone present. Bert McCabe has removed his glasses and teeth and is trying to break free from Ralph, Victor and Charlie to get at Joe Alf rushes to the bar to face Joe. Although quite upset he looks and also sounds very firm and determined.

"Right that's it Joe…You won't be getting any more to drink in here my Lad…You are barred!."

Joe reacts angrily.

"Oh I'm barred am I?....We'll soon see about that you dribbling Shithouse!."

With that Joe suddenly throws his empty glass at the hatch behind the bar causing broken glass to scatter. His tone clearly indicates that he has lost control of his temper.

"BARRED?....JUST FOR UPSETTING A MIDGET AND HIS PET COON!."

Eddie pushes his stool back, rising to his feet but before he can do so Norman leaps on top the bar counter He swiftly moves along the bar, saying.

"Me first please."

Norman then delivers a sickening smack to Joe's open mouth with his left fist. Joe falls backwards, as if pole axed. He lies on the floor spark out. Unruffled, Norman walks back along the counter to return to his stool. As he passes Eddie he remarks.

"Now if he requires any further attention Eddie.. It's your turn next."

To say everyone is viewing the scene with amazement would be putting it mildly. Bert strides over to Joe's limp body lying on the floor. He flips him over to take a firm grip on his collar and the seat of his trousers. With little effort Bert lifts Joe off the floor. He runs towards the front doors. One of the men seated near to the doors springs to his feet to ensure the exit is clear. Bert nods to him as he and the still motionless body of Joe Summers disappear into the darkness of the Car Park.

Alf and Woody are making sure that Denise has not been injured by the flying glass. Vic seems to be concerned about Bert. He anxiously enquires.

"Should some of us go outside to check if Bert is alright?...What a carry on....If anyone ever deserved to be locked up it has to be that idiot Joe Summers...The man is a menace to the Public at large when he has a drink."

Ralph is keen to calm things down. He makes a general address to all present.

"Please Gentlemen...Please...It's all over....Don't worry about Bert...Joe's no match for him when he's sober...Just leave Bert to deal with him...Please settle down everyone......Please....now carry on enjoying yourselves....Don't worry no-one has been injured behind the bar...Please accept my sincere apologies to all for any inconvenience... Please!....Please carry on everything's O.K."

By now everyone is turning their attention to Norman. He is the centre of attention and he is enjoying every minute of it. Wreathed in smiles, Alf places a full pint of beer in front of him.

"Here Norm...This is on the house and you deserve every mouthful of it...Bloody hell...I didn't think you had it in you...That's the best left hook I've ever witnessed outside a boxing ring...Well done Norman."

Smiling happily Norman responds to Alf's gesture.

"Thank you very much Alf...I wish you all to know that I am not normally a violent person but when the Gobshite picked on Eddie... Well...That was the last straw as far as I was concerned...I'm immune to people taking the piss out of me but I felt Joe went too far and there was no need for it at all."

Eddie tenderly places his arm around Norman's shoulders. His voice is tinged with emotion as he speaks.

"You deserve a medal Norman....I'm quite capable of fighting my own battles but I'll tell you this Mister...I could not have dealt with Joe more efficiently than you did...I was stunned when he hit the floor.... Just one smack."

Eddie looks around for support as he states.

"Not even Rocky Marciano would have got up from that....What a BLOODY SMACK!!."

Loud cheering and applause greet Eddie's remarks. Bert returns to the table, immediately replacing his glasses and false teeth. Victor anxiously enquires.

"Everything all right Bert?...That man really is a twenty four carat menace....Incarceration is needed I feel."

Bert carries out a couple of test bites with his teeth before he picks up his glass to drain it in one swallow. Alf gestures to Bert from behind the bar. He has a fresh pint of beer in his hand. Without speaking Bert takes the glass and after a quick nod almost empties it with one long swig. Bert wipes his mouth with the back of his sleeve before he speaks.

"How kind....How very kind Alfred...Let me assure everyone that Joe Summers will not be bothering anyone else this evening."

Ralph enquires.

"Have you locked him up for the night Bert?."

Bert looks slightly shocked.

"Locked him up for the night?...There was no need for him to be locked up Ralph...His mate is taking him home.. He was crying like a baby when he woke up...I doubt you'll be seeing his ugly face around these parts for some time...He'll be seeing me in my Office at the Nick tomorrow morning."

Bert turns to Norman.

"No offence Norman but your outstanding action demonstrated this very evening may well have destroyed Joe's hard man image a little around this particular of the woods...Eh?.... Eh?...Incidentally Ralph I'll be needing an estimate for the cost of any of the damage caused... Joe will be paying for that...He'll be getting the Bert McCabe Lecture on how to behave yourself in Public with both barrels in the morning.... I like to get them when they're still suffering from the nasty hangover Eh?...Eh?."

Denise is busy clearing away the mess with a brush and shovel, apparently unperturbed by the disturbance. Alf hears Bert's request to Ralph causing him to respond.

"I think he might be a bit lucky there Bert...The only thing he actually broke was the pint pot...And I'm not too bothered about that... Bloody lucky when you think about it...He could easily have smashed that row of Spirit Bottles lined up along there on the optics. Bloody close thing for sure."

There are gasps at the very thought of all that, Whiskey, Gin, Rum and Vodka, being destroyed by a tantrum. Bert nods an acknowledgement to Alf before he sums it all up.

"Yes...O.K. Alf as long as you're happy there's no point in complicating events....And you're right Alf it could have been a whole lot worse...Had anyone been injured...Even in the slightest way I would have to deal with Naughty Boy Joe in a very different way...

He's definitely not the whole shilling. He's fine when he's sober....A smashing Lad....Hard working Husband and loving Father to all his kids but once he gets some drink down him it causes his brain to slip into neutral...He reminds me of that fella in the famous horror story... You know Jeckle and some other bugger whose name escapes me?... Mind you I think tonight's little turn of events might have a long term and lasting beneficial effect on the bold Joe Summers...We can always hope so anyways....What a prize Tithead."

Bert drains his glass again. Ralph nods to Alf and he starts filling it up once again. Bert breaks out in a broad toothy grin as he acknowledges Ralph's generous gesture.

"Oh how kind...How very kind Ralph...Eh?...Eh?."

* * *

"Don't be daft Ricky…..I'd love to."

The glorious morning sunshine makes the Lapley Vale Nursery appear quaint, attractive and at it's very best. The neatness and divergence of the vast assortment of colourful flowers, shrubs, trees and delicately tinted ferns laid out in tidy allotments enhance the intrinsic charm and elegance of the large wooden structure, which is much more than a Garden Hut, standing proudly in the middle of all the foliage. The "Hut" has a dual purpose. Through the double glass doors on the front is the shop where members of the Public can place their orders for wreaths, select bouquets of cut flowers or purchase any of various ancillary gardening products displayed for sale. At the rear of the shop hidden from Public view is the work place where Dickie Mitchell and Eric McCabe carry out many of the various essential tasks required to maintain and service a thriving business as a Retail Nursery. There are three large greenhouses behind the work shop and office. These almost completely out of sight as one approaches the shop at the front. This is where all the specialised plants, requiring heat and protection or other individual attention in order that they can proliferate, like

tomatoes, geraniums, orchids and many others, are planted and encouraged to grow into healthy plants and shrubs and fruit.

Billy Dawes, looking resplendent in a white open necked shirt, sports jacket and cream coloured Panama Hat, normally worn only when he is bowling, walks through the gates to make his way towards the Shop. He walks past a collection of wheel barrows, bags of peat and assorted wooden bird tables. He pauses to admire a row of vividly coloured and sweetly scented hanging baskets, displayed on a firm trellis fence near to the entrance into the Shop.

Dickie Mitchell, the owner and Eric McCabe's Boss, is standing behind the counter putting the finishing touches to a wreath. Glancing up he is very surprised to see Billy striding through the open double doors.

"Good Morning Billy...Now this really is a rare treat...What can I do for you this lovely day?."

Billy's eyes are darting all around the room. He appears to be slightly nervous. He concentrates his attention on Dickie, smiling, rather weakly.

"Yes and a very Good Morning to you as well Dickie Yes...Thank you."

Billy pauses as Dickie waits. He notices that Billy appears to be unusually self conscious. Billy continues.

"Well...It's for the wife really Dickie.....It's her cockeyed birthday tomorrow and she's a great lover of flowers and the like and....Well I thought I might treat her to a nice bunch of cockeyed...."

Dickie is relieved that Billy's occasional visit is for a legitimate reason. He interrupts Billy.

"Well you couldn't have come to a better place than here Billy my Old Friend...Now tell me....How much did you want to spend on her?."

Billy is shocked by the directness of the question. He coughs and splutters before he manages a reply.

"Want to spend is putting the case a bit too cockeyed strong Dickie...I want to give her a pleasant surprise but I don't want to spend a cockeyed fortune in order to do so.. If you know what I mean."

Billy smiles weakly as Dickie thinks for a moment or two before he speaks.

"If you're prepared to part with a couple of quid Billy I could make up a really beautiful bouquet for her."

The mention of two quid stuns Billy. Dickie feels obliged to justify his opening offer.

"And that would also include all the fancy wrapping and delivery to your front door."

Billy cannot hide his shock. He tries to pretend that he has not been upset but fails to do so.

"Hell Fire Dickie....I'm only a poor old cockeyed Pensioner you know?...I'm not made of cockeyed money."

Dickie realises that Billy will need to be offered a bargain if he is going to make a sale. He tries to be as reasonable as he can be.

"Look Billy...Can you indicate to me just how much you were thinking of lashing out on this surprise gift...That'll give me some sort of an idea what I can let you have."

Billy shrugs his shoulders. He looks rather furtive as he replies.

"I think I can manage a cockeyed quid Dickie... Or maybe as much as thirty cockeyed bob but that would be my cockeyed limit I'm afraid."

Dickie decides to call it a day. He accepts that he will not be making much of a profit out of Billy Dawes. He seems resigned as he speaks.

"O.K. Billy I can do you a very nice bouquet for a quid...Christ... I'd hate to feel responsible for you and your family starving to death or anything like that...How does that meet with your requirements... Sir."

Billy immediately breaks out in a broad smile. He produces a pound note straight from his pocket. Dickie takes the note, placing it in his wooden till at the end of the counter

"Young Ricky will make up a nice fresh bunch of the prettiest flowers first thing in the morning Billy and he'll drop them off at your house first thing...You haven't moved house or anything have you Billy?."

Billy replies as only he can.

"Yes that's right Dickie...I haven't moved... I've lived there for more than fifty cockeyed years."

Billy is feeling pleased with himself because he is well aware of the prices Dickie normally charges for his splendid bouquets but he also knows that Dickie tends to charge his customers what he thinks they can afford. The bouquets are inevitably outstanding irrespective of how much they cost. Billy moves towards the double doors but suddenly stops, returning to the counter. He furtively speaks in a much lower tone.

"Keep this to yourself Dickie Boy…I don't want anyone to spoil Nan's cockeyed surprise."

Billy touches the side of his nose with his finger as he winks. Dickie plays along.

"Mum's the word Billy….Mum's the word."

Billy doffs his hat and swiftly disappears leaving Dickie shaking his head as he quietly chuckles to himself.

* * *

Eric McCabe looks anything but safe as he rides his delivery bicycle along the Street anxiously checking the numbers on the row of identical appearing terraced houses. A large bouquet of colourful flowers is lying in the basket at the front of the bike. He wobbles even more as he obviously sees the number he is seeking. Rather clumsily he stops. He pulls the bicycle forward onto the little legs provided for parking. He checks the number on the invoice against the number on the door of the house before he carefully lifts the flowers out of the basket. At this moment Jenny Dawes opens the door. She is wearing a stylish and very cute pink dressing gown. She steps forward, her arms outstretched.

"Hello….Can you hand them to me please?…I want to get them into water in a vase and well out of sight before my Nan gets back from the shops…I promised Granddad I would take care of everything for him."

Eric hands over the flowers without a word. He is strangely struck dumb by Jenny's stunning presence. She continues.

"Oh aren't they beautiful?…What a wonderful surprise for Nan… Mind you I must say I'm rather surprised myself…I didn't think for one moment that Granddad had a romantic streak in him…She's going to be absolutely thrilled."

Eric manages to speak, although he still seems oddly mesmerised being in Jenny's presence in her dressing gown.

"Yes they are nice and I can also tell you that I personally picked them this very morning...So that'll give you an idea about how fresh they are...I love flowers myself."

Although she is a little taken aback by Eric's honesty she cannot prevent herself from taking the opportunity to tease him a little.

"Well that makes a pleasant change I must say...I thought you Lads were only interested in Sport and Ale....I bet you get your leg pulled by your mates though don't you?."

Eric responds defensively and firmly.

"They'd get a good smack if they said anything to me...I've always liked flowers and all other things that grow in the ground for as long back as I can remember...I count myself very fortunate to have landed a job where I can not only grow nice things but I am able to learn more about them all the time."

Jenny, quite boldly, questions Eric.

"I thought you worked at the Bowling Club with Old Woody Green...That's what I heard anyways."

Eric is growing in confidence.

"Oh yes...Been making enquiries about me have you?"

Eric smiles. Jenny giggles in what he considers to be a very cute way. She adopts a rather false coy attitude.

"There's no law against that is there?."

Eric smiles as he shakes his head.

"Anyways it was Granddad who told me that you were working with Woody...That's if you must know."

Although Eric is enjoying their encounter he realises that their conversation is drawing to a close. He pulls himself together to project a more businesslike manner.

"Well I'd best be on my way now...I have to return this bike to the Nursery before I go to the Bowling Club...You see I actually work for both of them...Dickie Mitchell and Old Woody...Although I don't get paid at the Bowling Green Woody can't go on for ever and I think everyone acknowledges that he is the best authority on Bowling Greens and the like in the whole area….I want to be in pole position when he eventually hands over the reigns….It's not a bad arrangement actually because I'm learning from both of them all the time…I love it I wouldn't swap places with anyone in the World."

Jenny is more than a little impressed by Eric. She smiles sweetly whilst listening to his every word but she realises that time is against them both.

"I'd better get my skates on too…Nan will be back from the shops before I completed my mission…I promised Granddad that I would keep the surprise for him….So…Thank you very much…Er Ricky."

Eric feels strangely rewarded and flattered by Jenny, not only calling him by name but by the more familiar one used only by those people who know him well. She giggles and even blushes a little as she cheerfully adds.

"I'll see you around…I expect."

Jenny turns to re-enter the house. Eric calls upon all of his reserves of courage as he anxiously blurts out.

"There's a smashing picture on at the Ritz…If you fancy seeing it that is."

Jenny stops, she stares into Eric's wide open eyes. Again, she cannot stop herself from teasing him a little.

"What do you mean?.....Are you asking me out Ricky McCabe?."

Just for a fleeting moment Eric wonders if he has jumped the gun slightly. He can feel his face turning red as he backs off to add rather nervously.

"Well you don't have to if you don't…."

Jenny laughs aloud as she interrupts him.

"Don't be daft Ricky I'd love to go out with you…..What about tonight?...Or is that too short notice?."

Eric's heart is pounding as he eagerly replies.

"No…Not at all….Tonight is fine…That's just what I was going to suggest…Yes tonight….Great….That suits me fine."

He is hoping that he does not sound too keen in case he puts her off. He can hardly believe his luck as he continues.

"Shall we meet outside at say half seven?."

Jenny sounds delighted with Eric as she answers.

"Yes…That's fine Ricky…Half seven outside the Ritz…That's great…I must go now."

She closes the door, saying.

"Bye for now Ricky….See you later."

The door finally closes. Ricky stands in a trance for a few moments. He finds himself desperately attempting to come to terms with the turn of events which have just occurred. He immediately realises that he has just disclosed more about his personal feelings to Jenny, a girl he hardly knows, than he has ever revealed to anyone outside his Family and close Friends.

He takes the bike off the legs, almost falling over in the Street as he does so. He manages to concentrate his befuddled mind on the job in hand and, still smiling in a silly sort of fashion, he rides off down the Street. After moving a few yards along the Street Eric suddenly stands on his pedals, causing him to surge forward as He throws his head to exclaim, loudly.

"Y E S!!!!!!…."

* * *

"The double seats are always the first to go."

Mrs McCabe is busy in the kitchen in later stages of preparing the family evening meal. A quick glance at the clock tells her the time is rapidly approaching 6pm. She hears the sound of Bert driving his car into their integral garage which triggers off her dishing out onto two large dinner plates.

Bert, in full uniform, opens the adjoining door to step into the kitchen. He greets his Wife in his own individual style.

"Hello….It's only me….Is my dinner ready yet Mother…. Christ my stomach thinks my throat's been cut….I could eat a flock mattress….Well pissed….Eh?...Eh?.

Mrs McCabe frowns as she snaps at him.

"Bert I really do wish you wouldn't use talk like that in my kitchen… Of course your meal's ready…Hang your things up wash your hands and get yourself up to the table….Eric's already had his…It's a wonder that Lad is never crippled with indigestion….Came home early from Work bolted down his dinner and immediately flew up the stairs…"

She raises her voice so that Bert can hear her as he hangs his coat, tunic and cap on the coat hangers at the bottom of the stairs.

"I think there's something funny going on….Would you believe where he is now?....I'll tell you….He's only in the bath."

Bert is taking his place at the table, rolling up his shirt sleeves before he reaches for the local evening newspaper.

"Did you hear me Bert?....He's actually in the bath...I usually have to threaten him with a gun to get him to take his weekly bath...This is a definite first....A bath without being threatened."

Bert is more interested in the contents of the newspaper than what his Wife is saying but he nods and grunts. She places his dinner plate on the table in front of him and snatches the paper out of his hands.

"Come along please....There's time for reading and cursing at all the terrible atrocities related every night in that rag....Eat your meal whilst it's still piping hot."

Bert is about to complain until he sees his dinner. He immediately goes for his knife and fork with a vengeance. He devours almost half of the food on his plate before you could blink an eye. He then sits back for a moment, points to the discarded newspaper with his knife, and replies with half a mouth full of meat, which has to be chewed a little before it can be swallowed.

"You fuss too much Mother....Christ I wish you'd stop all this fussing...And it's a poor do when a man can't please himself when he reads his paper in his own bloody house....Eh?...Eh?."

Mrs McCabe ignores Bert's remarks. She places her own plate on the table and sits down facing her Husband. They are both eating quietly when their attention is distracted by loud thumping noises coming from the staircase as Eric bounds downstairs from the bathroom. He enters the living room wrapped in a large fluffy towel. His face is bright red and he appears to be glowing with cleanliness. He swiftly nods to his Mother and them speaks directly to Bert.

"Dad....I was just wondering if you'd mind if I used a little splash of the new after shave lotion you got last Christmas please."

The parents stare into each others faces searching for any reaction. Eric shuffles his feet and continues with his plea.

"Just a drop or two please Dad....My face is a little bit tender after a close shave...If you don't mind please."

Bert is sufficiently moved to put his eating irons down on the table. He seems to be stunned. He has an odd expression on his face. He glances at his Wife again before he answers his Son.

"After shave lotion?......After bloody shave lotion?...Hells fire Lad what's going on?....You given your Mother the beginnings of a very nasty shock by taking a bath without having received the statutory seven days written notice and now you want to borrow some of my after shave lotion....What the bloody hell is going on here....Eh?....Eh?"

They can tell Eric is embarrassed even though he tries his best to sound off hand and casual.

"Nothing!......There's nothing up at all....My face is a little bit sore after shaving that's all....Nothing else at all...Look if you don't want me to borrow yo...."

Bert eyes flash with annoyance as he sharply interrupts his Son.

"Keep your hair on Sonny....You're not too big yet for Daddy to place his highly polished size ten boot right up your ass you know…Eh?....Eh?....Anyways…Who said you couldn't use it?...I didn't did I?....You can pour the whole bloody bottle over your head as far as I'm concerned....If you wish to smell like a woofter that's your bloody funeral…Eh?...Eh?....O.K.?"

Eric turns to leave the room.

"Well that's fine then....Thank you...I didn't mean to cause an uproar...I like to look and smell at my best when I venture out for the evening....I don't thin they've made that a crime yet have they?."

Bert picks up his knife and fork again to remark to his Wife, loudly enough for Eric to hear as he ascends the staircase, with a hint of a chuckle in his tone.

"Well that's confirmed it for me then…You can bet a pound to a pinch of shit that Cupid has been firing his little arrows in the vicinity."

Mrs McCabe does not appear to immediately grasp Bert's meaning. He goes on, speaking even louder.

Oh yes....Mark my words Mother....My extensive experience and training as a Police Officer of great standing leads me to believe that Ricky has found a new love in his life....Eh?....Eh?."

Mrs McCabe rises from the table, picks up the empty plates and moves ponderously into the kitchen without comment.

* * *

A very smart looking Eric McCabe is standing on Huddersfield Road almost directly across from the Ritz Cinema. He is wearing his smart new suit, a neat white shirt and dark tie, even his shoes are polished. He anxiously glances at his watch before he manoeuvres his position to enable him to check his watch against the clock on the Town Hall. Both verify that the time is 7.20pm.

The Rex Cinema is extremely well illuminated. The bright lights, vivid posters and glossy photographs indicate beyond any reasonable doubt that the feature film being shown tonight is a eagerly anticipated Western starring the extremely popular Henry Fonda and Glenn Ford. Although the actual film being shown is not high on Eric's lists of importance or priorities at this particular time.

Suddenly Eric's attention is distracted as Terry Price, well known local prankster and possible future mental case gestures to him as he fervently darts inside the doorway leading into some shop premises just behind him. Terry then leans his head and shoulders out to sneakily peer up and down the road in a very purposeful manner. Whilst doing this Terry continues to wave to Eric inviting him to join him inside the door hole. Eric, reluctantly, moves towards Terry. He leans out to drag Eric, inside out of immediate sight. Smiling broadly Terry greets Eric in a cheerful fashion.

"Alright Ricky my lad?.....Christ!...Who got you ready tonight.... You look like a bridesmaid or the like....Not going to a wedding at this time of night are you?"

Eric smiles wryly. He tone indicates distain.

"Very funny indeed Terry....Still a bundle of belly laughs I see..... I don't have to go around giving explanations as to why I happen to be wearing my good clothes on a weekday....We don't all go round doing impersonations of tramps....Anyways...What do you want?....What are you up to tonight?."

Terry grins as he pokes his head out again to check that the coast is clear. He ducks back to pull a large white rat out of the inside pocket of the reefer jacket he is wearing. Eric jumps back more from surprise than a fear of the creature. Terry is grinning all over his silly face as he makes the introductions.

"Ricky you haven't met Ernest have you?....Ernest this is Ricky.... Ricky this is Ernest."

Eric nods and smiles, then feels a bit silly as Terry carries on.

"Tell Uncle Ricky where you're going tonight Ernest…Eh?...Come on tell him….Ernest is going to the flicks tonight Uncle Ricky aren't you Ernest?"

Eric laughs as he pretends to speak to the rat.

"Well Ernest I'm afraid Daddy won't be taking you into the Ritz tonight because he's barred since the night of the floating white glove and he'd never manage to get past Gordon the Doorman by himself never mind accompanied by you…So I'm sorry but you're going to be faced with a big disappointment……Sorry."

Terry appears to be hurt at the mention of the night when Gordon threw him out unceremoniously and barred him for life plus another ten years after that for frightening the life out of Jenny and her friend Kay. He feels the need to put his opinion forward.

"Some people have no sense of humour that's their problem Ricky….Life soon becomes very dull unless steps are taken to brighten things up a bit."

Eric dismisses Terry's remarks with a shake of his head. Terry looks very cunning and smiles sneakily.

"So you don't think I can get past that brain dead bastard Gordon eh?....Gordon's I.Q. is equal to that of a tadpole and mark my words Ricky he is no match for Terrence Price you can bet upon that Matey."

Terry places Ernest back inside his coat pocket before he leans out to have another look around. He then produces a knitted balaclava, which he pulls over his head. He then places an old pair of National Health Service Spectacles on the end of his nose. Eric stands back, unsure of what to make of the proceedings. Terry raises a finger by way of indicating that he had not yet finished. He pulls out a false set of buck teeth which he carefully fits over the top of his own normal sized teeth. Eric is astonished as Terry carefully checks his overall appearance in the shop window glass. He then steps back, obviously satisfied with his disguise and definitely pleased with himself. Eric wonders if Terry can actually speak with the ridiculous teeth in. Shoving the glasses back on his face he speaks, surprisingly quite coherently.

"There....Not even my own Mother would recognise me now....Will you please do me a big favour now Ricky?......Just go out and see if Gordon is actually on the prowl for me....Please."

Despite a very strong desire not to get involved with Terry's antics Eric steps out. He looks across to the Cinema where he sees Gordon, resplendent in his full uniform, standing proudly at the top of the steps leading into the auditorium. Eric chuckles to himself as he ducks back inside the doorway.

"Right in the front line Terry....You'll never make it...He'll twig you before you get your foot on the bottom step...You've no chance at all....Give up before you end up with another thick ear."

Terry dismisses Eric's observations and remarks with a wave of his hand. He removes his false teeth momentarily to enable him to speak distinctly.

"We shall see Ricky my boy....We shall see."

Swiftly replacing his teeth he shoots out of the doorway and straight across the road to the front of the Cinema. Eric is transfixed on the scene. Terry smartly ascends the steps and raises a friendly hand towards Gordon. Gordon stares at him for a second but then smiles before he salutes him, smartly opening the door to enable Terry to enter with a flourish.

Eric can hardly believe what he has just witnessed. He starts to quietly laugh to himself when he suddenly becomes aware of Jenny standing beside him. Jenny looks very smart and attractive. She pretends to appear concerned as she remarks.

"They do put people away if they find them laughing to themselves for no reason you know?."

She laughs as Eric blushes slightly, feeling a bit silly. He is delighted to see her. He attempts to explain.

"Believe me Jenny I'm not laughing to myself I'm laughing at that silly Pratt Terry Price…You know….The soft lad with the white glove and the…."

Eric shuts up sharply as he realises that Jenny is far from amused by any recollection she may have stored of the performance by Terry Price. She shrugs her slender shoulders, pouting

"The least said about that Twit is the better for all concerned if you ask me….Kay and I took ages to recover from that daft trick he pulled on us that night…..He's just a nut case."

Eric knows he must not laugh although he feels inclined to do so when he remembers the incident in question. Jenny quickly changes the subject.

"I'm sorry I'm a little bit late Ricky but we've had a bit of a party for my Nan…It's her birthday today as I'm sure you recall….And as it was her special day I cleared all the things away and did the washing up and all that sort of thing…Still I'm here now."

Eric is besotted and impressed.

"That was really nice of you Jenny…I dare say your Nan was well pleased."

Jenny smiles sweetly. She then sounds rather matter of fact as she explains.

"Oh I do my share around the house…Nan is not getting any younger….She was seventy today…I always help her whenever I can although she never asks me to…Her and Granddad have been very good to me."

Eric is not totally interested in what Jenny is saying but he listens sympathetically. He soon realises that she is about to relate some of her personal details to him.

"I never knew my Mum…Their daughter…She left home when I was a tiny baby."

Eric is aware that Jenny is starting to feel sorry for herself but he also feels privileged to be trusted with such personal feelings from this wonderful girl who he has only really met for the first time properly today.

"I've never been able to discover who my real Father was...All I know is they didn't get married."

Jenny checked momentarily to see if Eric was being shocked.

"But to be perfectly honest....I don't care...In fact I couldn't care less....Nan and Granddad have always been perfect parents to me and I wouldn't change my life for the world."

Eric feels awkward. He wants to hug and kiss Jenny but he knows that would not be appropriate as yet. He had not expected such stunning revelations on their first date but he was sympathetic and even more enchanted with her.

"It certainly isn't your fault Jenny...I have been brought up to judge people as I find them...I think that's the best policy...What do you think Jenny?"

Jenny looks deep into Eric's eyes as she asks.

"And what are your initial conclusions about me Ricky?...So far that is."

Eric gently takes hold of her shoulders. He looks straight into her eyes. He looks and sound sincere.

"Favourable Jenny....Very favourable indeed....We don't know each other very well yet but I have to tell you that you are the first girl I have even been out on a date with and I am over 19 years of age....The reason for that is nothing more than the fact that I am very choosy...So does that answer your question Little Miss Nosey?."

He smiles as he softly touches the tip of her cute little nose with his finger. She looks delighted as she happily giggles. Eric glances across the road towards the Cinema as he says briskly.

"Right....Well come on then...We don't want to be late for the main picture do we?......I bet there's a good few in tonight....Westerns are very popular around these here parts."

They happy couple stroll across the road. Gordon springs to attention, then salutes and bows as he opens the doors with a flourish. Eric approaches the ticket box inside the foyer. He carefully checks the prices shown for all the various parts of the Cinema. Swiftly pulling a crisp pound note from his trouser pocket he places it on the metal ticket machine which serves as the counter. Seated inside the ticket office, or box, is a rather over made up middle aged woman. She looks absolutely disinterested much more focussed on her knitting. Eric coughs politely to attract her attention.

"Two please....Upper Circle...Two please."

Without a glimmer of acknowledgement or a word she snatches his money as two ticket fly out of the machine, causing Eric to move rather rapidly to catch them before they shot onto the floor. She then rattles his change on the metal top and actually **speaks** without increasing her level of interest in the slightest.

"If you were hoping for a double seat **you're** too late I think you'll find several other couples have beaten **you to them**."

She looks straight at Eric, appearing **quite menacing**.

"You should've got here a bit earlier shouldn't you?."

Jenny is mildly embarrassed as Eric **gently** steers her away for the box.

"Yes thank you for the advice...We'll manage don't worry."

Eric nods towards a little sweet and popcorn kiosk in the corner.

"Would you like any sweets or anything Jenny?"

Jenny shakes her head as she replies.

"No nothing thank you very much...Like I mentioned I've been gorging myself at Nan's Party....Thanks all the same Ricky."

Jenny giggles as she takes hold of Eric's hand and they both skip up the stairs in the direction of the Upper Circle area.

Reaching the door, leading into the Circle Area, they are faced by the fairly elderly usherette, know to all as Florence Nightingale the Lady with the Lamp. Florence tears the tickets in half. She looks up at the young couple as he hands Eric his halves back before she speaks.

"You're too late for the courting seats they've all be taken you'll have to sit further down on the ordinary seats…The double seats are always the first to go."

Neither Eric or Jenny makes any comment as Florence backs into the cushioned double doors to the loud sound of Pearl and Dean adverts emanating from the screen beyond the darkness. She switches her large silver, metal, torch on. The couple follow but Eric almost falls over Florence as she suddenly stops in her tracks to whisper.

"I'm not sure how many of them have come here to actually watch the picture….If you know what I mean?."

She haughtily throws her head back as they stumble along behind her until she shines the beam on two empty single seats. She flashes the torch on the seats to indicate the place she was telling them to sit. She turns on her heels and disappears before they manage to reach their seats. They settle down and wait for their eyes to become accustomed to the subdued lighting just as the main feature film starts.

Soon able to see much clearer Eric glances around to their rear to notice that the back two rows or double seats are fully occupied. There are a few others dotted around the Circle but no many very close to them. Jenny wriggles out of her top coat, draping it across her knees with a self conscious little smile. Eric gets a waft of her sweet smelling perfume which made him feel quite light headed. Jenny realises what happened and smiled rather coyly.

The film has only been running for a short time when a loud piercing scream, emanating from the ground floor Stalls, makes both Eric and Jenny, and quite a few others, jump with fright. This scream is followed, initially, by muffled voices but then by more loud feminine squeals. Jenny grabs Eric's arm as the house lights suddenly come on. By now the noise of a fairly substantial disturbance taking place in the Stalls area can be heard in every corner of the Cinema.

The unexpected brightness of the lights cause immediate panic in the double seats at the rear of the Circle. Both Eric and Jenny turn their heads to witness numerous couples in various stages of undress, with others in embarrassing positions trying very hard to cover themselves up and adjust their poses. Some of the heavy petting has been so advanced that one or two couples can only slide off their seats onto the floor in a forlorn hope of maintaining some decency.

Fairly soon the noise of the commotion gradually dies down. The house lights begin to gently dim to return to the usual state of subdued darkness again. Jenny is still clutching Eric's arm. She looks up at him and laughs. Eric bursts out laughing in sheer relief as he holds her hand on his arm. He stifles his noise then leans over to whisper in her ear.

"You know who's responsible for that racket downstairs don't you?."

Jenny stares into his face vacantly.

"That daft bugger Terry Price."

Jenny gasps, covering her mouth with her free hand. Eric nods at her to emphasise his informed knowledge of the events taking place well out of their sight.

"He sneaked past Gordon heavily disguised…With his little friend Ernest."

Eric nods his head again a couple of times to show he is right in what he has just related. He glances away but Jenny grasps his arm tightly to earnestly enquire in a strained whisper with her lips very close to his ear.

"Ernest?….Who the hell is Ernest?."

Eric moves closer to Jenny to whisper in her ear.

"Ernest?….Ernest is Terry's pet rat."

It takes all her powers to stop herself from screaming out aloud. She stares into Eric's face with a sincere look of total disbelief. She can hardly mutter her question.

"Pet rat?….A rat?...are you sure?...That proves it then…He's cracked…He should be locked up in a padded cell in a Metal Home."

Eric nods his agreement and takes advantage of the opportunity to slide his arm around her shoulders. Jenny responds immediately by snuggling up to him. After a few moments he whispers, even softer.

"Did you clock that lot at the back?...Bloody hell."

Jenny nods vigorously as Eric chuckles. She reaches up to speak very quietly into his ear.

"Yes I did…And I recognised some of their faces too."

Chuckling Eric replies.

"Faces?....I never noticed their faces."

Jenny give him a playful nudge with her elbow before she snuggles up even closer to him.

* * *

The evening of Eric and Jenny's first date has moved on. The young couple have definitely enjoyed their initial experience together inside the Ritz Cinema, perhaps not altogether thank to the antics of Terry Price. Without his little intervention maybe they may not have bonded to each other so quickly. They have visited 'The Golden Chip', due to Eric having trouble with his stomach rumbling due to his early evening meal. Now they are slowly walking along the Street both eating chips from bags wrapped in newspaper. Jenny giggles, managing to speak without her mouth being full.

"I didn't think I wanted anything to eat until I caught that lovely smell coming out of Billy the Chip's."

They both smile as Eric finishes his chips and screws up the wrapping papers. Jenny shoves her chips towards Eric.

"Here Ricky finish these off please…I'm afraid my eyes were bigger than my belly….Come on it's a shame to waste them."

Without word, or sign of protest, Eric takes the package from Jenny and sets about polishing them off. Jenny keeps the conversation going as Eric munches away, merrily.

"What can anyone say about that prize nutcase Terry Price?…Do you know him well Ricky?."

Eric immediately ceases his attack on the chips to ensure Jenny is left in no doubt that there is no connection between him and Terry. He manages to speak through a mouthful of food.

"No not really!....We were in the same year at School but he wasn't in the same Form as Sam and Peter and I…But he was in the same year….He's always been daft…I remember once when we were in the Juniors everyone was asked to bring in any unusual pets and would you believe?….Terry brought in a tin of sardines."

Eric shakes his head as he returns to the chips. Jenny thinks for a moment before she roars with laughter. Eric grins as he finishes Jenny's chips, conveniently as they reach a litter bin. Eric makes a meal out of dunking the wrappings in the basket like a basketball player. They stop as Eric sums up his opinion on Terry.

"Definitely balmy….I don't suppose he'll ever grow up…Still…He's doing O.K. for himself…He works for his Dad…You know Price's Transport?…Gets to drive around all over the place…He'll probably end up owning the Firm and becoming a wealthy man…Makes you sick doesn't it?.

They very soon reach the corner of Jenny's street. With a quick glance up at the name plate on the wall Eric enquires.

"Looks like you're nearly home Jenny….What time do you have to be in?."

Eric moves around under the light of the overhead street lamp to get a clear look at his wrist watch. Jenny replies in a manner which indicates that she is serious about what she about to say.

"I'm never out later than eleven o'clock…I don't find this a problem….Nan usually goes to bed fairly early but Granddad…Well you know Granddad don't you?….If he gets drinking with his Mates he has been known to come home at all hours…Usually the worse for wear…It's a good job Nan doesn't see him sometimes…Still he's harmless and we love him to bits."

Eric smiles.

"Don't you mean he's…Cockeyed…harmless Jenny?."

They both laugh as Jenny agrees.

"Oh you're right there Ricky…Everything is cockeyed with Granddad."

They have almost reached Jenny's house. They stop by a narrow side entry at the side of Jenny's block of terraced houses. Eric does not want the evening to end but he knows he must not spoil their perfect first date. He is curious.

"Where does it all come from?....The cockeye and cockeyed."

Jenny is able to answer without a pause.

"Very simple answer Ricky...Nan has never allowed him to swear... Never has....She considers cockeyed to be a harmless substitute for any swear words...This goes as far back as far as the days when they were a young courting couple...So if you remove all the cockeyes from his normal conversation you will probably appreciate why Nan insisted upon stopping him from swearing in the first place."

Eric laps up every word. After a moment for consideration he realises that the answer is a very simple one. He chuckles, shaking his head.

"Yes...You're right there he'd hardly speak a cockeyed word.....I like him...He's always been alright with me and he's very palsy with Woody and Alf...And my Dad as well...He loves his bowling and there's not many players can give him a game especially on our own Green."

Jenny is delighted to hear Eric's kind remarks. She nods approvingly before she adds.

"That's what keeps him fit you know?....He's no spring chicken anymore."

Jenny pauses, wondering if she should continue. She decides to carry on.

"Mind you he does have another nasty little problem...Do you know what it is?....It tends to affect him when he's bowling specially if he's had baked beans with his dinner...You know?."

Eric cottons on immediately.

"Oh you mean his farting."

Eric laughs louder than Jenny. She thinks the conversation is turning a little coarse so she hopes to change the subject.

"Let's just call it wind for now please....Nan won't let him do it in the house....When he's been out for a dinner time session."

She breaks off to giggle.

"Poor man....He's like a cat on hot bricks...Keeps rapidly disappearing out of the living room."

Eric is visualising the scene, causing him to laugh louder. Jenny is now anxious about the time although she feels she could stay chatting with Eric until the cows came home.

"He's smashing really...I love him to little bits...But he would never go out of his way to upset Nan....Speaking of which...I had better get in...Thank you very much for a really wonderful evening Ricky...I have never enjoyed myself as much before going to the Pictures.... Thanks very much."

Eric knows that he must let her go although he wants her to stay all night. He takes his courage in both hands to gently steer Jenny back into the darker part of the Side Street. He stares into her eyes with a strangely determined expression on his face. Although Jenny is curious she does not feel threatened but she is wondering what is happening as Eric speaks.

"Say prune please Jenny...P R U N E."

Baffled Jenny starts to pronounce, "P R U" as Eric launches himself to kiss her full on the lips. Jenny shoves him away because his sudden move shocks her. Eric looks quite guilty and disappointed. Jenny steps back close to him. She places her arms around his neck to say.

"Hang on Ricky...There no need to leap all over me...Do it properly."

She pulls his head down to kiss him gently on the lips. She then kisses him on both cheeks. She feels him sway slightly as she whispers in his ear.

"There now....That's much better isn't it and we both get to keep all our teeth as well."

Eric lunges again but she swiftly places a finger on his lips.

"Steady...Steady lad...Try not to go raving mad."

The couple then kiss sweetly and softly again. Eric manages to respond without moving into any kind of attacking mode. They stand hugging each other tightly. Jenny then kisses him on the cheek, stepping back in a flash.

Forcing herself to speak with authority she insists.

"I must go…Sorry Ricky…But I don't want to spoil what I can only describe as a perfect day."

She gazes into his eyes.

"Will I see you again?."

Eric reaches out to grab her. He pulls her towards him. They kiss again. Jenny steps back.

"I take it that means yes does it?."

Eric realises that he is sounding soppy but cannot avoid do so.

"Oh yes please Jenny…Yes please."

He suddenly snaps out of his trance like state as he realises that he has a slight problem.

"I'd love to Jenny but I'm skint until pay day."

She straightens herself up. She looks and sounds positive.

"I don't care about that Ricky…I'm just pleased you want to see me again….Because I'd love to see you again as well…I'm exactly the same as you Ricky….Choosey…And you're the first choice I've ever made….Will you be able to meet me on Wednesday night…Say about seven…We don't need any money…We can have a nice walk and a chat so that we can get to know each other more."

Eric's enthusiasm is obvious.

"Wednesday?....Yes Wednesday will be fine for me Jenny…Where shall we meet?."

Jenny frowns anticipating a negative response.

"What about calling for me here?...At the house."

Eric replies without hesitation.

"Yes!...Why not?...Certainly…We're all above board…Yes Wednesday at seven…That's great with me…Yes."

Eric is now drooling. Jenny places her hand on his cheek to kiss him lightly on the lips, leaping back immediately to avoid his clutches. She darts to her front door, putting her key in the lock.

"Night and Bless Ricky….See you Wednesday…Night."

She blows a kiss before she disappears into the house.

Eric remains stationary in the middle of the pavement with a silly smirk all across his face. He feels unable to move for the time being. He is enjoying deep, pleasant, contemplation. He eventually shakes his head before breaking into a broad smile. Turning to walk back along the Street he talks to himself, quietly at first but then raising the volume.

"Bloody hell…..Bloody hell….BLOODY HELL!."

Eric then marches off with a spring in his step.

* * *

"Oh……Are you sure it was me?."

The Clubroom at Lapley Vale Bowling and Social Club is literally heaving with people utilising the facilities. There are a number of visitors adding to those present because a home darts match is taking place against the Grapes Hotel. Alf and Denise are very busy behind the bar. The majority of the men in the room are concentrated around the area in the vicinity of the dart board.

Charlie Walsh is stood by the scoreboard with a piece of chalk in his right hand. He has been persuaded not to wear his tin helmet and goggles by Alf who managed to convince him that, as the Club's official scorer, this would not be appropriate. Vic Callow and Bernie Price, the Committee man and Uncle of the infamous Terry, are seated at the table reserved for 'Officials only' along with Fred James the Licensee of the Grapes.

Eric McCabe is standing with his right foot close to the ochre, his right arm and hand are extended He is taking careful aim with a dart. Eric leans forward slightly as he dispatches the dart. It lands right in the middle the double sixteen segment on the board. This is greeted by loud cheers and applause. Smiling, Eric clenches his right fist, gesturing his delight, as he walks towards the board to retrieve his winning dart. Charlie declares loudly and clearly.

"Thank you Gentlemen….That is game to the Lapley Vale Bowling and Social Club….I thank you."

Eric is shaking hands with his losing opponent as Bernie rises to his feet holding an official looking clip board.

"Thank you....Thank you Gentlemen....The Lapley Vale Bowling and Social Club having won five games against the three won by the Grapes."

He pauses to glance at Fred, who nods in anticipated agreement. Bernie returns to his announcement.

"And the Grapes Hotel having conceded I do hereby declare that the Lapley Vale Bowling and Social Club are the winners of the contest.... I thank you."

Bernie's announcement is greeted by cheers and applause from all around the Clubroom. Eric is carefully placing his darts into his inside jacket pocket as he approaches the bar where Woody is seated on his usual stool. Woody has his close friends Eddie Brown and Norman Smith sitting with him. Noting the Lad's imminent arrival Woody makes a meal of ordering him a drink, shouting to Alf,

"Can you fill a pot with a pint of your finest ale for the 'Son of Old Eagle Eye' here please Alfred my good man?."

Eric feels a little self conscious. Woody places his strong arm around his broad shoulders, to add.

"You're getting quite good Ricky....Chip of the old block if you ask me Chaps."

Smiling and nodding they all agree.

"I suppose you'll be throwing out a challenge to our Norman here next will you?."

Norman stares at Eric eagerly. Eric feigns a false frown before he takes a deliberate step back.

"Not bloody likely....You must be joking...Challenge Norman... 'The Legend'?....Not me....I know my place Woody."

There is laughter as Norman enjoys yet another opportunity to bathe in his newly acquired fame. Eddie speaks to Eric pretending to offer him a very strict warning.

"Now just you be careful Young Ricky….Don't go upsetting Norman…He might decide to give you a bloody good smack for your cheek."

Norman is almost purring with pleasure as Eric carries on with the reverence, now undoubtedly required.

"Thank you for that Eddie but you can rest assured I will be minding my P's and Q's when I'm anywhere near Mr Smith….I don't want to be booking an appointment with the Tooth Fairy do I?."

Eric puts his hands over his mouth as he pretends to duck clear and away from the delighted Norman. Eric grasps his glass to take the top of his, most welcome, pint.

In the relatively short time they have become closely acquainted Woody has really grown very fond of Eric. This does not, however, stop him from pulling his leg unmercifully at every given opportunity.

"I'm pleased to see that this courting caper hasn't caused your eyesight to be affected too badly."

Eddie and Norman are anticipating more gentle amusement but, for a change, Eric refuses to rise the bait, Woody deliberately speaks directly to Eddie and Norman trying to antagonise the Lad.

"At least he's not walking around in a bloody trace anymore… Christ!....When he first met his precious Jenny I though he was losing the use of what little brain he possesses…Strutting around with a silly smirk across his face for weeks he was…I thought he needed a good dose of those liver salts or castor oil."

They are enjoying the 'leg pull'. Eric is managing to stand firm, clearly tolerating the playful attack. Woody presses on.

"Still you're only young once…Christ I've seen the day when I would have walked a mile for an inch of it….Nowadays I wouldn't even walk an inch for a bloody mile of it…Eh?."

They roar with laughter but Norman is aware that Eric does not like relish being the centre of attraction. He rallies to his defence.

"Take no notice of him Ricky….He's only jealous…anyone with one eye can see that…How long have you been seeing Jenny now?...It must be a couple of months or so…Eh?."

Eric appreciates the opportunity to talk about his Beloved Jenny. He looks and sounds extremely enthusiastic.

"About six months actually Norm…At times it seems much longer than that…I can't remember what my life was like without her anymore."

They all smile as they detect the Lad's genuine sincerity but Woody is determined to tease him.

"Bloody hell Boys it must be love…Eh?."

Eric is blushing, causing Woody to back off.

"Still she's a smashing girl…and in all fairness she could do worse than old 'Son of Eagle Eye' here…Eh?."

Eric is mistaken as he thinks the ribbing is over. Woody winks wickedly to Eddie and Norman before he adds,

"I just hope he manages to keep control of his trouser worm….You know what I mean Ricky?….Your velvet headed bed snake?."

Much to Eric's despair they laugh loudly encouraging Woody to go on further.

"He has been made well aware that amongst the many other considerations he does need to be very careful not to take any liberties….He doesn't want to be receiving a 'COCKEYED' pasting for his trouble."

Woody begins to regret his actions as Eric's naïve sincerity kicks in.

"No chance of anything like that….She won't let me…I've yet to break my duck…I still haven't managed to get started on bedroom athletics with anyone at all."

Woody sounds philosophical.

"Hey….Don't you worry about that Lad….Plenty of time for that sort of stuff…Many men, famous and infamous, if it come to that, have desperately tried to come to terms with what can be done to lessen the enormous pressures that nature bring to bear on the average adolescent youth…So we've all been in the same boat in our youth…What you may need is some mild practice…Just for the time being…..There's a few choices to be had in that department as well"

Woody cannot resist returning to mild teasing.

"There's always plenty of it about....That's if you know where to look for it....You'll just have to take yourself in hand as a last resort Ricky my lad."

Eddie joins in.

"He's right there Ricky....Worthington Mary is always making offers to him you know?....Isn't that right Woody?."

Eric screws up his face to indicate his abhorrence to even thinking about that as a solution. Woody begins to feel the attack swinging in his direction.

"Bloody hell Eddie....Do me a favour please...I think I'd rather have a nasty attack of the piles....Any day."

They laugh but Eric is anxiously trying to glean knowledge from his experienced Elders.

"I think I'd like to try it just the once...You know?...To see what it's like?....That's all....Trouble is I don't think I could fancy anyone else and in any case I wouldn't want to do anything that may cause me to lose Jenny....So I'm buggered."

Woody's arm goes around his shoulders again.

"Take no notice of us Ricky....You've got a wonderful treat waiting for you some day....Well worth waiting for too...Eh?...Am I right Norm...What do you say?."

Unwittingly Woody has possibly hit a raw nerve. He realises that he should have been more discreet. Luckily Norman does not take offence. He does respond rather curtly,

"What are you asking me for Woody?....I've only ever used mine to stir my tea with...You've asked the wrong fellow I fear."

These remarks are met with relieved laughter. Eddie joins in the general discussion.

"Don't worry Ricky you're day with certainly come....The first time you manage it you'll think a flight of swallows has flown straight up your arse...And you won't mind one bit."

Eddie's contribution is greeted by loud laughter. Eric decides it is time to make good his escape.

"Well thanks for all that advice but I really must be making tracks now…Perhaps I can buy you chaps a drink before I go…Eh?."

Woody glances keenly at their empty glasses but Eddie swiftly responds.

"No you can't Ricky….Thanks for the offer though…I am going to buy you one for the road as a little reward for being such a good sport…We were only pulling your leg…You know that don't you?…I think you're a lucky fellow to have met Jenny and I must add that she is a lucky Lady for meeting you….Don't let anything or anyone spoil what you've got Ricky….Alf…Fill them up for us please."

All agree with Eddie sentiments but Eric sticks to his guns, politely.

"Thank you kindly Sir…But I really must go….I have to be up very early in the morning….We do seem to be mad busy at the Nursery at this moment in time….And….I've had a long day."

Turning to Woody he adds.

I'm afraid you won't be seeing me until well after dinner time tomorrow Woody….I just hope and pray that you'll be able to cope without me."

Woody replies sharply, without venom.

"Listen Sonny I can manage without you even when I'm busy so you can bugger off…Sweet dreams lover boy….Don't forget all the useful advice and guidance you've received tonight it might just hold you in good stead for the future."

Patting Woody and then Norman on their backs Eric makes his bid for freedom. He speaks to Eddie as he indicates his determined intention to depart forthwith.

"Good night Eddie….I do hope that Mrs Brown doesn't know what sort of company you are keeping in here….I bet you'd be confined to Barracks if she did…..Good night all."

Denise draws their attention away from Eric's departure by placing three frothing fresh pints on the bar in front of them. After making sure Eric has left Woody speaks with genuine sincerity.

"What a smashing young lad he is….and he's a bloody good worker too….No wonder Bert is so proud of him….I bet any one of us would be happy to have him as our Son….Eh?."

Muttering and nods indicate agreement as Denise places Eddies change in front of him. Woody's face lights up as he turns to her.

"Hey Denise….I dreamed about you last night."

Denise is mildly flattered as she cutely replies.

"Did you Woody?."

Woody almost falls off his stool in his anxiety to launch into his well practised punch line.

"No Denise love I didn't….You wouldn't let me."

They all laugh as Denise starts to pull another pint for a man standing next to Eddie. Waiting for the hilarity to die down she stares curiously into Woody's eyes to enquire,

"Oh….Are you sure it was me Woody?."

All three men are left helpless with tears streaming down their faces.

* * *

"That's nothing to be ashamed of."

Just recently Eric McCabe's life seems to going Through, what can only be described as, a high. He has a full time job he loves at the Nursery. He has received a few nice pay rises because of the extra business they have been generating. He is unofficially 'Green keeper Designate' at the finest Crown Bowling Club in the District. As if that isn't enough he has now been paid a most acceptable little bonus for his work under the tuition of the famous Woody Green. This bonus has come out of the blue but is obviously as a result of the new found improvement in the Club's finances. Eric would not have dreamt of complaining about not being paid by the Club because he sincerely considers working under Woody is a privilege and priceless in value to the learning process he is willingly undertaking under both Woody and Dickie Mitchell. Building up a nice little savings account at the Post Office in addition to being able to afford to take, his beloved, Jenny out whenever the occasion arises makes Eric a very contented young man. His latest perk is having the use of Dickie Mitchell's small van inscribed, 'Lapley Vale Nursery', on both sides, after working hours for personal pleasure purposes.

* * *

The time is nearing ten o'clock in the evening and The aforementioned little van is parked in a secluded clearing deep inside Lapley Vale Woods. Although it is dark there are no lights on, either inside nor outside, of the vehicle. Inside the van, occupying the front passenger seat, Jenny looks red faced and frustrated. Her hair and clothing are disarranged as she pants and puffs shoving Eric away from her, back onto his own seat. Her desperation is clear from the tone of her trembling voice.

"Please Ricky....Stop....Please stop."

Eric throws himself back into the driver's seat with obviously disappointment. Jenny shakes herself gently in an effort to recover her composure, before she runs her fingers through her hair. She straightens out her clothing as best she can, before she exhales, in a, deliberately, loud way.

"I can't breathe Ricky."

Their eyes have become accustomed to the darkness so Jenny can clearly see the unhappy, tortured, expression on Eric's handsome young face. She appeals to him in a apathetic fashion.

"It's just as difficult for me Ricky…Believe me I want to give in to you just as much as you want me to…."

She stares, deeply, into his expressionless features. She shares his frustration.

"But you know we have to be sensible…You know that…If I did let you go any further I don't think I could stop myself and we would end up going the whole way…And….And you promised we would save that….We both know the dangers."

She is aware that Eric looks like a whipped dog. She desperately tries to reason with him.

"I know how much you love me and you know how much I love you but Ricky we also know that we must be responsible……Neither of us really knows exactly what we'd be doing…Would we?."

Eric finds himself unable to speak. He has allowed himself to become so excited that he feels sure that the pupils in his eyes are pulsating in unison with his pounding heart. Jenny reaches over to cup his face in her hands drawing him towards her. She kisses him wildly all over his face and forehead. She is near to tears as she roughly shoves his head back to look, once again, into his unhappy features. Shedding a silent tear, she relaxes back into her seat. With trembling fingers she unfastens all the buttons on the front of her blouse. She then pulls Eric towards her, gently guiding his right hand between her legs.

* * *

Although neither of them had actually made love before They each, subconsciously, felt that they had managed extremely well. They are lying, in the rear of the van, close together, with their arms holding each other. They had never even noticed how cramped the conditions had been. They are pleasantly savouring their enjoyable shared experience. They have not bothered to put their clothes back on. They are both in private heaven lying in each others arms.

The actual truth of the matter is that Eric wanted to commit himself, totally, to Jenny. He felt that fulfilling his overpowering urge to carry out the ultimate act of love with her would convince her, without a shadow of doubt, that she was his one and only true love and would be forever more.

Jenny, on the other hand, had finally submitted to him because she wished to give him what he wanted in an effort to please him. She was also afraid, deep down, that if she constantly refused him she might run the chance of losing him to another girl, who may not live up to her personal standards of moral behaviour.

It is hard to say just how long the young couple have been lying, still and silent, locked in their arms. Eric feels a warm, satisfying, glow inside as he eventually kisses Jenny on the neck before whispering in her ear.

"We really belong to each other now Jenny."

She kisses him as a tear rolls down her cheek. He hugs her tightly as he murmurs.

"We have shown our true love will last for ever."

He is aware, by her body movements, that she is crying to herself. He anxiously attempts to reassure her.

"That's nothing to be ashamed of…Please Jenny…Please don't cry."

He kisses her passionately as she tries to stifle her sobbing. He carries on.

"You and I will be alright Jenny....Hey come on...There's nothing to cry about...Jenny...What we have just done was wonderful....Wasn't it?."

Jenny nods into his neck as she bites her lip. Eric gently lifts up her tear streaked face to enable him to look deep into her eyes.

"We love each other....That's all that counts....Whatever happens we are deeply and passionately in love....It has nothing to do with anyone else...Just between us....You and I."

Despite being unable to stop weeping, Jenny manages to smile. Eric kisses her passionately once again. Hugging her closely he declares.

"Jenny....Jenny....I will never....Ever...Want anyone else in the whole wide world....I would rather die than live my life without you."

Eric is beginning to suspect that Jenny is regretting what they have done because she has not uttered a single word since their romantic interlude. As he stares into her eyes she detects his rising concern. With her left hand she grasps him around the nape of his neck to kiss him very passionately. She then reigns kisses on his face and neck before she releases her hold on him. She continues to kiss him briefly as she speaks to the, now, breathless Eric.

"Ricky....Oh Ricky....I love you with all my heart....You are wonderful and I will love you for ever more.....I didn't know what to expect from our first time...But all I can tell you is I now love you even more than I did before...If that's possible."

The couple clutch each other, both quietly smiling, both enjoying perfect contentment.

* * *

Eric made sure he was outside Jenny's house in the little van the following morning. He was anxious to check that she was alright after their first adventure into complete sexual behaviour. After finding her full of the joys of spring and clearly, still, very much in love with him, he dropped her off at work with a lingering kiss and loving hug.

After the comforting reassurance of their early morning encounter Eric feels on top of the world as he drives into Lapley Vale Nursery. As he parks the van he can see Dickie Mitchell is placing large bouquets of colourful flowers in large buckets in front of the counter inside the shop. Eric bounces into the shop to greet his boss enthusiastically.

"Good Morning Dickie....Those flowers are a treat to behold.... Absolutely beautiful."

Dickie stares at his young assistant, a little shocked by his exuberance, especially first thing in the morning.

"Morning Ricky...Christ you look like the cat that got the cream this morning....What have you been up to?."

For a fleeting moment Eric feels panicky, wondering if for some unknown reason Dickie actually knows the reason for his high spirits. He responds cautiously.

"Whatever do you mean Dickie?."

As soon as he detects Dickie's reactions to his question he realised that he was merely making conversation and could not possibly know why he was feeling so good. Eric continues before Dickie can offer a response.

"It's such a beautiful Morning Dickie...The flowers look fabulous and...Well... The whole world seems to be a wonderful place and... Anyways... What's wrong with being happy at work...There's no law against it is there?."

Shrugging his shoulders, smiling Dickie moves behind the counter.

"No....Not at all....Not at all Rickie....I wouldn't have it any other way...Listen....I wanted to have a private word with you before we start getting busy dealing with the demands of the general public."

Eric, somehow, realises that Dickie means to be serious by his stance and demeanour.

"What it is Lad...Well...I've been offered the lease on a small shop on the High Street....Bloody good offer it is too....It would prove a

little goldmine selling flowers and gardening equipment and the like....
I discussed it with Mrs Mitchell and she agrees that it would be a bit
too much to take on at our stage of life....But...I was wondering if
you could raise enough cash...And I'm not talking about a fortune
believe me...I would say about five hundred quid at the very most....
And we could be partners...My real love is here at the Nursery growing
the flowers and all that sort of thing....We don't want to interfere but
if you and Jenny are seriously considering your futures together we
could let Jenny run the shop....Paying her the same wages as Harry
Jeeps of course....And we could supply the flowers and so on from
here...All that's needed is the cash to buy up the lease and to set the
place up with initial stocks of hardware....We would share the profits
from the overall turnover and you could buy me out anytime you are
in a position to do so....I'm not looking to make much out of this......
Give me your answer when you've discussed it with all concerned....
I'll need to know fairly soon though....All I can say Rickie is this is a
chance you should grasp with both hands...No enterprise is certain to
produce profits without some element of risk being taken...But this is
worth the risk."

Eric's mood has changed in a flash. He has listened intently to
every word Dickie has spoken. He is thinking as hard as he can. He
already appreciates that this offer is an opportunity well worthy of the
most serious consideration. Dickie is anxious to hear his response.

"You've certainly given me food for thought Dickie...First of all may
I thank you for making me this offer...I know that you've always had
my best interests at heart...I do have some savings as it happens...I've
never needed to break into them before...But listen...I must discuss
this with my Mum and Dad and Jenny as well."

Eric pauses for a moment. He smiles as he continues.

"Right....It sounds like a step in the right direction to me Dickie...
How much time do I have before you'll require my definite answer?."

Dickie is pleased with Eric's initial reaction to his proposal. He
shrugs his shoulders as he speaks.

"Oh well….The sooner the better I suppose….I have to give my word on the lease by the end of the week….But listen Rickie…I don't want to get too involved if you can manage to raise the whole sum…. All the initial capital lay out….Probably less than I first anticipated. I can arrange for the lease to be signed over to you…We could draw up a contract for the supply of flowers….I wouldn't want you to leave my employment or anything like that…Anyways….See what you can come up with….If you take my advice you'll jump at it…It's an opportunity not to be missed…Someone will open a flower shop on that High Street before long…Nothing like being first past the post Ricky…Eh?."

Eric can feel himself buzzing with excitement as the prospects of owing his own business race through his mind.

* * *

"Is there anything the Trust could do for you Bert?."

Woody Green is sat on the bench outside the Pavilion at the side of the Bowling Green at Lapley Vale Bowling and Social Club. He is lighting up his pipe as he quietly admires the quality and colour of the grass. He realises that the green has never looked better. Since taking on young Eric McCabe as his understudy the whole area has been enhanced. Eric has introduced small, slightly raised, flower beds on each side of the square. Eric has grown all the plants himself at the Nursery with the full consent and connivance of Dickie Mitchell. The only expenditure incurred for this striking addition has been the small cost required for the seeds and compost.

Despite the fact that Woody is a flower lover he has always concentrated his full energy and ability to the provision of his, highly rated, grass. This involves enormous time and effort because of the care and maintenance required to ensure the constant high quality of grass on the surface of the Green.

Woody is the first to appreciate how much difference Eric's input has made to his beloved Green. He enjoys feelings of pleasure and tranquillity flowing through his body as he smells the sweet fragrances and gazes on the masses of vibrant colours in each of the four flower beds. The manicured grass is enhanced by the tidiness of the gutters, which are filled with white chippings and surround the entire perimeter of the Green. Woody is enjoying contentment.

Wallowing in his self satisfaction causes Woody not to notice the presence of a smiling Bert McCabe, in full uniform, standing directly behind him. It has amused Bert that he has been able to open the side gate and walk along the gravel path up to where Woody is sat without his old Friend being the slightest bit aware of him.

After the initial shock Woody greets Bert.

"Jesus Christ Bert....I was bloody miles away then...."

They both chuckle as Bert, shaking his head as a sign of disapproval, responds.

"I could have slit your throat without you even being aware that you were in jeopardy....Eh?...Eh?."

Woody, smiling, put his hand up to his throat.

"I'm bloody glad you didn't Bert...I'm about to treat it to having a nice pint of bitter trickled down it....Very shortly."

Woody makes room for Bert to sit alongside him on the wooden bench. Bert removes his cap, sighing in a sign of relaxation. Bert takes in the beauty of his surroundings before he compliments their Creator.

"Woody....Old Pal....I can honestly say....Without one word of contradiction....That I have never...Ever...Seen this Green look better than it does this very day...This must be the most beautiful spot in the whole of Lapley Vale and surrounding Districts...Even without the obvious added attraction of any Bowling taking place."

Woody smiles as he nods his agreement.

"And I'll tell you this Bert....I was only just thinking about it when you sneaked up on me actually...That young Lad of yours hasn't done it any harm either...He's responsible for all those flowers you know?......I wasn't sure it would be such a good idea when he first mentioned it but I'm very glad I let him have his way on it...I think it gives the whole place a nice finishing touch...Don't you?."

Bert is delighted to hear Woody complimenting Eric.

"That's nice to hear Woody....Thank you....I'm very glad things have worked out between you two....I don't think he's ever likely to say so but he's very fond of you....He's definitely your number fan in more ways than one....To tell you the truth I get sick of hearing him going on about Woody said this and Woody did that and Woody did the bloody other....If you ask me you come a very close second to that delightful little girl of his in his hit parade."

They both chuckle. Woody is well aware that Bert and his wife are very pleased with both arrangements.

After a short silence, Woody replies.

"Actually Bert....To tell you the truth and the truth be known...I'm very fond of the Lad myself...He's a credit to you and your Missus...And Jenny is a smashing young Hen....No wonder you're delighted with the way things are turning out at present....And if you're not you bloody well should be."

Bert nods and smiles. He then changes the subject slightly.

"Mind you Woody there's been a lot of happiness around these parts just lately...You know?....All those beneficiaries from that mysterious Trust Fund thing....Has anything come your way?."

Woody answers immediately.

"No...Not a thing Bert....And I'm not expecting anything either....As a matter of fact I can't think of anything I'm short of...I can honestly say that I enjoy the simple things in life and I easily manage to find contentment."

As Woody glances at him he is aware that Bert is staring, directly, into his eyes. He sounds most sincere.

"I think you've had all the pleasure you'll ever desire Woody....Seeing all the wonderful things happening all around you...Eddie...Alf...Peggy....All been recipients eh?....Even Old Doris Karloff from behind the bar touched out with a bit of good fortune which ended up as sweet relief to all of us eh?...eh?...Then the Club rises like a phoenix from the ashes at the very moment it was about to sink deep into the shit....Mind you nobody has any idea where all this money is coming from."

True to form, Woody had been nodding happily as Bert rolled off the list of his friends but his face immediately screwed up at the very mention of Doris. Bert continues.

"You're not the only one who won't miss her Woody…Eh?....Eh?...That Denise has made one hell of a difference behind that bar…Eh?...Eh?."

Woody has a horrible feeling that Bert has a hidden Agenda, as a short pause breaks up their conversation.

Bert's tone introduces a hint of curiosity creeping in as he breaks the silence.

"It's funny how everyone around these parts only know you as Woody isn't it?."

Woody is noticeably uncomfortable.

"Yes Woody….I wonder just how many people actually know your full name."

Woody is now twitching.

"Yes…I bet even your closest Mates are not aware of your God given name…..Isn't that right Woody?...Eh?....Eh?."

Woody turns defensive.

"Look Bert…I don't know what your working up to."

Bert realises the discomfort he is causing his old friend. He attempts to convince him of his good intentions.

"Wait a minute….Look Woody….There's nothing for you to worry your head about I'm on your side….Honestly."

Woody still looks ill at ease as Bert continues, now sounding rather cocky.

"I just happened to be glancing through the Electoral Register….You know the official book that lists all the registered voters….Street by Street….The Council supply us with one at the Nick…Comes in very helpful at times…Anyways I was checking up on the address of someone I wanted to speak to…Lives just around the corner from where you live…Well…On the very same page I was looking at I noticed the entry for your house Woody…."

Woody looks very apprehensive and is close to panic.

"There it was….Kenneth Gordon Green….Funny that I thought….Specially as that mysterious Trust is called the Kenneth Gordon Trust….Eh?....Eh?."

Woody stands up, not knowing what to do or say. Bert quickly reassures him.

"Look....Don't worry Old Pal....I've already made it clear I hope.... I'm on your side....Eh?...Eh?...Your secret is safe with me."

Woody sits down again. He looks rather shocked. Realising that Bert has uncovered what he considered he had carefully hidden. He stares into Bert's eyes. Initially feeling suspicious.

"What do you want Bert?."

Bert raises his hand aloft, empathising very clearly what his intention are.

"Woody I don't want anything from you....Nothing....Not a thing...I just wanted you to know that I accidentally became aware of your little secret....And let me say it one more time Woody....Your secret is safe with me....O.K?...Eh?...Eh?."

Woody appreciates that there is little point in him denying the facts to someone as cunning and shrewd as Bert McCabe. He drops his head indicating his acceptance that he had, beyond a shadow of doubt, been found out. Bert quietly enquires.

"What's it all about Woody?....What the hell is it all about?."

There is a pause as Woody re-lights his pipe. He draws on it a couple of times before he blows out a cloud of tobacco smoke. He looks into Bert's curious face. He glances all around to ensure they are not being overheard. He confesses.

"I might have known it would be impossible to keep my little secret safe from everyone for ever....Specially from a wise old bird like you Bert."

Bert pretends to be coy.

"A few months ago I had a most welcome visit from the man from Littlewoods Pools."

Bert radiates a knowing look. There have been many rumours circulating around the area about someone winning on the Pools but, to date, no-one had manage to prove, or disprove it. Woody, now feeling more relaxed, continues.

"It wasn't the actual Jackpot Win....As a matter of fact I hadn't even checked my coupon against the scores on Saturday night like I normally do...Anyways....It was a substantial amount of money...I didn't know what to do...I mean to say....I want for nothing in my life and my needs are precious few...Then I thought of all the good the money could do for many deserving people....Specially the one's I am fortunate enough to have as friends....Then I thought of all the possible repercussions open gifts might cause...You know?.....People feeling indebted or insulted or even being thought of as scroungers.... So I went to the Bank in Oldham after making doubly sure of the integrity as well as the confidentiality of Littlewoods Pools....I had a rather long chat with the Manager....A most discreet sort of a man.... He set about creating this Trust for me....So that I could give money away anonymously ....My first priority was to get this Club out of Shit Street...All the other little transaction were not as urgent in my estimation...That is...Except for that little bit of luck that Doris had....You're quite right there Bert I was very pleased to see her large arse disappearing over the horizon...I knew she'd be off the minute she had the funds to go...And...And...Well...I thought everything was working out great...The joy of seeing Eddie and Alf so happy and the change around in the fortunes of the Club....I admit a touch of self interest in the provision of the false leg for Peggy but I knew in my heart of hearts that it would spoil everything if the people were aware of where the source of the money lay."

Bert listened to Woody's revelations in a state of abject fascination. He also feels rather pleased with the value of his own powers of deduction. He appreciates that Woody's actions have all stemmed from a genuine affection for his friends and surroundings. He agrees wholeheartedly with Woody's need for secrecy sharing his opinion that this course of action is definitely in the best interests of everyone concerned. After allowing a few moments to absorb the magnitude of what has been related to him, Bert's face suddenly breaks into, one of his, beaming smiles.

"Fantastic Woody....Fan....Bloody....Tastic....How much did you actually win?."

Woody adopts a defensive stance.

"Let's just say a considerable amount of dosh shall we Bert?....I'd rather not disclose the actual figure but I have to admit it was more money than I have earned throughout my whole working life in total to date....There's not all that much of it left now...I've made what you might call a rather large dent in it....But there's still enough left to ensure that I never go short of anything until the day I die and then for another twenty years or so after that as well....I doubt that there will be too much left when I go under the sod...But I also made a will when I was going through with all the legal palaver over the Trust Fund and anything that survives me will go to the Club and it's Members.... I hope I can rely upon your total discretion in these matters Bert...I can...Can't I?."

Bert is slightly offended that Woody needs more re-assurance of his integrity but he manages to stress this without recourse to any offence being made or taken.

"Absolutely Woody....Not another living soul will get to know about this from me ....These lips are sealed....Take my word for it."

The two friends shake hands in a gesture of mutual trust and respect each other. Bert goes on.

"What has pleased me more anything else is the way you have taken that Lad of mine under your wing....I owe you a debt of gratitude on that score Woody....Anyways apart from all that let me assure you that I will not only keep it in the dark...Oh no...I will also strenuously deny any suggestion or rumour that you are involved in any shape or form...Eh?...Eh?."

Woody smiles but he still holds a niggling suspicion that Bert still wants some sort of compensation or reward for his loyalty to him.

"Is there anything the Trust can do for you Bert?."

Woody is quite surprised at how adamant Bert appears to be. Bert's tone is an indicator of his sincerity.

"Nothing whatsoever Woody…Definitely not…As you probably appreciate I'm nicely placed….I also noticed that those of your closest friends who are similarly placed to me missed out on all the treats…."

Woody nods, recognising, once again, Bert's insight and his unique level of understanding. They shake hands again. Bert keeps hold of Woody's hand.

"Without fear or favour Old Pal your secret is as safe as the Bank of England with me…I wish you all the very best for the future."

Woody radiates a satisfied expression as Bert adds.

"Mind you….I don't think I would make too much fuss if you were to offer to let me join you in a pint of Alf's finest Best Bitter…Right now would be nice…Eh?….Eh?."

Bert releases Woody's hand at last as they stand up together. Woody pulls a face as he manages to have the final word.

"No change there then….I've been buying your ale for as long back as I can remember….Come on Bert before I start spitting feathers."

Two happy men make their way towards the Clubhouse.

* * *

"I'm too much of a lady to repeat his actual instructions."

The small, newly opened, shop on High Street, Lapley Vale looks bright and inviting to anyone looking at it. The freshly painted sign over the front door and window proudly indicates, to one and all, 'BLOOMERS – Proprietor Eric McCabe'

The said, proprietor, Eric is in the process of filling a row of buckets, on the floor in front of the counter, with bunches of freshly cut flowers. Jenny Dawes, looking resplendent in a neat pink overall and short mini skirt is busy arranging an assortment of gardening tools, seeds, fertilisers and other ancillary goods on the shelves behind the small counter area.

Mrs McCabe, Eric's Mother, walks into the shop through a door giving access to the kitchen area and small storeroom at the rear of the premises. She is wearing a double breasted floral overall. She appears to be flustered. Exchanging a sweet smile with Jenny she speaks in a businesslike fashion.

"I think I can safely say that the last of the muck in there has been well and truly shifted."

Shaking her head in disgust.

"The person or persons responsible for leaving this place in such at state need to be put away for a very long and tedious time."

Neither Eric nor Jenny make any comment. She adds.

"Like a pig sty….You can't tell me there's any need for that…I can't understand people being dirty like that."

Standing up, Eric nods his agreement but feels he should clarify the circumstances.

"Well we did take over in a bit of a hurry didn't we Mother?…And in fairness the place had actually been empty for a couple of months after the previous tenant did a midnight flit…So what else can we expect…Still I have seen cleaner rabbit hutches."

Walking over, Eric places his arm around his Mother's shoulders. He sounds very smooth.

"It's a good job we have the European Super Champion of all Cleaners on our team…We couldn't be in better hands."

Mrs McCabe blushes slightly, waving away his compliment with a hand gesture. She responds.

"Get away with you young Eric McCabe….Flattery will get you everywhere…Do you know you're getting more like your Father every day….More patter than a duck's feet."

They all enjoy a little laugh.

Jenny finishes adjusting the shelves to her satisfaction. She exhibits genuine appreciation when she speaks.

"We'd have been in trouble without you Mrs McCabe…We didn't have time to turn around when we first opened up…What with all that stock arriving and needing to be sorted out and checked and trips up the Nursery and back…I definitely feel that the cleaning had to take a back seat until you came along to help…In our long list of priorities I'm afraid the cleaning up….Especially in the back…Has had to be the sufferer."

Eric grunts an agreement as his Mother walks around the shop flicking a yellow duster at everything in her path.

Mrs McCabe directs her remarks to Jenny.

"I can only speak for myself Jenny love…But I for one would not patronise a dirty shop and I think there are many more people around these parts who feel the same way."

Mrs McCabe changes the subject, speaking to Jenny.

"You'll be finding quite a difference working here after the Chemists won't you Jenny love....I don't imagine we're even half as busy in here for starters."

Jenny politely disagrees.

"If this morning is anything to go by I'm not too sure...Ricky has had to refill the buckets and we're not even close to visiting time at the Cottage Hospital yet."

She pauses to glance around the neat little shop before she declares, sincerely.

"I know it's still early days but I have a strong and growing impression that we are going to be on a real winner here....I hope I'm proved to be right on that score...Eh?."

Everything seems to be working out, exceeding all expectations. Eric used all his savings to purchase the lease. He even managed to scrape enough together to purchase the opening stock of hardware goods from the wholesalers. Even though all of this has cleaned out his Post Office Savings Account, he is delighted to have coped financially without having to take up Dickie's kind offer of a partnership. Eric is also confident that his Parents will stand by him in an emergency throughout these early, testing, days. He now has a business Bank Account which, according to the Manager, Edgar Thompson, will lend him money if the need should arise because they consider his little enterprise to be worthy of support and investment as a going concern.

Eric has been careful not to burn all his bridges. He remains in the employ of Dickie Mitchell and also works with Woody at the Bowling Club. He receives a regular income from the Nursery work and some acceptable bonuses from the Club. These injections of cash help to boost his total income when added to the profits from the shop. He has, to date, coped with the payment of Jenny's wages because she, obviously, still needs to hand over her keep money to Nan Dawes every week. He has signed up to a lucrative contract with Dickie for the supply of plants and flowers and has recently set up an account with the wholesaler who supplies their tools, seeds, fertilisers and the like.

A careful financial watch has revealed that so far Eric is covering all his expenditure with his wages and the small, but rising, profits from the turn over at the shop. So far, so good.

It pleases Eric that his venture has in no way been to the detriment of Dickie Mitchell's business. If anything it has proved to be a boon. Nearing retirement, Dickie has concentrated all his efforts on growing and the cultivation of Nursery products. He closed his little shop soon after Eric opened Bloomers. Dickie is content doing what he enjoys the most. Together with other long standing wholesale contracts and the business return from Eric's enterprise there have been no noticeable adverse effects being felt by Eric's original mentor. Eric would never have wished to have been in direct competition with Dickie for any length of time and the way things have worked out have been ideal for them both. Eric not only helps to grow the flowers, he also buys them at trade price to sell to the public at a profit but also offering them reasonable prices.

Having made sure everything has been attended to, Eric is preparing to go to the Nursery for the day. He turns to Jenny.

"Have you any orders for Dickie up at the Nursery Jenny?... Flowers?...Wreaths?....I can take them up with me...Save you phoning...Thank heavens we were able to get the phone reconnected without too much delay...We'd be knackered without that particular facility....That's one justifiable bill...Even if I might moan about it a bit when it arrives."

Smiling, Jenny opens the till to pass a number of invoices to Eric. They share a fleeting kiss but Jenny steps back, rather abruptly, as she realises his Mother is watching them.

Since their first nervous encounter with sex, they were now finding great difficulty preventing the inevitable from occurring whenever any suitable opportunity presented itself. She is well aware of Eric's strong sexual urges coming to the surface at the drop of a hat. In fairness, she no longer offers much resistance these days if the occasion is presented without any risk of disturbance or discovery.

Mrs McCabe open the door for her Son. He places his arm around her shoulders.

"Don't forget what we discussed Mother…I would be happier if you would take a wage out of the business…I don't know how…."

She interrupts him sharply.

"Don't you be silly Eric McCabe…I'm only too pleased to help….Anyways…I look upon it as helping to safeguard your little investment…Not that I'm the slightest bit concerned that you won't be able to make a roaring success out of it…If hard work could guarantee a lucrative future then you and Jenny will soon be absolutely rolling in dosh….So please…Don't talk about that again Rickie…That's a good boy."

Eric smiles as he places a kiss on his Mother's cheek. Stepping into the Street, he turns to remark.

"We won't forget what you and Dad are doing for us Mother…I'll tell you this for nothing….Without your moral support I doubt very much that I would have had the bottle to branch out into business on my own."

She is closing the door behind him as she half scolds him.

"You get yourself off to that Nursery my lad…Leave this shop to Jenny and I….Your Dad and I would never let you down…If Dad has to put his hand into his pocket it will made a pleasant change from him investing most of our money in the Breweries."

Waving, Eric blows a cheeky kiss as he roars away along High Street in the little white van.

With Eric out of the way Jenny decides to have a little chat with his Mother.

"I still wish you'd let me put some of my saving into the business… It isn't as if I have nothing in the Bank."

Mrs McCabe reiterates the family view.

"We all decided that we must not put all our eggs in one basket Jenny love….You never know when that rainy day will appear out of the blue…It's a great comfort to keep something in reserve…In case an emergency arises…Eh?."

Just for a second, Mrs McCabe thinks she detects all is not well with Jenny. Jenny loses her smile as she unnecessarily starts to shuffle things around on the shelves. Mrs McCabe is concerned.

"Are you sure you're alright Jenny love?...You look a bit peaky... Nothing's wrong is there?....Are you O.K. love?."

Instantly, Jenny snaps back to her usual self as she confidently replies.

"Yes of course I am....Don't be silly I'm fine...As Ricky's Dad would say I'm as happy as a pig in muck."

Mrs McCabe is convinced that her fears were unjustified as she, slowly, shakes her head to comment.

"Sorry Jenny love....His Dad would not say muck...You can take my word for that."

They both laugh. The telephone rings. Jenny answers it.

"Good Morning this is Bloomers...Can I be of assistance?...Oh yes....Yes...Hello Alf....No...You've just missed him....He's on his way to the Nursery....Can I take a message or will you ring him at Dickie's?.........What?.....Oh dear...He'll want to know right away...Can you ring the Nursery?...He should be there...Do you know the number?....Yes....Alright Alf...If you have any trouble ring me back because he usually keeps in contact with us during the day ....Right.... Oh dear....Yes....Let's hope everything is O.K....Bye."

Now Jenny's facial expression is a clear indication that all if definitely not well. She turns to Mrs McCabe. Her tone reveals great concern.

"It's Woody....Alf says he hasn't turned up this morning...He said he went home early last night because he was feeling off colour....He's never....Ever...Failed to turn up for work in Alf's living memory and he's very concerned indeed."

Mrs McCabe shares Jenny and Alf's concern.

"Oh dear....If Alf is worried there must be something very wrong.... He's not one to panic is he?....I believe you can set your clock by the time Woody walks into that Club each morning...Let's hope there's nothing too serious to worry about...Eh?."

* * * ...

The little white van skids to a halt on the Car Park in front of the Lapley Vale Bowling and Social Club. Eric is out of it, almost before it stops. He is met on the Car Park by Alf coming out through the Clubhouse door. Eric cannot understand why Alf does not appear to be too worried after what he had said to him on the telephone, only minutes before. The volume and tone of his voice clearly shows the level of his concern.

"Bloody hell Alf!....What's happened?...What's going on?...Your phone call has knocked me sick."

Aware of the state Eric is in, Alf attempts to cool things down. He speaks calmly and with care.

"Don't panic Lad....You didn't give me the chance to explain before you slammed the phone down on me....It's a wonder you got here without smashing into something or someone in that little contraption....Right...Let's calm down now....O.K.?..."

Still in a state of panic, Eric nods.

"Right....Thank you....It's the flu....That bloody Asian Flu that everybody is going on about....Doctor Berry has been to see him already and he says that Woody is ill but with his constitution he should pull through with care and attention....He has left medicine for him and I've sent Mavis round to his house to make sure he takes it."

The level of Eric's anxiety lessens but he still feels rather shocked. Even so, Alf last comments make him curious.

Although Woody is a friendly sort of person no-one has ever been invited into his house. Every person, in anyway associated with Woody, is aware of this as a fact. Eric looks over at Woody's house, which can been seen from his position on the Car Park. He recognises the fact that Alf's demeanour indicates a lesser state of emergency than he had at first anticipated. Some relief flows through the young man's body as he speaks.

"Bloody hell Alf....I definitely feared the worst when you phoned.... I know I panicked....I couldn't help myself....Sorry mate."

Alf shakes his head. He realises that he had be a little hasty ringing Eric at work. He is about to speak as Eric continues.

"What did you say just then?.....Mavis has gone round to Woody's house?."

Alf nods.

"Bloody hell Alf....A visitor in Woody's house is similar to finding a virgin in a brothel....I have never seen the inside of his house have you?."

Alf ponders, racking his brain.

"Not for many a good year Ricky....It was before his old Mother dies and she's been gone a long time now...He likes to guard his privacy does Woody....Still...I think he's become very fond of Mavis and let's face it....At this present time he needs all the help he can get."

Eric is rapidly returning to his normal self. Having had time to weigh up the situation he now feels much better.

"Yes....You can say that again Alf....He couldn't be in better hands if you ask my opinion...Safest hands I can think of anyways."

Having recovered from the shock, Eric now changes the subject, returning to more mundane matters.

"Right....O.K. then....What needs doing here Alf?....The shop's set up for the day....I have a number of jobs requiring attention at the Nursery but none that won't wait a while...Dickie's there....So everything seems to be under some sort of control....At least for the time being....Christ Alf....I think I'm going to shove a brush up my arse so I can sweep the floors as I'm dashing about....Talk about having a plate full....Eh?."

Alf is happy to see Eric back to normal. He also feels relieved that his own panic stations have not caused too much upset. Now able to genuinely smile, Alf sums up the current state of affairs.

"There's nothing too urgent Ricky....Only time will tell now....So....I'm going to put the kettle on for a nice relaxing brew....Fancy one?."

Despite having a lot of things to do Eric nods eagerly. They both feel that a cup of tea will be of great value to them after the ups and downs everyone has been through during the last couple of hours or so.

"Yes Alfred that would be very welcome….Can I use your phone to ring Jenny and Mother?….If you spoke to them before you contacted me they'll be as worried as everyone else."

Alf and Eric are sitting in their usual places around the table in the Clubhouse kitchen. They are slurping their tea from large stripped mugs, quietly contemplating the mornings events. The influence of Mavis and her tea pot have been put to one side due to the current circumstances. They are disturbed by the sudden sound of someone slamming the front doors of the Clubhouse, followed by the heavy clumping of feet walking, rather hastily, across the floor. Billy Dawes appears in the doorway. He looks flushed and distresses. He blurts his words out.

"What's all this about Woody?….I've been hearing all sorts of cockeyed rumours."

Alf, calmly, stands up to place the large, cast iron, kettle back on the lighted gas ring. He sounds casual.

"Morning Billy….Nothing to get yourself into a state about….Just a touch of Flu…He'll be alright…Fancy a cuppa whilst you're here?."

The relief is clearly visible on Billy's face. In a flash he is seated on a chair with his cloth cap off. Blowing air through clenched teeth, Billy mops his brow with his cap, clearly demonstrating his genuine disbelief, mixed with relief, evident as he speaks.

"Well….Thank God for that….I was more than a little bit concerned when I heard the news….It doesn't seem possible for our Woody to be struck down by a cockeyed illness…I've known him for more cockeyed years than I care to recall but this is the first time I've ever heard of him being ill….Just goes to show eh?….The cockeyed flu eh?….Still he's as cockeyed tough as an old boot so he'll soon get over it."

Billy attacks the mug of tea as soon as Alf places it on the table in front of him. Blowing on the hot liquid before taking a careful sip he carries on.

"Thanks muchly Alf…I understand there's a lot of this cockeyed flu going around…"

Without putting the mug down Billy turns to address Eric, who now appears to have almost completely recovered from the shock of the news.

"And how's the cockeyed Lad this hectic Morning?....Big responsibility on your shoulders now young Ricky….Still I must say on behalf of all the first team bowlers we all have complete confidence in your cockeyed ability to keep things up the Woody's high standards… How are thing at the shop…Typical something like this happened so soon after you've opened the cockeyed place…"

Eric has to stifle a laugh as he responds.

"No problems to report from the shop Billy…Everything well under control there….Thanks for your vote of confidence I can only promise to do my level best….Thankfully Woody has got things up and running for the Season so all I have to do is look after it for him…"

He suddenly remembers that the Ladies, are will still be waiting at the shop for any news, causing him to act immediately.

"Is it alright if I use your phone for a minute now please Alf?…. I promised to let my Mother and Jenny know what was going on…. They'll be worried."

Alf gestures with a wave of his hand.

"Yes….Of course Ricky….I bet they are concerned."

Eric leaves the kitchen but returns to stick his head around the door. He speaks to Billy.

"Any messages for Jenny?."

Billy swings around in his chair to respond positively.

"Aye there is Ricky….Tell her not to be late home for her cockeyed tea….The Missus won't let me have mine until she get in from work."

Eric, grins, shaking his head, as he disappears out of their view. They then hear the sharp sound of a woman's footsteps making their way through the Clubroom. Mavis, removing her top coat on the move, appears in the kitchen. Alf anxiously enquires.

"Glad to see you Mavis….How is the Patient then?....Responding to the prescribed treatment I hope."

Although she is obviously concerned, Mavis allows herself a brief smile as she hangs up her coat on the back of the door. She turns, straightening her apron with her hands. Placing her hands on her hips she responds in a rather resigned fashion.

"I think it would be fair to say the Woody is not the easiest person in the world to care for in a state of sickness….Mind you the poor man is bad…..He's as weak as a kitten….Needs an awful lot of rest…Still Doctor Berry says that provided he takes the medicine and stays in bed he should be up and about in a week or so."

Both men are pleased to hear the, reasonably good, news. Alf smiles. He decides to lessen the tension as Mavis put the kettle back on the lighted gas ring.

"I suppose you realise that you have created history this very Morning Mavis."

Mavis is curious.

"I would put money on the fact that you are the first female person to cross Woody's threshold since his late Mother passed away…. Donkey's years ago."

She pauses, momentarily, to think about what Alf has just told her. Her attractive features then erupt into a broad grin. She now looks very pleased with herself.

"Well you do surprise me Alf….Anyways….I'll tell you this there's nothing to be ashamed of in that house….I was most impressed with the neat and tidy way he keeps everything…He does marvellously well for a Chap living on his own."

Billy joins in the conversation, just as Eric returns from making the telephone call.

"That doesn't surprise me Mavis….He's one of a kind our Woody…. I wouldn't be surprised at anything you told me about him…There's no end to his cockeyed talents."

Mavis is about to react to Billy's comment when she remembers that she has an important message to pass onto Eric, who is noisily draining his mug, obviously about to move on.

"Just a minute Billy….Ricky I've got a message for you from your Lord and Master….The Great Woody….From his sick bed….He asked me to tell you not to make….Er….Shall we say…Make a mess of his beloved green….Or else…Er…Again shall we say…He will be annoyed with you."

Eric nods and smiles.

"Oh yes….I bet I know exactly what he said Mavis…Mess doesn't immediately strike a cord with me as the sort of word he would normally use in these circumstances."

Mavis colours up instantly as she experiences slight embarrassment. She coughs politely before she speaks.

"I'm too much of a lady to repeat his actual instructions….But you're right of course Ricky…..And I guess you know exactly what he means."

Mavis rolls up her sleeves on her blouse as she glances around the room. She looks as if she means business.

"Right….Now then…Give me some space Boys….I'm way behind with my proper work today….I'd better start cleaning this place up for a start."

Alf places his arm around her shoulders in a friendly way as she turns the taps on in the sink. He sounds grateful, blended nicely with sympathy.

"Hey slow down Mavis love….Sit yourself down and have a nice sup of tea before you start on anything….Here let me make it for you….It'll make a pleasant change for one of us to wait on you."

She tries to resist, Alf gently but firmly guides her away from the sink into a chair by the table. She reluctantly conforms to his wishes, realising that Alf will not take no for an answer anyways. She acknowledges his kind, understanding, nature.

"Well alright Alf….Thanks very much…I really must press on though….I want to finish my work here before I dash home to make something tempting for Woody's tea….So I'm going to need to get my skates on."

Billy pretends to be upset by her remarks.

"Hey steady on Mavis…..It sounds to me as if that Woody is being cockeyed spoiled….."

The smile vanishes from Mavis's face as Alf smacks a large stripped mug of steaming tea on the table in front of her. As she suspected her attempts to raise the standards around the table at Lapley Vale Bowling and Social Club still have a long way to go.

* * *

"And we thought this was just another ordinary day."

Having enjoyed his evening meal Bert McCabe is sitting in his armchair reading the local evening newspaper. Mrs McCabe is sat at the, now cleared and tidy, dining table, knitting. They are both quietly enjoying the tranquillity as they digest their food.

Their bliss is disturbed by the sound of a key turning in the lock on their front door. Eric pokes his head around the living room door. He nods a greeting to his Parents. He enters the room pulling, a very upset and pale looking, Jenny behind him. Mrs McCabe stops knitting to smile and greet the young couple.

"This is a pleasant surprise....We didn't expect to see you two tonight."

She detects that all is not well but continues.

"Hello Jenny love....Is everything alright?."

Jenny starts to cry, softly, as Eric steers her towards a chair. By now, they have both realised that something is wrong. They can see pain in Eric's eyes as he comforts Jenny before he speaks.

"Well....That's just it Mum..."

Bert is dreading bad news as he give his full attention to his Son. He folds the newspaper, anxious to get it over with. Eric, choking back his tears, continues.

"Mother....Dad....I can't think of any easy way to say this...But.... Well...Jenny is pregnant."

Mrs McCabe gasps, Bert is visibly shocked. Jenny tries to hide her face in Eric's jacket. Eric feels the need to explain, exactly, what he means but does so rather badly.

"She's….Well….What I mean to say is….We are….We are going to have a baby."

Eric stares at his Parent desperately searching for a suitable reaction from them, although he is not sure what that would be. Mrs McCabe goes over to place a, comforting, arm around, the weeping, Jenny's shaking shoulders. This makes Jenny cry even more.

Bert slam's his paper onto the table. He responds quite sharply.

"Yes thank you very much for the full explanation….If she's pregnant she will be having a baby….That's bloody marvellous that is…Just what we need….I don't think."

Mrs McCabe, who has tears running down her cheeks, turns on Bert with a purpose.

"Now you can pack that in for a start Bert McCabe….Can't you see how upset the girl is?."

These remark annoys Bert.

"Upset!....Up…Bloody…Set!....I should think she is upset!...Bloody hell!....What on earth were you thinking about?...Christ….You're not much removed from being babies yourselves."

Mrs McCabe takes over the comforting duties completely. She looks and sounds rather philosophical.

"I think you're forgetting that Jenny is nearly eighteen years old Bert….Only a couple of years younger than I was when you got me pregnant….Remember?!!!."

These comments are met with a stunned silence. Bert is stopped in his tracks. Eric stares at his Mother because this news is a revelation to him. Mrs McCabe instantly regrets her need to be so honest but she is also very annoyed by her Husband's attitude.

"I'm sorry you've had to learn something so personal in such a cruel manner Ricky but I think your Father needs to think twice before he sits in judgement…I'm not saying that I relish the situation but recriminations are not going to help to solve anything."

There is what might, in other circumstances, be aptly called a pregnant pause. Jenny is clutching onto Mrs McCabe's arm. Eric, almost crying, reaches over to kiss his Mother, softly, on her cheek. Bert stands up. He walks over to the other three. He kneels on the floor in front of the chair to gently stroke Jenny's hair. His attitude has done a ninety degree turn. He clears his throat, choking back emotion, to speak with sincerity.

"You're quite right as usual Mother….We've got enough problems without me kicking off…What they need now….More than anything else…Is our love and support."

Jenny breaks away from Mrs McCabe to hug Bert tightly, crying even louder than before. Bert is moved as he kisses the hair on the top of the girl's head. He then pulls himself together, ready to take control of the situation.

"Right!...The question now is…What are we going to do about this?....Eh?...Eh?...Any suggestions?....Mother?....Ricky?."

Eric is still slightly stunned by his Mother's personal disclosure but he is beginning to realise that they have just started to overcome a very trying and sticky experience. Although very close to tears, he manages to maintain his composure.

"Thanks Dad….Thanks for being….Well…Look thanks anyways…I know Jenny has dreamed of a white wedding at the Parish Church….You know?...In about twenty or thirty years when we could actually afford to pay for it…But…The present circumstances demand a quick response…The sooner we make the necessary arrangements at the Registry Office the better for all concerned."

Mrs McCabe, eagerly, nods her agreement. She speaks sympathetically to Jenny, who by now, is recovering slightly.

"Are you sure that's what you want Jenny love?."

The all wait a few seconds to allow Jenny to compose herself. She wipes her face with her handkerchief before she gestures to Eric to sit with her. His Mother moves away to allow Eric to put his arm around Jenny. There is no doubt that she is speaking straight from her heart.

"I have no doubts whatsoever Mrs McCabe…I love Ricky very much indeed….There could never be anyone else for me….And I know he loves me as much as I love him…We both appreciate that we have made a mess of things but nothing could ever change our feelings for each other.."

Eric hugs Jenny before he kisses her sweetly on her lips. He is proud of her. Bert places his arm around his wife to declare.

"And we thought this was just another ordinary day… I'll say this for that Son of yours Mother….He certainly knows how to command my full attention when he wishes to do so….Eh?....Eh?."

They all hug each other in a small scrum. They start to laugh, as much as a relief than from amusement caused by Bert's closing remarks. Bert then decides he will maintain the much lighter ambiance, which has now, thankfully, entered into the proceedings. He sounds as if he is back to normal.

"Hey!....Hang on….Just a minute….I'm going to have to stop calling you Mother you know?....Nana….Or Nan….Or Granny or Gran…which would you prefer dear."

Mrs McCabe brushes him away with a swift retort.

"Alright…..Granddad!!."

Bert pauses to contemplate. She comes back at him again.

"And there's a lot of water has to flow under the bridge before you have the excuse to start wetting the baby's head."

As tensions are dying down, Mrs McCabe feels the need to ask Jenny some further questions in order to clarify all the facts.

"Have you told your Nan and Granddad yet Jenny love?."

This enquiry almost causes Jenny's tears to flow again but she manages to stay calm.

"Nan knows because she went up to Doctor Berry's with me… She's O.K. about it…She says it will be best if she tells Granddad…. Especially after all the trouble they went through with my Mother."

Mrs McCabe nods sympathetically. Bert intervenes, much to his wife displeasure.

"He'll have a cockeyed fit….Eh?...Eh?..."

They all laugh.

"Don't worry I'll sort things out with Billy….He's bound to be a bit upset….But…Mark my words children….I am confident that we will all be pulling in the same direction….Eh?....Eh?."

Mrs McCabe is fairly tentative as she addresses Jenny.

"Jenny love….I think you should stop calling me Mrs McCabe from now on don't you….I'd be very pleased if you were to call me Alice….Or even Mum….That's if you'd like to…What do you say?."

Jenny's tears start to flow, instantly, as she kisses and hugs Eric's Mother. She has some difficulty speaking due to rising emotions. There is no doubting how much she wants to call her Mum.

"Mrs McCabe….I mean Mum….Thank you…I would love to call you Mum…I've not had much opportunity to call anyone by that name and I would be thrilled and delighted to call it to someone who is as loving and caring as you are….Thank you…Thank you Mum."

All four persons present are now, openly, crying as they, once again, form a small scrum in the middle of the room.

* * *

"Look there's no need for panic…"

Woody is delighted to be back at work. He is busy inside the pavilion at the side of the Bowling Green. His attention is drawn to the sound of someone approaching along the gravel path. Glancing up he sees the smiling face of his understudy, Eric, peering through the door. Woody, pleased to see him, he is conscious of the Lad's apparent high spirits.

"Morning Woody….How the hell are you this lovely bright morning?."

Woody nods, putting his tools down. He walks outside to join his young friend. They casually stroll over to the bench. Woody now speaks.

"Well I'm not sure why you look so pleased with yourself but thank you for asking I feel much better thank you….I think I'm well on the way to a full recovery now….That bloody flu….Didn't half knock me about Ricky….Being able to get back to work has caused my improved health to feel a lot more permanent….And hey….I don't want to give you a bigger head than the one your wearing but this green doesn't appear to have suffered too much in my absence….In no small way down to your efforts….Thank you Ricky… You more than anyone know just how much this green means to me."

Woody lights his pipe. They are sitting back quietly admiring the magnificent sight of the vivid green turf and the profusion of colourful flowers and bushes in the neatly laid out and well tended beds, enhancing the main feature of the grassed surface of the impressive manicured square.

"You're a quick learner young Ricky…It's a pleasure to teach someone who shows keenness to learn and the ability to put his new found skills into practice."

Eric is grateful that Woody has seen fit to compliment him. He is well aware that Woody is not normally prone to pass on many favourable remarks or comments about people or things. He is a little embarrassed but is also very pleased. Woody snaps out of his softer, kinder, frame of mind, turning to more urgent matters.

"Anyways never mind me….How are you Buggerlugs?.....Have you managed to sort yourselves out yet?."

Woody is relieved to note that Eric is fairly relaxed, He responds positively.

"Yes….Thank God…Everything has been fixed for the Registry Office next Friday…The ceremony starts at half past two….As a matter of fact that's one of the reasons I called to see you this morning to keep you up to date and verify that all seems to be going to plan at this present moment in time."

Woody nods and smiles but he is more interested in ensuring that they are alone and are not being overheard. Satisfied, he speaks, furtively, almost in a whisper.

"Yes thanks I've been well briefed on those matters thanks….Listen Ricky…."

Woody re-checks that they are alone. He moves closer to Ricky, continuing.

"Right….Are you listening?....I don't want this to become general knowledge Ricky but I've got an appointment there myself at two o'clock…Half an hour before you and Jenny."

Eric is struggling to understand. Before he can appeal for clarity Woody adds.

"You see Mavis has asked me to marry her and I've accepted."

Eric can hardly believe his ears. Woody senses the turmoil going through his young friends brain so he strives to explain himself.

"I know you'll have difficulty believing that an old confirmed bachelor like me is even thinking about marriage but it's true…Your Dad and Alf are the only other persons who are aware of this forthcoming arrangement…Oh….And Mavis of course….So think yourself honoured to be getting the information straight from the horses mouth…So to speak."

Eric is genuinely stunned. He stares into Woody's eyes, establishing his sincerity. He is half convinced but still needs to ask to be sure.

"You're not trying to pull my leg are you Woody?."

An excited Woody is nodding his head vigorously.

"I'd hardly pull your leg over something as important as this Ricky….Would I?.

Eric is instantly convinced. He springs to his feet to grasp Woody's right hand. Shaking it warmly he finds himself unable to think of the right things to say. He splutters.

"Bloody hell fire!....Congratulations!....You're a dark horse and no mistake….When was all this worked out….Hey!....I hope you're not in the same trouble as Jenny and I find ourselves in…You're not are you?."

Woody roars with laughter. Shaking his head he responds.

"Hardly….Don't be daft…I leave all that sort of thing to you….. You randy little get."

Both chuckle, happy to find themselves enjoying the run up to the current, unexpected, but nevertheless eagerly anticipated, future events. Woody attempts to rationalise the topic under discussion.

"No Ricky….All that love and romance stuff is for the young and fit….I've grown very fond of Mavis since she came into our lives…She was really wonderful to me when I was ill….I don't know what I would've done without her…She's the best thing that's happened to me for many a good year….It has to be said that she has been a lonely widow for many years…Completely on her own…And…Well…Let's say it's a mutual arrangement….You see…She loves looking after people….Well you've seen that yourself with all the scones and cakes and that eh?......But I've got to face the facts Ricky…I need her to look after me…That nasty attack of flu made me think very long and hard about my future…I was fond of her from the very first day we met and then the way she responded to my sudden problems…Well…I was able to appreciate all her caring qualities first hand….I'm not sure what love is Ricky but I'll tell you this for nothing….My future would seem very bleak without her by my side…She informed me that she neither wants nor expects me to alter my ways…She's prepared to take me as I am…So the bottom line is we are committing ourselves to each other for our mutual future benefit."

Eric has absorbed every word related by his old Friend. He finds himself buzzing with sheer joy. He nods his whole hearted and unreserved agreement with everything said.

"Woody….What can I say?.....I am very happy for you….And Mavis of course….I'm sure you'll be very good for each other…There's no doubt in my mind…Anyways….How come my Dad knows all about it?."

Woody, surreptitiously, glances all around, once again, before he speaks. His volume decreases, his tone denotes sincerity.

"For personal reasons….I don't want every Tom Dick and Harry knowing all my private business…So your Dad…And your Mum have kindly agreed to be the required witnesses for Mavis and I at the Registry Office….We don't want any fuss….Probably the fact that you and Jenny are getting hitched put the whole idea into our heads in the first place….So your little mishap shall we say eh?....Well…You have accidentally done Mavis and I a very big favour….But listen to me Buggerlugs… Promise me that you'll keep our little secret to yourself for the time being…O.K.?....Keep it under your cap….People will get to know all about it in due course….O.K.?....Catch my drift?."

Eric does not envisage any problem adhering to Woody's wishes but is still curious about his Parents, obvious, involvement.

"You have my word of honour as a fellow son of the soil Woody…. But….I'll tell you what….My Dad and Mother play their cards very close to their chests….This has all come straight out of the blue for me…"

Woody interrupts.

"Exactly my Boy…..That's why we asked them to stand for us…I can guarantee Old Bert can keep a secret."

Momentarily, Woody pauses to reflect before he adds.

"Listen Ricky….I've had good cause to have the utmost confidence in your Dad's loyalty and trust in the very recent past….Anyways…Let's change the subject for now….Let's talk about you and your Jenny…. Where are you going to live?….Or haven't you sorted that out yet?."

Eric appreciates the relevance and legitimacy of Woody's enquiry. He attempts to sound as happy and confident as he can be.

"Yes….We're going to stay at her Nan's….At least for the time being….We have to carefully consider all our pressing priorities…. Fortunately the shop is really doing well….And Jenny will be able to carry on working for a while yet…So we can stay with her Nan and Granddad until we are in a position to sort out something more permanent in the future."

Woody seems very pleased with himself.

"Hang on a minute Ricky….I think I might have some good news for you on that particular front…."

Eric is puzzled.

"Just think about it….I have my own house and Mavis has her own house….As a Bride and Groom….Legally bound together…. Under the law of the land….We only need the one house….So…. Mavis and I have discussed this….I am sure we will be able to come to some amicable arrangement….That is if you and Jenny are interested in Mavis's house… Mavis is all for it and hopes you will be as well."

Finding himself experiencing great difficulty coming to terms with all the information Eric's, poor, brain is being asked to process at very short and unexpected notice, Eric has to think hard before he is able to speak. His face suddenly erupts into the biggest smile anyone could possibly imagine. He is unable to disguise his sheer delight.

"Interested!?…..Interested!?….Too true we'd be interested…. Bloody hell Woody….Jenny loves Mavis's house….She's told me so often enough….We often visit her as you know….As a matter of fact

I think Jenny passed comment when we were there....She even told Mavis....."

Eric stops mid sentence, suddenly realising how all the pieces are beginning to fit together in a logical way. Obviously matters of great importance have been discussed in their absence. Woody has a knowing look.

"Exactly Ricky....Listen....I'm not saying that you and Jenny alone have been responsible for Mavis and I making our decision to get married...But....When we were into our discussions it soon became apparent to us that we could boost our own personal happiness even more if we were able to be of assistance to our friends....Shall we say.... In a time of need."

Eric is finding, great, effort is required stopping himself from throwing his arms around Woody. He risks it. To his relief and surprise Woody does not kick him or shove away, on the contrary, he responds by hugging Eric back. They both enjoy mutual back slapping. Tears of joy are streaming down Eric's face.

"Bloody hell Woody....I just....I just don't know what to say.... Jenny?....Well Jenny will be over the moon when I tell....Thanks Woody....I'm beginning to realise why even my Dad thinks a lot about you...I am completely bowled over...It's hard to take all this in in one go...."

Woody breaks into the conversation.

"Look....Steady down Lad....There's no great rush required...Let's not panic just yet....Once we get over the formalities at the Registry Office and the dust starts to settle down a bit...We can all get together and sort out the finer details....Incidentally Ricky your Dad and Billy are aware of all this."

Eric gasps.

"But let me finish off this conversation by assuring you that you can be certain of one thing....It will be an offer you will find very difficult to refuse."

Eric is speechless. He desperately wants to express his gratitude even more but his mouth will not move. Woody appears to be understand just how the Lad feels. He is very pleased with himself as he stands up, breaking the mood by adopting a, false, bossy attitude.

"Well come on Buggerlugs....Don't stand there with your gob open catching flys....We've got a lot of work to do if we intend to earn our keep today....Come along now....The sooner we start is the sooner we finish and then you can cut a dash up to that little goldmine you've opened for a long and pleasant discussion with that pretty girl of yours....I'd love to be a one of your flys on the wall when you tell her all the latest news....Eh?."

Shaking his head and smiling, Eric can scarcely belief how well things appear to be turning out for everyone concerned. He does have time to savour the moment for long because Woody gives him a playful kick up the backside. Two very happy men return to the pavilion to get the ball rolling.

"The drinks are on the house.... Steady now!!!!"

There has not been a Thursday night to compare with the one the Members are sharing in the Clubhouse at Lapley Vale Bowling and Social Club for as far back as anyone present can recall.

Some younger men are playing darts and snooker and some older ones are playing dominoes and cribbage. Every available table in the room is occupied by friends and relatives of Woody and Eric, who are celebrating their joint Bachelor Night.

There is a large group of men seated and standing around in the vicinity of the bar. Alf and Denise are working flat out to cope with the demand for drinks.

Woody is on his usual stool, alongside the bar, chatting with Norman and Eddie. Eric, Bert, Billy Dawes and Charlie Walsh are seated around a table close to Woody and his friends. Ralph Jones, the Chairman, Vic Callow the Secretary/Treasurer and Bernie Price are seated on stools on the other side of the open bar from Woody, Norman and Eddie. Everyone appears to be in high spirits. Obviously, a great deal of alcohol has passed many lips.

Bernie shouts across the bar.

"Hey Woody!....Ralph Victor and myself wanted to assure you that we'll be on hand for you tomorrow night....You know when you're enjoying your nuptials?....We have all volunteered to lift you on...It's the very least we can do for an Old Mate."

Woody takes the remarks in good humour. He has had more than his normal quota of drink but he is still quite capable of making a swift retort.

"Hey....Clever buggers....It's not the getting on that worries me.... No that isn't a problem....It's the getting off again afterwards that's concerning me....Anyways....I thank you lot to stop being so bloody rude....You'll have me blushing next."

Everyone is enjoying the convivial atmosphere. Norman swings around on the top of his stool to speak to those at the table.

"I don't think young Ricky will be needing any assistance will you Ricky?."

This comment produces nods and laughs.

"Perhaps you can find the time to give Woody a quick lesson before it's too late."

More laughter. Woody responds, almost spilling some of the beer he was drinking from his pint glass, in his haste.

"Don't you worry about me Boys....I'm not exactly a novice you know?....It may have been a long time but they tell me it's a just like riding a bike...You never forget how to do it once you've learned."

Getting the worse for drink, Billy nudges Bert.

"Did you hear that Bert?....I think you'd better have a quick word with Woody....It sounds as if he's thinking of taking a cockeyed bike to bed with him."

The laughter is dying down as Victor rises to his feet. His raises his glass aloft in a gesture to draw everyone's attention to what he is about to say.

"Gentlemen.....Gentlemen please!....Can we have a moment of order please....For a toast!."

Smiling, Vic turns to signal readiness to Ralph with a flourish from his free hand. Ralph stands up. There is a certain amount of order. He coughs into his left hand, holding a full pint of beer in his right.

"Yes....Thank you Victor....May I on behalf of the Committee and Members of our beloved Club ask you all to charge your glasses and be upstanding for a toast to our good friends....Enjoying their last night of freedom…Good health and happiness to Woody and Eric and of course….Not forgetting their blushing brides as well…"

There is a certain amount of shuffling and re-adjustment as those concerned prepare to stand up. However Ralph, realising that he now has the floor carries on.

"Now I want to take this opportunity to offer you both some sound advice….Given in friendship….I want you both to pay particular attention to what you will be asked tomorrow during the solemn marriage ceremony….Because….I well remember my own wedding day many….Many years ago…Up there in the Parish Church….As it so happens….The Vicar said to me loudly and clearly….Wilt thou take this woman to be thy lawful wedded wife and naturally I replied I wilt… The Vicar then paused to look more closely at my Missus…He then looked me in the eye and said….Look I'm only going to ask you one more time…"

Roars of laughter are quelled as Ralph raises his glass high to exclaim with authority in his tone.

"Gentlemen!.....All joking apart….Seriously Boys….Gentlemen!.... I give you the Brides and Grooms."

A quick slurp is followed by cheers and applause.

Bert glances across their table wondering why Eric is so quiet. Seeing that Eric is showing clear signs of being the worse for wear. He nudges Charlie and then Billy.

"I'll tell you what Charlie…Billy….It's a bloody good job it's not tonight…Just look at the state of the Lad….Christ he'd have difficulty raising a smile at the moment….Eh?...Eh?..."

Charlie intervenes.

"Go easy Bert….Hells fire if a Lad can't get pissed on his Bachelor Night when can he….Eh?."

Billy takes the opportunity to express his views.

"And by reference of your past record of getting pissed Charlie…. You must have had a few cockeyed Bachelor Nights…Eh?."

Although they are all enjoying the fun, Bert discloses his now rapidly rising concern for his Son's welfare.

"Hang on….Bloody hell….Look at the state of him now…This means I'll have to stay sober so I can smuggle him into the house past his Mother….If she sees him like this she's bound to blame me…Eh?...Eh?."

Bernie, overhearing Bert's comments as he returns from a visit to the toilets, comments.

"I'd like to have shares in the Brewery that could produce and sell enough ale to get you pissed Bert….Most people around these parts think your leg is as hollow as Old Peggy's…"

Bert treats Bernie's remarks as a compliment. He shrugs his shoulders to reply, calmly and casually.

"Years of practice….Yes….Many years of dedicated practice…And incidentally Bernie….May I say that if you had spent as much money on your education as I have spent developing my drinking skills and technique….You would not be so bloody ignorant today."

Immediately realising that he is well out of his depth in any verbal contest with Bert, Bernie backs off.

Sweating profusely, but happy with the fantastic trade, Alf bangs an empty beer bottle on the top of the bar to instantly capture everyone's undivided attention he shouts.

"Gentlemen!......If you would be kind enough to pass your empty glasses over the bar to either myself or my beautiful assistant Denise…"

Alf waves his arm in the direction of Denise who smiles sweetly and curtseys.

"You may be interested to know that thanks to the generosity of Mr Woody Green and….Prepare yourselves for a shock Gentlemen…. Sergeant Bert McCabe…The drinks are on the house….Steady now!."

There is a surge similar to a stampede as the throng make their way to the bar. Alf is now pleading with them.

"Steady now!....PLEASE!....Take your time….You'll all be attended to….Thank you!."

* * *

"I must have been soft asking you Lenny."

Although he feels rather delicate, Bert is seated at the table at his home, really doing his level best, eating a full English breakfast. The time is approaching 8.45am. Today is Woody and Mavis's, followed by Eric and Jenny's, big day.

Mrs Alice McCabe is fully dressed, including her top coat. Flushed and flustered yet, reasonably, under control. She constantly Peers out through their front windows, anxiously, awaiting the arrival of Jenny and her Nan. They are all booked in at 'Short Cuts', their local, Hairdressers on the High Street. The appointments are for 9am. Turning her attention to Bert, she barks out her orders.

"Right….Well I hope they won't be much longer…I'm meeting them at the end of the Street because I don't want Eric to see his Bride on their wedding day before they meet at that Registry Office…It's bad luck….They're cutting it fine…Bert….BERT!...I wish you'd wake up and pull yourself together….Pick us up outside the Hairdresser at eleven o'clock sharp….Don't dare be late….Are you listening?....Then you can drop Jenny and her Nan off on the way back….Right….Where's Ricky?...Get him up as soon as I've gone will you….I don't know what time you crawled in here last night or should I say this Morning but I hope you haven't made that Lad forget what an important date he has lined up for later today….There's still loads to do….He needs to pick up those button holes from the Nursery and the rest of the flowers…….I'll come to the Bakery with you I don't trust you with two wedding cakes....They'll end up as wedding cake crumbs if I know you Bert McCabe so we'll call there after dropping Jenny and Nan off at home...Are you paying attention Bert?.."

Bert tries to smile but fails. He is bravely trying to attack the delicious, if a little greasy, contents of his plate.

"Oh.....They're here....Right....Don't forget what you've got to do will you?.....See you later Dear...Get Ricky up NOW!...Bye for now."

Mrs McCabe disappears in a flash. Bert cringes at the bang the front door makes as it slams shut behind her. Bert pushes his, half eaten, breakfast away from him. He walks across to the window, checking that the Ladies have actually gone, before he takes the plate through into the kitchen. He thinks of scraping, the considerable, left overs into the pedal bin but immediately thinks better of it. He quickly opens the back door to put the rubbish straight into the outside bin. Even though his head is pounding he still has some of his cunning and wits about him. He notices Eric's breakfast plate inside the oven, on a low light, through the glass inspection window. He is making his way to the bottom of the stairs when he spots Alf walking up the garden path. He opens the door to let him. Alf smiles through an obvious hangover.

"Morning Bert....Jesus my head....I thought I'd just check if you and Eric were alright because I can't properly remember you leaving last night. Charlie's in the shit with his Missus...Slept at the bar all night...Or at least until early this morning when he need an urgent piss...I remember Eddie and Norman taking old Billy home and I vaguely recall helping you to put Eric into your car but I must confess it's all a bit of a blur really...Still you're O.K. that's the main worry over with...Is there anything I can do to help Bert?....I'm using my new limousine to collect the bread and pies and what have you from the Bakery on Rochdale Road first then later on I'm to chauffeur Denise and a few of the other surprise Guests from the Club up to the Town Hall...So I hope I get the full use of my head back before then."

Bert is desperately trying to snap himself out of, his current, bleary, much less than vigorous, mood.

"Thanks on both counts there Alf….We're O.K. don't you worry…Christ I hope that Bugger never gets married again…I don't think I could manage another night like last night…Eh?...Eh?....Everything's under control thanks Alfred….You stick to your agreed schedule that'll be for the best…I'm going to arouse sleeping beauty up there now before he rots in his pit."

Alf departs as quickly as he arrived.

Bert shouts upstairs.

"RICKY!......RICKY….Come along now….Daddy needs you to be up and about…Pull your finger out….Mummy's made you a lovely big fried brecky…Daddy's already had his….COME ON!....SHIFT YOURSELF!."

There is no response. Bert, not pleased, climbs the stairs to wrap sharply with his knuckles on Eric's bedroom door. Still no response. Bert is losing patience as he, violently, shoves the door open. His knees buckle with shock when he sees that the bed has not been slept in. He, pointlessly, looks around the room, even gets down on his knees to search under the bed, but there is no sign of Eric. He checks the bathroom. He is now conscious of, large scale, panic rising up inside of him. He knows who will be blamed if anything has happened to Eric on their way home from the Club. Returning downstairs, Bert decides to start by carrying out a quick search for Eric using the car. He grabs his coat to dash through the kitchen into the garage. He is climbing into the car when he sees Eric, fast asleep, on the rear seats.

His panic is now mixed with a little relief. He quickly drags the snoozing Lad out of the car and into the kitchen. Eric wakes up, not knowing where he is, or even who he is for that matter. Bert realises that he has to work fast.

"Jesus Christ Ricky….Look at the state of you….I thought I was bad….Get your ass up them stairs and take a cold bath….Go on…It's cruel but you'll have to do it."

Eric is, gradually, coming round, although he is far from firing on all cylinders. Bert pulls him onto his feet. He checks that Eric can stand by himself. Glancing at the oven, he remarks.

"Come on Son….Look your breakfast is going to be cold."

Eric forces himself to look into the oven. He immediately needs the sink as about a gallon of beer decides to leave his system, all at once, via his mouth.

Strangely enough vomiting seems to improve his all round demeanour. Eric sticks his head under the cold water tap and, to Bert's joy, actually manages to speak.

"Christ Dad…..What happened?."

Bert is aware of the urgency necessary to get them through, what is already proving to be, a very trying Morning.

"Never mind that now….Come on Son….This your big day…. Remember?…Don't be letting me…Or should I say your Jenny down… Come on Son you've got to get shaping…And fast."

Eric staggers through the living room to haul himself up the stairs. Bert waits for a second or two then nods his approval as he hears the sound of the taps filling up the bath.

* * *

The clock on the Town Hall strikes three. The doors of the Registry Office burst open. A small but very joyful group of people emerge onto the top of the steps. Bert and his wife are the first to appear, closely followed by Billy and Nan Dawes. Eric, Jenny, Woody and Mavis come out together. All are wearing delightful button holes and both the blushing Brides are carrying their wedding bouquets.

Woody is hardly recognisable, dressed in a smart blue suit, with waistcoat, a white shirt and dark tie. He is minus his cap, a very rare sight not witnessed by many people ever before. Both the Brides are dressed in pink. Mavis wears a neat suit with matching hat, gloves and shoes. Jenny looks absolutely stunning in a pink dress with a matching wide brimmed hat. With Eric in his new three piece suit, Bert and Billy in their Sunday best suits, Mrs McCabe wearing a very small but attractive hat to go with her smart suit, they really do look splendid.

They are merrily descending the steps when, almost out of nowhere, they find themselves surrounded by their friends cheering and applauding as they throw handfuls of confetti and paper streamers.

Ralph, Victor, Charlie. Eddie, Bernie, Dickie Mitchell and their Wives, Alf and Denise, Eric's mates Sam and Peter Peter, Jenny's best friend Kay Brown with some of their other girl friends are all in attendance.

A couple of them have their box cameras with them and attempts are being made to organise photographs of the happy couples and their guests. The are slowly getting into some sort of suitable shape for the amateur photographers but it needs Alf to take a prominent, central, position before there is any semblance of order. He shouts to Woody over the racket being caused all around them.

"You didn't think you could just sneak off to get married without all your friends being present to wish you all the best did you?."

Woody is glowing with happiness as he places his arm around the shoulders of his new Bride. A number of disorganised snaps are being taken as Ralph demands every one's attention.

"Hello!....Can you hear me?!....Hello!...Will you all kindly makes your way to the Clubhouse?....We have a little surprise laid on for the happy couples."

There are cheers as the couples beam with joy. Victor cannot stop himself from supporting his Chairman as usual.

"Yes come along every one....We've all be at it all morning and I think I can say without fear of contradiction that we've managed to prepare for you and your honoured guests the finest wedding breakfast it has ever been anyone's pleasure to witness...."

Eddie joins in.

"Yes and it's all bought and paid for....That oven has been in overdrive....It'll be best if we hurry up now."

As the happy throng linger, chatting and giggling on the steps Bernie makes his presence felt.

"If we don't start making tracks soon...and by that I mean... Tout...Bloody...Suite....Some robbing bastards will have eaten it all for us….So come on pull your fingers out…I've not had any dinner today….My guts think my throat's been cut."

At last they are making a positive move when Lenny Jopson, the local newspaper reporter from the Lapley Vale Examiner, dashes up with a flash camera in one hand, carrying a large tripod under his arm. He is almost breathless but he desperately attracts their attention.

"Wait!....WAIT A MINUTE PLEASE!....Please!."

He glances up to note the time on the Town Hall Clock.

"Christ is that the bloody time?."

Sheepishly he nods to Bert, who appears to be annoyed.

"Sorry I'm a bit late Bert….I've been run off my feet today with one thing and another…Still I'm here now…I've made it."

Bert glares at Lenny, shaking his head in disbelief.

"I must have been soft asking you Lenny….You'd be late for your own bloody funeral you would…But at least you're here…Now hurry up….PLEASE!...The ales going cold so you'd better put your skates on if you intend to be one of the breakfast guests…Eh?...Eh?."

Lenny has managed to set up his camera on the tripod whilst being chastised by Bert. Realising that Bert is not the best person in the Town to upset, especially on such an important day, Lenny masterfully completes the group photographs without falling down the steps and breaking his neck.

Half a dozen bright flashes from the camera and then a couple more of the two couples together and then by themselves are a prelude to a mini mass exodus of the wedding party moving off towards the Lapley Vale Bowling and Social Club.

* * *

Soon the delighted Brides and Grooms are seated at the top of the rows of trestle tables, tastefully covered with linen table cloths, There is an abundance of colourful floral tributes, generously distributed, along their entire length. There are two beautifully decorated wedding cakes, with little brides and grooms, on the top, on the couple's table.

The bakery have actually managed to put a cloth cap on the model of Woody, much to the delight of all present.

The spread is lavish. There are sandwiches of all kinds, pies of many varieties, sausage rolls, things on sticks not to mention jellies and cakes. Eric nudges Jenny before he turns to address his remarks to Woody and Mavis.

"What a wonderful surprise eh?.....I don't know what goes on in big cities like London and these Swinging Sixties or whatever they call them….If you have friends, relatives and neighbours like these I for one wouldn't swap places with Her Majesty the Queen herself or anyone else…What do you say Woody?."

Nodding and smiling, Woody puts his arm around his new bride to kiss her briefly as Eric made a much better job of putting his lips on Jenny. Their actions are met by loud cheers and applause. Lenny, cream all around his mouth, shouts from behind his camera at the foot of the table.

"Right thank you…Can the Brides and Grooms please cut their cakes for the Albums now….Ready."

The flash of the camera records the event for posterity.

* * *

"Worry not my son…..Worry not."

Several months have passed since the memorable day when Mr and Mrs Green and Mr and Mrs McCabe (Junior) each celebrated their marriages. Although the Town of Lapley Vale continues to plod along at it's own familiar pace, a number of changes have taken place. Some are for the better and others are not quite so clear cut.

There is a prevailing atmosphere of tension in the Vestry/Office at 'All Souls', the Parish Church of Lapley Vale. The Vicar, Reginald Blackburn, a kind, elderly man with friendly inviting features, is gazing, sympathetically into the eyes of the much younger, gormless looking, recently appointed Curate, Jeremy Smith- Eccles.

The Reverend Blackburn has been the spiritual leader for the whole District for many years. He is generally well accepted and respected by the vast majority of his Parishioners. He enjoys his fair share of popularity and regard in most quarters, irrespective of individual religious beliefs or leanings.

A genuinely sincere and loving person, the Reverend Blackburn has one, rather obvious, Achilles heel. He has fairly large, protruding front teeth. Strangely enough, these actually go quite well with his face but, unfortunately, they do cause him to emit the occasional, involuntary, whistle when he is speaking. Years of practice have helped him to control his impediment to a certain extent but, the truth is, many people find it difficult to take him too seriously, especially when he speaks in earnest, causing the affliction becomes more acute an noticeable.

Jeremy Smith-Eccles is a recently ordained Priest, emanating from one of our lesser known aristocratic families in the South of England. He was fortunate enough to grow up within a very close, protected, group of relatives and friends. A sheltered upbringing in almost every respect. He had been educated through the public school system, followed by an, undistinguished, degree course at a top University and finally, a Theological College. Obviously well educated, Jeremy is naïve, totally incapable of dealing with the basic needs of ordinary working class families. Without putting too fine a point on the matter, Jeremy finds himself completely out of place in Lapley Vale.

As if this poor man is not handicapped enough due to his privileged background, he has also earned quite a reputation for being naturally accident prone. In all honesty he is proving to be a challenge to the experienced Vicar, who has been delegated by their Bishop to be his Guide and Mentor.

Jeremy, sitting in front of Reginald's desk, appears to be forlorn and dejected. Reginald is earnestly attempting to console and comfort him. His voice has an encouraging tone, despite the involuntary whistling noises. He is being helpful and positive, there is no trace of blame or retribution.

"Jeremy….My Boy…..Every one of us has had to learn…Even the Bishop many years ago….I know Jeremy….In my heart of hearts… That you will never….Ever….Stand too close to the hole in the ground whilst you are conducting a Funeral Service….Ever again."

Listening intently, Jeremy sadly shakes his head. He is close to tears, a mixture of shame and frustration. The Vicar leans forward across the top of his desk, desperately trying to comfort his unfortunate Charge.

"I'm only grateful it happened to you and not myself Jeremy….I swear you came back out of that hole quicker than you went in…"

Reginald emits a half hearted laugh to no real effect. He feels incapable of bringing Jeremy out of his current state of abject misery. Desperate to succeed, he really begins to emphasise what he is saying. He gazes deep into Jeremy's eyes.

"I....I....I am sure Jeremy that all those Mourners were very.... VERY....Relieved and thankful....Yes thankful Jeremy....That you were able to carry on and eventually get the right person into the grave."

Jeremy cringes. He makes a soft, low, whining sound. Reginald is not deterred, he continues, positively.

"Be thankful for small mercies Jeremy....It was nothing more than an unfortunate accident....Bear in mind that the edges of those holes can be treacherous....Especially when we have been experiencing inclement weather conditions."

There is a pause. The two men stare into each other's faces. Jeremy, eventually, regains enough confidence to speak.

"I can't help wondering what the family thought Reginald....I mean to say....They were gathered there together....Sad and sobbing one minute and then....Then....I could swear that I heard stifled laughter as I clambered out of that hole Reginald...And again...Later on when I was continuing with the service...More pronounced."

Reginald can sense Jeremy's suffering in. He tries, once more, to cheer him up.

"Well there you are Jeremy....You see...You may well have brought a little ray of sunshine into an otherwise very sad occasion."

Considering that he was, at last, making slight headway, Reginald decides to change the subject.

"Now do come along Jeremy........Do pull yourself together there's a good Chap.....How are you progressing with your preparation for your very first....Solo....Sermon?....Have you completed it as yet?... Do you need any further assistance from me?."

Surprisingly, the young Curate seems to snap out of his depression as a swift reaction to Reginald's question. He sounds keen.

"That is very kind of you to offer Reginald but thank you all the very same No....I have prepared a comprehensive text."

He actually pauses to smile.

"I know just how vitally important it is to one's future development to get the first one right.....Off to a good start you might say."

He emits a tense sort of laugh, before he emphasises his point.

The first....Live one....Across to the jolly old Congregation....What?."

He appears to slip back into to former depressed state or a moment as he obviously reflects on possible consequences.

"I just hope and pray that nothing goes wrong…I know I am quite capable....But....I just hope my nerves do not get the better of me on the actual day Reginald."

Not wishing to lose the Curate to the doldrums again Reginald responds very confidently.

"Worry not my Son....Worry not....I have every confidence in you and your ability....Would you like me to pass a cursory glance over your prepared text Jeremy…I do not wish to interfere…Perhaps it may by ancillary to the strength of your own self confidence....A little boost…What do you think?."

Jeremy nods, enthusiastically, he rummages through a large leather brief case at the side of his chair to pull out a wad of papers.

"Oh yes....YES....Thank you Reginald I would appreciate that....Be silly not to use the wealth of the experience you can call upon....Thank you Reginald."

He passes the papers across the desk. Reginald is pleased that he has been able to shake his Protégé out of depression into a state of keen participation. He pats the papers, gently. Smiling broadly as he does so. He sums up their deliberations.

"Leave it with me Jeremy....I am sure we have both benefited immensely and will be able to profit greatly from this little friendly discussion....Fret not....God....And I…Will look after you."

* * *

"If I'd hadn't seen it with my own eyes....I wouldn't have believed it."

Eric McCabe has, once again, found it necessary to adjust his comprehensive work schedule. He has to look after 'Bloomers', the shop he now jointly owns with his Wife, whilst Jenny has to make her regular visits to the Ante Natal Clinic at Lapley Vale Cottage Hospital.

Eric's Mother is usually a very useful stand-in but today, due to unforeseen circumstances, Eric is in sole charge.

The shop has turned out to be a dazzling success. Their initial investment has been recovered and they are now enjoying a more than adequate profit margin.

Taking into account the income from Eric's other commitments, at the Nursery and the Bowling Club, the young couple can pride themselves on being well on the way to becoming financially sound. No mean feat at their age in any reckoning.

Because of the generosity of their close friends, Woody and Mavis Green, they have a manageable mortgage on a very desirable property. Finding her home was surplus to requirements after her marriage to Woody had allowed Mavis to come to the assistance of their young friends at a time of dire need. Eric and Jenny had insisted on paying the current market value for their house but because of their close personal relationship with Mavis and Woody they had been able to enjoy the convenience and comfort of their own property a couple of months before any of the legal documents had been drawn up and duly signed. The actual valuation had been arranged by Mavis and Woody. Eric and Jenny were never in any doubt that they had secured their house at a very fair price. Because of the urgency of their marriage, due to Jenny's pregnancy, which coincided with the opening of the shop Eric and Jenny had been glad of any, and all, the assistance they could get. Both Eric's parents and Jenny's grandparents had given them all the love, support and guidance they could ever have wished for. They are now closely and permanently bonded to Woody and Mavis and, bearing in mind the trials and tribulations they have had to face together, Eric and Jenny are very fortunate to be a happy and perfectly contented couple.

Kneeling on one knee, Eric is attending to some flower arrangements in the buckets on the floor in front of the counter. The tinkling of a bell indicates a customer is entering through the shop door. Eric glances round to see the figure of John Brooks, a local businessman in his late forties, standing before him. Eric recognises John as he is being greeted by him.

"Hello Ricky….How are you doing?....I was just passing so I thought I'd call in to settle up with you for all the wreaths and flowers and what have you provided for my Granny's funeral yesterday morning."

Eric rises to his feet, wiping his hands on his overalls. Nodding and smiling he walks behind the counter.

"Oh hello John….Hey….That's very prompt of you…There's no mad rush you know….I do hope everything was to your satisfaction."

John is nodding and grinning. He then bursts out laughing. Eric is bemused. John realises that an explanation must be forthcoming to justify his odd behaviour.

"Sorry….Sorry Ricky….Yes….Oh yes everything was fine the wreaths and floral tributes were all first class….You did us and Gran proud…Thank you."

He breaks off to laugh again. Pulling himself together, he continues.

"Sorry….Sorry again Ricky…I'll explain in a second."

To Eric's frustration, John is unable to control his emotions. He doubles up laughing, leaving Eric grinning without knowing what he is grinning at. Eric finds the invoices and bills for the wreaths and flowers inside the till. He stares at John. He wants to join in the fun but is, so far, unable to do so. John manages to pull himself together sufficiently to carry on with his explanation.

"Yes….Sorry….The flowers and what have you were smashing thanks Eric but…."

He pauses to laugh again but this time he notices that Eric is beginning to look a bit frustrated. He calls upon all his inner powers of self control. Firmly gripping the counter with both hands he speaks, with some difficulty.

"You are aware that my Gran had a bloody good innings aren't you?."

Eric nods keenly, still waiting to be put fully in the picture. John continues.

"Ninety-three…Bloody good going….And she passed away peacefully in her sleep…."

Eric is still nodding.

"Well….After the short service inside the Church…The new Vicar or Curate….Whatever….Whistling Reggie's new sidekick…Have you met him yet Ricky?."

Eric shakes him head this time. He is anxious to hear the John's story. John carries on.

"The Vicar's apprentice he is….Jeremy…Oh I don't know… Something double barrelled."

Eric nods but is not really too interested.

"Well….We all went out into the Churchyard and gathered round the open grave….And….The Vicar or Jeremy…Anyways he has just started the proceedings….Pissing down with rain it was….And I must say I saw it coming…."

John almost collapses on the floor. He has to hold his sides. Tears are rolling down his cheeks. He desperately pulls himself together, once more, in an attempt to finish his story.

"Jeremy comes prancing forward...Slips and disappears down into the grave on top of the coffin...Went in like shit off a shovel..."

John loses control for a moment as Eric starts to smile as he begins to visualises the scene as described. His voice is increasing in volume, well on the way to a scream.

"And....And I don't know if it was assistance coming from above... On high."

He points towards the ceiling and nods.

"But....But....I swear he came back out of that hole quicker than he went in...."

John has to wipe the tears from his eyes.

"The poor bugger....He was covered in mud...But...He just carried on as if nothing had happened....Old Reggie was standing close by.... I took one look at his face and I thought he was going to need a new plot dug for himself next to where my Gran's hole..."

Eric is relieved to be able to join in the laughter with John. John is on his knees, thumping the floor with his fists. He drags himself up, using the counter.

"We were all feeling a bit sad....You know?....But when that happened....Well I nearly pissed myself trying not to laugh out loud...And I wasn't the only one I can tell you....Unbelievable...If I hadn't seen it with my own eyes....I wouldn't have believed it....Christ Almighty what a bloody fiasco."

Both men are roaring with uncontrolled laughter. John wipes his eyes so he can check the bills. Opening his wallet he hands over a few pound notes. Eric places them in the till, handing John some small change in return. Eric gradually calms down, summing up with a air of disbelief plainly detectable.

"Bloody Hell John....I have heard one or two funny stories about this new Vicar bloke but I haven't come into contact with him myself as yet....I bet he'll be much more careful in the future....They're bloody deep them holes you know?.....It's a wonder he didn't do himself some sort of injury."

John is now able to laugh in a more control fashion.

"I doubt if the poor bugger is able to help himself Ricky....He appears to be a born twit....I mean to say Old Reggie Blackburn is a funny old bird but he's usually fairly sensible...I'm telling you Ricky that Jeremy's one in a million."

John really composes himself properly. Shrugging his shoulders he walks towards the door.

"Christ Ricky look at the state of me....I'd better pull myself together and think about something else....If people see me walking down the main street laughing like a daft bugger the day after burying my Granny they'll have a right to wonder what sort of person I am... Well....Anyways...Thanks again Ricky....Must press on....See you."

The bell dings as John opens the door. He waves with one hand as he disappears from Eric's sight. Eric pauses trying to assimilate the contents of the conversation he has just endured. Just for a fleeting second he wonders if John had been pulling his leg. Dismissing this thought he shakes his head rather vigorously. He convinces himself that John could not possibly make up a story like that. He briefly laughs out aloud before he continues to re-arrange the flowers in the buckets on the floor.

* * *

"Just find a cubicle….Doctor will see you in a minute."

Jenny McCabe is well advanced into her pregnancy. She is approaching the Entrance into the Ante-Natal Clinic at Lapley Vale Cottage Hospital. Jenny waves as she meets up with the two friends she has recently made, due to them being in a similar situation as herself.

Lynda Chumley is a young woman, not much older than Jenny. Susan Summers is about ten years older. Susan is the long suffering wife of the notorious local troublemaker Joe. All three have reached the same stage of their confinements. Their friendship has developed through their regular visits to the Hospital over the previous few months. For both Jenny and Lynda the imminent birth of their baby's will be a new experience for them. Susan is having her fourth child.

Jenny is slightly out of breath as she greets the other women with a happy smile.

"Hiya…..Sorry I'm a bit late girls…Have you been waiting for me for long?."

Susan answers for them both.

"No you're alright Jenny….I've only just arrived myself…I've had a bit of trouble with my lot this morning….First it was getting HIM off to work…Followed by the nightmare of getting the kids off to school….It's a major operation most days….I find it's a real pleasure to get away from them all for a few hours….It's my only chance of peace and quiet and of course I'm always ready for a good natters...Girl to girls."

Lynda greets Jenny with a smile.

"Hiya Jenny...I was lucky...I got a lift here this morning.... It's starting to be a bit too much for me on the bus...Lugging this about."

She leans back to pat her protruding, large, lump. The other two, grinning, pat theirs, nodding sympathetically. Smiling, brightly, Lynda adds.

"I'll be glad when it's all over and done with."

Susan shakes her head.

"Take it from me girls....Your troubles really begin when we get past this stage in the proceedings."

The younger women gaze at Susan, expecting a fuller explanation.

"You'll have to take the word of someone who knows."

She pats her bump again.

"Wait until you've got your little bundle of joy in your arms....You will soon find that you won't know if you're coming or going...You might even meet yourself on the way back...I just hope....For your sakes....That your Fellas are more help to you than that useless swine of mine is to me....Joe puts a gob on if he has to stir his own tea."

Jenny and Lynda have become accustomed to listening to the vastly experienced Susan. Both are also well aware of the low opinion she appears to hold of her husband.

Attempting to break away from discussions about the more unpleasant side of life, Jenny is mildly sarcastic.

"Well thank you very much Su....I was feeling quite good this morning...."

Lynda interrupts, supporting Jenny.

"Jenny's right....You're a proper little ray of sunshine today Susan.... My Malcolm isn't like your Joe thank God....I think he'd be prepared to have the baby for me if it was possible for him to do so...."

Susan laughs in an ironic way as she intervenes.

"Perhaps you're right Love….But if he did I can tell you one fact for sure….You'd only be having the one….Believe me."

Jenny does not like Susan being negative. She hopes to snap her out of her present mood.

"It doesn't seem to have stopped you Susan…How do you explain the fact that you're about to have your fourth baby?."

Susan realises that she is on the brink of causing upset to her young, naïve, friends. She smiles, adopting a different attitude, immediately.

"O.K…..I have to admit certain aspects of the process involved in having children is quite pleasurable…."

They all giggle before Susan continues.

"And I suppose I wouldn't know what to do with myself all day without my little lot….Demanding attention….Morning….Noon…And Night…I'm definitely going to tie a knot in it after this one….Or send Joe to the Vet's….Enough is enough."

She breaks off to glance all around her. She suddenly takes on an air of urgency.

"Hey come on girls….We better join the happy throng inside…..Chop!….Chop!."

As they enter the building Lynda gets between the other two to link arms with them both. She appears and sounds to be a little concerned.

"I have to admit that I feel a bit embarrassed today…I couldn't find a suitable bottle for my water sample….I was sure I had something….But anyways….I couldn't find it….So as time was pressing I empties his sauce bottle."

She causes them to stop as she, furtively, shows them a H.P. Sauce bottle, concealed, inside her bag. She blushes, turning bright red, as she continues.

"So I gave it a quick wash and I've used it."

Initially shocked, Jenny soon giggles. Susan does not appear to be concerned in the slightest. Jenny speaks.

"Oh Lynda…I feel for you…. Honestly….Perhaps it might have been better if you'd taken the label off the bottle."

Lynda is defensive.

"I didn't have any time….Anyways it's obviously a sauce bottle…Anyone can see that and in any case I think it's much better than arriving without a sample and having to go through the rigmarole of providing one here."

Lynda is feeling rather self-conscious until Susan intervenes in a casual, matter of fact, way.

"I don't know what you're getting your knickers in a twist about….They empty them out as soon as you hand them over….Anyways….Listen."

She pauses to ensure she has their full, undivided, attention before she adds.

"On one of my previous encounters with child birth I found myself standing behind a lady…At this very Clinic….You know?...Just like we are standing here now?......And she handed over her sample to the Nurse in a jam jar."

Jenny and Lynda both gasp.

"And it was one of those two pound one's as well."

They all chuckle.

"I thought the Nurse was going to give her a goldfish in return for it."

All three roar with laughter. Susan ushers them along.

"Hey….Come on….We'll be right at the back of the queue again…Let's get a move on eh?."

They book themselves in at the small reception desk. They cannot help themselves from giggling as they handed over their sample bottles. They look around before selecting one of the rows of plastic chairs to sit on.

There are quite a few women in varying stages of pregnancy seated all around them Where they are sitting faces directly towards another large counter area. A Sister and a Nurse appear to be sorting through a large pile of files. They are obviously very busy. Lynda leans over to speak, quietly, to her friends.

"My God....Am I glad that part's over and done with...Did you see that snotty look the Sister gave me....I wanted the earth to swallow me up."

She pushes her face towards Jenny.

"Am I still red?....It crossed my mind to give her the full explanation but I soon decided against it....I'll tell you something though....That is never going to happen to me ever again."

Shrugging her shoulders, she sits back in her chair, glaring at the Sister behind the counter, who is ignoring everyone as she hunts through all the files. Susan recognises who the Sister is.

"Oh take no notice of her Lynda....That's Sister Murphy...I've met her before....She's a right Madam....It would do her good if some man was brave enough to put her up the duff...She might be a little more sympathetic towards the likes of us then."

Jenny's face screws as she stares at Sister Murphy. She is apprehensive as well as curious.

"They're not all like that are they Susan?."

Jenny's expression now indicates horror.

"Oh God....I feel ill....Please tell me that she's the exception to the rule Su....Please."

Lynda is as anxious to hear the reply as Jenny. They are both hoping for a positive response. Susan, identifying signs of nervousness, immediately, puts their minds at ease.

"No...Not at all.....They were all smashing in the Maternity Ward....Well....Should I say most of them were anyways....Mothers themselves you see....It does make a lot of difference to their attitudes."

Susan can tell that her answer has given both her young friends a certain amount of relief and has helped to renew their fragile confidence. They all sit back on their chairs for a few moments. Lynda leans across to ask Susan another question. She speaks, cautiously, in a quiet voice.

"Susan....Su....Can you give me any idea how long you have to wait....Er...."

Susan and Jenny are unable to comprehend her meaning. Neither can understand her, incomplete, question. Lynda blushes again and seems embarrassed.

"Well....You know?....After the baby has been born...."

Her friends are still in the dark. She feels they are not helping her at all. Frustration rising, she splutters out her words.

"Before you can....Well shall we say.....Resume normal married activities?...."

Susan stares, blankly. Jenny has a vacant expression on her face. Lynda is desperate to ask her question, this causes her to splutter even more.

"You see....I think my Malcolm is getting a bit restless...At the moment....It can't be much fun for him if you catch my drift....What I actually need to know Su....Is how soon after you've had the baby can you start letting him have his little treats back again....You know what I mean?.... His....Nookey?."

At last, the penny drops. Linda is visibly relieved that her enquiry has, at last, been understood. Jenny is just as curious to hear Susan's response as Lynda. Susan attempts to hide a cheeky, mischievous, expression, which is starting to spread slowly across her face. She tries hard to sound informative and casual, without laughing.

"It all depends on the Sister on duty in the Ward."

Jenny and Lynda both look puzzled.

"You know?...The Ward Sister....If she's prepared to draw the curtains around your bed when your fella come in to visit you and the baby."

Lynda, gasping, is genuinely astonished. Jenny notices the cheeky expression on Susan's face. She is wise to her little attempt at humour. She wags her finger before she replies.

"Ah....Ah....Pull the other one Susan....You must think we're both a little bit softer than we actually look."

Laughing, confidently, shaking her head to reflect her delight in her powers of detection, she nudges Lynda.

"Depends on the Sister in charge of the Ward!....Really Susan Summers you are really awful."

Susan winks and smiles. They all need to stifle their laughter.

Appreciating how the two girls hang on her every word, Susan decides to give them a sensible answer to the genuine question posed. Making sure she has their full attention, she speaks.

"The true answer to your question is it depends upon a lot of different things....But if you're anything like me it'll put you off for quite some time....It certainly won't be before you are given the all clear from the Post-Natal Clinic....And absolutely not by the Ward Sister after you have just given birth...You were too sharp to fall for that bit of leg pulling... Anyways Lynda....What did you mean when you said it's not much fun for your Malcolm?...I suppose you're having a ball are you?....If he wants to be the Father of your children then he has to be prepared to make a few sacrifices....I'm beginning to suspect that you might be a little too soft on that fella of yours Lynda."

She springs to Malcolm's defence.

"Oh no....No....He's always been very understanding....But when he's been used to having...."

She leans forward to mouth her next few words.

"A full....Sex life."

Lynda glances all around her to check that her revelations are not being overhead by anyone else. She continues.

"It must be a bit of a strain on him....If you know what I mean."

Susan can scarcely belief what she is hearing. She accepts their need for her, essential, words of wisdom but she is beginning to get annoyed by Lynda's attitude towards Malcolm's creature comforts actually being interfered with and even spoiled.

"Oh Yes I think I can safely say that I know exactly what you mean Lynda....but that doesn't alter my response in the slightest bit....My answer is still the same....He has to be patient."

The younger women appear to accept Susan's conclusion without further question. Susan now starts to really vent her true feelings on the delicate subject, which are clearly influenced by her own experiences with her husband, Joe.

"They're all swine…Men!....Some more than others…I'll grant you that….Take their little pleasures away from them and they act like baby's who have lost their rattles."

She sits back to emphasis her words as she pats her large, protruding abdomen.

"Look at this….My youngest if four and half years old…Started at the Infant School this Term…A couple of years after she was born I split up with Joe….I decided the kids and I were better off without him….I was fed up with all his capers…Getting drunk…Getting himself locked up in the Police Station."

Jenny and Lynda are rapt. They hang on each word.

"Then after a couple of years…He came round visiting the kids as usual….And I felt sorry for him….He never left us short of money or anything I'll say that for him….And he loves those kids as much as they love him….Anyways….He managed to convince me that he was a changed man….After listening to his patter I was beginning to believe he would be in line as a candidate for the World's Greatest Husband and Father of the Year."

Breaking off, pausing to wearily shake her head, she now looks and sounds like a whipped dog as she continues.

"I still cannot understand how I could be so bloody stupid….So bloody gullible….But anyways we made up….I let him back into the house again."

She pats her lump again.

"And this is my reward for my soft-heartedness….And of course…. As we are only too aware Ladies….A leopard cannot change his spots…. Although he's not quite as bad as he used to be he still manages to be a complete pain in the arse at regular intervals…I have to watch him like a hawk…I have to meet him outside the Mill….Where he works…Every pay day to get our share before he disappears into the nearest Ale House…Still….I suppose we all have our little crosses to bear....I'm sorry I've gone on a bit but it was listening to Lynda being so reasonable about her fella that set me off.........Sorry Ladies."

Jenny and Lynda are stunned by Susan's frankness. Jenny leaps to Susan's defence in her own particular way. She snaps, angrily.

"If my Ricky ever turned out like that I'd swing for him."

There is a short pause as Lynda adds her opinion.

"I don't think that's ever going to be on the cards for you Jenny...I mean...I don't know him well but your Ricky seems to be a smashing bloke to me."

Susan snaps back into the conversation.

"Oh they're all smashing until you give them what they want... Then....Well then...Well that's when all the trouble starts."

Lynda hopes that Susan is merely speaking for herself.

"Well I'm very sorry that you ended up with...Well...You said it...A swine...But I don't think it's fair to say that all men are the same...Jenny's Ricky is alright and then there's my Malcolm...Well I can't honestly say a bad word against him....I love him to bits."

Susan adopts her wise and experienced pose. She appears to have calmed down after her outburst.

"I really do hope that everything works out as you would wish girls...I really do....But there are no guarantees...None at all."

They sit reflecting on what has been an interesting few minutes. Jenny changes the subject.

"It looks like my Family are keeping this Hospital going at the moment....My poor old Granddad is lying in a bed in Entwistle Ward as we speak."

Both are concerned. Lynda speaks.

"Oh dear....Nothing too serious I hope."

Although the extent of her worry is obvious, Jenny manages to sound quite positive as she responds.

"Well thankfully it's not as bad now...It was touch and go last weekend when we had to have him rushed in here by Emergency Ambulance...Trouble with his gall stones....They operated on him right away...Thank God he seems to be well on the way to recovery now…But my Nan says she could manage very nicely without shocks like that…You don't want any shocks like that when your over seventy years of age do you?."

Her friends agree with the comments made. Lynda asks.

"And how has your Nan taken it Jenny…I really must have been a terrible shock for her….Never mind her age."

Jenny nods.

"She's taken it very well considering….Considering that they have been married for nearly fifty years and this the very first time that Granddad has suffered from anything more serious than colds and chills….Oh and the odd bad hangover….If think he's always managed to drown all those nasty germs that fly about with large quantities of beer….Still….He seems to be O.K. again…They're keeping him in for another few days whilst they carry out some more tests and things…We're all most relieved I can tell you….I hope to be able to pop up to see him for a few minutes after we have finished our business in here."

Jenny sits tall on her plastic chair to she if she can notice any signs of movement. On noticing this Susan, sounds expresses her observations in a sarcastic manner.

"It's great isn't it?….We've been sitting around on our arses most of the morning….Patiently waiting….The don't even offer you a cup of tea or anything like that."

Lynda attempts to be helpful.

"There's a machine Susan….Just along that corridor…Near the Out-Patients waiting rooms…I could soon…."

Jenny grimaces as Susan interrupts.

"You've forgotten haven't you?.....We tried some once….Remember?....Tasted very much like fermented badger piddle….We had to buy some sweeties to take the nasty taste away."

Lynda, obviously, remembers as she pulls a suitable face. Jenny is actually starting to feel sick as she recalls how foul the drink had been.

They are suddenly startled by Sister Murphy prancing out from behind her desk carrying a number of large files under her arm. She glances towards the rows of waiting Ladies. Her tone is arrogant enough to be called cocky.

"Mrs Donald….Mrs McCabe….Mrs Chumley….Mrs Summers."

They all rise instantly. Excusing themselves as they push and wriggle their ways past other women waiting on the same rows of seats. Sister Murphy nods in acknowledgment to their response, saying, rather curtly.

"Follow me please….Just find a cubicle….Doctor will see you in a minute."

The patients, obediently, follow the Sister into the Examination Rooms where several curtained off cubicles as situated. Murphy rushes along, casually, throwing back the curtain on the first cubicle on their left. As she does this they can all see the, big, bare backside of the, unfortunate, woman patient still inside as she tries her best to get dressed again following her examination. This Lady, instantly, emits a loud scream. The girls all have to stifle their, rather unsympathetic, chuckles.

* * *

"ME?.....There's nothing wrong with me Arnie...."

Billy 'Cockeye' Dawes, looks pale and wan as he lies in his Hospital bed. He appears to be sleeping. He has a drip attached into his left arm. He seems whiter in his face because he is wearing bright red pyjama tops. There is a small bowl of fruit and a bottle of orange squash on top of the locker next to his bed. Mary York a, young and inexperienced, Student Nurse walks up to Billy's bed to start fluffing up his pillows. Billy awakens with a start. Nurse York smiles down at him.

"Sorry Mr Dawes....There now that's much better....You weren't asleep were you?."

Billy struggles to recover his senses. He is irritable.

"Weren't asleep?....I was just enjoying that....It's the first cockeyed rest I've had since you brought me into this cockeyed place...What do you want?."

Nurse York is smiling sweetly as she answers him.

"I only came to see if there was anything you wanted."

Irritation turns to annoyance. Billy snaps at her.

Anything I wanted?....Well for your information....Nurse cockeyed Clever clogs...For your information....I wanted to have a cockeyed kip....That's all I wanted....And that's just what I was having until you arrived on the cockeyed scene."

They are joined by Sister Mead, an older, much wiser and experienced, nurse. She is in charge of the Ward. She wants to know what all the fuss is about. Nurse York is slightly upset by Billy's rather unnecessary attack on her. Sister Mead is able to quickly assess the situation.

"Now then….What's all this about?...Eh?....Feeling a bit out of sorts today are we Mr Dawes?."

This comment is the final straw. Billy erupts.

"Feeling out of sorts?....Listen Missus….Er Sister….I was perfectly happy lying here on my sick bed…Having a most welcome and refreshing kip….When Nurse cockeyed Nightingale here………."

Billy lurches forward pointing an accusing finger directly at Nurse York, who is now close to tears.

"Wakes me up to ask if I……"

Sister Mead interrupts Billy, purposefully.

"Now now Mr Dawes….Tut tut….We mustn't allow ourselves to be an old grumpy must we?....Eh?."

Despite his pain, Billy is almost out of his bed, due to His, ever increasing, rage level.

"WE?.....WE?....What all this cockeyed WE?...If you and young Florence here would care to make yourselves scarce…I…"

Billy pauses to vigorously thump his finger into his own chest.

"ME….Not WE….Will be able to get on with my cockeyed kip…. And….Let me add….I will be happy to do so."

His demeanour and performance cuts little ice with Sister Mead. She shoves him back under the covers. She leans over to fluff up his pillows even more. Nurse York, standing on the other side of his bed tries a little smile as she enquires politely.

"I know what it is Mr Dawes….It's that nasty operation scar giving you trouble isn't it?....I understand."

Billy patience has run out. He now threatens.

"I you two don't leave me alone to enjoy my little kip….WE…. WE….Will ALL be having cockeyed scars to be worried about."

The two Nurses, calmly finish off the adjustments to Billy's bedding. A smiling Sister Mead nods to Nurse York and they walk away. Billy is growling and muttering to himself as he tries to settle down again.

His is one of ten beds in the Ward. Five on each side of the long room. All the beds are occupied by male persons. One or two are wearing clumsy looking plaster casts others are in their dressing gowns lying on top of their beds reading books and newspapers.

Directly opposite Billy is the bed being occupied by Arnie Brooks, the Member of the Liberal Club Crown Bowling Team. They are well known to each other. Arnie was on the receiving end of a dreadful thrashing from Billy in their last game after Nan Dawes had given her husband baked beans for his lunch, causing him to have, quite memorable, flatulence. Arnie has recently undergone an operation on his nose and sports a large plaster across his face. Arnie has been watching all the antics around Billy's bed with more than a little amusement. Chuckling to himself, he shouts across to Billy.

"You can be a cantankerous old get when you put your mind to it Billy."

Billy is offended. With a deep sigh he abandons his forlorn attempts to catch a short nap. He snarls.

"ME!....ME!....It's not down to me that fiasco Arnie....Did you witness that cockeyed performance?....I was having a nice little kip.... Then over they came....Interfering...ME!....There's nothing wrong with me Arnie."

Arnie tries to reason with him.

"She's only a young girl Billy....Christ give her a bloody chance.... She was only doing her duty....It can't be easy for the likes of her having to put up with nasty old gets like you all day for a living."

Fortunately Billy's blood pressure is not being monitored. He is close to bursting a blood vessel through rage and frustration.

"Listen to me....Mr cockeyed perfect....I am the last person in this world to cause trouble for anybody...I've got enough on my plate trying to cope with this dirty great scar...."

Billy tugs his pyjamas up to expose his bandaged abdomen.

"Across my cockeyed belly region....Without Nurses and other interfering people trying to give me a hard time..."

He pauses to look up towards the ceiling.

"Is it too much to ask?.....All I want is to be left alone so I can have a cockeyed kip...."

He breaks off to talk directly to Arnie.

"Incidentally Arnie....If you insist on calling me those nasty names....You're going to end up having another operation on that cockeyed hooter of yours.....So wind your neck in please."

Arnie, noisily opens up his newspaper. He spreads it as far as he can across his face to avoid being able to see Billy. There are now two muttering, annoyed, old, patients on Entwhistle Ward.

* * *

"Don't worry Mavis….I won't let you forget."

Woody Green and Alf, the Bar Steward, are seated at the table in the kitchen at the Lapley Bowling and Social Club. They are both, carefully, sipping hot tea from large steaming mugs. Woody's wife Mavis is busily engaged cleaning and dusting in the Clubroom. Eric McCabe enters through the front doors. Mavis pauses to greet him with a smile.

"I swear you can hear tea brewing Ricky….Come on through Woody and Alf are having theirs in the kitchen."

Eric nods and smiles broadly.

"Good Morning Mavis…I'll have you know that I can home in on a fresh brew within a radius of several miles….Especially when you're brewing it Lovey…..Is it scone Morning?....I do hope so…. I'm starving….As usual."

Mavis ushers Eric into the kitchen. Leading the way, she calls out to the others.

"Visitor for you Boys….You can't fault this Lad's timing."

There are exchanged grunts and half smiles of greetings as Eric takes his place at the table. Mavis is already pouring his tea into his mug. Woody speaks between sips of tea and mouthfuls of scone.

"Alright Young 'un?....I didn't expect to see you till much later today…What with all those balls you've got up in the air at this moment in time…. Never mind not knowing if you're coming or going…You'll be meeting yourself on the way back….Mark my words."

Mavis places Eric's mug and a side plate in front of him. Eric is unable to respond to Woody because he already has a mouthful of scone taken before he had his plate to put it on. He gulps the food down to reply with a little difficulty.

"Don't lose any beauty sleep over me or my balls in the air Woody… Taking everything in my stride at present thanks very much I'm sure…. It isn't a problem to a multi-talented person such as myself."

They chuckle as he continues.

"Seriously….Things are going remarkably well considering…."

Alf intervenes.

"And how's that little Mother to be of yours.?....Not much longer to wait now is there?."

Eric is always delighted to speak about his beloved Jenny,.

"She's fine thanks Alf…Touch wood….Getting bigger every day…. When I woke up this Morning I had to kneel up in bed to see if it was daylight….It's a bit like sleeping on the side of a mountain actually."

The men laugh but Mavis is not as amused. She soon rushes to Jenny's defence, without being aggressive.

"Oh Ricky….You are awful….Poor Jenny….It can't be much fun for her at the moment….Try not to be unkind Dear….I'm sure you don't mean it for one moment."

Woody joins in the conversation.

"And old Billy Cockeye?.. What's the news bulletin on Billy?...Last we heard he was well up the road to recovery."

Again Eric is delighted to reply positively.

"Yes…Thanks….They say he'll soon be back to normal…Or should I say as normal as he is ever likely to get….Should be released from the Cottage Hospital within the next couple of days or so."

He breaks off to chuckle.

"I bet the Nursing Staff will be pleased to see the back of him….I understand he's managed to be a complete pain in the arse to most of them."

Mavis now comes to the defence of Billy.

"Don't be cruel Ricky…It must be a terrible shock to his system….Finding himself in Hospital for the first time in his long life….Must be really upsetting for him….Thank God he's making such a good recovery…Those Doctors and Nurses do a really fine job don't they?."

Woody considers Mavis's statement for a few moments before he is prepared to give his opinion on the issue.

"Given half a chance Old Billy has always had a tendency to be a pain in the arse….I think we've become used to him over the years…He doesn't try it on with us anymore….Speaking for myself I like to keep my distance from Doctor and Nurses and the like if I can possibly avoid them but I agree with you Mavis they do a great job without too many thanks."

Agreeing in principle Alf sums up.

"That's good news all round then…And whatever anyone has to say about Billy….He's a fabulous Character….There's not many around like him….One in a million."

Eric suddenly remembers some extra new information he has to pass on to his friends.

"Guess who's sharing Entwistle Ward with him?...You'll never guess."

Eric does not expect, nor get, any reply. The others are agog with interest as he carries on.

"Arnie….You know Arnie Brooks?….Bowls for the Liberal Club?."

Woody realises to whom he is referring, with some instant amusement.

"Bloody Hell Fire….Arnie will be suited…I don't think."

He nudges Alf, who does not seems to know Arnie.

"You remember that game Alf…."

Woody nods in the general direction of the Bowling Green.

"Out there….On the Green….When Billy almost blew poor Arnie off the bloody grass….Blamed his Missus for giving him cockeyed beans….You can't forget those sort of games can you?."

Alf's face lights up. He nods as Woody continues.

"You would hardly refer to those two as Mates…Would you?."

Eric has managed to dispose of two large scones which now enables him to join in the conversation, without spraying every one with crumbs. He, readily, confirms Woody's opinion.

"You can say that again Woody….Arnie was telling me last night… When I had a few words with him….He reckons he's suffering enough having just had an operation on his sinuses without being trapped in a confined area with Billy and his musical arse."

Eric pauses as they all laugh.

"The poor old bugger has got his hooter in a sling…No kidding…. He really has had an operation on his nose…I had to stop myself chuckling when I saw all the bandages across his face…I think we can safely say that between the pair of them they are managing to keep the Doctors and Nursing Staff on their toes at all times…Eh?."

They are all laughing as Eric, rising to his feet, finishes off his mug of tea. He sounds as if he is ready for immediate action.

"Well come on Woody….Pull the finger out please….I can't sit around here gassing all day….Come on….Chop!....Chop!."

Before Woody can give him a deserved return blast, Eric turns to Mavis. He pours out his natural charm.

"Thank you most awfully kindly My Dear…I think I can honestly say that was the finest cup of tea I've had since the last one you made for me…..And the scones…Well….What can I say?…Please promise me that one day you'll teach Jenny how to make them like that…. Promise…."

Mavis enjoys the flattery but is defensive, once again, towards any veiled attacks on Jenny.

"It takes many years of experience Ricky…And if you remember?…. She does have other….More pressing and urgent things on her mind at present….But don't worry…She'll soon pick it all up…Just as soon as she settled with Baby….After that you'll need to remind me again to give her my special recipe to follow….She can't fail with that."

His arm goes around her shoulders as he kisses her lightly on the cheek. He turns to leave the room but pauses to add.

"Don't worry Mavis….I won't let you forget."

Woody is now standing in the doorway, pretending to be bored. He, playfully, scolds his young friend.

"Come on Lover Boy….I thought you were threatening to do some work."

They smile at each other as they leave the room to make their way out onto the Bowling Green. Mavis turns the taps on in the sink as Alf clears the mugs and plates off the table.

* * *

"I think someone has been pulling your leg."

The Curate, Jeremy Smith-Eccles, appears to be very cheerful and full of self-confidence as he begins conducting the Bible Class in the Annex at Lapley Vale Parish Church. Despite some unfortunate set backs and little mishaps in his early experiences, so far, as the Vicar's Understudy, he is sure he can handle a Class of six young boys and five little girls. They are all aged about ten years old. He had even been looking forward to this particular encounter. He feels that he will be able to perform well within his, acknowledged, limited capabilities.

He can tell by the expressions on the tiny faces that they readily accept him as being in full charge. He smiles to himself as he genuinely believes that nothing can, or will, go wrong on this type of elementary occasion.

He has, carefully, chosen a non-controversial theme, yet, after about fifteen minutes or so he is suddenly aware that the children seem to be wearing odd expressions, tending to indicate that they no longer fully convinced by what he is saying.

Jeremy smiles, broadly, hoping that his pleasant self assurance and confident demeanour will convey a message across to the children that there is nothing in what he is telling them that could possibly give them cause for concern. This cunning ploy does not appear to be having the immediate desired effect, causing a pause.

Tommy Summers, son of Joe and Susan, is fairly typical of any boy of his particular age group. A likeable Lad, he has never been afraid of speaking up to ask any questions if he does not fully understand. Tommy breaks the silence as he, politely, enquires with genuine sincerity.

"Where is he then?...."

The Curate stares into Tommy's eyes. He does not understand his question but he still remains confident that he will be able to respond to any query posed by a small child.

"Where is who Tommy?."

Tommy quickly glances around the expectant faces of his peers before he responds.

"God?......Where is God?."

Jeremy feels, somewhat, relieved to field such an easy enquiry, despite his obvious, continuing, confidence.

"He's up in Heaven Tommy....That's where God is....Up in Heaven?."

He is surprised that his prompt, stock, response does not appear to be instantly accepted by any of the children. His fears are justified as Janet White, sitting next to Tommy, joins in the discourse.

"I suppose we just have to take your word for that do we Sir?."

Jeremy is shocked, realising that further information will be helpful to all his little charges.

"No....Well...What I mean is yes......Look....Everyone knows that God lives in Heaven."

There is a tense silence for a few moments. The Curate is now experiencing some difficulty in coming to terms with the situation he is facing. Unexpectedly, he has discovered that small children do not automatically accept the basic religious concepts. He is aware that none of them is prepared to take his answer as final but he cannot think of anything else he can say which could rectify the dilemma he now faces.

Tommy breaks the silence.

"Listen....I would like to know a bit more about this Heaven place."

There are murmurs and nodding heads all around the room. A very clear indication that Tommy is speaking for them all. Jeremy is still unable to find inspiration. Tommy elaborates.

"When my Granddad died they told me there was nothing to worry about because he had gone up to Heaven."

Jeremy nods, eagerly, thinking he may be on the brink of a break through. Tommy, with unanimous support, carries on.

"And as far as I can tell….No-one has laid eyes on him ever since."

Vocal agreement is heard from many of the children. Little Richard Briggs is bold enough to speak out.

"Yes….Exactly the same thing happened to me with my Nan."

Richard's comments cause most of the children to shout out the names of their loved ones who had died and gone up to Heaven, never to be seen again.

The Curate is now losing his confidence. He struggles in a vain attempt to offer an acceptable explanation.

"Look….Look children….I appreciate that it may not be easy for you all to understand….I realise that….But…Well…I'm afraid you are going to have to take my word for it…..There certainly is a place called Heaven….And that's where God lives….All our loved ones who have passed away are….."

Tommy interrupts Jeremy to ask him directly and bluntly.

"Have you ever seen him then?."

The others emit sounds of approval of the question. The Curate is slightly bemused.

"Seen who Tommy?."

Tommy stares at him in disbelief that he does not know who he is enquiring about. His response is rather sharp.

"GOD!....That's who you've been going on about…GOD!...Have you ever seen him?."

Beads of sweat are now trickling down the Curate's face. He knows he cannot evade Tommy's question but he is struggling to find a suitable answer. Every child is waiting for his response. He manages to splutter.

"Well No....I...Well....No-one has ever actually seem him....But he is there.....Up in Heaven....And....And everywhere."

Jeremy throws his arms out wide to show what he means by everywhere. This action causes all the children, as one, to carefully, look all around the room for any signs of God.

After checking with each other, they realise that there is nothing at all to be seen. Again, Tommy speaks for them all. He sounds rather patronising.

"I think someone has been pulling your leg...."

All the children nod, smiling their agreement. Jeremy is completely lost for words. Tommy stands up.

"Have you finished with us now Sir?....Can we go?."

With a shell shocked expression across his bemused features, the Curate, unable to utter a word, gestures his consent to Tommy's opportune request with a wave of his hand. Every one of the children quits the room in a flash. Leaving Jeremy placing his head between his hands. After a few moments he exhales loudly before he stares up to the ceiling. He appears to be making a pathetic, direct, appeal to God on high. Jeremy Smith-Eccles is very close to tears.

* * *

"There are more urgent priorities than a van Lad."

Alice McCabe is turning the 'Open' sign around to 'Closed' on the door at Bloomers Flower Shop on High Street, Lapley Vale. Jenny is behind the counter, counting money from the till. Jenny is wearing a floral apron which protrudes, rather comically, over her extended abdomen. Placing the cash and notes inside a Bank Bag she sighs, stepping back. Grimacing, she places both of her hands in the small of her back. She stretches and sighs again. Mrs McCabe is quietly watching her. She takes the opportunity to express her empathetic concern for the girl's current predicament.

"Oh Dear....I can almost feel that for myself Jenny Love....You're going to have to leave this place in my hands very soon...I know you want to carry on doing your share but it's getting to be far too much for you now."

Straightening herself up, Jenny attempts to sound casually confident.

"Don't be silly Mum....I just get a bit stiff if I stand in one place for too long....I'm O.K....Honestly....There's a couple of weeks to go yet and I can't leave it all to you just now...That wouldn't be fair....You deserve your rest as well you know?.

Mrs McCabe sounds quite determined.

"Listen Jenny Love....You mustn't worry about me....You're the one we're all concerned about....I can manage here without you Jenny

Love….Ricky knows that….He wants you to get more rest as well you know?....We have to think of baby as well."

Jenny waddles across to place her arm around her Mother- in-Law's shoulders. Her tone expresses her genuine sincerity.

"I don't know what we would have done without you Mum…And Dad…He's been really smashing as well….It made things worse with Granddad being in Hospital…Ricky and I couldn't have coped without your help….The last thing we want to do is abuse your kindness."

Alice looks into Jenny's eyes.

"Jenny Love….How can you be accused of abusing a labour of love?....We feel as if we've got a purpose in life again….I love being useful and after all is said and done….We're all family….Aren't we?."

Jenny, gently kisses her. She is about to hug her Mother- in-Law until she finds that her lump is in the way. They are both laughing in a girlish way when they are disturbed by a sharp wrapping noise on the shop door. Peering through the glass on the closed door is Sergeant Bert McCabe. Mrs McCabe pretends to be alarmed.

"Hey up Jenny Love….I think we may be getting propositioned…. There's a strange man peeping at us through the door."

They are laughing happily as Alice unlocks the door to allow Bert to come inside. She greets her husband cheerfully.

"Good timing Bert….We've just finished for the day…As soon as we get our coats on we'll be ready for the off."

Bert nods and smiles at his wife but addresses his remarks to his Daughter-in-Law.

"And how's my little plum pudding today then?..."

He walks over to put his arm around her shoulders. Turning to Alice, he says.

"Hey Mother just take a look at the glow in those lovely rosy cheeks…Eh?....Eh?....Having babies must be good for her."

They hug, as best as they can. Alice walks through to the rear of the shop to return with their coats. Jenny picks up the heavy Bank Bag from the counter, handing it to Bert. She sounds pleased with herself.

"No complaints here Dad…If this keeps up we'll be able to retire soon….In about twenty years that is."

They all laugh. Jenny sounds more serious.

"No kidding….I think the profits are now exceeding our wildest expectations…By a long chalk.."

Bert nods, cautiously.

"Make the best of it while you can Jenny Love….You never know when the bad times might be lurking just around the corner… It's nice to know there's still rewards there for those prepared to put the grafting in….Eh?...Eh?."

Alice helps Jenny to put her coat on after she has attended to her own. She frowns, not too pleased with Bert pessimistic comments. Noticing this he quickly continues.

"Still thank goodness there'll always be a place for flowers and the like….Eh?....Eh?....Do you want me to drop you off Jenny Love…. Or is that big ugly husband of yours picking you up?."

Jenny glances through the shop window towards the street outside.

"Well he said he would but you know what he's like when he gets together with that Woody and their beloved Bowling Green…They tend to lose track of time completely."

As she speaks a van screeches to a halt outside the shop.

"Oh….Speak of the Devil…I spoke too soon."

She glances down at her wrist watch.

"I must apologise to him….He's actually a minute or two early for a change."

Alice unlocks the door again. Eric gives her a passing kiss on the cheek as he makes his way towards Jenny. Placing his arms around her, adjusting his stance to allow for the lump, he kisses her full on the lips. They hug before Eric turns to speak to his Father.

"What all this then?......A Board Meeting is it?....Have I been sacked or something?."

The ladies laugh but Bert pretends to scold his Son.

"You want sacking....You're a bloody tearass you are....I've spotted you whizzing around the Town in that heap of a van....It's a wonder the bloody thing doesn't disintegrate it's that old the wings are flapping in the breeze."

Eric is defensive with the aid of some sarcasm.

"Rubbish!.....I hate you Coppers....Always on the look out for a pinch....I know bloody Gestapo..."

They all smile as he adds.

"You know very well that Dickie's van is the best we can do for the time being....It shouldn't be too long before we can afford a nice new....Or should I say a nice new to us....Mode of transportation Anyways we can't keep using Dickie's vehicle for ever...It's seen better days and all being fair....We should supply the replacement...It's our turn."

Bert looks and sounds quite serious.

"There's more urgent priorities than a new van Lad."

He casts an eye towards Jenny's lump.

"I foresee a considerable amount of expenditure in the very near future....What do you say Mother?....Eh?...Eh?."

Mrs McCabe does not wish to interfere.

"It has nothing to do with me Bert...I've got every confidence in your Son....Anyways there's no wonder he's having to move about rather swiftly....The poor Lad is working his fingers to the bone at the moment....And you know it Bert McCabe."

Bert back off immediately.

"All right Mother.....Keep your shirt on....Bloody hell."

He glances to see if he can expect any support from Jenny. She quickly looks away from him.

"She does tend to get very shirty sometimes....Don't you Dear?....Eh?....Eh?...Listen....I'm not trying to be over critical....All I want to say....Before we close this whole subject under discussion...Is.... It won't help anything at all if Stirling Moss here wraps himself and his van around a lamppost....Eh?...Eh?."

They are about to vacate the premises as Bert adds.

"And if you all keep on picking on me I won't take you out for a nice drink tonight....So there....Put that in your pipes and smoke it..."

No-one appears to be taking the slightest bit of notice of anything Bert has to say. Resenting the lack of response to his invitation, Bert is shaking his head in a gesture of disbelief.

"Bloody hell....Please....Don't get too excited will you?...Eh?...Eh?...You'd think I'd just offered to give you all a good hiding...Eh?...Eh?."

As the last one out, Eric switches off the lights and locks the shop door behind them.

* * *

"I think I'd rather have my leg off."

All appears to be peaceful and under control in Entwistle Ward at the Lapley Vale Cottage Hospital. It is mid-morning. Most of the Patients, at least all of those who are able, are seated on chairs alongside their beds. Those who are bed bound are propped up on their pillows reading or listening to the radio through their, rather primitive looking, head phones. Billy Dawes is, totally engrossed, reading the report on the Crown Bowling Green matches, contained in their weekly local newspaper, The Lapley Vale Examiner. The paper has just arrived, hot off the press. Only one between the whole Ward.

Excitedly, he looks up and across the Ward to where Arnie Brooks is quietly relaxing in his chair, awaiting his turn to read.

"I see my Team only managed to squeeze a very close victory out of the Constitutional Club....At home as well."

He is, clearly, teasing.

"Missing their star player you see Arnie."

Arnie, showing initial interest, realises that Billy is talking about himself. Arnie tuts, shaking his head. Billy goes on.

"Woody murdered their Captain...As usual....And Young Ricky.... Now there's a promising player if I ever saw one....Managed to notch up 15 cockeyed points against Old Johnny Westwood....Good going that....I mean to say....He's only a cockeyed learner Arnie....And Johnny has a pretty good reputation around the cockeyed greens."

Arnie nods an acknowledgment before he enquires.

"How did my lot get on playing against the Flying Horse Billy?."

Billy takes his time carefully checking through all the results printed in the paper. Arnie waits patiently for a reply. Billy's face lights up. He seems pleased to suddenly answer.

"Won....Beat the Flying Horse on their own cockeyed green...I dare say that's got you a bit worried Arnie....They appear to be doing better without you in the cockeyed Team...."

Billy laughs mockingly as Arnie enquires.

"How did the Buffaloes go on against the Free Masons Billy?."

Billy rustles the paper as he searches for the desired result. Mysteriously, he shakes his head as he reads.

"Doesn't say Arnie....Oh yes...Hang on....Here it is....The Free Masons won the Match....Yes home win for the Masons."

Arnie nods as he awaits further information. Billy puts the paper down for a moment to shout across to Arnie.

"Apparently they can't publish any of the details of the score....It was a cockeyed secret."

Arnie thinks for a moment and then has to choke a laugh as Billy throws his head back to laugh with gusto.

Their tranquillity is suddenly interrupted by the clatting sound of a metal trolley being pushed up the Ward by, a nervous looking, Nurse York. She give them a, fleeting, sickly smile as she loudly announces.

"Medication....Time for your medication please Gentlemen."

She is attempting to read a large chart on the top of the trolley as she is pushing it along. She suddenly trips over her own feet sending the trolley flying along, up the Ward, by itself. The Young Nurse falls over and skids along on her back across the, highly polished, floor. Her uniform rides up, almost over her waist, as she desperately tries to regain control of her movements. She exposes a full view of all her most intimate underwear to all present in the Ward. Sister Mead appears from nowhere to, casually, stop the trolley just before it is about to crash into the wall at the opposite end of the Room. Nurse York is struggling to get back to her feet. She is frantically pushing her clothing down with decent haste. Sister Mead is not, in the slightest bit, flustered.

"Ups a daisy Nurse York....Do try to be more careful please...Dear....Oh Dear....You are in a state....Try not to flash next week's washing Nurse....It could prove to be too much for some of our more poorly patients...."

Nurse York is blushing with acute embarrassment. Sister Mead soon snaps her out of it by saying, firmly.

"Now come along Nurse...Stop playing about...There's lots needing to be done....Put your hat straight as well....Come on."

Sister Mead examines the chart on the medicine trolley, the one partially responsible for Nurse York's little mishap, she quickly scans it.

"Yes here we are....Now you can attend to Mr Dawes and Mr Brookes with their injections."

Billy and Arnie both cringe. Nurse York heads towards Billy first. He protests.

"Hey!....Hang on just a cockeyed minute Missus....Er Sister...You are joking I hope....We are getting better now....We don't want to be suffering a cockeyed relapse."

Mead, ignoring Billy's comments, joins York at the bedside carrying a metal kidney dish. There are two rather big syringes in the dish. Billy is climbing back into his bed, looking for any sort of sanctuary. Mead remains positive as she addresses him.

"Now come along Mr Dawes....We're not going to be a little baby are we?."

York is poised, syringe in hand. Mead attempts to comfort Billy.

"Just a little prick Mr Dawes."

Billy is instantly offended. He protests.

"Who are you calling a little prick?....I'm not having this...Hey!...Watch what you're doing with that cockeyed needle."

Before Billy can utter another word, Mead turns him over, pulls down his pyjama bottoms and York sinks the syringe into the meaty part of Billy's bare backside. Billy goes rigid, yelling.

"J E S U S..... CHRIST!!."

Nurse York, uses her free hand to briskly rub his bottom before she gives it a playful smack. She pulls his pyjamas back into place and heads over towards Arnie's bed, where Sister Mead awaits her. Arnie is considering a bid for freedom but before he can get up to his feet, Sister Mead yanks him up into a standing position. Still grasping both of his hands she, snappily, remarks.

"Now then you're not going to make a fuss are you Mr Brookes?.... We don't want any further trouble today...Thank you very much indeed."

Before Arnie can reply, Mead quickly bends him over his bed. She pulls his pyjama bottoms down. York nips in to do the business with the needle. Arnie issues a yelp. Mead tugs his bottoms up and in a flash the two Angels of Mercy turn on their heels, heading back towards their trolley. Other patients in the Ward, realising that there is no escape, quietly await their turns with trepidation.

Both victims are feeling very sorry for themselves. Billy looks across to, the pathetic sight of, Arnie saying, with empathy.

"I'll tell you what Arnie....This is no place for a cockeyed sick person to be."

Rubbing his backside, Arnie nods in agreement.

The Ward has settled down again after every patient has had their turn with the Nurses. Billy notices the impressive figure of Bert McCabe, in full uniform, including his thick woollen overcoat, standing in the doorway at the top of the Ward. On seeing Billy, Bert waves and smiles broadly as he makes his way towards Billy's bed. As he moves there is a very distinctive clinking sound coming from Bert. He stops at the foot of the bed. Still smiling and now nodding as he greets his old friend.

"Billy....My Old Pal....How the Devil are you?....You remind me of someone who has just had his full pint knocked over...Cheer up Billy....How are you?....Eh?....Eh?."

Billy is delighted to see Bert. Smiling, he rubs his tender backside, trying not to sound too pathetic as he responds.

"Hello Bert....You've no idea...The things we are being put through in here....Honestly it's nobody business what the Nursing Staff are getting up to....It's cockeyed murder Bert....Cockeyed murder.... Anyways what are you doing in here at this time of day...It isn't visiting time for cockeyed ages yet."

Bert winks, touching the side of his nose with a Finger in a sinister manner.

"Special dispensation Billy....For the Police..."

He touches the side of his nose once again. Speaking in a lower tone.

"Say no more Billy Boy....The enormous pressures brought to bear upon me through my duties make it impossible for me to conform with the normal visiting arrangements designed for ordinary people... Hence the dispensation and here I am...Eh?....Eh?."

Before he takes a seat on Billy's bedside chair, Bert, sneakily, glances all around the Ward. He then discloses the reason for the chinking noises emanating from the region of his overcoat. He pulls two bottles of beer out of each of his pockets. Giving Billy a sly wink he whispers.

"Slip these into your locker Billy....Doctor's orders....Doctor McCabe that is....Eh?....Eh?....They will definitely do you good....Alf and Woody have sent them to you."

Billy is very pleased with the gifts. He caresses and kisses one of the bottles. Bert is happy to see Billy's reaction. He swiftly places the bottles inside the locker, closing the door. Another glance around the Ward reveals that they have not been observed by any one of significance. Bert sounds, quite, confident.

"Better than grapes eh Billy?....Eh?....Eh?."

Billy almost falls out of his bed ensuring that the locker door is secure. Bert casually shoves him back onto the bed.

"Thanks Bert....Thanks for the beer....They'll be like a cockeyed transfusion....I've almost forgotten what the taste of beer is like.... Thanks Pal....And thank the boys at the Club for me please...Cockeyed heroes that's what they are....Cockeyed heroes."

Bert spots Arnie. He waves as he greets him.

"Now then.....Hello Arnie...."

Arnie responds with a nod and a weak smile. Bert pretends to be shocked.

"Bloody hell they must have half the population of this Town in here….How are you Arnie?….How's your hooter?."

Arnie, very gingerly, touches the bandages on his face.

"Not too bad thanks Bert….Mustn't grumble….But sharing a Ward with Billy and….."

He breaks off to gesture around the Room with a wave of his hand.

"And all these other blokes as well….I'll tell you what Bert…It's a bit like a brass band tuning up in here at night….As soon as those lights go out…They start up….And I'll tell you this as well…I'm beginning to wish I'd left my nose blocked up."

Bert shakes his head and grins. Arnie continues.

"I didn't know when I was well off Bert."

Bert turns to Billy.

"See that Billy…Some people are never satisfied."

He addresses his next remarks to Arnie.

"You won't be moaning when you catch the scent of a nice piece of roast beef cooking….Or a warm steak and kidney pie…Eh?...Eh?."

Arnie reacts instantly.

"Some bloody chance of that in here Bert….I thought my Missus was a bad cook but at least her gravy usually manages to move around a little bit."

Billy grunts his agreement. Bert enquires.

"Don't they feed you well in here then?."

Billy blurts out a reply before Arnie can respond.

"Feed us well?.....Feed us cockeyed well?...I reckon you could get a better meal by emptying the cockeyed dustbins at the back of Billy the Chip's Fish Shop on Huddersfield Road."

For once, Billy and Arnie are in total agreement with each other. Bert shakes his head in a sympathetic fashion.

"Still….Never mind Boys….You'll both be going home soon."

Bert suddenly remembers that there are plans for a celebration in the Club on Billy's release.

"And then....Then...We will be enjoying a night to remember and a half...Eh?...Eh?....You'll have to invite Arnie Billy....Eh?...Eh?."

Billy is not too sure about that suggestion but he smiles briefly before he starts feeling sorry for himself again.

"Can't come soon enough as far as I'm concerned Bert....I've had more than enough of this cockeyed caper....I was just remarking to Arni8e before you came in that this is no place for a cockeyed sick person to be."

Bert is laughing, shaking his head as Billy sounds more positive and hopeful.

"All being well I should be out tomorrow Bert....Speaking personally....I cannot cockeyed wait."

Bert glances at his wristwatch. He stands up, buttoning his overcoat.

"I'd love to stay chatting to you pair all day but duty calls."

Billy is interested.

"Working on a big case are you Bert?."

Bert has the decency to look a little guilty as he lowers the tone of his voice.

"Well not exactly Billy....I've got to meet up with the Inspector.... For a spot of lunch and a game of bowls at the Flying Horse.."

Billy wishes he was going along with Bert. Bert attempts to be more serious. In his own inimitable way.

"It's all go in today's modern Police Service Billy my boy...I don't know how I manage to stand the pace at times....Eh?,,,Eh?."

Billy throws his head back to chortle loudly. Bert nods.

"Anyways....I really must take my leave of you....I will slip into the Club....Provided I can find the time with my busy schedule...I must warn Old Alf and all the others of your imminent re-appearance on the scene...Eh?...Eh?."

Billy's eyes glaze over as he dreams of the Club and all his friends and relatives. Bert waves goodbye to Arnie. He stands in the middle of the Ward, between the two beds, to deliver his leaving remarks.

"Now I want you both to promise me on your words of honour that you will stop yourselves from getting too fresh with all these pretty Nurses in here Boys....They say you must be ready for home when you start to fancy them...Eh?....Eh?."

Bert and Billy laugh but Arnie seems disgusted at the very thought. He really means what he is saying.

"Some bloody chance of that happening as far as I'm concerned Bert....Bloody hell fire....I think I'd rather have my leg off."

Bert pretends to be alarmed. His speaks loudly.

"Hush up Arnie....Watch what you're saying...They may be listening in....They have been known to do that sort of thing you know?....Eh?...Eh?."

Billy and Arnie wave a fond farewell as Bert, noticeably, laughing to himself, vacates the Ward, allowing for the return of peace and tranquillity.

* * *

"Good afternoon Reverend....
How nice to see you."

The Parish Vicar, Reginald Blackburn, and his new Curate, Jeremy Smith-Eccles, are engaged in conference in the Vestry/Office at the Parish Church of 'All Souls' Lapley Vale.

For a welcome change, the Vicar is in excellent form. He is delighted that his young protégé is, at last, showing signs that he is, after all, capable of carrying out his duties without being, utterly, accident prone as well as, naturally, naïve and gullible. His delight is mixed with a tiny element of pleasant surprise, as he passes a large ledger type book and a thick file of papers across his desk into the waiting hands of his proud looking Curate. His high level of excitement is responsible for his slight impediment, emitting the involuntary whistle when pronouncing certain words, becoming over active. Jeremy's familiarity with Reginald means that he does not even notice this unfortunate handicap, although many people might find it quite bizarre, distracting or even very amusing. (As a reminder pronouncing anything beginning with the letters 'C' or 'S' causes him the biggest problem.)

"Well....I must say that does seem to be most satisfactory Jeremy... The way things are progressing we should very soon be in a happy position when we can engage the necessary skilled craftsmen with a view to the commencement of the most urgent work desperately needing attention on the aged roof of our beloved Church...I am very impressed by the way you have presented the accounts to me for my inspection...It has been an arduous task gathering together such an enormous sum of capital but I was confident that with maximum effort from everyone concerned we would eventually succeed and…Of course.…In the long term I was convinced that the Lord would provide…"

Both men, clasp their hands together before they avert their eyes in an upward direction, each smiling gratefully. Reginald coughs politely, before he continues, enthusiastically.

"I re-iterate Jeremy it has been a most challenging task raising such a large amount of money.…But.…Thanks to the many fund raising activities and many dedicated endeavours undertaken with zeal and steely determination by a number of individuals I think we are now beginning to see the light."

Jeremy is placing the book and papers inside his large open briefcase when he suddenly has a compelling urge to be humorous.

"I was under the impression that it was because we could see the light.…Through the roof.…That you were obliged to commence all these money raising ventures, appeals and activities in the first place Reginald."

His face distorts into a rarely seen smile. The Vicar stares at him, momentarily, then laughs in a deliberate manner. He slaps his thighs with both hands before expressing his appreciation for Jeremy's, surprising but most welcome, injection of humour.

"Oh by Jove Jeremy.…That's a good one.…I'll say."

Both men enjoy a moment of merriment. Reginald is also pleased to witness a marked improvement in Jeremy's attitude, confidence and his overall general demeanour.

"It is wonderful to see you perking up a little after some of the unfortunate setbacks and mishaps that have unfortunately come your way recently.…I must confess I was beginning to become a bit concerned about your general well being Jeremy.…I think it may be fair to remark that you have encountered more than your share of minor upsets and what have you in the past few months.…Still.…Well done with the accounts and very well done with your very amusing jest…Oh yes…Yes indeed….Very witty….Most amusing….Seeing the light through the roof eh?….Yes good one Jeremy."

They sit back to enjoy a few precious moments of jolly reflection, indulging themselves in some well deserved, if rather rare, self satisfaction.

Reginald lurches forward in his chair, indicating that he is ready to move on to some of the more mundane and pressing matters requiring further discussion between them. He adopts an encouraging tone as he speaks.

"Now I hope I can count upon you to call at Lapley Manor this afternoon Jeremy."

Jeremy sits forward on his chair, nodding eagerly.

"Fine…Excellent…Thank you Jeremy…Lady Lapley has long been a most generous benefactor to our little roof appeal fund…I cannot say how much her cheque will be made out for on this particular occasion but I can assure you that it will be for a substantial amount….Yes indeed….Her Ladyship's generosity knows no bounds when she is approached in an apt and suitable manner…."

Jeremy is starting to get a little dizzy because he continues to nod, vigorously and enthusiastically, at every word spoken by the Vicar. Reginald continues.

"She has specifically requested your attendance upon her today Jeremy…She not only wishes to hand over her cheque to you personally I think she also wishes to become better acquainted with you on a face to face basis."

Reginald is hoping that he has been able to impress upon Jeremy the vital importance of his mission without being too direct or intimidating. Jeremy, cautiously, nods and smiles, brimming with apparent confidence and earnest motivation.

"You may depend upon me Reginald."

Rising to his feet, he brushes down his cassock with both hands before he lifts up his rather heavy briefcase. He looks and sounds businesslike as he smiles, quite naturally for a change.

"And…Incidentally Reginald….Thank you for your offer to look over the sermon I have been preparing…I have prepared it now so I would appreciate you taking up your kind offer….I am sure that with your guidance and support I need not be apprehensive about my first attempt to go solo…So to speak."

The Vicar, smiling, is hopeful that a significant break through is, at long last, about to happen in the ongoing training experiences of his fledgling Cleric.

"Whenever it is ready for my perusal Jeremy…I don't need to remind you…I am sure…That there is no necessity for you to be hasty because time is on your side….We all have to learn."

Jeremy puts his briefcase down whilst he tightens the broad leather belt around his waist, worn over his cassock.

"Well thank you Reginald….I have worked rather hard upon the text and pray that it will meet with your approval….Well…Tempus fugit eh Reginald?…Our chatting merrily in this way will not replace even one of those defective slates upon our roof…If there is nothing else you wish to discuss Reginald?."

Reginald shakes his head.

"Right….Fine….I will now mount my trusty velocipede and make my way up to the Manor…."

The Curate places his bicycle clips around the bottom of his trouser legs. He picks up his briefcase as Reginald walks over to open the door for him.

"Good show Jeremy….That's the ticket….Incidentally…How are your motor car driving lessons coming along?."

Jeremy's head drops. He, swiftly, pulls himself together, trying to look and sound positive. He puts his case down again.

"I'm afraid I'm not finding them too easy Reginald…Mr Longfellow….My instructor….Is a very patient man and I feel sure I will be able to grasp the fundamental skills required under his expert tutelage….I am certainly willing to give it my best shot…I am extremely keen to transfer from my two wheels to the comfort of four."

He is about to take his leave when he turns to add.

"I find it all a little frustrating at the present time Reginald.... Mr Longfellow does seem to be extremely busy recently...I have been attempting to make contact with him in order to arrange my next lesson for quite some time now....I always miss him for one reason or another...Well...I mean to say his little car was only off the road for a short period after that unfortunate little accident I had with a tree...He did make quite a fuss about it...You remember Reginald?.... I mentioned it to you when it happened."

The Vicar nods sadly.

"I was attempting to carry out one of those manoeuvres he is teaching me....What was it?....Oh yes....The five point turn...That was it....It was hardly my fault Reginald....Indeed I was acting under Mr Longfellow's direct orders...He should have seen the tree on my behalf because I was finding it difficult enough to steer in a backwards motion without having to look where I was going as well."

Reginald appears to be stunned by Jeremy's, flippant, attitude. Jeremy emits a sickly sort of laugh as he adds.

"Still I think his insurance company will be very well equipped to deal with the results of these minor unavoidable mishaps... I dare say they probably expect a good many of them from learner drivers...Still Mr Longfellow does see some potential in me."

Reginald half smiles.

"Oh yes....He thinks I might be unique because in all the many years he has earned his living as a driving instructor he has never encountered anyone quite like me before....Stated that he thinks it must be impossible for anyone to be totally lacking in any sort of co-ordination...Really Reginald...He considers me to be his greatest challenge....He is sure I am a worthy of being identified as a complete 'Pratt'."

The Vicar appears to be shocked, causing the Curate to reassure him without delay.

"That's a technical word used by driving instructors Reginald....I had never heard it before....Apparently it means..."

Jeremy raises his hands to indicating a quote in the form of two inverted comas.

"A challenging yet nevertheless promising student."

Reginald can scarcely believe his ears. He stares into Jeremy's eyes in total disbelief. This causes Jeremy to emphasise his interpretation of the word 'Pratt' in finer detail.

"Really Reginald....I had to ask Mr Longfellow to explain the meaning to me....It was after he had referred to me as a 'Prize Pratt' on a number of occasions when I was having one of my really off days behind the wheel....He seemed a little embarrassed at first but then he realised that I was not familiar with many everyday terms of expression in this particular part of our beloved Country...He did assure me that it was not uncommon for instructors at one time or another to refer to some of their students as 'Pratt's'."

He smiles, shaking his head.

"He is quite a character my Mr Longfellow...Forever using strange and obscure Anglo Saxon words and expressions...At least that is what he calls them....I am looking forward to being able to place myself back in his most capable hands...He has explained that I will need to progress to his classification of 'Pillock'....That's another of his unique words Reginald... Before the day arrives when I might be ready to face a driving examiner in test conditions...."

Jeremy nods and smiles as he is leaving the room.

"Thank you and God Bless you Reginald."

Reginald is speechless. He remains, stunned, holding the door open for several minutes after the Curate had disappeared from his view.

* * *

Jeremy is at peace with the World as he cycles, slowly, along the, long, impressive, private drive leading up to Lapley Manor. His bicycle is one of those, elderly, 'Sit up and beg' machines. He holds his head up high, quietly, singing to himself.

"Onward Christian Soldiers."

As a safety precaution he has the bottom edges of his cassock drawn up and carefully tucked into the broad leather belt worn around his waist.

He is gathering a little speed as he passes a large clump of rhododendron bushes on his left side when, suddenly, a cock pheasant shoots out from the cover of the bushes across the drive directly into the Curate's path. Jeremy brakes and swerves. He manages to avoid a collision with the bird but in doing so he, together with the bicycle, disappears out of view into the thick undergrowth, accompanied by a loud scream.

After a few minutes Jeremy's head and shoulders appear from the midst of the bushes. He furtively glances up and then down the drive before he ducks down, disappearing from view again. He then emerges carrying his bicycle up over his head in order to clear of the foliage. He checks, once again that his accident has not be observed and, after ensuring that his machine is undamaged and roadworthy, he re-mounts, in a rather wobbly fashion. He manages to maintain his balance, enabling him to proceed on his journey along the drive. Thankfully, uninjured and able to, slowly, regain much of his composure, Jeremy is undoubtedly shocked. The carefree singing has ceased, his full concentration is now focussed on his riding.

At the end of the drive he reaches a large open courtyard, situated at the front of the Manor House itself. Jeremy glances all around scanning for any signs of life. He notices the Butler, in full morning dress, emerging from the large, very ornate, front doors. He descends a number of wide steps leading into the courtyard. Jeremy steers his bicycle towards him. He comes to a stop with a slight squeal from his brakes. The arrogant looking Butler does not seem to be much impressed by the Curate's manner of arrival. He raises his hand in front of his mouth, coughs, saying in an exaggerated and clearly false tone.

"The Reverend Jeremy Smith-Eccles I presume?."

Jeremy nods vigorously, causing him to wobble on his stationary bicycle.

"Her Ladyship is expecting you Your Reverence."

The Curate smiles rather weakly.

"She has instructed me to take you directly to her."

Jeremy removes the tails of his cassock from his belt. He attempts to brush himself down whilst holding his bicycle but almost loses his balance. The snobbish Butler is now, deliberately, looking down his, red, bulbous, nose at the Curate.

"Shall I arrange for your….."

He glances up and down at the bicycle with an undisguised air of disgust.

"Your…Ahem….Transport….To be…Ahem….Parked for you Your Reverence?."

Jeremy looks at his bicycle and then at the pompous Butler. He manages to blurt out his reply.

"Yes…Well No….Not really…Oh how kind….Do you think it might be in order for me to leave it propped up against the wall?.

Although he is being courteous and polite, the Butler is clearly unimpressed to the extent of outright disapproval with the Curate and his mode of transport. He actually snaps, without seeming to sound too offensive.

"As you wish Sir….Be kind enough to follow me if you please…."

He steps off heading towards a very large, manicured, lawn at the side of the Main Building.

"Her Ladyship is taking advantage of the clement weather by relaxing on the lawn near to the kitchen garden….Follow me."

The Butler is striding out briskly. Jeremy is struggling to keep up with him because he is attempting to remove his bicycle clips on the move. Walking around a neat clump of well established trees and bushes the Curate sees Lady Lapley seated on one of the highly ornate metal chairs positioned around a cast iron table.

Lady Lapley is quite elderly. She is stylishly elegant, projecting a serene ambience. She is wearing a large white, wide brimmed, hat, which compliments her, expensive and dressy, floral summer frock. The sunlight is glinting off the jewels encrusted on her necklace and matching bracelet.

On becoming aware of the approach of the two men she places her book on the table, allowing her to pay full attention to imminent their arrival. The Butler stops abruptly, clearing his throat to make an announcement in clear, audible, tones.

"The Reverend Smith-Eccles Your Ladyship."

Smiling in a friendly, welcoming, fashion Lady Lapley, rather limply, extends her right hand. She speaks with a refined and cultured accent.

"Good Afternoon....How do you do Reverend?....How nice to meet you at last."

They shake hands gently. Lady Lapley then addresses her remarks to the Butler.

"Thank you Smithers....We are ready to take tea now."

Smithers almost doubles over bowing before he turns and walks away. As he heads towards the Manor House, Lady Lapley makes a gesture with her, gloved, hand. She addresses the Curate.

"Won't you please be seated Reverend."

Jeremy is about to sit on one of the other chairs when he is suddenly aware of a large golden Labrador dog bounding around the side of the walled kitchen garden heading straight towards him. The Curate is alarmed and startled, Lady Lapley calls out to the animal.

"Bruce....BRUCE!.....BRUCE!...Heel boy!....Down boy!."

The over excited dog pays her no heed as, with his tail wagging furiously, he leaps up at the terrified Curate. Bruce is a large beast and his weight is pushing Jeremy back towards the table. Almost bending over backwards across the table, Jeremy is really struggling to control Bruce. Managing to roll out from under the animal for a moment, Jeremy breaks free. Lady Lapley anxiously shouts to him.

"Kick his balls Reverend!....Kick his balls!."

Without hesitation Jeremy lands his right foot between Bruce's back legs. The dog yelps and runs away at an even faster rate than the speed he had approached them in. The dog can still be heard whimpering as Jeremy attempts to recover from his dishevelled state. Lady Lapley, rapidly, surveys the scene before, shocked, she exclaims.

"No....I didn't mean those ball's I meant the other one's lying over there on the lawn...The one's he chases."

She gestures in the direction of two colourful rubber balls on the grass.

The Curate immediately realises the gravity and possible consequences of his misunderstanding. His obvious distress leaves him totally speechless as the pathetic sound of the dog howling can still be clearly heard.

* * *

Back in the Vestry/Office at the Parish Church, Reginald Blackburn, the Vicar is leaning over his desk desperately speaking into the telephone. He is most concerned. He holds the telephone receiver to his right hand and he has a finger from his left hand in his ear as an aid to clarity of hearing. His whistling affliction is in overdrive.

"Yes....Certainly...Well I must confess I was worried about you.... Yes....Well...You seemed to be in excellent spirits when you set off on your bicycle to make the appointed and most welcome visitation upon the Lady of Lapley....Yes....Oh were you?.....Hmmmmmm..... Perhaps it would be best if you have a little lie down then....Yes....Well if you are feeling so out of sorts a reflective rest should be beneficial....I became concerned when Lady Lapley's Head gardener called here with the cheque from her Ladyship....Hmmmmmmmmm....Well really Jeremy I must say that the cheque is made out in a very generous sum indeed....Much in excess of expectations...Obviously I am delighted by that....Hmmmmmm....Well I think you may be doing yourself a grave disservice here Jeremy...I do not think she would have seen fit to be so benevolent if you had not made a good impression of yourself upon her....Jeremy....JEREMY!....Are you still there?...."

Reginald bangs the telephone earpiece on the flat of his hand. He then shakes it before he returns it to his ear.

"I'm sorry Jeremy but there seems to be a whining noise on this line....Perhaps it is what I have heard people refer to as atmospheric interference....Hello....HELLO!....Hello....Are you still there?....

Jeremy!....JEREMY!....Oh yes....There you are....It is merely that I became somewhat confused when I read the hand written note Her Ladyship was kind enough to place inside the envelope containing the cheque."

He shuffles all the papers on the top of his desk until he finds the actual note. He holds it out in front of him so that he can read and refer to it directly.

"Yes...Here we are....Her Ladyship sincerely hopes that you are all right Jeremy."

He pauses, smiling as he reflects.

"She is such a caring person...Now this is the portion of the letter I find rather confusing....She says that they eventually managed to find....Er....Bruce....He is fine and is not suffering any permanent ill effects...Now tell me....Does this make any sense to you?.... Hmmmmm...Well I have to admit I do not know who Bruce is Jeremy....But Her Ladyship states that he is well and taking everything into consideration I must say that it would appear that your venture has turned out to be a good job well done....Hello....HELLO!.... Jeremy!....Are you still there?...Those whining noise have returned on the line once again...Oh dear."

This time Reginald knocks the receiver on the top of his desk. Retuning it to his ear. He is now quite frustrated.

"Jeremy....Oh there you are Jeremy.....Hmmmm...."

As he listens he moves around his desk to open a deep drawer. He pulls out a full bottle of vodka, placing it on the desk. He is caressing the bottle with his free hand whilst listening to the Curate.

"Hmmmmm....Incidentally Jeremy...I think I may have found the solution to combat your tendency to become apprehensive.... You know?....For when you deliver that first sermon of yours?... Hmmmmm....Well as I have related to you before Jeremy on several occasions it is not my intention to rush you into doing anything until you feel competent in your own skills....Hmmmm...No....No I do not think I could possibly describe this remedy as divine intervention.... No....That would be asking quite a lot....Hmmmmm...No....Oh no let me assure you categorically Jeremy....I have faith and confidence in you and your eventual ability........You will have to trust my judgement....Hmmmmm....Well in me and the Lord....Hmmmmmm....Yes....Are you feeling somewhat happier now Jeremy?. I think I detect an improvement in you there....Please try not to worry too much I think worry may be the root cause of many of your problems...Yes....Well you take that well earned rest now Jeremy....Hmmmm...Goodbye and God Bless for now....Yes....Oh Jeremy before you go...I almost forgot....Good news....I did manage to speak to Mr Longfellow....Your instructor chappie...Yes....By telephone....He promised me he will continue to provide you with his expert driving tuition...Hmmmm...Yes....But he did emphasise that he was only prepared to do so wearing a crash helmet....Ha....Ha....I feel certain he was just having his little jest Jeremy...Don't you?....Jeremy....JEREMY!....Are you still there?....That peculiar noise is back on this line again...Anyways I hope you can still hear me....Mr Longfellow told me he would be in touch with you tomorrow....Yes....So you get on with your little rest now...Yes.....Bye....Bye for now....Sweet dreams....Bye Bye Jeremy."

Reginald replaces the telephone receiver. He picks up the Vodka bottle. He stares at the bottle for a few moment before he throws his head back to state up to the ceiling. Reginald has his eyes closed tight, praying under his breath.

* * *

"It's great to see old Billy back in circulation again."

As the time approaches ten o'clock in the evening, Billy Dawes finds himself the centre of attraction in the crowded Lapley Bowling and Social Club Clubroom. Discharged from the Cottage Hospital, he is thoroughly enjoying the, promised, celebration taking place in his honour. Billy is seated at a table in the middle of the room with his Wife, Bert and Alice McCabe, Eric and Jenny McCabe and Mavis Green. Woody is occupying his usual stool at the side of the bar with Norman Smith and Eddie Brown his closest friends.

Although the clientele appear to be in several individual Small groups there is a constant flow of banter being exchanged between those seated at the tables and others at the bar. Ralph, the Chairman, Vic Callow, Bernie Price and Charlie Walsh are, as usual, seated at the bar opposite Woody and his friends. Alf, the Steward and Denise, the Barmaid are busy serving drinks from behind the bar.

A discernable aura of anticipation is evident throughout the Clubroom. A delicious aroma emanates from the kitchen where a huge, home made, pastry crusted, meat and potato pie is warming in the oven. This simple dish is an must at any gatherings for any sort of celebration in the Clubroom. Served with a generous helping of mushy peas and pickled red cabbage, in separate dishes, as an added extra, this offering is preferred by the good folk of Lapley Vale to anything the Ritz Hotel could possibly provide. The plates and cutlery are provided by the Club with the Member's Ladies ever willingly to accept all responsibility for the dishing up and serving of the food. They also end up dealing with all the washing up afterwards.

Billy appears to be the worse for drink and his Wife is, quite naturally, concerned about him. She politely, yet firmly, warns him.

"Billy....You will remember what Doctor Berry said about taking it easy won't you?....At least for a while....Until you get your bearings back after that long stay in the Hospital."

Considering himself to be in a strong, privileged, position as the guest of honour, Billy, for a change, is quite defiant. However his brave display only extends to him picking up his glass, taking a deliberately long drink from it, no actual words. Jenny, heavily pregnant, has orange juice, Nan has a port and lemon and Alice McCabe is nursing a small sweet sherry. Jenny supports her Nan, appealing to her Granddad.

"Nan's right Granddad....You don't want to end up back in that Hospital again do you?...."

This comment instantly hits a nerve. Billy stares at Jenny and then at his Wife and the others. His tone reveals genuine and heartfelt sincerity.

"I think I'd rather have a cockeyed good hiding than spend another cockeyed second in that cockeyed place."

He then appeals to Bert, who is keeping a low profile.

"I told you Bert didn't I?....It was no place for a sick person to be in there....Didn't I?....."

Bert smiles, nodding his agreement as Billy reiterates.

"Cockeyed murder in there it was....COCKEYED MURDER!."

Jenny latches onto his remarks.

"All the more reason for you to take things easy for a while...Please Granddad."

Billy is about to protest but realises that Jenny means well. He, rather sulkily, drops his head as she adds.

"Don't forget....You've got to have your supper yet....Leave some room for that eh?...."

This comment snaps Eric out of his quiet supporting role.

"Just wait till you taste Mavis's meat and tatter pie Billy…"

Eric rubs his stomach as he licks his lips. He turns to, the now blushing, Mavis, who swiftly adds.

"Not to mention the mushy peas and red cabbage to go with it.… Kindly provided by Alice.…Do you think it's time to start serving up Alice?.…If that pie rests in the oven for too long it may start drying out.…That'll never do will it?."

Alice and Jenny rise to their feet. Mavis, concerned, attempts to intervene.

"Hang on a minute Jenny.…Why don't you stay here to keep an eye on the men?.…Alice and I can manage."

Jenny is haughty as she dismisses Mavis's suggestion.

"I'm not an invalid you know?.…I want to do my share."

Realising that Jenny would be hurt if she is left out, the two older women concede. Mrs McCabe, smiling, shakes her head.

"O.K.….O.K. Jenny love.…You win.…But you're not allowed to lift anything heavy.…And that's an order."

Woody has perceived the movement taking place at the table. He shouts.

"Good show Ladies.…Time to get the old feed bags on…I don't know about the guest of honour but my belly thinks my bloody throat's been cut."

Winking to Eddie and Norman he directs his next remarks to Billy.

"We're actually using the money we collected for your wreath Billy.…When we thought you were going to snuff it we had a whip round…It's a shame to waste the money so we're about to gorge ourselves on the biggest and best pie you've ever seen in your life."

He shouts to Alf, still dashing around behind the bar.

"Isn't that right Alf?.…"

Alf smiles as he carries on serving, confirming Woody's words.

"Let me say this.…The old legs on that oven have been placed under the most severe pressure this very evening."

He shouts across to Mavis and the Ladies, who have reached the kitchen door.

"Mavis....Can you manage love?....I can spare Denise if you need a lift."

Mavis is about to reject Alf's offer but sees the willing look on Denise's face. She can tell that the barmaid really wants to help the Ladies. Mavis replies.

"Well thank you kindly Sir....Yes....Thanks Alf....The more the merrier....The sooner we get dished up is the sooner we can clear away again afterwards....Marvellous isn't it?."

Turning the Ralph and Vic she, politely, asks.

"Can some of you Boys fix up a nice firm table for us just outside the kitchen door please Ralph...We'll need it to do all the dishing up in an orderly fashion."

Ralph is delighted to respond, positively.

"Certainly my Dear....Say no more....Charlie....Bernie."

In view of the facts that the aroma being emitted from the kitchen smells really delicious and tempting that they are all ready to eat there are many volunteers and the task is soon completed.

In no time at all the huge pie and bowls of mushy peas and dishes of red cabbage are ready for distribution. Mavis gives a nod to Ralph, who is poised, ready to make the announcement.

"Ladies and Gentlemen please....Here we go now....Can we form a nice orderly queue on the left please....Billy....Come along Billy.... As guest of honour you must be served first...Come on....Let's get stuck in whilst it's still piping hot....Come along now..."

Bert and Eric nudge Billy. He rises to his feet. There is a round of applause and some cheering as Billy makes his way to the servery. Touched by the response, Billy starts to wave his hand, then both hands. He almost trips over a chair but is rescued by his two close attendants. The whole Clubroom soon, suddenly, falls strangely silent as refreshments are taken and enjoyed by one and all.

The Ladies are busy clearing away and washing up as Woody slips off his stool to walk across to the table where Billy, Bert and Eric are seated. Bert smiles as he sits back on his chair to rub his stomach.

"If that's an example of your Wife's cooking Woody…You'll soon have a belly on you like a poisoned pup….Eh?….Eh?."

Woody smiles politely as Eric chips in.

"And that's not all Dad….You want to taste her scones."

Woody feels very proud. He pretends to carefully study the current state of Billy. He sounds alarmed.

"Bloody hell Lads…..I'm not too sure about Billy and those mushy peas….It's a bit like asking for trouble if you ask me….Like loading the gun…Whistling up the wind you might say."

They laugh as Billy responds, casually.

"Look….Don't you worry about me Woody….That was the best cockeyed meal I've tasted since I was taken bad….Now I can see how Mavis managed to get a old confirmed bachelor like yourself up that cockeyed aisle."

Everyone around them roars with laughter.

Bert notices that most of their glasses are empty. He pretends to be upset and alarmed.

"Christ…..Look at this….A crisis….We've only run out of Ale again…..Same again is it Lads?."

Woody intervenes.

"Hold onto your horses Bert…It's my shout…You've been seeing to Mavis's drinks all night….Fair's Fair."

Bert, about to protest weakly, allows Woody to head back to the bar. He calls out after him.

"How kind Woody….How kind…I'll give you a lift with the glasses….Eh?…Eh?."

Woody is at the bar as the Ladies come out of the kitchen, switching off the light behind them. Vic nudges Ralph who immediately springs to his feet.

"Gentlemen.....Ladies and Gentlemen please....Would you please show your appreciation to Mavis and her happy band of helpers in the traditional Club manner...I Thank you."

There is an instant round of raucous and prolonged applause and cheering. Mavis and the others modestly wave as they make their ways back to their tables. Ralph manages to clap longer than anyone else before he adds.

"Thank you....And once again....I thank you."

Sitting back on his stool, Vic remarks to him.

"What an excellent repast....I do hope I have not overdone my eating at the expense of my drinking."

Bernie, as quick as ever.

"I bloody hope not Vic....It's your shout."

Vic is ordering the drinks as Charlie nudges Ralph.

"I'd like to witness the day that anything put Bert McCabe off his drink....Or Billy Cockeye if it comes to that."

Laughing and nodding his agreement, Ralph responds.

"You're right there Charlie....Fair comment...You have to admit though....It's great to see old Billy back in circulation again....And looking as fit as a cockeyed butcher's dog....Eh?.

The Ladies arrive back as Woody places a tray full of drinks on the table. He is more polite than usual.

"I had to assume you were all having the same again Ladies...I do hope that will be acceptable to you....Thank you awfully much I'm sure."

Bert, assisting by passing the drinks around the table, comments with genuine sincerity.

"Well Boys....Mavis....And Ladies and all....I have to say that you've done us all proud here this evening....I think it would be fair to say without fear of contradiction that...That was the finest supper we've seen in here for many a year...And in here that's saying something... Eh?.....Eh?.."

Nan Dawes is looking at Billy. His eyes are starting to roll in his head. He is displaying a silly, vacant, smirk on his face.

"I would hasten to agree with you there Bert....But....Take a look at the guest of honour.....I think it would be most sensible for me to take him home now."

Billy would have protested but he is now incapable of forming the words correctly so he just settles for looking disgusted instead. Eric shares Nan's concerns.

"Can I borrow your car keys please Dad?....I'll see to taking them home....I've been taking it easy all night....Still sober."

Bert rummages through his pockets as Alice comments.

"I think it's time we all started to make tracks...We don't want to spoil what has been a splendid evening."

The Ladies agree but Bert does not seem too convinced, as Alice continues.

"Look....Ricky can take us home first and then he can call back for his Dad?....No point in us all being squashed together is there?."

She notices a sneaky smiles spreading across Bert's face. Instantly, she turns on him.

"And that's not an invitation for you to stop out all night Bert McCabe....Ricky needs to be up first thing in the morning so bear that in mind will you?."

Bert nods in a sickly fashion as he hands the keys to Eric. This memorable evening is still far from over for some of the main party.

* * *

"Why me?........WHY ME!!!!?."

Amongst the best known and respected persons in the whole of Lapley Vale is Doctor Malcolm Berry. He has practised in the same place in the Town ever since he initially arrived, as a young man, from the University of Liverpool with his newly gained M.D. many years before.

He is intimately known to many of the local families. Over the years he has become their friend as well as their medical practitioner. He has been privy to many little secrets. A thoroughly trusted and appreciated man, he is now in his late fifties. He has a sturdy, possibly tending towards the rotund, domineering appearance and impressive presence. He is no stranger to the Pubs and Clubs in the area although he would not be regarded as a regular at any of the many haunts he has been know to visit. His fondness for strong liquor over a long period of time has resulted in him sporting a bright red face and boozer's nose, although these are partially concealed by his large bushy moustache.

A brass plaque bearing the name, Doctor M.T. Berry M.D. is exhibited on the wall next to a door with a, large and prominent, sign over the top saying, 'SURGERY'. The plaque has weathered considerably over the years despite the regular attention it has received from his cleaner, Nellie Dawson and her trusty tin of 'Brasso'.

Anyone, vaguely, familiar with Doctor Berry is aware that he can be quite fearsome if upset. He has been described on more than one occasion as having a short fuse. The generally held view in the area is the Doctor does most of his drinking behind closed doors. This is due to frequent occasions in the past when, idiots, have approached him with their various ailments when he has been in Pubs or Clubs relaxing, trying to get away from his professional environment for a little while.

Doctor Berry is seated behind his desk in his Consulting Room. His half moon spectacles are perched on the end of his nose. His stethoscope is draped around his neck. His concentration is focussed on what he is writing on the patient's card. His patient, Charlie Walsh, is behind a screen getting dressed, after being examined. There clinical appearance to the room. There is a rather bland looking examination table next to the screened off area. A small wash basin and toilet are situated in an alcove set into the corner of the smallish room.

The Doctor is glancing over his notes as he addresses Charlie, who is still out of his sight behind the screen.

"You say you're feeling generally out of sorts and lacking in your normal energy levels....Is that correct Charlie?."

Charlie emerges into view, pulling on his jacket. He walks over to sit on the patient's chair, which faces the Doctor's. Settling himself down he replies.

"Yes that's it Doctor....I just don't seem to have either the energy nor the inclination to do very much at this present moment in time.... Nothing specific just jaded really."

The Doctor sits back in his chair, screwing the top back onto his fountain pen. Placing the pen on his desk in front of him, he looks deeply into Charlie's eyes as he speaks.

"Well....I've given you a full examination Charlie...And...Well... I'm afraid I can't find anything wrong with you at all."

Charlie is puzzled. He shakes his head as the Doctor adds.

"I think we'll just have to put it down to the booze."

Charlie stands up to shake hands with the Doctor. He finishes fastening his jacket as he walks towards the door. He sounds rather patronising as he speaks.

"Well…Thank you Doctor….Don't worry about it too much…I can always call back when you're not pissed."

The Doctor, who has been nodding and smiling, suddenly changes his expression. His annoyance is obvious in his tone as he replies.

"When I'm not pissed?....When….I!....AM NOT PISSED!...You cheeky bastard Charlie…..Go on….Piss off you cheeky bastard…Go on stop wasting my valuable time….Go on!....Before I sling you out of here."

Genuinely shocked by the Doctor's reaction Charlie decides not to prolong the consultation as he swiftly leaves the room.

Doctor Berry is muttering to himself as he reaches forward to pick up his little brass bell, used to indicate to those waiting that he is ready for the next patient. He rings the bell in a vicious way, continuing to mumble under his breath.

He hears a faint rapping noise. He looks up to see Wilf Wood's head appearing around the partially opened door. Wilf is a local plumber in his mid to late forties. He is a well liked and respected man mainly because of his good manners, honesty and politeness, which he readily extends to everyone he encounters at all times. Wilf appears to be nervous, having heard the Doctor's raised voice and witnessed Charlie, hastily, quitting the premises.

"Er….Good Morning….Er….Doctor Berry….I….Er."

Doctor Berry looks up. He realises that Wilf appears to be rather self-conscious and uncomfortable. Wilf, hesitantly, continues.

"You did say you would fix me up with that medical examination I require for my life insurance policy this morning Doctor…But I can come another time if it's not convenient…."

The fact that Malcolm Berry receives a nice little cheque from the insurance companies for carrying out these type of examination is responsible for snapping him out of his bad mood almost immediately. He greets Wilf in a, calm, friendly fashion.

"Yes….Of course….Good Morning Wilf….No problem….Have you brought the forms with you….I have to fill them in as we go along…So I'll need them before we can start."

Wilf, nodding eagerly, pulls a large envelope from his jacket pocket. The Doctor gestures him to be seated as he passes the papers across the desk.

"Yes....We'll soon see to this Wilf....How are you feeling in yourself?....Any problems I should know about?....Feeling fine as usual I hope."

Wilf, still slightly tense, replies.

"Oh yes...Thank you Doctor....Never felt better actually...Fit as a flea on a butcher's dogs back...You know me well enough."

Wilf grins, nervously, as Doctor Berry picks up a small fluted glass from the top of his desk. He points towards the alcove, where the wash basin and toilet are situated, as he puts the glass in Wilf's hand.

"Yes that's fine....I thought you would be Wilf...Just step over there and pass me some water in this please."

Wilf responds instantly. He walks over to the alcove where he looks closely at the glass. He glances back to see the Doctor is busy ticking boxes on his insurance forms. He coughs politely as he enquires.

"Hot or cold Doctor?..."

Malcolm looks up from the forms to see the hapless Wilf standing in the alcove, holding the empty glass in his hand. Shaking his head in disbelief he is desperately trying not to lose his temper for the second time in quick succession.

"Hot or Cold?....Hot or bloody cold?....Christ Wilf....What are you going on about at all?....Just piss in the glass will you?."

Wilf realises what he is required to provide although he wonders, for a moment, why the Doctor did not ask him properly in the first place. Wilf turns towards the wash basin to fill the glass as prescribed. Doctor Berry exhales loudly, looks up to the ceiling and in a pitiful voice, pleads.

"Why me?............WHY ME?....."

* * *

"Come on give us a kiss and lend us a shilling."

Bert and Eric McCabe with their wives Alice and Jenny are dressed in their Sunday best clothes enjoying a meal out at the up market Vaughan Arms Hotel. The Vaughan deserves the reputation it has earned with the locals in Lapley Vale as the best place to eat out in the whole surrounding District. The high prices charged are a true reflection of the quality of the food and service provided.

Bert is looking particularly pleased with himself as they sit around a table for four in the quiet, secluded, annex of the well appointed restaurant area. Bert is piling on his natural charm as he addresses Alice.

"Well Mother…..Have you enjoyed your little birthday treat?...That is…Up to now of course….We haven't finished yet….Eh?...Eh?"

Alice smiles and nods as Bert is in danger spoiling the developing ambience by overdoing the charm offensive.

"Nothing would be too much for you my Dear…..Now would you like me to go to the bar to get you another nice little drink?."

Alice is flattered if not slightly overcome with all the attention her Husband is lavishing upon her. She replies coyly.

"Oh I don't know Bert…..I think I might have already exceeded my normal limit of alcohol….That wine we had with the meal was really delicious….Just right for the food we were eating too."

Taking her right hand in his, Bert gently pats it as he Speaks to her tenderly.

"Look Mother....It is your special day today....If you can't have a little extra treat on your Birthday I don't know when you can....Eh?....Eh?."

Eric and the heavily pregnant Jenny are rather embarrassed by Bert's open display of attention and affection. They are also a little surprised. Eric attempts to encourage his Mother.

"Come on Mum....Dad's right....It's your day....Have another drop of that nice sherry you always enjoy....Anyways....It's my turn to pay for the drinks.....Dad hasn't let me put my hand in my pocket all night so far...."

Bert, nodding, instantly agrees to accept the offer.

"Alright then Ricky.....How kind....How very kind....I think I can just about manage to force another pint or two down....And what about our Jenny....Ricky is having the annual public opening of his wallet so what can you be tempted to have?."

Jenny glares at her empty orangeade glass, shaking her head.

"Oh I'd better stick to soft drinks I think Dad....I've already been naughty taking a glass of wine with the meal."

Eric places his arm around his Wife's shoulders. He attempts to emulate the performance of his, well practised, Father.

"You heard what Dad said Jenny love....Nothing is too good for the Ladies of the McCabe family."

Giggling as she snuggles up to him she replies.

"Well thank you kindly Sir....But I still want an orangeade if you please."

She pats her very large and protruding lump.

"Got to think about baby."

Eric kisses her on the cheek before he rises to his feet. His Father gets up with him.

"I'll give you a hand with the drinks Son....Anyways....I haven't managed to have a quick word with Keith yet...You know?...Keith the Landlord of this fine establishment?."

The two Ladies are sitting back with expressions of contentment clearly identifiable on their happy faces as their Husbands leave them to make their way to the bar.

As the evening progresses several more drinks have been purchased and consumed. They have all had a wonderful night out at the Vaughan. Bert and Eric are merrily chatting away to each other as Jenny, who appears to be experiencing a little discomfort, whispers something into Alice's ear. Alice's reaction is sharp. She turns to speak to the men.

"Right come on Bert Ricky….We have to go."

Bert glances at his wrist watch and then both men, in unison, check the time showing on the clock on the wall. He sounds stunned.

"What on earth are you going on about Mother?...Look it's not even closing time yet….Christ it's only quarter to ten…Have you gone raving mad or what?....Eh?...Eh?."

Eric is nodding in agreement with his Father until he notices the look on Jenny's face. Alice leans forward to speak to them calmly and distinctly.

"Bert….Ricky….We have to leave right away….Jenny has started to have contractions."

Shocked, both men stare at Jenny, instantly realising what this means, as Alice quickly adds.

"Yes that's right….Baby has decided to make an appearance."

Bert and Eric both spring to their feet. Alice attempts to calm them both down.

"Look don't panic…Let's just leave in a nice and easy fashion…. Take us back to the house first please."

Eric cannot hide his rising state of panic.

"The house?.....Back to the house?.....What do you mean Mother….. Surely we should be going to the Hospital."

Alice is still trying her best to calm him down.

"Look we don't require your opinion on the matter just yet Ricky… Stop panicking….There's loads of time to go before Baby arrives…. Let's get back to your house where you can telephone the Hospital and

we can gather Jenny's things together...Leave it to the Ladies please....
Now let's get moving....Right away."

Bert and Eric get on either side of Jenny to assist her out of her chair and on their way out to the car park.

* * *

Eric is standing at the foot of the stairs back at their home. He is wearing his flat cap and overcoat. He sounds agitated as he shouts upstairs.

"Right....O.K.....I've rung the Hospital and they are expecting us....Mother!.....Jenny!....What the hell are you doing?."

On hearing water slashing, he bounds up the stairs, two at a time. He peers into the bathroom to see Jenny sitting in the bath with his Mother kneeling at the side, gently bathing her.

Eric can hardly believe his eyes. He is astonished.

"Christ Mother!....What the hell are you doing?....Dad's got the engine running outside ready for the off....Let's go!."

Alice rises to her feet to usher her Son clear of the bathroom. She adopts a calm tone, hoping to calm Eric down a little.

"Look Ricky I wish you men would just leave things to us... Good Lord I've never seen such panic...Now Ricky...Go downstairs and wait in the car for us...Go on....We won't be long."

Eric is speechless but he allows himself to be steered towards the top of the stairs. He is white with worry as he, slowly, descends the steps.

* * *

Bert McCabe's Ford Prefect saloon car screeches to halt on the tarmac outside the entrance into the Maternity Ward at Lapley Vale Cottage Hospital. The front passenger door flies open immediately the vehicle stops. Eric leaps out to open the rear passenger door. Jenny, sitting with Alice's arm around her shoulders, is breathing very deeply and deliberately. With assistance from Bert, Eric manages to carefully extradite Jenny's swollen body out of the back of the car. Alice takes Eric place, supporting Jenny, as Eric dashes up to the closed doors to press the emergency bell. Bert and Eric both remain in a state of near panic but the Ladies appear to be taking everything in their stride. The door is opened, almost instantly, Sister Murphy peers out into the gloom. She completely ignores Eric to gesture an invitation for Bert and Alice to bring Jenny inside. As they carefully guide Jenny towards the open door, Sister Mead directs them.

"That's right….Gently does it now….You'll be alright now my Dear….Come inside….Nice and easy."

Sister Murphy shoves Bert out of his position to assist Alice in supporting Jenny. The men are very much on edge but all three women are handling the situation in a calm and controlled manner. Murphy steers Jenny towards a wheelchair which had been placed just inside the door. They very gently lower Jenny into the chair. Alice brushes her hand across Jenny's hair and kisses her on the cheek. They hug for a moment. Jenny catches a glimpse of the two, helpless looking, men which almost causes her to burst out laughing, however a sharp contraction puts paid to that. Murphy grabs both handles on the wheelchair as she swings it around. She speaks with urgency and obvious authority.

"Right….Say goodnight to your family….You've got some hard work in front of you before this night is through my Dear….Let's not delay…Come along."

Jenny smiles weakly as a distraught appearing Eric moves towards her. Even his voice seems strained as he addresses Sister Murphy in a rather pathetic way.

"I thought I might be able to stay for a while Missus…Er Nurse…I mean Sister."

Murphy dismisses his comment with contempt.

"You just take yourself off home and kindly leave things to those people who happen to know what they are doing….Say Goodnight if you please….We must move on."

Alice hugs and kisses Jenny.

"Goodnight Jenny love....Don't worry sweetheart....Everything will be fine....You're in good hands."

Murphy is starting to push her away. Jenny stretches out her hand to grasp Eric's. Seeing how upset he is, she ties her best to console him, as Murphy pauses momentarily.

"Go home now Ricky...There's nothing for you to do now....You did your bit a few months ago."

Her attempt to make her Husband laugh fails miserably. She is still attempting to ease his obvious deep concern for her.

"Go home Ricky....The Sister will ring you there....They have the number and all that....If there's any news she will ring you....Won't you Sister?."

Murphy nods before she throws her head back in a haughty fashion. Jenny pulls Eric closer to her. She kisses him as Murphy makes an issue out of staring at her watch, hanging over her left breast on a small chain. Jenny smiles.

"Come on give us a kiss and lend us a shilling."

She hugs and kisses Eric until Bert pulls him away from her and Murphy whisks the wheelchair in the direction of the Labour Ward.

* * *

The noise of very loud banging on the front door causes, fully clothed, Eric to wake with a start. He has fallen asleep on the settee in front of the fire. Rubbing his eyes, he stares at the clock on the mantelpiece. It is 10.30am. Still bleary eyed he stumbles over to open the door. Bert is standing there, still banging on the door with both fists, almost falling into the house, Bert grabs Eric's right hand in his, he shakes it vigorously.

"Congratulations Son....I bet you're relieved it's all over with.... Eh?....Eh?."

Eric is still coming around from a deep sleep. He half smiles and then realises the significance of Bert's remarks. His excitement is beginning to rise rapidly as he enquires.

"What?....Do you mean that?.....Has she had?....Has the baby arrived?....What's going on?....What do you mean Dad.?"

Bert is nodding and beaming with a broad smile.

"What?....Jenny?....She's had the Baby?...Has she?."

Bert is now beginning to feel dizzy because of his continuous nodding. Eric reflects for a moment, then splutters.

"Oh bloody hell fire....Am I a Mummy or a Daddy?."

Bert is still trying to understand his question as Alice pushes past him to give her Son a reassuring hug, followed by a kiss.

"It's alright Ricky I know what you mean love....You have a little baby daughter...Just over seven pounds in weight and what's most important of all....They are both fine...Are you telling us that you didn't know?....When we phoned the Hospital they told us they had tries to phone you about an hour ago....They said they had been unable to contact you...We assumed that you'd gone up to the Hospital...When they said they hadn't seen you Dad and I decided to come around here to check....Good job we did by the look of things."

Still dazed, Eric glances over at their telephone. Immediately he sees that the receiver has not be replaced correctly. He smacks his forehead with the back of his hand, sounding and looking exasperated.

"Bloody hell......I phoned at half seven the last time...They sounded as if they were getting a bit fed up with me...They asked me not to ring again...They would ring me...I had to promise them....I admit that I did ring quite a few times during the night but I was so worried...And that Sister....Murphy....Well she got a bit nasty and I got annoyed...I remember slamming the phone down....Bloody hell....It's no wonder they couldn't contact me....I don't remember falling asleep but I must have done....Bloody hell."

Eric's parent's smile sympathetically. His Mother steers him back to sit down on the settee. Before his backside hits the cushions he rises to his feet sharply. There is panic in his tone.

"Bloody hell....What about the shop?....Look at the time."

His Mother forces him to sit down.

"Calm down Ricky....It's Sunday...Please try to stop panicking so much....I think we saw enough of that last night."

She casts her eyes in Bert's direction.

"Yes....From both of you."

Bert and Eric look at each other, then burst out Laughing, nervously. Bert sounds enthusiastic.

"Right come on Buggerlugs....I want to see my little Granddaughter...Even if her Father isn't all that bothered about meeting his first born daughter for his very first time...Eh?...Eh?."

This remark shocks Eric.

"You must be joking.....Bloody hell....But listen...That does sound good doesn't it?....My daughter...Eh?.....My daughter!....Bloody hell!."

Contentedly they all reflect for a few moments. Eric suddenly remembers.

"And let's not forget the brand new Mummy....I can't wait to see Jenny...Is she pleased?...Oh no there's no point asking you...You wouldn't know either would you?...Anyways....I don't think I have the foggiest idea what I'm rabbiting on about at this moment in time.... Bloody hell...My Daughter....Bloody hell!."

Alice shakes her head, smiling.

"Get your skates on Ricky....Get yourself smartened up a bit.... Have a nice wash and shave....You want to make a good impression on them....Both of them that is....Eh?....Don't you?."

There is no disguising Eric's sheer delight as he bounds up the stairs to the bathroom. As he disappears from their view the happy new grandparents hug each other. A loud voice is heard coming from the bathroom upstairs.

"My daughter.....I'm going to meet....My daughter....My lovely Wife and my brand new daughter....YES!....Bloody hell fire."

* * *

"What was the problem?....
Not enough milk?"

The newly opened Crump Ward situated in the recently built Maternity Ward at Lapley vale Cottage Hospital is a pleasant, bright and airy, room accommodating four beds. Two of the beds are occupied. Jenny McCabe is in one. Next to her is her older and more experienced friend Susan Summers. Although both women are flushed in their faces there is no doubting that they are happy and contented. Susan is, lovingly, feeding her new baby daughter with a bottle. She turns to speak to Jenny.

"Well…Now that's it all over and done with….Was I kidding about the birthing experience or not?."

Jenny has to force a little smile.

"If anything Susan you didn't even tell us the half….Perhaps it was as well that I didn't know what I was letting myself in for…."

The two fiends pause to laugh together. Jenny continues.

"This might sound weird and funny Susan but I've almost forgotten all the nasty bits already….The sheer agony seems to be well worth it when you see the end result."

Jenny carefully adjusts her position in her bed to sit up slightly. She is peering, anxiously, down the Ward. Her high level of anticipation and excitement is pain for all to see.

"I wish they would hurry up and bring my baby to me…I want her to be here when her Father eventually arrives."

Susan is gently rubbing her daughter's back to bring her wind up as she replies, rather casually.

"Don't worry Jenny….There are going to be times when you will be sick of the sight of her before too long….Believe me…You can take my word for that."

Susan recognises one of Jenny's little warning looks. Jenny chooses to ignore her remarks, maintaining her enthusiasm.

"Perhaps they'll let Ricky see her on his way up to the Ward."

She appears to be comforted by this thought. She smiles, snuggling down on her pillows. She soon sits up again as she catches a glimpse of Eric entering the Ward. She leans forward with outstretched arms to greet him. Eric almost falls over his own feet as he dashes to her bedside. He hugs and kisses her until she screams and forcefully pushes him away. He is leaning on some places which are very sensitive and sore. Eric, horrified, gasps wondering what he has done, hoping that he has not hurt her. Jenny, merely, very tenderly, places her arms around him and they gently hug each other without a word.

Witnessing the tender scene as she eventually manages to get her baby's wind up, Susan cannot stop herself from being mischievous. She catches Jenny's eye, whilst she is still enjoying the loving clinch with Eric. Her tone is deliberately teasing.

"Jenny……Shall I shout the Sister to see if she would be prepared to pull the curtains around your bed for you now Dear?.

Susan throws her head back to roar with laughter. Jenny is genuinely shocked and horrified. She exclaims, loudly.

"SUSAN!....Susan Summers…Behave will you!?....You have got to be joking.….Hell fire Susan….What are you like?."

Jenny joins in the uncontrolled mirth. Eric, looking utterly bemused, has no idea what they are talking or laughing about. Perhaps as well.

Eric waits until the laughter subsides before he nervously, anxiously, enquires.

"Are you alright Jenny?......I've been worried sick…And then I fell fast asleep…And then Mum and Dad had to wake me up….Are you sure you're alright Jenny?....You look smashing to me....Are you sure Jenny?"

Jenny smiles at him in a loving way, allowing him to hopelessly ramble on.

"I've seen her Jenny....She's absolutely gorgeous...Mum and Dad are still staring at her through the glass window....Nan and Billy have been informed...Dad's going to pick them up to bring them here to visit you tonight....And...Oh Jenny....Are you sure you are alright?.... I've been worried sick about you."

Jenny hugs and kisses him all over his face and neck. She, calmly, attempts to reassure him.

"Of course I'm alright Ricky...I'm a bit sore...But that's only to be expected...My eyes still tend to water a bit when I think about what happened to me in that Labour Ward....But it was all worth it in the end...Are you disappointed that I didn't manage to produce a Son for you?."

Eric is stunned by her question. He can hardly speak with built up emotion playing havoc with his tone of his voice.

"Disappointed?.....Disappointed?...Jenny I think I must be the proudest....Happiest and luckiest man in the whole wide world...And several other places you might care to name....I don't think I could possibly be any more delighted and thrilled than I am today....I love you Jenny....I will always love you....I don't care who hears me say it...I love you Jenny McCabe."

Jenny hugs and kisses her Husband again. She notices a young Nurse wheeling a small canvas cot into their Ward. She checks the label hanging from the cot against the name on the chart at the bottom of Jenny's bed, smiles, and steers the cot to her bedside. The friendly Nurse smiles as she addresses Jenny.

"Here you are Mum....She should be ready to feed now... Sister says she'll be along to see you in a few minutes if you have any difficulty.... Don't worry you'll manage fine."

She peers down at the tiny baby.

"Oh isn't she lovely?."

She glances at Eric.

"I think she has her Father's eyes."

Eric, looks, and feels very proud as he, also, gazes at his baby daughter. The Nurse is still smiling as she walks away. Eric now feels that he could quite possibly burst with happiness and pride. Jenny snaps him out of his partial trance. Her arms are extended.

"Pass her over here then…Dad."

Eric is apprehensive. He is uneasy about touching such a small and delicate looking infant. Jenny reassures him.

"Come on….It's alright….She won't break…Just make sure you support her little head."

Using extreme caution and care, Eric lifts the child out of the cot to gently pass her over to her Mother. Jenny's face is a picture of sheer love and delight as she speaks to her daughter.

"That's right my little darling….Come to your Mummy…There's a good girl…You must be starving."

Considering her inexperience and the shortness of time since the actual birth, Jenny adeptly makes the necessary adjustments to her nightdress before she begins to feed the child. She ensures that the baby is suckling before she turns to, the astonished, Eric.

"That's it….Now then….Daddy and I have got to sort out what we are going to call you….Haven't we Daddy?."

Eric is mesmerised by the sight of his wife and child in perfect harmony. He suddenly manages to respond.

"What?....Yes….Well….I don't really mind Jenny…I leave it entirely to you…I'm just delighted that we've got her."

Jenny is much more positive.

"I think we can forget your Mum and Nan for a start…She doesn't want to be called either Alice or Emily…Do you know the name I really like Ricky?."

She is gazing, deeply, into his wide open eyes.

"And I think it suits her as well…Remember it?."

Eric is desperately trying to remember one of the many dozens of names they had discussed over the previous few months. He is not prepared to chance the selection of one as her actual favourite. He stammers, starting to panic slightly.

"Oh yes….Er….You mean….."

To his great relief, Jenny interrupts him.

"Yes that's right Ricky…Amy…Our little Amy."

Thankful that he was not called upon to remember the exact name, Eric's face breaks into a broad smile.

"Absolutely perfect Jenny….Absolutely perfect."

He carefully leans over to kiss Jenny gently on her lips. He then uses even more caution to kiss Amy on the top of her tiny head.

Despite the indisputable fact that he would be happy to remain alongside his wife's bed for ever, Eric is aware that he was privileged by the Nursing Staff when they allowed him to make his first visit outside the normal visiting hours. He is mindful that he promised he would not stop for too long. He reluctantly rises to his feet, preparing to take his leave of them.

"Well Jenny….Amy….Much as I'd like to stay I'd better honour my promises and make myself scarce…It was very nice of the Sister to let me up…The laid down visiting hours don't start until this afternoon…. Thank heavens she did bend the rules for me….And…And well…. I just want to go outside and announce to the whole world that my beautiful daughter has arrived and both she and her equally gorgeous Mother are both extremely wonderful and they are doing exceptionally well."

Jenny gazes into his eyes returning his love with a bonus. Eric is close to tears.

Jenny….My darling Jenny….You are a bloody marvel."

She swiftly moves Amy out of the way to allow Eric to kiss her fully on her lips. Realising that they are being watched, Jenny breaks off, pretending to chase Eric away.

"Off you go then….Leave us girls to get better acquainted…We'll be looking forward to your visit later on…Both of us will….Won't we Amy?….Yes we will…."

Eric is walking backwards with a silly smirk on his face. He is making a waving motion with his right hand but he is clearly having to force himself to leave. At the last possible moment, just before he reaches the way out, he calls out to them.

"Bye…Bye….See you both later then….Bye."

Jenny feels tears welling up inside of her as she looks down at her child, contentedly, feeding. She glances over to see that Susan is taking the opportunity to take a very close look at her new daughter. Her look of adoration is obvious. Jenny manages to interrupt her concentration.

"I think we can safely say that our Daddy is pleased with…Ahem…. Baby Amy…Yes Amy….And I."

Susan instantly understands the significance of the decided name. She suddenly feels pangs of being sorry for herself in her marital situation. She dismisses these feeling as soon as they arose. She is happy to share Jenny's happiness.

"No doubt about that Jenny….I reckon you have both made an excellent and what is more….Lasting impression there."

She is fighting off her own disappointments again.

"I suppose I should be grateful that Joe managed to get here in a reasonably sober state last night….I bet that didn't last for long when he got out again….Still my Mother is there keeping an eye on the kids….No worries there."

Susan gazes at the sight of Jenny and Amy together. She is now battling against unwarranted envy as she announces.

"He's a smashing fella your Ricky Jenny ….You're both very lucky."

Susan swiftly changes the subject, only slightly.

"I hope you're going to be alright with the breast feeding Jenny….I tried it with my first…Little Tommy….But we had to put him on the bottle after a few days or so."

Jenny is concerned.

"What was the problem?....Not enough milk?."

Susan is conscious that she must not do or say anything that may spoil Jenny's happiness. She reverts to her natural, spontaneous, sense of humour.

"Oh no....The quantity was there although I don't think the quality was up to the required standard....So rather than take a chance we decided to send the milk back and started him on the bottle right away."

Jenny is nodding in a sympathetic fashion causing Susan's wicked streak to come to the fore.

"And of course we mustn't forget the other big problem we had to face Jenny....Joe was smoking a pipe at that time."

Jenny is puzzled as Susan delivers her punch line.

"Baby didn't like sharing it with a St Bruno smoker."

Jenny stares at Susan in astonishment. She gradually works out the hidden implications in Susan's statement. Knowing her quite well after all the months they have been acquainted, she soon enjoys roaring with laughter together with her cherished friend and welcome companion in the face of adversity.

* * *

"Carry on please…..Everything is under control."

The time is 7.25pm by the clinical looking clock on the wall in the waiting room outside the entrance into Crump Ward at the Cottage Hospital. There is a large notice exhibited on the wall under the clock.

'Two visitors only allowed for each patient.

Visiting hours will be strictly enforced.

By order of the Matron.'

Eric is seated on one of the, basic, plastic chair with Billy and Nan Dawes, dressed in their Sunday best clothes, alongside him. The large double doors which give access through to the Ward suddenly swing open. Sister Murphy, looking anything but friendly, appears in front of them. Giving them a quick once over, she clears her throat to make an announcement.

"I hope you understand that the rules and regulations in here are made for very good reasons and they must be obeyed at all times…."

She draws their attention to the notice on the wall.

"And let me make myself perfectly clear….VERY CLEAR!....I will not stand for any nonsense from anyone…Especially tonight."

She pauses for a moment, gauging their stunned reactions.

"We are scheduled to have a very special visitor here tonight….No lesser person than His worship the Mayor of Lapley Vale himself… Councillor Crump."

She stops to point at the sign over the double doors.

"Crump....As in Crump Ward....Yes that's right....Get it?....Understood?...Now as you may or may not know the Local Health Authority have been responsible for the provision of this new....And in my considered opinion...Magnificent Wing...To this Hospital...And as a sign of our respect and gratitude this Ward has been named after the Mayor...And he's coming here tonight to officially name and open it."

Murphy pauses. Placing her hands on her hips.

"Right....Any questions?."

Eric, Billy and Nan, still shocked, shake their heads in perfect unison. Murphy starts up again.

"Now I will be ringing the visitor's bell at 7.30pm precisely...AND....AND....I will be ringing it for the second time at 8.30pm precisely...At which time I will expect all visitors to vacate the Ward quickly and quietly allowing myself and my Staff to get on with our duties which as you may appreciate are looking after mothers and their babies...Not catering for visitors...Without any further unnecessary interruption....Do I make myself clear?."

Waiting a brief moment for any reaction, she turns on her heels, disappearing through the double doors into the Ward.

The three visitors remain stunned for a few moments. They anxiously gaze into each other's eyes in amazement as much as anything else. Eric breaks the silence.

"Bloody hell....Just for a while there I thought we were getting a lecture from Hitler....With tits."

He suddenly remembers that Nan is present which causes him to blush before he, swiftly, continues.

"She definitely likes to leave us in no doubt whatsoever eh?....Mind you I suppose she has to warn us if we're going to be mixing with the cream of Lapley Vale Society."

Billy, shaking his head, intervenes.

"The Cream of Society?.....It's only old 'Oily Crump' not cockeyed Royalty....Yes that's correct Old Oily Crump is the Mayor alright....When he's not engaged on his civic duties he's a cockeyed train driver...

Usually wearing oily and smelly overalls....I've known him most of his cockeyed life....I don't think we need to be dressed in our best clothing to mix with the likes of him."

Annoyed, Nan tutts, shaking her head. She is about to say something to Billy when the outer door into the waiting room opens. Lenny Jopson, the local reporter for the Lapley Vale Examiner, struggles through into the room carrying his large tripod and flash camera. He smiles, nodding a friendly greeting as he scrambles around attempting to sort himself out. He recognises them.

"Oh hello Billy Alright?....I hope I'm not late again...He hasn't arrived yet has he?...The Mayor?."

Lenny, anxiously, attempts to gain a view inside the Ward through the small round windows on the double doors. Eric puts his mind at ease.

"No you're alright Lenny....Anyways....What are you doing here?."

Lenny is pulling out his cigarettes and matches as he takes a seat. He does not sound over enthusiastic.

"Orders from on high....Carrying out my orders Ricky...I've got to take pictures of His Worship the Mayor visiting the Ward they've named after him."

Billy is unimpressed by his comments.

"His cockeyed Worship the Mayor?...."

He stares at Lenny and then at the others. He sounds rather exasperated.

"It's only Oily Crump...He's not cockeyed Royalty."

The men chuckle but Nan is embarrassed by Billy's brash conduct and his derisory expressions.

Lenny sits back, drawing on his cigarette. He suddenly springs forward, having had a thought.

"I wonder if the Sister will let me in to set this lot up in advance of the formalities?."

He leaps up to peers through the round windows again. Eric shakes his head.

"I wouldn't build your hopes up there Lenny…She's already been out here laying the law down…I don't know her name but I think I'm going to christen her Attila the Hen."

Eric's comments amuse Billy and Nan but they cause Lenny to panic.

"Oh bloody hell….Don't tell me it's Sister Murphy on duty…. That's all I need."

Eric, Billy and Nan all nod their heads in unison once again. Lenny is distraught.

"Wonderful….Sister Murphy….That's all I need….I knew things were going too bloody well today."

The loud, clanking, noise of a hand held bell being rung inside the Ward causes all four of them to spring to their feet. The double doors swing open exposing, an even nastier looking, Sister Murphy, holding the brass bell in her right hand. Eric nudges Lenny as they are walking past Murphy.

"Good luck Lenny….Looks like you'll be needing it."

They start to snigger but stop instantly when they notice the, evil, expression on the Sister's face.

Nan reaches Jenny first. They hug and kiss each other with sincere and loving affection. Nan, weeping tears of joy, steps back to allow Billy to greet his Granddaughter . Eric walks to the other side of her bed awaiting his turn to kiss his Wife. After briefly kissing and hugging her, he glances around rather nervously. He speaks in low tones, expressing genuine concern.

"I'll have to wait outside while you have a chat with Nan and Billy Jenny…We have been left in no doubt that you face the death penalty if you break any rules in here….Don't worry…I'll be in the room just out there….Are you feeling alright?."

Jenny nods, looking rather disappointed as Eric backs away. He stops at the bottom of the bed to catch a quick glimpse of Amy in her little cot. He is about to get a closer look as he spots Sister Murphy. She is standing in the middle of the Ward, ferocious with her arms folded across her buxom chest. He raises both his hands over his head indicating his total surrender. Keeping his hands aloft he swiftly sweeps past her and through the doubles doors into the waiting room.

Eric is met by a dejected appearing Lenny. Sitting back on a plastic seat in the small ante room. Eric guesses that his reasonable approach to Sister Murphy had received the predicted and inevitable response. He is about to speak words of consolation to Lenny when Billy's head and shoulders appears around one of the double doors. His face indicates that he may be the bearer of glad tidings.

"Come back in Ricky....It's O.K....The lady in the bed next to our Jenny has no cockeyed visitors and she says she's not expecting any either....So you can come in....Pretend you're visiting her...Come on."

Eric is not totally convinced but is brave enough to follow Billy through to the Ward. He is relieved as Susan waves and nods to him. Although he is happy to back in the Ward he is, nevertheless, apprehensive. He has no wish to do anything which could possibly upset Sister Murphy. In the relatively short period of time since their first encounter, he has concluded that she is not the type of person he should take any sort of liberties with.

Nan has lifted Amy out of her cot. She is cuddling and cooing to her as, clearly delighted, Billy looks on. Eric gazes, lovingly, at Jenny. In such a touching family setting, she is clearly feeling as proud as punch.

Suddenly everyone's attention is drawn to a loud clattering coming from the entrance into the Ward. Joe Summers, obviously worse for drink, soon appears at the foot of Susan's bed. He carries a sad looking bunch of half dead flowers in his hand. Susan is horrified. Joe smiles as he exaggerates his joy at seeing his Wife.

"Hello Su....My little darling....I nearly didn't make it....I just called in the Pub on my way here to wet the baby's head and some of the Lads made a bit of a fuss of me...But I'm here now....How are you sweetheart?."

Joe lurches forward, attempting to kiss Susan. He stumbles, tripping over the leg of the bed He falls flat on his face on the floor at the side of her bed. He is laughing in a silly fashion as he hauls himself back onto his feet, using the side of the bed to do so. Susan wants the Earth to swallow her.

"Oops a daisy…Oh Shit…..I nearly fell then….Have that bed leg whitewashed…Eh?....Sorry about that Su…You'll be most relieved to know I haven't hurt myself…."

Susan's face is bright red, a mixture of rage and embarrassment. Joe glances around the Ward, declaring in a loud voice.

"Highly polished floors….Typical Hospital bullshit."

He tries to laugh off the whole incident but fails to impress any of those present.

All attention is diverted away from Joe as Sister Murphy sweeps into the Ward, announcing in a loud, clear voice.

"O.K. Pay attention everybody….He's here….The Mayor is here."

The Mayor is a small, round, baldy headed man in his mid fifties. He is smartly dressed in a dark three piece suit. His decorative chain of office is worn around his neck. He smiles in a friendly way as he approaches Jenny's bed. Lenny is scrambling about with the photographic equipment. The Mayor is accompanied by the Matron, a distinguished, elegant, elderly Lady, who looks about as friendly as Murphy. Resplendent, in full uniform with medals, standing discreetly behind the official visiting party is Sergeant Bert McCabe. Bert is smiling from ear to ear as he nods, silently greeting all his friends and relatives in the close vicinity of Jenny's bed.

The Mayor shakes hands with, a rather bashful, Jenny and then does the same with Eric. He then recognises Billy and Nan so he smiles as he nods to them. He, very politely, asks Jenny.

"Would you care to have your photograph in the Lapley Examiner this week my Dear?....With me…Oh and your little baby of course…. And your Husband if you like."

He gestures to his rear, where Lenny is having trouble with his tripod, as usual.

"We have the Press here with us….Are we alright for you here Lenny?."

Harassed, Lenny nods and smiles to the Mayor as he manages to set the camera on the tripod after several attempts to do so. The Mayor continues.

"If you could hold the baby in your arms my Dear...And if your Husband stays where he is with Matron alongside him...That's it...Oh yes....This should make a nice little group photograph."

Without any further delay, they all conform to the Mayor's wishes. Billy and Nan move out of the way behind Lenny. Lenny ducks down behind his camera to look through his lens.

Whilst all this is going on, Joe is sitting on Susan's bed scowling. Lenny stands up, gesticulating with his arms.

"Can you all stand a little closer together please?....And Mummy.... Can you show us a bit more of baby's face if you can?...That's fine.... Thank you."

Jenny does her best to expose Amy's face towards Lenny and his camera as the others shuffle closer together as requested.

Lenny disappears under the cloth but continues to Dish out his orders.

"Yes....Right....That's fine....Ready?....Stay still please...Ready.... Say cheese please."

There is a bright flash of light which frightens little Amy. This causes her to, softly, cry. Everyone's attention is immediately drawn to the child as Lenny pleads with them all.

"Please....Wait.....Hang on a minute please....I'll just take another one for luck....Keep your positions please...Right...Here we go."

Another bright flash of light illuminates the area.

They are all becoming aware of Joe's menacing presence. He now appears to be seething. He snaps at the Mayor.

"I hope you're going to have one taken with me and my family now."

Bert, for the first time, is aware of Joe's presence. His proud, smiling, friendly expression disappears, instantly. Before anyone can respond, Joe turns aggressive.

"COME ON!....Fair's Fair!....That's always been my motto.... Come on I'm waiting."

The Mayor, knowing what Joe is capable of, decides to make a hasty retreat. Joe detects this move which angers him more.

"HEY!.....Where do you think you're off to?....I've got as much right as this mob here."

He gestures towards the whole McCabe party with a dismissive wave of his hand. Billy steps forward. He is angry.

"Hey….Come on Joe….You want to learn how to conduct yourself in Public you do….You're a cockeyed menace you are….A cockeyed menace…Try to remember where you are….That's the cockeyed Mayor of Lapley in person you're talking to you know?….Behave yourself."

Joe snarls at Councillor Crump, who is nervously fiddling with his chain of office. Joe's sounds most derogatory.

"Oh really…I suppose you're referring to this little twit here are you?....Well I for one am not impressed in the slightest… Everybody knows that all shithouses have a chain."

Bert McCabe has had enough. He strides forward, his anger etched across his face. Susan is close to dying with shame. Bert spits out his words.

"Right Joe….You're leaving….Right now!....You can choose the easy way or the hard way…."

Bert is fumbling in his tunic pockets trying to locate his handkerchief to enable him to begin his false teeth ritual. Bert is removing his glasses when Joe recognises the procedure. He immediately backs off. He scrambles past the end of the beds, making a dash for the exit. As he reaches the double doors he turns to shout.

"Alright!......Bloody hell…It's a fascist State if you ask my opinion…. I don't need you to tell me when I have to leave."

Unable to trace his handkerchief, Bert's teeth are placed directly into his tunic pocket. He lurches forward as Joe flies out through the doors before Bert can reach him.

Sergeant Bert McCabe pushes the double doors ajar to look through into the waiting room. There is no sign of Joe. He adeptly replaces his glasses and teeth. After a couple of test bites. He announces in a calm, controlled manner.

"Your Worship....Madam Matron...Ladies and Gentlemen...If you would be kind enough to excuse me for a few moments."

He pauses as he sees Susan crying with shame.

"I will just check that the Er....Gentleman....Leaves the premises... Thank you awfully much.....Carry on please....Everything is under control....Eh?....Eh?."

He disappears from their view in an instant. Jenny turns to Susan displaying her heartfelt sympathy without speaking. The Mayor is desperately attempting to regain his dignity. Lenny Jopson has dismantled his equipment and is ready to leave. All the other Ladies are stunned by the performance they have witnessed. Billy takes hold of the Mayor's elbow. He speaks with an apologetic tone.

"Sorry about that Oily...I'm afraid some cockeyed people just don't have any cockeyed respect."

The Mayor nods, visibly nervous. He quickly makes his exit with the bristling Matron and shocked Sister Murphy on either side of him.

* * *

"Natural has got to be best."

The news of little Amy McCabe arrival has, quite naturally, been welcomed at the Lapley Vale Bowling and Social Club. At 9.30pm on the day of her birth a certain amount of celebration has already taken place in the absence of any of the main players.

Woody, Norman and Eddie are in their usual positions at the bar with Ralph, Vic and Charlie Walsh opposite to them. There is a considerable amount of activity taking place. There are dart players, domino and cribbage tables in action and there is also a queue of others waiting for their turns on the snooker table. Alf and Denise are being fully occupied behind the bar serving them all with drinks.

A loud cheer erupts as Eric and Billy walk through the doors. Eric is a bit embarrassed, not too happy to find himself in the limelight, but Billy is loving every minute of his new found fame.

On arrival at the bar, Billy stands back to allow Woody, Norman and Eddie to congratulate and shake the hand of the proud new father. Ralph gestures for Eric to join them and he receives the same warm treatment from the others. Woody and his friends are now heaping the attention on the new great granddad. Denise is smiling sweetly at Eric as Alf stretches his hand across the bar to offer his congratulations and best wishes to him.

Before an order has even been placed, Ralph is up on his feet, making a formal announcement.

"Ricky....On behalf of all the Committee and Members of the Club...May I extend our warmest congratulations to you....And of course to your lovely Wife Jenny....On the occasion of the birth of your daughter....Your daughter?...."

Ralph stares at Eric who immediately realises that they are not aware of Amy's name. He blurts out his answer.

"Amy....Yes Amy....We're calling her Amy."

There is a hum of approval. Ralph nods, continuing.

"Yes...Thank you Ricky...As you have now informed us...Your lovely daughter Amy."

Ralph nods to Alf behind the bar.

"Alfred would you please offer the proud father a drink from me on this auspicious occasion?....Now what will you have Ricky?."

Before Eric can respond, a rather upset looking, Billy intervenes.

"And what about the cockeyed GREAT!... Get that Ralph.... GREAT!...Grandfather...Eh?....What about him Ralph?."

Roars of laughter greet Billy's remarks. Ralph adds.

"Yes please Alf....And whatever the...Cockeyed GREAT! Grandfather wants as well...Cheers Boys....All the very best....Give our love to Jenny....And of course....To little Amy... Won't you?."

Ralph sits down to a polite ripple of applause, led by Vic. All present are now happy to settle down with their drinks. Eric and Billy raise their pint glasses to Ralph. They nod and smile to each other across the bar. Woody slaps Eric on the back.

"There now....I did tell you that everything would work out fine in the long run...Didn't I?....You randy little swine."

Eric takes no offence. He sounds as happy as he looks.

"Thanks Woody...Yes thanks for reminding me of that....Thanks Boys....Thanks everyone really....My Dad will be certain to make an appearance before very long....We did experience a little incident involving that daft bastard Joe Summers up at the Hospital and Dad left us to deal with him."

Eddie, springs forward on his stool.

"Hey you should have sent for Norman."

They laugh as Norman relives his famous incident. Eddie is careful not to nudge Norman too hard before he directs his next words to him.

"Soon sorted him out eh Norman?...No problem...Send for big hitter Norman....Joe won't start anything if he's about...He's not that daft."

Norman feels obliged to respond. He surprises even himself as he sounds defensive toward Joe.

"He's a bloody menace that Joe....There's no doubting that for a fact... Why can't he behave himself?....I bet booze was involved.... He's a different person when he's sober you know."

There is general agreement with Norman. Eric speaks.

"Well....I have to admit that I don't know her very well...But Jenny tells me that Joe's wife....Susan....Is a smashing bird....She's in the next bed to Jenny and they have attended all the ante natal classes or what ever they do before they have the babies and all that together... Been friends for months now....Jenny really has taken to her...It's a bloody shame isn't it?....She was crying with sheer embarrassment at his drunken performance wasn't she Billy?..."

Billy nods but suddenly shakes his head.

"I'm sorry to say this but somebody should drown that cockeyed Joe....I mean it....Really....Do us all a cockeyed favour...And that includes his own cockeyed family as well."

Everyone sadly agrees with Billy sentiments without making comment. Woody turns to Eric.

"So our little Jenny is O.K. is she Ricky?....No problems?."

Eric is delighted to be able to reply in the affirmative.

"Yes thank you Woody...She looks wonderful and she's so happy.... If she was a top she'd be spinning...And the baby...Sorry....Amy... Well she is absolutely gorgeous."

They are all pleased to join in Eric's obvious delight. He carries on.

"I'm not too sure about the feeding arrangements though...But Jenny knows best....It's what she wants to do."

Denise has been eavesdropping.

"Oh is she feeding Amy herself Ricky?."

Eric nods.

"Oh that's smashing....Just the way nature intended it...They don't seem to be encouraging it these days...You'll find that little Amy will really flourish on Mother's milk...You mark my words...You'll see... She's definitely doing the right thing....Good for Jenny."

Woody is smirking as he questions Denise.

"Oh you think babies grow up bigger and better if they're fed on Mother's milk do you Denise?."

Denise has no qualms at all.

"Without the slightest of doubts Woody....I don't care what anybody else might have to say....Natural has got to be best."

She is confident that she has made her point. Woody, slyly, winks to his friends.

"Far be it for me to contradict you Denise...My little flower.... But although I have to admit that I am getting a bit long in the tooth now...When I was in my prime....As a youth....There's many here will be able to testify that I was a fine figure of a man...Agreed?."

Eddie, Norman and Alf support his claim.

"And if my dear old Mother was alive today."

Woody pauses to, briefly, cast his eyes upwards.

"She would tell you that I was seventeen and had started courting before I ever had a woman's breast in my mouth."

Denise gasps for a moment but then roars with laughter. Tears are running down her cheeks, spoiling her heavy make up, as she cries out.

"Oh Woody....I don't know why I ever take any notice of you at all....You're a nine carat teaser...You really are....Seventeen and started courting indeed...."

They are all laughing uncontrollably. The men are almost helpless, not just because of Woody's remarks but also with Denise's reaction to them.

* * *

"I'm not here to cause any sort of trouble."

Jenny and Susan, both appear somewhat preoccupied, as they sit in their beds in Crump Ward at the Cottage Hospital. Their attention is focussed on one of the other beds, situated on the opposite side of the room, the curtains are drawn closed around it. The Ward has been spruced up and they are awaiting the arrival of visitors at 2.30pm. Sister Murphy and a young Nurse are busy inside the Nurse's Station, close to the double doors.

Although both new mothers appear to be glowing with health and look radiant there is, obviously, something spoiling their state of contentment. Susan turns to speak to Jenny.

"Don't worry Jenny....I've seen all this kind of thing before.... They're becoming more common these days...These Caesarean Sections....Lynda will be alright....Honestly....She's knocked out by the anaesthetic that's all....You can take it from me Jen....She'll be O.K.....Especially when she hears that her baby daughter is fine...Just imagine....Over ten pounds in weight....And her first as well....Bloody hell Jenny....My first two put together didn't weight that much....It's that poor husband of hers...What's his name?...Oh yes....Malcolm that's it....He really did look dreadful when he was guided in behind that curtain last night...Poor bugger looked as if he's been mauled by a lion or something...The poor man...Still....Like I said Jen.... They'll be fine....Don't worry....Wait and see...Everything will turn out fine."

Although she is consoled by Susan's experienced comments, Jenny cannot dispel her heartfelt concern for her friend Lynda. She nods.

"Yes....I suppose you're right Susan....I know we should be thankful for normal deliveries...Mind you....I wasn't too happy about it at the time."

They both chuckle, easing the tension. Susan, rapidly, changes the subject.

"Who's coming to see you this afternoon Jenny?....Will your Ricky be able to make it?."

Jenny shakes her head but smiles as she responds.

"No....Ricky has to look after the shop today to allow his Mum to come....She hasn't seen Amy yet...And hopefully my Nan will be with her...I hope so anyways."

Susan appears to be slightly embarrassed.

"I just hope that a certain...You know who?....Doesn't dare to show his face in here again....I nearly died of shame last night Jenny...Fancy calling the Mayor a shithouse....I hope your father-in-law didn't hurt him too much....Mind you....He deserves all he gets."

Jenny's empathy is sincere as she listens to Susan.

"Trouble is....He loves the kids to bits....And they adore him.... He's never ever raised a finger to any of us....They think the sun shines out of him...."

They shake their heads in unison. Susan continues, attempting to rationalise the unfortunate situation.

"The innocence of children eh?....Mind you...It could be much worse for us....He's always looked after his work....He's never been without a weekly wage packet for as long as I have known him...And as it has been pointed out to me on many occasions in the past....I was daft enough to marry him in the first place...I was warned by several people including his own Mother."

Although she is very interested and wants to know more, Jenny is careful not to pry too deeply into Susan's private affairs.

"Well Su....You must've loved him once otherwise you would never have got married to him would you?."

Susan scoffs at Jenny's remark.

"I hardly knew him at all when we first got married....I did fancy him a lot though....I don't think my brain had been fully formed when I allowed myself to get pregnant...Marriage seemed to be the best solution at the time...It was expected by my family."

Susan breaks off to lean over, closer, to Jenny. She lowers the tone of her voice.

"You won't mention any of this to anyone who doesn't need to know will you Jenny?."

Jenny stares into Susan's face as she laugh ironically.

"Well I could hardly say much about anything like that myself... Could I?."

They both giggle.

As the fingers on the clock moved to 2.30pm precisely, Sister Murphy rings the brass bell to indicate that visiting time has arrived. Nan and Mrs McCabe appear immediately. Both are smiling and waving as they rush to the side of the bed. Nan goes to one side, Alice the other. After hugs and kisses both visitors are glancing towards the tiny cot at the bottom of the bed. Alice politely enquires.

"How are you today Jenny love...You look very well indeed....And how's our little precious?."

As she asks she is moving toward the cot. She and Nan meet at the bottom of the bed. They are drooling as Jenny responds.

"She's fine....Fast asleep I hope...And I feel great...We can't wait to get out of here and home where we belong."

Nan moves away from the cot to allow Alice to get a closer look at Amy. She sits on the chair next to the bed.

"Sergeant Bert brought us here in his motor car today Jenny.... Picked me up at home and then we called for Alice at the shop...Your Ricky is in charge there this afternoon....Oh...He is proud Jenny....I think we might have to buy him a larger size in caps."

Alice glances at Susan. She is pretending to read a magazine. She has heard about Joe's performance. She feels sorry that Susan has no visitors. Alice is friendly as she speaks.

"And how are you today dear?....Everything going alright I hope...."

Susan is delighted to be involved.

"Oh hello...Yes...Thank you Mrs McCabe....Thank you for asking."

Susan looks humble as she directs her next remarks to Nan, on the far side of Jenny's bed.

"I wish to say how much I regret that awful incident in here last night with...Well....I'm sure you must know what Joe is like."

Nan stands up. She walks around to Susan's bed. She gently takes hold of her hand.

"Listen to me my dear....If we were all held responsible for the stupid actions of our husbands I don't think too many of us would want to show our faces outside out front doors...Don't worry love...I know your Joe....And I can tell you that I've known him much longer that a lot of those people who are always sitting in judgement over him...Joe is basically a good man.....But...When drink is in...Sense goes out...."

Susan is bravely fighting back tears as Nan nods to Alice before she continues.

"There's quite a few of us around here who have been placed in very similar situations from one time to another....Don't think you're on your own dear."

Alice agrees.

"So don't you give it another thought Susan...We've all had our share of being in the same boat as Nan quite rightly pointed out.... We girls have got to stick together."

Alice pauses. She appears to be a little nervous.

"He's not expected here this afternoon is he?."

Nan anxiously switches her gaze to the double doors. Susan sees the funny side of their actions. She laughs, assuring her.

"No....Don't panic....I'll be very surprised if he shows his face here today....Mind you he is on early morning shift...I've a feeling that he will be making himself rather scarce...For a little while at least."

Alice McCabe is changing Jenny's flowers. Nan is carefully wiping an apple before she passes it to Jenny. All are relieved that the air has been cleared. Jenny, eagerly, rekindles the conversation.

"Did I catch it right?...Did you say that Dad is here?...."

They both nod as Jenny warns them.

"Mind you....Even he might have some difficulty getting past Sister Murphy...She's a real tyrant...Well... I think we all know what she can be like."

Nodding, in unison, they all glance towards the Nurses Station. Alice is first to speak.

"He's here alright...He's gone to visit someone on the Surgical Ward....But....He'll be here when he's ready...Not even someone as formidable as Sister Murphy will be a match for Bert...Believe me she's not even in the same league as him....Bert could get in to see the Queen if he had a mind to do so."

Her love for him becomes apparent as, smiling, she shakes her head, adding.

"I've heard people swear that he could take a nut off a monkey and I've no reason to doubt that he would."

Their mirth is cut short as they become aware of Bert's voice coming from the Nurses Station, just inside the Ward. Bert is in full uniform, without the actual medals on show this time. He addresses Sister Murphy and her Nursing Staff with authority.

"Look I don't want you to be worrying yourself Sister....If it makes you feel any happier then we'll call it official police business...But let me tell you this....So there can be no mistake...Eh?...Eh?....I am going to visit my granddaughter and her mother whilst I'm here....O.K.?....Is that settled now?....Oh...And incidentally I'll thank you not to quote rules and regulations to me if you don't mind....I might suddenly decide to turn nasty myself and start asking people for their driving licences and quite a few other things I could mention....Eh?....Eh?.... Anyways Sister you've got a bloody short memory when it suits you.... Eh?....Eh?....You were very glad to see me here last night...Eh?....Eh?.... Ask his Worship the Mayor if you require a witness....Now I'm sure you have lots of paperwork and things to see to and I am also a very busy person…Eh?....Eh?."

Bert walks away from a, stunned and deflated, Sister Murphy. He shakes his head as he stresses his opinion to his family.

"Bloody hell….You give some people a little sniff of power and they tend to go raving mad."

Bert stops, abruptly. His facial expression changes immediately to one of gentle friendliness. He throws open his arms, beaming broadly, emphasising his delight.

"Ladies….My dears….How the hell are you all?…Eh?…Eh?…"

They are nodding and smiling as Bert peers into Amy's cot at the foot of Jenny's bed.

"And my little darling….You're alright I hope?."

Jenny responds on behalf of her daughter.

"Hello Dad….She's fine….She'll be awake anytime about now…. She's due a feed."

Bert blows a kiss to his granddaughter before he walks up to kiss Jenny on the cheek. He then turns to speak to Susan, who looks rather uncomfortable in his presence.

"Hello Susan….And how are you and your little precious one today…Both fine I hope….Eh?....Eh?."

Susan smiles, rather nervously, Bert moves to the side of her bed to enable him to speak to her in a lower, more confidential, tone.

"I have to tell you that I had to have strong words with Joe….You know after last night's little episode in here….No harm done….I think he saw the sense in what I was telling him…He was genuinely sorry for causing such a fuss and well…Let bygones be bygones….EH?....Eh?.... No harm done."

Everyone can see, welcome, relief through Susan's attitude and demeanour. Bert switches his attention to Linda's bed, still with curtains draw around it. He is curious.

"Hello hello what's all this?....What's going on over there then?… Eh?…Eh? "

Jenny reveals her own deep concern in her tone.

"It's our friend Dad….Lynda…Lynda Chumley….She's had a bad time….Had to have a caesarean operation…But she's going to be fine….She's had a lovely little girl as well."

She turns to direct her next remarks to the Ladies realising that they are more likely to appreciate what she is about to disclose to them.

"Over ten pounds she was….And her first baby as well."

They gasp and look over at Lynda's bed with genuine sympathy.

Bert, seeing the reactions of the Ladies, remarks.

"Oh yes….Quite common these days…Or so I'm told…Did you know how you can identify someone who was born by caesarean for the remainder of their lives?….Eh?….Eh?."

There is no attempt to respond. Bert's face, instantly, lights up, his eyes gleaming with devilment.

"Oh yes….You see they always leave a room through the window instead of using the door…Eh?….Eh?."

They all chuckle. Jenny pretends to scold him.

"Oh Dad….You are awful…And look at us…All laughing and enjoying ourselves whilst poor Lynda is lying over there probably still unconscious….And her poor Husband…Malcolm….Well the man is beside himself with worry….He's never left her side."

They all, rapidly, pull themselves together. Nan who is sitting on a chair facing the entrance into the Ward suddenly changes her facial expression to one of fear and apprehension. They all turn towards the double doors to see Joe, smartly dressed in a neat suit, clean shaven and sober, standing inside the Ward. Susan is horrified. Bert leaps to his feet, growling. Joe raises his right hand, speaking very calmly.

"Alright….Don't panic….It's alright Bert…I'm not here to cause any sort of trouble…In fact I have come to apologise to each and everyone for my dreadful conduct in last night"

He, swiftly, produces a large bouquet of flowers which he had been hiding behind his back. They are beautiful.

"I've just been to see Ricky in the shop."

He walks forward, rather sheepishly, thrusting the flowers towards Susan.

"These are for you sweetheart....Sorry."

Susan hesitates for a moment but soon realises that everyone, including Bert, is smiling and nodding their approval. She accepts them, glances at them with pride and appreciation, before she reaches up to pull Joe's head towards her for a well deserved hug and kiss. Tears are running down both of their cheeks as she pretends to chastise him.

"I should bloody well think you are sorry as well Joe Summers.... You big crate egg."

Susan kisses him with feeling. Joe now has recovered his confidence. He decides to amplify his apologies.

"Yes....And whilst it is still fresh in my mind Ladies...And Bert of course..........And before I forget to do so."

He has everyone's attention.

"I would like to take this opportunity to humbly apologise to you all for making such a prize twat of myself last night."

Joe is nodding and smiling. The ladies do not know whether they should laugh or cry. Bert glares at Joe as he slowly shakes his head in disbelief.

* * *

"Not a dirty dish to be seen and spotless."

The scene inside Ricky and Jenny's house is one of intense activity. Eric is carefully hoovering the carpets in the living room and Mavis Green is in the kitchen, up to her armpits in soap suds. Mavis is bravely tackling a huge pile of dirty pans, dishes and cutlery. Eric switches off the Hoover. He stands back to admire his work. The whole house is clean, neat and tidy.

Mavis is quietly singing to herself. There is a delicious smell wafting out of the oven. Eric winds the flex of the Hoover around the handle before he places it in the cupboard under the stairs. He walks into the kitchen, sniffing the smell.

"Mmmmmmmmmmm....I hope that cake will taste as good as it smells Mavis."

She throws him a smile over her shoulder as he adds.

"You do realise that I will have to tell her that you baked it Mavis don't you?....She is well aware of the fact that I would not be capable of such a feat."

Mavis laughs.

"I'll have to go along with you there Ricky."

She pretends to chastise him.

"I'm not sure how you managed to leave so many dishes and what have you for washing up....I've seen smaller piles of dishes after a supper at the Club."

Eric appreciates that he is out of order.

"Sorry Mavis...To tell you the truth I was beginning to run out of dishes....I'd of had to do something about them then...I kept meaning to do them...Still not to worry....I bet Jenny and Amy will just be pleased to get home....Out of that Hospital."

He stands back, deliberately posing, he coughs behind his hand before he speaks using a, very false, cultured voice.

"My wife and daughter...Mrs and Miss McCabe will soon be in residence at their home abode.......Sounds pretty good to me Mavis.... Eh?."

They are laughing as the telephone rings. Stifling his mirth, Eric answers.

"Yes....Hello...Oh Hiya Jenny....Really....What you mean?... NOW?....What right away?....Yes....Oh smashing....No....No problems...I think I can safely say that I'm well and truly prepared to greet the pair of you home....Yes....O.K. then....Fine....About half an hour then?....Bye for now...Yes..."

He turns to check if Mavis is listening to him. He noticeably lowers the volume of his voice as he continues.

"Yes....Me too..."

Turning to check again, he drops his tone even lower.

"Yes I love you....Now go and get yourself ready...Yes....Bye Jenny....Love to Amy....Yes....Bye."

Mavis, having attended to all of the kitchen needs, walks into the living room, drying her hands on her apron. Eric replaces the telephone receiver.

"That was Jenny Mavis."

Mavis acts surprised as she replies, sarcastically.

"Oh really...I'd never have guessed that Ricky...By the way....I'd have something to say if I ever heard you telling someone else that you loved them on the telephone."

Eric blushes as Mavis laughs.

He, swiftly, changes the subject.

"I don't know what I would have done without you Mavis love…. Things have been going raving mad all around me for these past few days or so…And I really do want things to be nice for Jenny and Amy's homecoming…I would have been struggling….Tell me Mavis…How did you know I needed help?."

Mavis flashes a knowing look.

"Call it female intuition if you like Ricky….In my experience all you men are very much the same when left to your own devices…..I think the correct word to describe you all would be useless."

Eric places his arms around her, kissing her on her cheek. Mavis is delighted but she gently pushes him away.

"Get away with you….You'd better get your skates on if you're not going to be late…You don't want them to be sat waiting in that Hospital Ward do you?..."

He turns and is half way up the stairs in no time at all. He stops, abruptly, to shout back.

"Can I drop you off on my way Mavis….At the Club or are you going straight home?."

Mavis is now, carefully, removing a rich fruit cake from the oven. She shouts back to him.

"No you carry on…I've still got a couple of things to attend to before I leave….I'll close the house up behind me when I go….You just concentrate on the job at hand Mister…And HURRY UP!."

* * *

Fully dressed for the first time in many days makes Jenny feel quite strange. She is pleased that the, seemingly, ever growing lump she had been exhibiting has disappeared and she has, almost instantly, recovered her trim and attractive figure. She looks delightful in a new floral mini dress. Susan Summers has already gone home with her baby. Jenny smiles as she observes Lynda, back to her usual self after a traumatic couple of days, sitting up in her bed feeding a bottle to her daughter.

The curtains have been drawn around the bed next to Lynda's. Lynda does not know the expectant mother but, obviously, has great empathy with her current plight.

Lynda calls across the Ward to Jenny.

"I bet you can't wait to see the back of this place eh Jenny?.....Don't you worry Ricky will be here to free you both before very long….You lucky girls."

Jenny is carefully checking that she has put all her clothing and cards and odds and ends into her suitcase.

"I won't be sorry to get out of here Lynda and that's a fact….It was smashing having you and Susan here with me but I hope I never lay eyes on a certain Sister with a face on her like a jar of pickles ever again as long as I live."

Jenny nods towards the Nurse's Station and grimaces.

Satisfied that she has everything, Jenny closes her Suitcase, with a little difficulty. She looks over at the bed next to Lynda's. Her sympathetic observations are heartfelt.

"Here we go any Lynda…I don't think I know her….Do you?...The poor thing."

Lynda carefully shakes her head, so that she does not disturb her child feeding.

"No…I don't think I do either….Still I bet I soon get to know her in here…Especially as we will both have something in common to talk about."

Lynda looks up to the ceiling, exhaling, loudly, indicating her displeasure at the experience she has suffered. Jenny is still quite concerned about Lynda's welfare.

"How is it now Lynda?....Still a bit sore?."

Lynda nods but soon breaks into a broad smile.

"Yes it does but it was all worth it….Your Amy was thoughtful enough to be about the right size for beginners….Trust me to produce a whopper….Mind you big babies tend to run in our family…My brother was over twelve pounds when he was born…And…There were no caesareans in those days either…Mother has always said it took a few weeks before her eyes stopped watering altogether....I can believe that now...Thank God for these advances in medical skill and science...Mind you I think it was the aesthetic that did for me...I kept hearing that song by that new rock and roll group...You know the Beatles?....'She loves you....Yea...Yea...Yea.'.....I don't know why....I was out for the count but I could still hear that going on and on."

Remembering the actual time when Lynda came out of her deep sleep to rejoin the conscious, Jenny's conclusion, really. is inspired.

"That was definitely being played on the Radio when you eventually came round Lynda...Yes I'm sure it was....That could well account for your musical mystery...They seem to be playing those Pop Records all the time now....I must say I quite like them especially the Beatles... They look a bit odd though don't they?....Someone was saying that all the young Lads are having Beatle haircuts to attract the girls...I think it may take some time before it catches on around these parts... Ricky needn't bother....I have to say I quite enjoy listening to most of it but I'm not sure how long this new musical revolution will last... Older people simply call it making a loud noise...Nothing like proper music...Still...If it entertains some and cheers other people up....Who knows?....Let's wait and see eh?....We've got more pressing things to occupy our minds for the foreseeable future eh?."

Their little chat comes to an abrupt end as the double doors at the entrance into the Ward swing open. Eric comes into view, struggling, as he tries to manoeuvre a brand new carry cot through the spring loaded doors. He appears to be in excellent spirits.

"Good morning Ladies...I trust I find you all well...You don't happen to know if there are any new mothers and their babies looking for a quick escape route out of here do you?."

Jenny moves over to him and they enjoy their first hug, in a standing position, for quite a few days. They kiss briefly. Eric does not attempt to hide his obvious excitement.

"Bloody hell Jen....I just realised how nice it feels to hold you in my arms....All of you that is....Not just the top bit...And it's great to be able to get so close to you again."

Eric playfully pats Jenny's flat abdomen. They both laugh. Jenny is as pleased with the situation as Eric is.

"I agree Ricky but don't think you've got rid of that big lump altogether will you?....I think you'll find most of it is fast asleep in that cot over there....Or have you forgotten about your new daughter already?."

Eric pretends to be horrified.

"Forgotten?.....Forgotten?....How could I possibly forget my little Amy?."

He strides over to the cot, leaning in, grinning.

"I've got everything ready for you both at home Jenny....Even baked you a nice cake."

Jenny nods even though she is doubtful that his statement is actually true. Her suspicions are soon confirmed as Eric continues to boast.

"Not a dirty dish to be seen and spotless."

Jenny has an inquisitive look.

"All your own work I suppose?....You didn't need any outside assistance then?."

Eric prevaricates.

"Well Mavis did drop in for a few moments this morning.... Nothing much for her to do really....Still it was a nice gesture...Much appreciated I'm sure."

Predictably, Jenny does not believe him at all.

"Ricky!...It's a wonder a streak of lightening doesn't come through that window to strike you down...I bet you managed a little light dusting and a whip round with the Hoover...Eh?....If that house is clean and tidy it will be nothing to do with your efforts...I'm right aren't I?"

Eric grins, dropping his head, pretending to appeal for clemency.

"Hit the nail on the head have I?."

They laugh, hugging each other again. Jenny, suddenly, breaks away, now sounding as if she really means business.

"Well...Come on....Let's get out of this place...I want to call in at the shop on our way home to say hello to your Mum....And have a decent cup of tea for a pleasant change....So finger out...You'd better let me transfer Amy into her carry cot...Can you deal with my suitcase and what have you?....Make sure you get all my stuff...I don't want to have to come back for anything....No thank you...Come on....Chop....Chop."

Jenny manages to move Amy, tenderly, into her carry cot, without waking her up. Jenny places her on the top of her bed. She walks across to Lynda. After smiling sweetly at her baby Jenny leans over to gently kiss Lynda on both of her cheeks. They both have real tears in their eyes.

"The McCabe family are about to love and leave you now Lynda....I hope everything will be O.K....I know it will be...Keep in touch like we promised you've got both the telephone numbers haven't you?....Give me a ring...As soon as you can....We can arrange to have a day out with our daughters... A nice foursome....Eh?."

Lynda, smiling as she nods, pulls Jenny back to hug her again, kissing her on both of her cheeks with genuine affection."

"Bye for now Jenny love....Look after yourselves..."

She shouts over to Eric.

"You're in charge of these two now...Mind you make a good job of it or you'll have me to contend with...O.K.?"

Because of the luggage Eric is unable to wave. He smiles and nods to Lynda. The happy trio reach the double doors. Jenny is the last to leave, with a fond wave to her friend left behind.

* * *

"O.K…..Time I pulled my finger out."

Jenny is seated in the comfortable armchair in her own living room feeding Amy. Billy Dawes is present, on the sofa, gazing, lovingly, at his granddaughter and great granddaughter, smiling proudly. Nan is busy in the kitchen doing the families weekly wash. The sounds of the Hoover being used upstairs indicates that Mavis Green is also present giving a helping hand. Jenny breaks off Amy's feeding to gently rub her back, getting her wind up. Billy in awe of what he is witnessing speaks.

"Isn't she a little love Jenny?....I don't think I've heard her cry yet…. When you think about it….It really is a cockeyed miracle."

Jenny does not respond. She appreciates how much pleasure Billy is getting from being in the same room as his great granddaughter. Billy continues.

"It is Jen….It's a cockeyed miracle and no mistake."

Shaking her head, Jenny replies.

"You keep on saying that Granddad….You'd think I was the first woman in the whole world to have a new baby….There are hundreds and thousands of babies born every day…All over the wide World."

Billy is not impressed by this comment.

"I dare say you could well be right there Jenny…But I bet we have the bonniest little darling of them all."

Jenny smiles, proudly, as Billy reiterates.

"As I say Jen…It's a cockeyed miracle…."

She joins in by mouthing the words she knows he is about to repeat.

"A cockeyed miracle."

Wiping her wet hands on her apron, Nan walks through from the kitchen. She is obviously a very contented woman as she speaks to Jenny.

"Right....That's the washing all done and out of the way....Now our next priority is to put the kettle on so we can all enjoy a nice cup of tea....No arguments there eh Jenny?."

The sound of the Hoover stops as Nan speaks. She walks to the bottom of the stairs to call up to Mavis.

"Have you finished up there Mavis....I'm about to make a pot of tea....I'll bet you're spitting feathers like the rest of us."

Mavis makes a suitable noise in response to Nan, who then comments, as she quickly turns to go back into the kitchen.

"Good show....I think we all deserve a nice cuppa."

She glances towards Billy.

"With one possible exception of course."

Billy reacts by looking hurt.

"I suppose you've come to give us your moral support have you Billy?....Not to actually help by joining to do anything in particular."

Billy really is really upset now.

"Just a cockeyed minute Nan....If a great....Note that please.... GREAT!...Grandfather can't sit and admire his loved ones for a few moments in between jobs...It's a poor show....Anyways...I'm about to cut the grass for Ricky as soon as you get round to making the cockeyed tea."

Nan makes a fist but smiles as she shakes it at Billy. She realises that he is completely smitten in the presence of the mother and child. She sounds conciliatory.

"Keep your shirt on Billy....There's no call to turn nasty...You know I don't like it when you turn ugly like that...I do realise that you....William Dawes Esquire dead horse and donkey buyer....Must be the one and only GREAT grandfather ever heard of in the whole Country and many other places as well."

Mavis, the sleeves on her blouse rolled up and wearing a loose scarf around her head, carries the Hoover into the room. She places it under the stairs, commenting.

"There we go….A little work but carried out often….That's always been my motto….I like to keep on top of any housework…A stitch in time always saves nine…I've always believed in those little words of wisdom."

Jenny expresses her gratitude.

"I wonder what on earth we would have done without you and Nan and Rickie's Mum…I really am very grateful to you all…I wish there was something we could do for you all in return."

Mavis dismisses her comments with false contempt.

"What nonsense….Dear Dear….Seeing you with Amy… and Ricky so happy…That's reward enough as far as I'm concerned…I can't speak for the others but I bet they all feel the same as I do."

Nan reappears with a tray containing all the teas things. She immediately enters into the conversation.

"Quite right Mavis….You mustn't think you're putting on anyone Jenny…It's a genuine labour of love and we're pleased to be able to help out in any way we can…Now come on….Let's have a nice cuppa…. I'll be mother."

Jenny, gently, places her hands under Amy's arms to lift her up. She dangles the tiny, limp, child in front of her. Shaking her head, she speaks, smiling adoringly at Amy.

"I think we'd better do something about a certain little lady's full nappy before we tackle anything else…Eh?."

She speaks in a babyish voice to Amy.

"Shall I take that nasty nappy off you…Eh?."

Mavis reaches over with her arms outstretched.

"Here let me do the honours Jenny…You enjoy a nice little rest whilst you have your cuppa."

Jenny thinks about protesting for a second but instantly realises that it would be pointless. She kisses the child and hands her over to Mavis.

Mavis kisses and hugs Amy as she moves her over to the table under the window. Jenny stands up to pass her a large basket containing clean nappies and many other necessary items. Nan is passing the cups and saucers to Jenny and Billy.

"Now come on Jenny....Take Mavis's advice...Sit down and drink your tea whilst it's still hot."

Nan cuts a large slice of cake, passing it, on a small plate to the eager Billy, who adjusts his position to receive incoming treats.

"I dare say we can depend upon you to force down a large piece of this delicious home made cake can we Billy?."

Billy bites off a large piece, smiling and nodding and chewing, all at the same time. She leaves Mavis's tea on the tray before she sits down with an, exaggerated, sigh of relief.

They are quietly sipping their tea as Mavis attends to Amy when Jenny speaks.

"Ricky is going to see the Vicar sometime today to see if he can make the arrangements for Amy's Christening...All being well we should be able to go ahead as soon as a week next Sunday afternoon.... I hope so anyways....There's no point in waiting...It'll be a nice family day out for us all."

Nan keenly nods her agreement.

"Oh good show Jenny....That's another fine treat to look forward to....I really love christenings...I always have....Better than any other family gathering in my opinion."

Having changed Amy into a clean, dry, nappy, Mavis carefully passes the child to an expectant and delighted, Nan. She then carefully lifts up the dirty nappy to walk behind Billy on the sofa on her way to the kitchen. Billy, who has demolished his cake and drunk his tea, screws his face up into a grimace.

"How can something as sweet as our little Amy produce something that smells as bad as that....It's making my cockeyed eyes water."

Mavis and Jenny laugh but Nan is not amused.

"Well....If you've got any complaints in that department Billy perhaps we should all remember who the child's... Ahem....Great...Great Grandfather is...."

Billy is embarrassed as she teases him.

"Old Billy the POO!...Eh?....That might account for it...Eh?....I must say I admire your nerve Billy Dawes."

They all laugh with the exception of Billy. He rises, swiftly, to his feet. He chooses to ignore Nan's comments completely as he makes for the door.

"O.K.....Time I pulled my finger out....Let me get at that cockeyed grass....Thanks for the tea and all that."

* * *

"Quite a character old Mabel Brooks."

The time has now moved on to half past nine in the evening. Eric walks into the Clubroom at the Lapley Vale Bowling and Sports Club. Woody and his friends Norman and Eddie are in their usual positions at the bar. Alf is behind the bar. There are a few men playing snooker and darts but it is fairly quiet by the recent, new, standards of attendance being set by the Club Members.

Eric does appear to be preoccupied as Woody digs his hand into his pocket.

"Now then Daddy....I bet you're ready for a nice pint of Alf's best bitter eh?."

Eric nods a greeting to them.

"Cheers Woody....'Evening Gents...I definitely do need a pint.... You can say that again.

As soon as Alf places the drink in front of Eric he takes a long draught out of it, much in the style of his Father. He nods his appreciation.

"Thanks Alf...Cheers."

Woody has detected that all is not well with his young friend. He cautiously enquires.

"Something wrong young 'un?....You don't appear to be at your radiant and sparkling best....What's up Lad?."

Eric seems ready to get something off his chest in the company of people he trusts. He lowers his tone.

"Well... After closing the shop tonight...I needed to go up to Dickie Mitchell's for an hour or so to finish off a couple of things I was doing and....Well...I called in a the Parish Church to see the Vicar....You know old Whistling Reggie?...To sort out some of the arrangements for Amy's christening."

Woody interrupts him, he sounds concerned.

"Bloody hell Ricky....I hope you're not going to say that you've made a balls up of those arrangements....Mavis is really looking forward to that little ceremony."

Eric, instantly, puts his mind at ease.

"Oh no there's no problem with the actual arrangements....A week on Sunday at half three in the afternoon...There's no problem there... All fixed up that is...No...That's not it....It's that new Curate."

They are not able to understand.

"You know....That new posh fellow....Jeremy....Jeremy whatshisname...Something double barrelled...The Curate....Reggie's latest understudy."

The three men are still waiting to be made aware of the cause for Eric's obvious concern.

"Well...We've got to have him to conduct the Service in the Church...."

They are all staring at him. None of the three Have yet detected anything to be concerned about. Norman speaks, Somewhat, sarcastically.

"Far be it from me to interfere with any ecclesiastical matters Ricky....But I think you'll find....Unless I am severely mistaken.... That's what Vicars and Curates and the like are there for isn't it?."

Woody and Eddie eagerly nod their agreement. Eddie comes into the conversation.

"Norm's right Ricky....You can't have a proper Christening without a Vicar or the like being present."

Eric is getting frustrated. He bangs his fist on the bar, now shouting.

"Bloody hell fire!....I know that....But it's this new bloke.....Have you been listening to some of the tales that have been circulating about him?"

They, quite clearly, have not, Eric continues.

"Did you hear about John Brook's Grannies funeral the other week?."

Again, nothing, blank stares.

"Christ!....Apparently this Jeremy is such a twit that he almost buries himself in the grave with John's Gran......By accident."

There is still no, expected, response. Eric is now beginning to lose his cool altogether.

"Honestly!....He shot into the grave.....On top of the coffin.... Look....It was John Brooks who told me about it....It was nothing short of a bloody fiasco....He slipped and fell into the open grave...In the middle of the service....In front of all the mourners and everyone."

Woody, Norman and Eddie are all desperately trying to visualise the unlikely scene, as described. Eddie asks.

"Did he hurt himself Ricky?."

Eric is struggling to keep his temper under control. He hopes that a break through might be imminent.

"No....Apparently not Eddie...Because....According to John's version of events he came back out of the hole quicker than he went in....But you see that's what I'm worried about....Old Reggie....You know the whistling Vicar?..."

They keenly nod.

"When I spoke to him....At the Vicarage....When I called round on my way to the Nursery...I ask him if he would be doing the honours himself....Personally....He said it was one of the Curate's duties....He did explain it all to me....Bloody hell...He said it would have to be the Curate....I couldn't talk him out of it...Well not without becoming a bit too personal....I haven't mentioned anything to Jenny yet...All she know is the Christening in on and she is really looking forward to it..."

Woody interrupts.

"And so are a few other people I could mention Ricky....You don't think John Brooks was pulling your leg do you?."

Eric looks as if he is about to explode.

"I mean to say....A Vicar falling into the grave...It does sound a little far fetched to me Ricky."

Norman and Eddie nod. Eric grasps the bar with both hands. He adopts a very determined tone.

"Look....All I can tell you is that I spoke to John Brooks....Just after the funeral....Christ....He came into the shop to pay for the wreaths and flowers and all that...He nearly pissed himself laughing as he was telling me the story....He almost ended up being a stretcher case...In the shop....And that's not all...I've been hearing other stories about Jeremy....I met Harry Longfellow...You know?...He owns that driving school?....He was up at the Nursery the other day....You should've seen Harry's face when someone happened to mention the Curate's name... He was on about him backing into a bloody tree....Nearly wrote the car off and had the nerve to blame Harry for it....Harry described him as a complete and utter Pratt with a total absence of any sort of normal coordination....Listen....I have to admit it...I'm a worried man."

It is obvious that Eric is genuinely concerned but the older men suspect that he may be guilty of being slightly over sensitive. Woody laughs, shaking his head.

"Look Ricky....Just because he may have had a couple of unfortunate accidents doesn't automatically mean that he can't be trusted to carry out a simple christening service...Bloody hell...I don't know much about it but I would image that they are one of a Vicar's easiest jobs."

Norman and Eddie agree but Eric, remains, far from being convinced.

"Well....I just hope you're right Woody....Christ if he manages to bury himself at funerals what is he capable of doing at a christening."

Norman laughs and rather unwisely decides to be funny.

"He probably ends up drowning himself in the font eh?..."

He chuckles but soon realises that his comment has not be helpful. Eric's knuckles are white as he grips the bar again.

"Never mind drowning himself....I'm not bothered about him doing that....It's little Amy....Now....Now can you see why I'm a worried man?....I can't get it out of my mind....I feel sick...Just the thought of it."

Eric is comforted by the feeling that his friends are now, at last, aware of the reason why he is so worried. Eric attempts to adopt a more positive approach.

"I have managed to convince Reggie that he must be there.... Said the family would expect to see him...Even if he wasn't actually doing the job himself...He assured me that he will be present...Said he wouldn't miss it....I did detect a slight element of anxiety being present whenever Reggie actually mentioned Jeremy's name...I don't know it was just a hint of concern but he covered it up very well....Anyways.... We're stuck with Jeremy....He'll be performing the service....I've tried my best to alter things but I got nowhere....Bloody hell fire."

All four of the group are now looking quite glum. They are joined by Bert McCabe and Billy Dawes. Bert is smiling from ear to ear, eagerly anticipating a pint of best bitter. Eric sneakily signals to Woody, Norman and Eddie to keep quiet about the Curate. Bert notices their expression, he addresses Billy, loudly.

"Well we have come across a happy band of pilgrims here Billy.... Christ just look at them....They've all got faces on them like smacked arses...Eh?...Eh?."

Billy, who is slightly out of breath after keeping up with Bert on their way in, responds.

"You can say that again Bert....Looks like we're in for a fun filled night of cockeyed belly laughs...What's up with you all?"

No-one knows how to react because of Eric's indication that he does not want them to discuss his concerns. Eric steps into the void. He acts as if he is surprised to see them. Laughing, falsely and unconvincingly, he splutters.

"What?....No....Oh hello Dad....Billy....No....No we're alright.... We were just saying how sad it was about....Er....John Brook's

Grandmother dying and having to have a funeral and all that….You know?…How sad it was for them and….Er everyone."

Eric feels that he has escaped by planting a red herring and is quietly pleased with himself, in the circumstances. Bert pauses to glare at Eric. He comments, with a tinge of disbelief apparent in his tone.

"Sad?….Sad?…Well yes of course sad….But I feel I should point out that she was well over ninety years of age…You could hardly say she had been cut down in her prime…Eh?….Eh?…Quite a character old Mabel Brooks…."

Bert looks around their faces as he grins.

"Liked her drop of whisky….Never let a day go by without a swig of her medicine as she called it….Christ….It had to be a burial…. There would have been an objection from the Fire Brigade if they'd even mentioned cremating her….They'd never have been able to put the bloody fire out…Eh?…Eh?."

Bert and Billy laugh but the others are a bit half hearted in their response to the injection of McCabe humour.

Bert, becoming impatient, shakes his head before He, deliberately, nudges Billy.

"There's even more sadness about than that you know Billy."

He has everyone's attention.

"Yes I'm afraid so….Billy and I have been standing here with our tongues hanging out for the last five minutes without any mention of us getting a pint from anywhere….Eh?….Eh?."

Eric, resigned, nods to Alf, who is already pulling two pints. Eric gets his money out. Billy declares.

"Two grown men….Dying of thirst….Standing at the bar….Now that's what I call cockeyed sadness."

They all end up laughing as Alf pulls them all another pint.

* * *

"Everything arranged for the Christening Ricky?."

Jenny has taken Amy around to visit her Grandparents, Bert and Alice McCabe at their home. All are seated in the front room. Alice has Amy on her lap and Bert is looking on with genuine affection. Jenny is pouring tea into china tea cups from an ornate tea pot. There is a delicious assortment of cream cakes on a glass stand next to the tea things. Jenny passes a cup and saucer to Bert, who can hardly take his eyes of the baby. After almost dropping his cup and saucer he manages to adjust himself before speaking affectionately to Jenny.

"Oops a daisy....Thanks Jenny love.....I'll tell you what...If there was ever a bonnier child than our Amy then I would like to see it...Eh?...Eh?.."

They all smile in agreement. Alice speaks to Amy.

"You had better go back to your Mummy for your tea darling....I'm sorry but Grandma is unable to be of assistance to you in that particular department for the time being....You'll have to go to Mummy for a little while yet...Yes you will...."

Alice kisses Amy on her head as she gently passes her over to Jenny, who is now seated. Jenny soon has her baby feeding. Alice smiles as she admires the spectacle.

"Oh....What a sight....Perfectly natural just as God intended....I really am so pleased that you decided to breast feed Jenny love....I don't care what anyone says it's got to be better for both mother and child."

She speaks to Amy again in a babyish voice.

"Yes your Mummy is a very clever girl isn't she?...Even your Grandpa would like to oblige you if he could….Perhaps it's for the best that he can't….It wouldn't be nice….No….Probably taste of beer…Yes it would."

Jenny laughs. Bert pretends to be offended.

"Now then Mother….Sorry…I mean Grandma….You must try to stop yourself from being indelicate….If it was up to me Amy could have the whole world and sixpence to go with it for good luck."

The ladies smile contentedly.

Alice opens a cupboard on her sideboard. She turns to Jenny.

"I'm not sure if you'll want this Jenny love but I've got it ready just in case you do."

She removes a large brown paper bag which contains an infant's christening gown. It is sparkling white and most ornate. She carefully shakes it out to display it fully. Jenny gasps as Alice comments.

"There it is….It still looks as good as new…It's hard to believe that both Bert and Ricky were christened in this."

Bert is embarrassed.

"Christ Mother….I was only a baby myself at the time….Still it would be nice if you decided to use this treasured family keepsake for this most important of days….Eh?...Eh?....We would be very proud and pleased if you did Jenny love."

Jenny is stunned. She is clearly enthusiastic when she responds.

"Apart from the fact that it is the most fabulous thing I think I have ever seen….And that Amy would be proud and honoured to wear it….We wouldn't like to be faced with the added expense of buying a new one anyways….It's beautiful Mum….Amy will be delighted to be christened in it…Oh I hope I haven't given you the wrong impression…. Ricky and I are doing fine financially but we are just having to watch the pennies for the time being.."

Bert and Alice are concerned. Alice speaks.

"Look Jenny love....I hope you will never leave yourselves short of anything when you can approach Bert and I....I mean to say.... We aren't exactly rich but we are fairly comfortable...And we are well aware of the difficulties a young couple may have to face when they start their married lives together but we are a family and I think you realise that we will help each other whenever we can."

Bert is smiling, nodding.

"Yes that's quite right Jenny love...Mother and I have had to go short a few times over the years...Eh?...Eh?."

Alice turns on him, sharply.

"I don't remember too many occasions when you had to go short of your precious beer Bert...Now that would be a serious state of affairs."

They all chuckle as Bert attempts to be wise.

"Ah yes Mother...That may well be true...But...What you have to bear in mind when making that sort of statement is the fact that it's not always my money that has ended up paying for the beer...Eh?...Eh?."

They instantly appreciate what he means.

"Take it from me ladies....It's not all beer and skittles in today's modern Police Service...As a matter of fact....Getting free beer is one of the very few perks still available to the more popular and successful Officers nowadays...Eh?...Eh?."

They are still laughing as Eric pulls up outside in the van. He walks up the path and through the front door. Bert nods and to his Son as he holds the door open.

"Just checking up on your Wife and Daughter are you....Or did you hear the sound of tea brewing...Or did you see your Mother coming out of the Bakers shop this morning...Eh?...Eh?."

Eric nods, kisses his Mother on her cheek and moves towards Jenny and Amy. He notices the cakes. He turns to Bert.

"Neither of those reasons Dad....I thought I had better get round here before a certain well known gannet demolishes all the best cakes."

Both men make a lunge for the cakes but Alice sweeps the plate off the table to offer the first choice to Jenny. Jenny quickly makes her selection but Eric, deliberately, makes a meal out of his turn. He just manages to get his favourite chocolate éclair before Bert whips the plate away from him. Bert pretends to be upset.

"Bloody hell Mother....We're back to being the swift and the hungry in this house again are we?...Eh?...Eh?."

Turning to Jenny he remarks, sarcastically.

"I see your Husband hasn't lost his appetite...Mind you he always used to pick at his food like a bird when he lived here Eh?...Eh?...Yes a bloody VULTURE!....Eh?...Eh?."

Everyone enjoys a laugh before they start on their cakes and tea. Bert manages to carry on talking to Eric.

"Anyways buggerlugs....I wanted a quick word or two with you.... Yes....I called in the Vicarage today to see old Reggie the Vicar....Just as a matter of routine....No special reason at all...He seemed a bit defensive to me....I wasn't sure but I gained the impression that he was apologising to me about something...I couldn't get to the bottom of it...But he did say that you had visited him to make all the arrangement for the Christening service....Said he managed to recognise you after all those years since you and your little friends attended his Infant's Sunday School classes...Eh?.....Eh?....Now tell me Ricky...Did anything happen between the two of you?....What the hell is going on?...I knew something was amiss... Reggie doesn't usually get the communion wine out when I pay him a social visit?...Eh?...Eh?."

Eric, feeling guilty, replies defensively.

"What do you mean?....No....Nothing....Well actually all I asked was for old Reggie to do the service for us himself....You know?.... With our family connections and what have you?...That was all."

Bert is, genuinely, shocked.

"What difference does it make?....What the hell are you going on about at all?....Eh?....Eh?....His Curate does most of the routine tasks around the Church....Old Reggie has more than one Church to look after....In any case Reggie wouldn't dream of undermining the authority of his Curate....You can't expect an important man like old Whistling Reggie to drop everything just to give us personal attention Ricky....It wouldn't be right....Anyways....Since when did you become so interested in Church Services and the like?....Eh?....Eh?."

Eric realises that his Father would not be interested in his personal fears regarding Jeremy Smith-Eccles. He decides to quit whilst he is ahead.

"No....Well you're right there...I'm not remotely interested if you must know....It's just I thought it might be better for Jenny and Amy and everyone else if we had the Big Boss himself...No...I'm not bothered really....Old Woody was telling me that christenings are a piece of cake for Clergymen....Their easiest job of the lot he said...No nothing's amiss....Everything is fine....No problems."

Although Bert is far from satisfied he decides to let the whole matter drop. Jenny is quietly rubbing Amy's tiny back, resulting in the emission of a surprisingly loud burp. Any remaining tension is instantly dispelled as they all laugh at Amy. Alice quips.

"Now that's the first time I've seen her Granddad Billy in her Jenny love...Sounded just like him when he drinks his beer too fast."

Everyone nods, laughing as they agree. Jenny speaks.

"I just hope she hasn't inherited some of her Great Grandfather's other little traits....If you know what I mean?."

They all chuckle as Bert retorts.

"Yes I think we all know exactly what you mean Jenny love...We certainly...Cockeyed do....Eh?...Eh?."

Alice attempts to restore some sanity into their conversation.

"Everything arranged for the Christening Ricky?....No snags or anything we ought to be told about in advance is there?....I'm really looking forward to it."

Eric has to reply through a mouthful of his second cream cake.

"No....No....Everything's on the ball Mother."

He feels less than convinced in his own response. He makes a determined effort to sound really confident.

"Alf has set aside the Clubroom for a little family celebration after the service....I understand there were no objections from the Police...."

Actually smiling now, he nods towards his Father. Bert grins in a cocky manner. Eric continues.

"Woody and Mavis have been briefed on their duties and what have you....And Jenny has seen Kay....You know Kay Brown?....Her friend?....She's going to be the other Godmother...So as you can see everything is boxed off and we're ready to go."

Eric is relieved that he has convinced his family that all is well. He still wishes he had no lingering doubts himself. Alice smiles as she speaks.

"Oh that good Ricky...Your Dad and I are so pleased that you have asked Woody and Mavis to stand for Amy...I know some people might think they are a bit old but I for one don't care...I don't think our Amy could have more loving Godparents than those you have chosen for her...."

There is total agreement. Alice now spoils it.

"And of course Woody has been present at all of the numerous head wetting ceremonies that have been taking place since Amy was born."

Alice pulls a face as she nods towards the two men. They back off because they know exactly what she is hinting at. Alice Then, purposefully, crosses her arms across her chest, she sits back to conclude.

"It's a miracle that the poor little thing hasn't been drowned with the amount of wetting that's been going on in that Club and some other licensed premises I could mention....Involving you all...And I included her Great Grandfather in that as well."

Bert and Jenny laugh. They wonder, for a brief second, why Eric almost choked at the very moment when his Mother mentioned the word 'Drowned'.

* * *

"Thank you Gentlemen....That appears to be unanimous."

Ralph Jones, the Chairman, has called an afternoon meeting of the Committee at the Lapley Vale Bowling and Social Club. As is their usual practice, the snooker table has been covered with a large piece of plywood and a table cloth. The stools from around the bar have been utilised because ordinary chairs are be too low.

Ralph is seated at the head of the table with Vic Callow, the Secretary/Treasurer, at his right hand, as usual. All the other Members of the Committee, Eddie Brown, Billy Dawes, Bernie Price and the Steward Alf, are present.

The Chairman sounds confident, even chirpy, as he addresses his Committee.

"Right....Thank you Gentlemen....We're making very good progress with this very long agenda today...And may I take this opportunity to say Vic....Er Mr Treasurer....That I am delighted to hear how well our beloved Club is doing from a financial point of view as well as any other view you may care to look of...Yes....Nice isn't it?."

Victor coyly nods as he smiles. Ralph goes on.

"There has been no turning back since the day we received that generous donation from the Kenneth Gordon Trust...God Bless it.... Whoever...Or even whatever it may be...."

This comment is greeted by spontaneous applause.

"Now....Victor....If I may request you to put on your other hat..... I think that Er....Yes....Mr Secretary has a couple of pressing matters to raise with us....Isn't that right Mr Secretary?."

Vic, nodding eagerly, clears his throat before he rises to his feet to speak.

"Thank you Mr Chairman...First Item....Letters received...The first is from Mr Leonard Jopson recently appointed to the dizzy heights... On promotion...To the Editor of the Lapley Vale Examiner."

Lenny is well known to everyone present.

"Mr Jopson wishes to expand his circulation figures by specialising in the inclusion in the newspaper of certain items of particular local interest...He is sure this will definitely do the trick."

They are all listening intently, determined to understand what Victor is saying, without having to ask. They are all curious wondering what on earth Lenny could possibly have in mind that might be of any possible interest to them.

"In short....Mr Chairman....Members of the Committee...Mr Jopson wishes to include a full page feature on our beloved Club in his highly acclaimed journalistic publication."

They are dazed, taking in the information, not quite sure if they understand what Lenny wants, hidden somewhere in Vic's exaggerated communication.

"I have conversed with Lenny and I understand he wishes to take some photographs...Which he intends to use together with some old photos recovered from the Newspaper Office's Archives...Which he had in his possession... Also borrowing some of the ones we have displayed around the walls of our Clubhouse...He intends to cover the complete history of the Club from the earliest beginnings up to and including all our excellent present day facilities...And well....In addition to the photographs he needs plenty of first hand information from us to authenticate the completion of his article in style."

Bernie interrupts.

"Tell the nosey bastard to knob off....What's our Club got to do with him?....What's in for him I'd like to know?...Christ he'll be asking us to sell copies of his rubbishy rag in here next…Cheeky bastard Lenny Jopson…..Always was nosey….I suppose that why they've made him the new Editor…Bloody cheek."

Ralph, instantly, realises that Bernie's, rude, comments will upset Vic. He steps in to take control.

"Now…Now…Bernie….Let's not be too hasty eh?....We all know Lenny….And he is a fully paid up Member…And he likes the odd pint or two in here does our Lenny."

Bernie jumps in again.

"Aye he does….But only if some other poor bugger pays for it…. Christ….What with him and Bert 'Tightassed' McCabe some people think they are having their pockets picked every time they show their faces in here."

Ralph is aware that Bernie's comments are annoying and upsetting all present now. He is close to losing his patience with his constant carping. He leans forward to speak directly to him, using a sharp tone.

"Look Bernie….I wonder if you would be kind enough to keep your big clanking gob shut for a change…Please!...I've heard it said that you could give an Aspirin a bloody headache and I'm beginning to believe that is correct now…So right….Can we please continue?.... Victor….What are your considered views on this very interesting suggestion?."

Vic pauses long enough to see Bernie sink back onto his seat with a sullen expression written all across his face. He offers a nod of approval to the Chairman for his punitive action and then speaks with vigour.

"Thank you kindly Mr Chairman….After carefully consideration I wish to report that I think this would be a wonderful idea….Apart from any other selfish motives it must be the best possible way to advertise without it costing us a penny….And let's be honest about this….None of us would strongly object to our photographs being displayed in a good light by our local media…And…Finally Mr Chairman….We have got a great deal to be proud of here."

Bernie is still sulking but the others are impressed by Victor's assessment of the offer. They grunt and nod their tacit approval. Victor, seeing his chance, continues.

"Lenny wishes to draw particular attention to what he describes as our excellent...Consistent...Playing record and of course the magnificent work undertaken on the general maintenance of the grass and the green by Woody...And not forgetting young Ricky."

They are quietly absorbing the possibilities the offer has provided for them but Bernie is sullen and still wants to be obstructive, even destructive. He suddenly lurches forward.

"Well that knackers up his plans to increase the circulation of his rag then...Eh?..."

He looks for support. None is apparent. He stresses his point with enthusiasm.

"If they publish a photo of that ugly bugger Woody Green on their front page only persons over the age of eighteen will be able to buy the paper...It'll have an 'X' certificate."

Bernie throw his head to roar with laughter. The others are not amused. Eddie, as one of Woody's best friends, speaks, trying to conceal his obvious contempt for Bernie.

"Mr Chairman....Please....Could I please ask that we attempt to discuss these matters placed before us without the constant interference we are getting from Bernie?...I'm afraid he's starting to get on my wick now and we are not making any progress with our deliberations....Are we?."

Billy is brave enough to support Eddie.

"Here....Here...Why don't you give your cockeyed gob a long rest Bernie?....I think we already know that you're anti-cockeyed everything."

Bernie responds with an aggressive glare. Billy immediately backs of. The Chairman regains control of the meeting.

"Gentlemen....Gentlemen please....Look Bernie....Can I through the Chair....Request you to confine your comments to relevant matters under discussion please?....And...And to stop subjecting us all to a constant barrage of your own personal and usually border line out of order comments?....Now pack it in!...Perhaps the best course of action for us to take is an adjournment on the issue to enable us to speak to Lenny in more detail and hear more about his legitimate and interesting request....Now I don't know about anyone else but I am now spitting feathers."

Ralph winks at Alf. There is a general movement which swiftly ceases when a smiling Mavis enters the room. She is carrying a large tray with steaming cups of tea and a plate of buttered scones on it. She politely addresses Ralph.

"Excuse me Mr Chairman but Alf is wanted on the telephone…It's the Brewery Alf…And I thought you must all be ready for a nice cup of tea and a scone."

Although this is not what Ralph had in mind, he nods his consent to Alf as he leaves the room and he makes a gesture to Mavis with his hand for her to carry on serving the refreshments. Eddie, ever the Gentleman, gets up to assist Mavis with the heavy tray. Ralph submits to the inevitable. He politely thanks Mavis.

"Thank you most kindly Mavis my Dear…I'm sure I speak for us all when I tell you how much we appreciate your most welcome contribution to what is proving to be a long and arduous meeting… Thank you."

Mavis smiles and quickly leaves the room. There is an instant rush for the biggest scone. There now follows a natural break whilst they all quietly sup their tea and munch their scones.

Ralph leans forward to enable him to catch a glimpse of the time on the clock over the bar. He immediately injects a sense of urgency back into their proceedings.

"Bloody hell fire….Look at that time…We really must press on… What else is there on the agenda Vic?."

Victor pulls himself together, spitting a few crumbs on his paper as he does so. He wipes his face with his handkerchief and brushes the crumbs off his papers before he speaks.

"Thank you Mr Chairman…Sorry about that…Er yes…There is a second letter…It's from a Mr Joe Summers."

Joe's name is greeted by moans and other signs of general disapproval.

"Yes…I know….But he has taken the trouble to write to us… Actually it's a nice letter in which he apologises from his inexcusable and much regretted behaviour and disgraceful conduct in the past… And he requests that his suspension from membership be revoked and lifted forthwith."

There is instant uproar around the table. Bernie's voice can be heard above all the others.

"The cheeky bastard….Bloody hell….What a cheek."

A brief stare from Ralph causes Bernie to shut up immediately. Ralph attempts to be rational.

"Yes…Thank you Vic….I have to report that I had prior notice of this letter…Joe approached me personally…Outside the Post Office on the High Street…After quickly ascertaining that he didn't want to smash my face in we had a long chat…I advised him to write the letter to be considered by us as the Committee."

Ralph appreciates that they all share the same low opinion of Joe. He continues.

"He informed me that he is now a much reformed character…A happy family man….He told me that he had recently been fortunate enough to acquire a good quality set of second hand woods…In short he wishes to avail himself of the facilities provided by the green as well as those at the bar."

There is silence as each man considers Ralph's additional information…. Billy is first to speak.

"I've never been one to hold grudges…But I'm afraid I find it hard to believe that Joe Summers could possibly change…Not without a cockeyed brain transplant."

Bernie blurts out.

"Listen Billy....If that man had a new arsehole transplant it would probably reject him...The man is bad news....Always has been... Always will...."

Eddie, abruptly, interrupts.

"Wait a minute Bernie...I think we should try to be reasonable here....If Joe has actually gone to the trouble of...You know?... Writing a letter to us...I for one say we must consider his request in a fair and open minded fashion."

Vic nods, raising his right hand to indicate his wish to speak. Ralph, who was about to speak himself gives way.

"Thank you Mr Chairman....I think Eddie has made a valid point there...And....I must draw to your attention to the written rules of our beloved Club which dictate....I quote....That having made a written request to the Chairman with a subsequent rejection....A suspended member may....And is entitled to....Make a personal appearance before the whole Committee to present his case."

This information stuns them. Ralph asks.

"Bloody hell Vic...Are you sure about this.?

Victor nods. He then passes him a copy of the Club Rules Book, opened at the relevant page. Ralph, swiftly, peruses it before he addresses them.

"Well...What can't speak can't lie Gentlemen...Shall I put the matter to a vote?."

Glancing around the table, Ralph sees that Eddie has raised his right index finger. He invites him to speak. Eddie clears his throat before he says.

"Thank you Mr Chairman....I know this may sound a bit silly but I think we ought to give Joe one last chance...Making it very clear that any further nasty misbehaviour would definitely result in him receiving a ban for life."

Eddie's submission is met with genuine sounds of approval. Eddie continues.

"And anyways...If he does act the Madam in here again little Norman will soon sort him out."

They all roar with laughter. Billy enhances the final comment made by Eddie.

"He really must be desperate to get back in here....You'd wonder why he's want to show his cockeyed face in here after the way he was chinned by Little Norm."

They continue to chuckle as Ralph draws them back to the matters in hand.

"Right....Anyone got any further comments on this application?... No....Fine....Those in favour of the...Stressed....Conditional reinstatement of Joe Summers as a Member."

They all raise their hands, although Billy needs to give Bernie a little nudge before he, reluctantly, does so.

Smiling broadly, Ralph declares.

"Thank you gentlemen...That appears to be unanimous."

Alf has returned from his telephone call and is standing a short distance away from the table. He is silently inviting Ralph to join him at the bar for a drink by moving his right hand up and down in front of his face. Ralph needs little encouragement. He briskly announces.

"Right...That's enough then....Meeting over."

Before anyone can argue or say anything else, Ralph tidies up his papers, rising to his feet.

"I think you should know that Alf has switched the beer on whilst he was attending to Club business."

The Members of the Committee needed no further discussion as they rapidly make their ways to the bar where six freshly pulled pints are standing on the bar awaiting their pleasure. In grabbing his first Ralph almost downs the whole pint in one swig. Alf, happily, shakes his head as the others construe this gesture as a challenge and attempt to emulate their Chairman, with relish.

* * *

"It's a pity they didn't knock me back in 1944.."

The most popular venue for the many senior citizens in Lapley Vale and surrounding districts on any Thursday morning is the local General Post Office on the High Street.

Saying it is a popular place to visit could be a bit misleading because most ordinary people enter those premises in a state of apprehension or even trepidation. This is entirely due to the attitude and behaviour towards their customers by the two female Clerks who serve behind the counter.

Bella Briggs is now in her sixties. She is an old fashioned spinster, who, together with her life long friend Lily Forest, has worked behind the counter for as long back as anyone, still alive, cares to remember. Bella has a very short fuse. She has never been noted for her approachability, patience or polite manners.

Lily is about the same age as Bella and there is little to choose between the two when it comes to being obnoxious. They look very similar with their grey hair tied in tight buns behind their heads. They always seem to wear the same outfits, which would not be out of place in the 1920's. Although they are unrelated Bella and Lily are generally known as the 'Terrible Twins'. Others call them 'Sodom and Gomorrah'. Their efficiency can not be questioned but the two women are suspected by many people of openly competing against each other in the nastiness stakes. Neither of them would ever miss an opportunity to be officious or starchy. If these public servants had anything to do with it, a visit to the Post Office would prove to be an ordeal for anyone of a nervous disposition. This is especially so on during their busiest period, which happens to be, on Pension Day.

Billy Dawes, collecting his own and Nan's Pensions, enters the Post Office to find he has a choice of two long queues stretching from the long service counter, behind which the two clerks sit, to the rear of the room, where there is a long shelf or desk used by the customers for writing addresses or sticking stamps on packages or letters or for any administrative purposes at all.

Although there are quite a number of persons waiting there is a strange air of reverence prevailing, similar to that found in a Church. There is a complete absence of any chatting or, indeed. talk of any kind. Billy chooses to stand in Lily's queue.

As he waits his turn he notices Peggy Hackett standing almost at the front of Bella's queue. Peggy, who is wearing his new artificial leg, appears to be unconcerned and at peace with the whole world.

The lady in front of Peggy steps back from the counter, looking shocked, clutching a large package and some stamps. Peggy, confidently, steps forward, placing his Old Age Pension and War Pension books on the counter. He pushes them towards Bella under a glass screen. He nods giving Bella a friendly smile.

Peggy's cocky demeanour is brought to an abrupt halt as Bella shoves the two books back to him. She snaps.

"You've signed the wrong week on that one…Go and put your glasses on and try again….NEXT!."

Peggy stares down at his books. Bella, sighs, then leans forward to point to one of Peggy's books with her pen. She is clearly condescending by her tone.

"You've signed the voucher for next week in that book….Look at the date….Look!"

Bella leans forward again attempting to peer around, the bewildered looking Peggy, to call out, even louder.

"NEXT!."

Peggy, realising his mistake, appeals to Bella.

"Alright....Bloody hell Bella....It's a genuine mistake...Lend me your pen for a second will you so I can sign the right one?....It'll only take a second."

Bella is horrified at the thought of her being Helpful or reasonable to one of her customers. She rises up on her stool to snarl at him in a very nasty fashion.

"Certainly not!...."

She glances at Lily who is nodding her agreement with her actions. This only serves to make Bella even nastier.

"The pens provided for use by the general public are fastened on chains at the back...Over there....NEXT!."

Realising that his appeal has no chance of being successful, Peggy snatches his books off the counter and lurches off towards the desk at the rear of the room. A frightened looking lady steps forward to take Peggy's place at the front of the queue.

Billy watches the antics and although he sympathises with Peggy and would like to say something in his support, he decides to keep his head down, pretending not to notice his old friend.

For some strange reason Bella's queue disappears quicker that Lily's and Peggy finds himself back at the front at the same time as Billy reaches Lilly. Peggy is obviously annoyed, he does not even notice Billy.

Peggy bangs a coin against his metal leg, making a loud metallic, chinking, noise. He sounds very upset.

"It's a pity they didn't knock me back in 1944......From the front line....Before I got this...Eh?."

Bella has her hand outstretched behind the glass partition waiting to take hold of his books again. Peggy rants.

"Yes...Whilst I was over there fighting to save the likes of you from the ravages if the advancing Nazi hoards...Nobody asked me if I had signed on the correct line when I volunteered for the Army in 1939.... You seem to forget that I fought for you Bella."

Bella is also experiencing some difficulty controlling her temper.

"You'll be getting a chance to fight for yourself in a minute Peggy Hackett!....One more word from you and I'll come round there to shuffle your teeth for you."

Billy has received his money but he remains transfixed as he anxiously awaits the outcome of what has now become a battle of two very strong wills. Peggy is not intimidated by Bella's remarks. He steps back slightly, tapping his false teeth with his coin.

"No....Wait a minute Bella....Don't get up of that fat arse of yours...I'll pass my teeth through to you so you can smash them to pieces with your stamper."

For one tense moment Bella actually thinks that Peggy is going to take his false teeth out in front of her. Seeing that he has achieved a partial victory by Bella's facial expression, Peggy grins, passing his books through to her. Bella almost sends her stamper through the wooden counter as she franks his books. She glares at him as she silently counts out his money before ramming it and his books back to him under the glass window. Peggy places the money and the books in his pocket. He emits a cavalier laugh before he places two finger up against the glass screen causing Bella to jump back with surprise. Peggy then throws back his head to march, smartly, away towards the exit. All those present are quietly impressed as he loudly bangs his false foot on the floor whilst making a dignified departure. Billy dashes out behind him.

On the pavement outside Peggy notices Billy for the first time. He nods a greeting.

"What a carry on Billy....That's no way to treat a bloody war hero....Did you see it?....That woman is a bloody menace."

Billy nods, eagerly. He thinks for a moment before he responds.

"Yes I did Peggy....Dreadful to behold...It's a cockeyed disgrace.... Incidentally Peggy when was it you were actually named a cockeyed hero?."

Peggy chooses to treat Billy's remark with contempt. He turns on his heels to walk away on his own, muttering under his breath.

* * *

"Bert McCabe…..You're one in a million."

Jenny McCabe and Susan Summers are pushing their new prams along a tree lined path inside Lapley Vale Memorial Park. The sun is shining brightly and the birds are singing. They veer off towards an vacant park bench. They manoeuvre their prams into safe positions and set the brakes. They both check that their tiny infants are fast asleep before actually sitting down on the bench.

Susan sighs deeply as he opens her packet of cigarettes. She offers one to Jenny, who politely but firmly declines to take one. Susan takes one out for herself as she speaks.

"Sorry Jenny….I forgot for a minute…You don't do you?."

Jenny shakes her head as Susan lights her cigarette, taking a long draw from it. Blowing the smoke out she sits back, relaxed, enjoying a perfect day in pleasant surroundings. She calmly turns to ask Jenny.

"Still coping O.K. with the breast feeding Jenny?."

Jenny is happy to respond.

"Oh yes….No problems in that department and Amy is thriving on it….They do say there's nothing finer."

Susan takes a furtive look along the pathway, first to her right and then to her left. She takes another quick glance both ways to ensure they are not being overheard or observed before she slyly nudges Jenny.

"You're quite right there Jenny love."

She thrusts her chest forward to display her form as she starts to giggle.

"I did think hard and long about it when I had to stop with my first…You know our Tommy?....Even allowing for what you say is correct.…At that particular time it was the most sensible thing for me to do.…I was sorry at the time but I'm bloody glad I did now.…If I'd have done it for all four of mine…"

Susan glances all around once again before she continues. She cups her hands under her breasts as she speaks.

"I would have needed to lift my tits up to put my shoes on by now."

Jenny seems shocked for a moment but they soon roar with laughter. Jenny gives Susan a playful shove.

"Susan Summers.…You are awful.…The things you say."

Both are enjoying their little chat when Amy starts to cry. Jenny immediately tends to her. Leaning into the prams she talks to her baby.

"There…There little one.…Did the naughty Mummy and Auntie Susan wake you up with their wild laughter then."

She fishes around inside the pram and then places a dummy in Amy's mouth. Amy settles down instantly. Jenny looks at her wrist watch. Pulling herself together before she speaks.

"I'd better be making tracks Susan.…Amy will be due her next feed at four o'clock and I don't fancy feeding her out here in the open air."

Susan puts her cigarette out, rising to her feet.

Jenny smiles as she remarks.

"It's been really smashing meeting up with you both today Susan.… And I'm very pleased to hear the good news about your Joe…You know?...A changed man.…Behaving himself and all that."

Releasing the handbrake on her pram, Susan looks and sounds rather cautious.

"Yes.…Oh aye…Credit where credit's due…But I won't be banking on it being a permanent state of affairs.…He's usually fine until he gets into one of his drinking modes.…Fortunately with an extra mouth to feed there hasn't been all that much money left over for his beer.…

I know it will end some day soon but I must say I am enjoying the situation for as long as it lasts."

Chuckling merrily the two women push their prams away from the bench, heading back along the path.

They are strolling through a very sheltered stretch of pathway when they both stop, jumping back with fright. A scruffy looking man in his thirties, wearing a full length raincoat, suddenly leaps out of the bushes about ten yards ahead of them on Susan's side.

He has his hands deep down inside the pockets on the raincoat and although the buttons are undone he is holding the coat closed across the front of his body with his concealed hands. He has a weird expression on his spotty face as he speaks in a nervous, slightly teasing, tone.

"Bet you can't guess what I'm holding in my hand girls....Eh?."

He leers at them as Susan grabs hold of Jenny by her arm. Jenny is terrified but Susan shoves her along using her shoulder, encouraging her to move in a forward direction with their prams. Susan throws her head back, speaking to the man in a defiant, controlled, way.

"Listen Sonny....If you can hold it in one hand we aren't interested."

She is leaning against Jenny forcing her to keep moving. They are level with the man, who appears to be a little confused by Susan's bold reaction. Still holding his coat together he confidently exclaims.

"Well you wouldn't want it on the end of your nose as a wart Missus...And I'll tell you......"

Susan stops, turning quite vicious as she interrupts him in mid sentence.

"Look Mate if you don't piss off and play with your little toy somewhere where you won't be annoying decent people...I'm going to give you a sharp kick in your couple and then you can take them up to the Hospital to show all the Nurses...Now PISS OFF!....I won't warn you again Mister."

The bewildered flasher thinks for a second or two but decides to give up. He turns to disappear back into the undergrowth where he had come from.

Jenny has turned white and is shaking. Susan cajoles her along until they reach a clearing. She places her arm around Jenny trembling shoulders. Her tone is concerned and soothing.

"It's alright now Jenny....He's gone....We're safe now...Are you alright?."

Jenny just about manages to speak.

"My God Susan I never thought that would ever happen to me.... Especially not in Lapley Vale in the middle of the afternoon...Oh Su....You were marvellous...I think you may have frightened him to death...He'll definitely think twice before he leaps out on anyone else for a while...Really Susan....You were great....You showed no fear...I don't know what I would have done without you."

Susan, relieved to see her friend has recovered, smiles and they walk along in reflective silence for a few minutes. Susan stops to speak.

"I'm glad you think I'm so brave Jenny love...Come on let's get out of here...Eh?....It's not only the babies who will need to be changed now...I'm not kidding neither."

Jenny is shocked for a moment but then realises that Susan's sense of humour is coming to their rescue once again. She giggles and then they both laugh as Jenny says.

"Oh Susan...You really are awful...Come on."

They laugh for a few moments before Jenny returns to a more serious tone.

"Anyway....I am glad you were here with me....I think I might have died if I'd been on my own...Really Su....If you hadn't shoved me along I would have remained rooted to the spot."

Susan is now feeling quite proud of herself. She laughs again before she remarks, with genuine sincerity.

"I'm glad I was able to help Jen....But just in case you though I was being brave let me tell you... I really was shitting myself....I mean it Jenny....I can still feel my insides quaking...But there was no way a little pervert like him was going to know it..."

Her face erupts into a devilish grin as she deliberately glances all around before she says.

"Come on Jenny love....Let's make ourselves scarce before we meet up with another one....I don't think I could manage two in the same day without really having a very nasty personal accident...Eh?."

They both roar with laughter. Susan nudges Jenny before they move off again.

"Perhaps it's the weather.

* * *

Having taken Susan home, Jenny pushes her pram around to the Bowling Club. Woody and his wife Mavis are taking afternoon tea on the veranda with Alf. They have been anxiously waiting for Jenny's arrival since they had received a telephone call from her informing them about the incident in the Park.

Jenny enters through the side gate. She stops the pram alongside the table where her friends are seated. Mavis immediately checks that Amy is all right. They are waiting to hear the full story. Jenny sits down before she speaks.

"I don't know what I would have done if Susan hadn't been there with me....She was marvellous...."

All are relieved because they can see for themselves that Jenny does not appear to be any the worse for her ordeal. Alf is the first to enquire.

"Did you recognise the dirty swine Jenny?."

Jenny shakes her head.

"No...No well I didn't really look at his face.."

She breaks off to laugh with irony.

"Oh hell what am I saying?....No...It was all over so quickly.... And I was so shocked at the time that I didn't pay any attention at all to his appearance...I couldn't give a good description of him...Really."

They shake their heads sympathetically as she adds.

"The only thing I can say for sure is I have never seen him before."

Woody tries to console Jenny.

"Look Jenny….A bloke like that…It won't be long before your Father-in-law or one of his Bobbies will have him under lock and key where he belongs…From what little I know about what actually happened it doesn't sound to me as if this bloke can be the whole shilling and….."

Mavis interrupts him, sternly.

"Well I must say that I think it's absolutely disgusting that a man like that can just wander around….Doing unspeakable things with his fly buttons…In the middle of the afternoon….In a quiet Park….In Lapley Vale….I think Jenny and Susan have both been very brave and sensible in the circumstances…Do you know if Bert knows about it yet?."

They await Jenny's response.

"Well Yes…At least I think so…We spoke to Mr Snooks…The Park Keeper….As we were coming out of the Park…He said he would ring for the Police right away…We didn't want to wait for them…So I can only assume that the message has got through to those who can do something about it."

Alf speaks with genuine disgust.

"I don't know what this World is coming to…I agree with everything Mavis has said…It's coming to something when young mothers can't take their prams out for a push without being attacked or molested by…Herds….Bloody herds!...Of perverts."

The ladies agree but Woody is surprised at Alf's unaccustomed outburst.

"Steady on Alf….You're going slightly over the top there aren't you?...Bloody hell….I don't recall anyone mentioning herds….Herds?….Of perverts?."

Alf is temporarily hurt but soon appreciates that Woody is making a fair observation.

"We must try to keep the whole thing in some sort of perspective.... He didn't actually do anything did he Jenny?...Just a flasher wasn't he?.."

Jenny nods her head but then changes, shaking it.

"Yes…Well no…What I mean to say is….No…No he didn't even show his….Well you know?....He kept his raincoat over it…I certainly didn't see anything…But I definitely think he would have done if Susan hadn't chased him off."

Mavis tuts, Alf looks very angry. Woody is still attempting to calm things down.

"I'm not saying for one moment that this has not been a very nasty shock and all that…And I'm not saying that I wouldn't pay a King's ransom just to be able to place my size ten boot right up this bloke's arse…But…When you think about it…What sort of a person would be capable of doing this sort of thing…You've got admit it's all a bit pathetic…Isn't it?."

They are listening without making any comment.

"If you ask my opinion I would have to say that he must be a butty short of a picnic."

They all nod.

"Definitely got a slate loose to do that sort of thing….Stands to reason that does."

They are all in agreement. Before any further comment can be made Bert McCabe suddenly appears, in full uniform, on the veranda. He is smiling as he nods.

"Now then….This is where I find you all is it?...Eh?...Eh?."

Bert looks at Jenny, who bursts into tears. He puts his arms around her, giving her a tender hug.

"Are you alright Jenny love?....There…There…There's nothing to be worried about sweetheart….I've locked the culprit up and he's now on his way back to Hospital in Royston."

Jenny is instantly impressed. Her sobbing stops.

"You see….Everything's alright….It's a sad story really."

Everyone is listening with baited breath but Bert breaks off to exclaim.

"Bloody hell Alf….All this catching flashers doesn't half dry your throat out…."

Mavis reaches over for the tea pot but Alf is aware of what Bert means. He jumps up.

"Message received Bert….But hang on a minute….I'll just pop through to fetch you a nice pint of bitter….Don't tell them the story until I get back…I won't be a minute…Woody do you fancy a little refresher?."

Woody nods eagerly. Bert take his cap off and sits down. He shouts after Alf.

"Does Old Woody fancy one?….Eh?….Eh?….The chance of a freshly pulled nicely chilled frothy pint of your best bitter?...Eh?...Eh?….Is the Pope a catholic?....Does a bear shit in the woods?...Eh?...Eh?."

He instantly realises that he is being indelicate.

"Ooops….Oh sorry ladies….Er Mavis…Er Jenny…Slip of the tongue…I'm sorry about that."

Bert clears his throat and speaks in a false upper class BBC Newsreader's voice.

"Yes thanks awfully my man….Mr Green can be persuaded to partake on this occasion….Thanks awfully much."

Bert grins from ear to ear as the Ladies chuckle. He winks at Woody.

"Eh?......Eh?."

He gets to his feet to peer into Amy's pram. Jenny warns him.

"Please don't wake her up Dad….Let her sleep…She's not long finished her feed….I fed her when I called in at Susan's to use the phone to tell Mavis what was going on….I thought Ricky might have been around here."

Bert steps away from the pram. He smiles cheekily.

"Don't you worry about old Granddad Bert…Now don't you be fussing yourself Jenny love….I wouldn't want to wake the little darling up….Eh?...Eh?....I just wanted to take a little look that's all….I think this child is getting bonnier every day…If that was possible…Eh?…Eh?."

Alf returns with three frothing pints on a tray. Bert appreciates that they are all anxious to hear the details about the capture of the flasher. He takes a long drink first. Sits back and starts to explain.

"It's a long and sad story really….He was a brilliant young man….An accountant or the like….Wonderful prospects until he got jilted at the altar on his wedding day."

The Ladies gasp.

"Oh yes he was left standing at the altar…It transpired that his fiancée had more than one string in her bow and she vanished off the scene with a lingerie salesman from the other side of Oldham…Never to be seen around these part again…Eh?….Eh?."

Although they all know Bert well enough to be suspicious about the validity of whatever he says, no-one can avoid feeling, just, a shred of sympathy for the offender. Bert takes another swig from his pint, almost finishing it.

"As you can well imagine he lost his bottle completely…And then….Eventually….He fell off his perch good and proper…Suffered a complete nervous breakdown…Ended up on a Psychiatric Ward in the Hospital over Oldham way where he still remains to this very day…Eh?….Eh?."

They are shaking their heads, trying to understand.

"Had to be put away permanently for his own good…Sad….But there you are….That's what happened to him…It certainly doesn't explain his disgraceful conduct but at least it puts it into some sort of perspective…Eh?…Eh?."

Bert breaks off to drain his glass. He wipes his mouth with the back of his hand before he continues.

"They say that he's very docile normally…Probably the medication they give him…Eh?…Eh?….But every now and again he takes off from the Hospital and decides to show his crown jewels to anyone who might wish to see them….Or anyone who doesn't wish to see them if it comes to that…Eh?…Eh?….They assure me that he's quite harmless really…Apart from the nuisance value….But they said he has never ever flashed to any young girls or children…He always picks on married women pushing prams…So I suppose we should be grateful for some small mercies there…Eh?…Eh?."

The whole group are totally absorbed in Bert's revelations. All shake their heads, reflecting, quietly, on what they have just heard. Mavis speaks.

"Thank goodness you caught him Bert…It's a shame for the poor fellow but I'm afraid you cannot allow a man like that to wander around unsupervised….I dare say he must realise that he has been put away for his own good as well as that of others."

Alf is placing the empty glasses back on the tray intent on re-filling them. He comments.

"You've got a point there Mavis love…Any normal bloke catching him up to his tricks would definitely thump him…There's no doubt about that…They wouldn't wait to hear his life story."

Mavis is sorting out the tea things as Jenny is preparing to move on. She addresses her remarks to Mavis.

"I must make tracks now….We've got Nan and Granddad coming round to our house for supper tonight…And Ricky won't want to wait for his meal neither."

Lifting up the heavy tea tray, Mavis responds.

"Hang on a minute Jenny love…Woody will be expecting his meal on the table despite all these events and goings on today…I'll walk along with you if you don't mind."

Nodding and smiling, she adds, playfully.

"Anyways…There's safety in numbers…Eh?."

Bert laughs.

"Let's hope that we've got more serious than a misguided flasher to worry about…Eh?…Eh?…Thank goodness we don't have a permanent flasher around these parts…A few years ago I had to deal with a flasher who had a regular round."

All are curious, not knowing what was coming next.

"Oh yes….Had regular customers….Oh Aye…He was always in position just inside the park gates….In all weathers….Mind you in the Winter….You know when it's really bitter cold….He wouldn't flash himself then….Oh no…He would stand there describing himself to all his victims….Eh?……Eh?."

Although they had all anticipated that Bert was trying to pull their legs, they all roared with laughter. Mavis wipes a tear from her eye as she lifts the tray up again. She walks off towards the kitchen as she comments.

"Bert McCabe….You're one in a million….I never know what you're going to come out with next….But having said that…Well done Bert….I'm sure everyone appreciates what a first class service you have performed for the public today by capturing that poor man and then making sure he was put back where he quite rightfully belongs…You're my hero Bert….Thank you on behalf of all of us girls you're a comfort to us all….Despite that wicked sense of humour of yours."

* * *

"And that's for forty years after you die."

Later the same day, in the evening, Woody and his friends Eddie and Norman are seated in their usual places at the bar in the Clubroom at Lapley Vale Bowling and Social Club. They are lauding and paying humble homage to their current local hero Sergeant Bert McCabe. Because of the swift and efficient manner in which the flasher had been dealt with by the local Police, the sorry incident is the main topic of conversation throughout the entire neighbourhood. Bert is 'reluctantly' accepting credit and accolades from his friends for what many people are describing as an excellent piece of Police Work.

Alf and Denise are busy behind the bar. There are groups of drinking men playing darts and snooker and there are queues waiting their turns to utilise the Club's facilities. There are quite a few, more sedate, domino and cribbage players seated around tables.

Eric McCabe accompanied by Billy Dawes joins Woody and company at the bar. Bert is the first to notice their approach.

"Now then....Alright Ricky...Hello Billy."

He continues as they nod their greetings.

"Everything O.K.?....Has Jenny recovered from her ordeal yet?...Eh....Eh?."

Woody is ordering two pints from Denise as they soon realise that Eric is quite upset. He nods to the others.

"Hello Dad....Gents....Yes....I think she's O.K. now....Even having a little laugh about it all."

The expression on Eric face changes as, suddenly, his anger is apparent for all to see.

"By Christ I wish I'd been able to get my hands on the bastard…It would've been his very last appearance as a flasher…And I'm not kidding neither."

There are sympathetic grunts and nods from all the others. Billy adds his comments.

"Those sort of blokes should have their cockeyed cocks cut off."

Eddie is about to laugh at Billy's remark but realises how upset both Eric and Billy, genuinely, are. He shakes his head, offering empathy.

"They do say that it takes all sorts to make a world but I feel sure we could all manage quite nicely without his sort of pervert in a place like Lapley Vale."

Norman agrees.

"Here….Here….But let's not forget."

He pauses to gesture to Bert.

"Our local Chief of Police."

Bert exhibits false modesty.

"Soon had him sorted out and no messing….Eh?...Smart piece of work in my books."

There is total agreement with these remarks. Bert continues to pretend that he is a reluctant hero but, in reality, he is loving every minute of the hero worship being heaped upon him. He attempts to look and sound off hand and casual.

"Well…When there's a job to be done….You know?...It's got to be done irrespective of the risks and danger that it may entail….It's not all beer and skittle in today's modern police service….Oh no….I was only making that very same remark to Ricky the other day…Wasn't I Ricky?...."

Eric, proudly nods. They are all looking on with admiration. Bert continues.

"Mind you….I have to say….I do find that the rigours of law enforcement give me one hell of a thirst…Eh?...Eh?."

They smile, shaking their heads. Alf has been listening in to their conversation.

"O.K. Bert....Message received and understood....Come on boys drink up...I'll see to these drink myself personally."

Bert's glass is first to empty. His face breaks out in a broad, ear to ear grin.

"How kind....How very kind Alfred."

The others quickly follow suit. Alf is filling their glasses as Woody comments.

"From what Bert was saying...Earlier on today...The poor bastard can't help himself."

They are curious.

"Yes....More to be pitied than blamed b y all accounts...Isn't that right Bert?."

Bert is now concentrating on taking the top off his fresh pint. Eric takes the opportunity to intervene.

"It's alright saying that Woody but...But when it's your Wife and Daughter involved....Well I find it difficult to have any sympathy with him....It's a bloody good job Joe Summers's wife Susan was with them at the time...My Jenny could tell you....Susan really put the skids under him."

Bert is now taking a further swig from his glass. Woody responds.

"I agree with you there Ricky....Mind you Susan Summers must be well used to handling dangerous nut cases...Eh?...She's been married to Joe for long enough."

They are smiling and nodding their agreement as Alf places the last two pints on the bar. He has been eavesdropping again.

"And that's something we'll all be getting a chance to do very shortly....The Committee have lifted his ban....We'll be having that soft bastard amongst us once again...Very soon."

They gasp with shock. Eddie, as a Committee Member, looking rather guilty, feels he must explain.

"Yes…Well yes….But listen….Everyone should be entitled to second chance….You know?....It's very easy to give a dog a bad name…"

Woody interrupts him in a derogatory fashion.

"Give a dog a bad name?....No self respecting dog would dream of being associated with that daft bastard….Christ almighty….The man is a well established head case of the first order."

Having started what has now become a heated debate, Alf attempts to lighten things up a little.

"Well I won't worry too much as long as I have little Norman at my side…Eh?....Joe won't step out of line if he thinks he might be upsetting the big hitter again….Eh?."

Norman is delighted to received this continuing adulation for his past actions against Joe's nastiness. Whilst they all enjoy a chuckle, Eddie takes the opportunity to explain further.

"Anyways….This is his final chance….If he causes any sort of trouble ever again he will be barred out for life and both the Chairman and the Committee have made this very clear to him."

Bert drains his glass. He is assessing the possibility of a swift refill. He addresses them.

"Going back to what Woody was saying before it is true to say that this offender is definitely a slice short of a loaf and unfortunately these type of situations can arise from time to time…He occasionally escapes from his keepers at the Hospital and then….As someone else has already pointed out…There has to be a responsible….Fully trained…Experienced criminal catcher available to deal with him…. Fortunately the good folk of Lapley Vale just happen to have the…. World's greatest…As their protector…Eh?....Eh?."

They shake their heads and smile as Billy reaches forward to lift up Bert's empty glass. He signals to Alf as Bert expresses his delight at his gesture.

"How kind….How very kind William…I'm glad to see that at least one of my adoring public is not backward at being forward when it comes to levels of appreciation being shown to a hero."

Billy grimaces as he addresses Alf.

"Give Sherlock cockeyed Holmes another cockeyed pint will you please Alf....And see to these other chaps as well please....I'm just very pleased that the flasher is back under lock and key where he belongs.... I have no time whatsoever for any of these cockeyed perverts."

Denise is assisting Alf with the order. Woody nods and smiles to her, then, politely, enquires.

"What do you think about all this Denise love?...This flasher?... What's your opinion about it all?."

She shakes her head, rather carefully, as she is giving most of her attention to the provision of a foaming head on the pint of beer she is pulling from the pump. She places the full glass on the bar before she speaks, quite calmly.

"Well...I'm very pleased that all the Ladies involved are O.K. and I hope they will not be any the worse for their very nasty experience."

She pauses to smile and nod at, the now smirking, Bert.

"And I'm very impressed by the efficiency of our local Constabulary... But....Speaking for myself personally...His trouser worm would've needed to be adorned with a set of flashing fairy lights for me to have even noticed it these days."

Harry Longfellow, the local driving instructor, joins them at the bar as they all laugh at Denise's remarks. He smiles, nodding to Bert.

"Evening Sergeant....Everything O.K?....I must say I was very glad you arrived back at the Police Station when you did this afternoon Bert..."

They are all listening to Harry, much to Bert's rather strange discomfort.

I thought that poor bloke was going to break the bleeding door down."

Bert is wishing Harry would shut up but the others are keenly interested.

"I went past three bleeding times with Mrs Sinclair in the car and each time he was banging on the door with his fists...Clawing with his fingernails...Boy...Was he desperate?."

409

Bert now exhibits a tight smile. Harry adds.

"The way he threw himself at your feet when you eventually showed up....Bleeding hell Bert that man looked to be in a dreadful state of terror and no mistake."

Bert is still hoping that Harry will just go away but Woody is getting more curious.

"This bloke Harry....The one who was trying to break into the Police Station...Was this bloke wearing a raincoat by any chance?....One of those long ones?."

Harry nods vigorously as he picks up his pint of the bar.

"Yes that's right Woody...A scruffy bleeder...He was in a right state of panic I can tell you....If Bert hadn't turned up when he did I was going to get Mrs Sinclair to stop so that I could find out what was upsetting the poor bleeder so much."

Accusing eyes are now beginning to focus on Bert. He realises, immediately, that he is now required to offer a very good explanation. In view of all the circumstances he bravely decides to accept defeat.

"Well....Some of these villains are sometimes easier that others to capture."

His companions are unimpressed. He adds.

"You never know which way things will turn out when you're on the track of a dangerous felon...Eh?...Eh?."

All those present are quietly making their own assessments of the situation. Eric throws his head back, a clear indication of his rising state of indignation, as he enquires.

"Are you telling me that this....Flasher....This dangerous felon....That you led us to believe you captured with utmost skill and efficiency....Actually....Actually gave himself up?."

Bert is now having to think on his feet but his back is, well and truly, up against the wall.

"Yes that is correct Son."

This reply is met by gasps of disbelief. Bert is struggling but is not, as yet, completely lost.

"Yes….He could feel the net tightening around him…He realised that it was hopeless for him to carry on….He knew what he was up against….The odds were stacked high….He knew he was beat."

Unfortunately none of the group are too impressed. Woody, lifting his cap to scratch his head, taunts Bert.

"You bloody old toe rag Bert McCabe…You didn't mention that this bloke gave himself up….Did you?."

They all glare at Bert, who is sweating slightly. Woody presses on.

"You bloody old swine…You were quite content to let us think that you had tracked him down…..Using unique skill and determination."

Although he knows the game is up, Bert's defence mechanism swings back into action.

"I don't think I used those actual words Woody…But I must confess that the poor bastard was so frightened that Susan Summers was going to get him he was very relieved to be taken into my custody….Eh?….Eh?…Wanted to be put in the safety of a strong cell immediately."

There is an air of disappointment, which enhances Bert's built in defence system even more.

"Mind you he had to be very skilfully dealt with…I bet I had him back inside his rubber room at the Hospital within the hour…He actually closed the bloody door behind himself…Eh?…Eh?."

Bert appreciates that all his efforts are failing to impress his friends. He adopts a silly smile, shaking his head. Woody speaks firmly.

"Right!….Get the bloody ale in Bert."

Acting even more sheepish than he now looks, Bert pulls his wallet out. His actions bring instant smiles to their faces. Alf springs, smartly to attention to give Bert a mock salute.

"Yes sir!….How many pints would the Sir like to pay for?….Sir!."

Bert gestures that he will pay for a full round. He then turns to speak directly to Harry.

"Well thank you very much Harry…You've no idea just how pleased I am to have run into you this evening…You've dropped me right in it you have….Eh?…Eh?."

Harry begins to panic slightly because he does not wish to get on the wrong side of the law. He starts to sweat as he stammers nervously.

"Bleeding hell Bert....What have I said?....I'm sorry but I couldn't help noticing that poor bloke outside your Police Station this afternoon....Honestly I thought he was going to rip the bleeding door off it's hinges...But...What have I said to drop you in anything?.... What did he do?."

The old friends are really enjoying the unexpected change turn in events. Bert has well and truly capitulated as he pretends to be shocked at the lack of change he receives from paying for the round of drinks. He laughs before he reassures Harry that he has not made an enemy of him.

"It's O.K. Harry....Never mind....No serious harm been done....I suppose you'll be wanting a pint as well will you?."

Harry, eagerly, drains his glass and nodding places it on the bar where a grinning Denise takes hold of it. Bert, sadly shakes his head.

"That's right Denise love...Give Harry one as well...Harry.... Harry the Gob....Have one for yourself dear and you'd better not leave Alf out....At least you've managed to keep your sense of humour intact despite all these tragic happenings....Eh?...Eh? Bloody hell...I'll think I've been robbed when I wake up in the morning and take my wallet out from under my pillow....Eh?...Eh?."

Denise is delighted to accept the offer.

"Thanks very much Bert....I'll only have a small gin and tonic with you...I don't fancy ringing for an ambulance at this time of night...It's a real honour and privilege to be present at the annual opening of your wallet....Cheers."

Harry is still slightly concerned about his relationship with Bert. He raises him glass.

"Cheers Bert...A toast to Lancashire's finest policeman bar none."

There is a resounding echo of 'Cheers' from all the group as they happily raise their glasses. Billy waits until there is a pause before he adds.

"Now that is something I haven't heard so cockeyed often in all my many years of drinking in here....Cheers Bert...But I have to admit... Sounds cockeyed good to me....Cheers Bert."

Smiling wryly, Bert nods and raises his glass to them all before he takes a long draught from it. He turns his attention to Harry.

"Anyways....How are things with you Harry?....Still managing to get lots of paying clients for that driving school of yours?...Eh?...Eh?."

Relieved that Bert is obviously not at odds with Him. Harry responds positively and enthusiastically.

"Fine...Yes....Great really Bert....Making a nice comfortable living...That's good enough for me...Mind you there is one bleeding client I would willingly do without."

The others are listening, interested in what Harry is about to reveal to them all.

"Aye...It'sthatnewCurate....Youknow?....JeremyWhatshisname.... You know....Something double barrelled...I've had to deal with some very sorry cases in my many years as a driving instructor Bert but he's got to be the worse prospect I have ever encountered...Ever."

Eric suddenly coughs and almost chokes on his drink at the point. Eddie slaps him on his back. Eric, now looking pale and worried, waves him away, anxious not to miss a word that Harry has to say.

"The man is a bleeding plonker....Completely uncoordinated.... I never thought I would ever see the day when I failed to teach any person under my instruction the basis skills required to drive a motor car but I'm getting desperate with him....I'd need a month of bleeding Sundays and then some more."

Harry shakes his head as an indication that he really is trying to rationalise his situation with Jeremy.

"The pity of it is he's such a nice bloke...Seems to have come from another planet at times....I dare say he's learned a few new words from me over the past few weeks or so...And then to cap it all....Now listen to this...."

Harry is receiving maximum attention from all present, Eric appears to be close to fainting.

"He had the bleeding nerve to bollock me....Yes...He actually.... BOLLOCKED ME!....When he!....HE!....Reversed straight into a bleeding tree....More or less told me it was my bleeding fault....It was my responsibility to watch where he was going....Said it was difficult enough for him to move in a backward motion in the first place...Never mind having to look where he was bleeding well going as well..."

There are grunts of disbelief as Harry adds.

"Honestly....My bleeding car was in Billy Hancock's garage for two whole days and the soft bastard kept ringing up and leaving messages all over the place for me...'When's my next lesson?'.. I should bleeding well coco...I don't think he will ever learn how to drive as long as there's a hole in his arse."

They all laugh, Woody chuckling adds.

"And that's for forty years after you die."

Everyone, except Eric, roars with mirth. He feels that he must speak. His nerves are jangling as he addresses Harry.

"Well you've certainly built up my confidence for our family christening Mr Longfellow...I am definitely going to be shitting myself until Amy's service is over and done with."

Woody scoffs at Eric's remarks.

"Come off it Ricky...What can possibly go wrong at a simple christening ceremony?.."

There are general nods and grunts of agreement but Eric is still far from happy. He makes an impassioned appeal to his Father.

"Bloody hell Dad are you sure you can't persuade Old Reggie to do it for us?."

Appreciating his Son's genuine concern, Bert looks him straight in the eye as he tries to sound as convincing as he possibly can.

"Look Ricky....You know what your trouble is don't you?...Eh?...Eh?...You worry too much....Don't worry....Everything will be alright....You'll see....We'll all be there with you....Won't we boys?."

There is a positive response with shouts of affirmation. Bert continues.

"Do you think for one moment that I would let anything nasty happen to our little Amy....Eh?...Eh?...Come on Ricky....Think about it... You're definitely screaming before you've been hit....Do...Not... Worry."

Bert decides that enough has been said about the impending christening. He is anxious to change the subject. He grins, in a cheeky fashion, as he nudges his Son.

"Anyways let's forget about all that for the time being...Eh?.... And look Ricky....Daddy's glass is all empty and needs filling up with beer....And there is one fact that is beyond any dispute whatsoever.... IT'S NOT MY BLOODY ROUND AGAIN!....Eh?.....Eh?."

Bert grins from ear to ear as Eric shoves his glass forward, indicating to Alf he wants him to set up another round of drinks. Alf springs into immediate action. Billy places his empty glass on the bar before he rounds the conversation off as only he can.

"No....That's true...Not for a cockeyed year or so at the very least."

Eric manages to smile as he pulls out his wallet. Woody and Eddie both slap their young friend on his back, both relieved that he is at last appears to be coming to terms with his unwarranted state of anxiety.

* * *

"I'm sure that was just a slip of the tongue."

There is a tense atmosphere of expectancy, tinged with excitement, in the Vestry/Office at the Parish Church of 'All Souls' at Lapley Vale as the long awaited Sunday morning arrived. The Vicar, Reginald Blackburn is seated behind his desk. The Curate, Jeremy Smith-Eccles is seated on a chair facing him.

Jeremy appears to be a little apprehensive but Reginald is attempting everything in his power to encourage him. Jeremy speaks, unable to hide the tension in his tone.

"Well here it is Reginald....This is it....I have to admit that I do feel somewhat nervous...Yet at the same time I am looking forward with keen anticipation to my first experience in the pulpit delivering the entire sermon by myself....I have rehearsed and prayed and I am confident that my text embraces a little of something that should at the very least be certain to suit all varied tastes and persuasions....But.... I'm sorry Reginald....I am unable to rest at ease with my nerves...I think my present state must have a bearing on the way things have been progressing for me of late....One mishap or accident after another...I fear that I am still woefully short of that essential element of confidence in my own ability."

Reginald has listened patiently. He smiles in a reassuring manner, sounding calm and comforting.

"Jeremy....Jeremy my Boy....You do not have to doubt that I have the utmost confidence in your ability...I have studied your prepared sermon and find it to be of excellent quality and adequate content… Absolutely first class preparation Jeremy…I do mean that most sincerely…So it merely remains your objective to match that up with your delivery this very morning…And then we have the christening of little Baby Amy McCabe for you to attend to after a well deserved luncheon with Sybil and I at the Vicarage….Indeed a wonderful day to look forward to in many respects Jeremy…Sybil is preparing your favourite repast….Roast Duckling with all the trimmings…So pull yourself together and let us all enjoy what will be a most memorable and enjoyable milestone in your blossoming career."

Jeremy is doing his level best to control his emotions but he continues to have, lasting and nagging, doubts. He does appreciate the support Reginald is providing for him.

"Thank you most kindly Reginald and your beloved Wife Sybil also…You are my rod and my staff….I fear that I cannot dismiss from my tormented mind the distinct possibility that something will go dreadfully wrong….I am not at all perturbed by the expected multitude of worshippers in the congregation for the Morning Service and I know to expect a large gathering for the christening of the infant Amy this afternoon….But….I am so sorry Reginald….I really do find great difficulty allowing myself to relax for even a short period of time."

Jeremy clasps his hands together, looks up to the ceiling, praying, silently, under his breath. Reginald leans forward, lowering his tone considerably.

"Jeremy….Look Jeremy."

The Vicar, enthusiastically, opens one of the deep drawers in his desk to reveal an almost empty vodka bottle. Jeremy is unable to immediately appreciate the significance of the bottle. He stares into Reginald's face after he returns the bottle to the drawer, out of sight.

Reginald places his hands in front of him in a praying posture. He clears his throat before explaining.

"Jeremy I have taken the unprecedented step of providing you with some added comfort and support when you are up there in the pulpit delivering your sermon."

The Curate is still unable to understand.

"Yes....Now I know that you are not over fond of alcoholic beverages as a rule Jeremy and hence the significance of vodka.....I am assured that it has little taste and even less smell...Now we must keep this strictly between ourselves and the Lord Jeremy."

Both men glance all around the room in a rather furtive manner before Reginald continues.

"The glass decanter....On the shelf....In the pulpit....Out of sight...."

They look through the open door across the altar area to where the pulpit is situated. Jeremy, suddenly, nods as Reginald carries on with his instruction.

"Has a fluid therein which to all intents and purposes has the outward appearance of common and ordinary water."

Jeremy still cannot fully understood what Reginald has been telling him but he is trying very hard to do so. The Vicar leans forward to say.

"I have exchanged the usual water therein with confidence building vodka."

Jeremy is shocked as he, at last, realises the implications of Reginald's actions. He strains to get a better view of the decanter from his seated position in the Vestry/Office. Because the decanter is placed on a shelf under the top of the pulpit it is difficult for him to see it properly. He is spellbound as Reginald adds, with a hint of craftiness.

"Should you be overcome by an attack of nerves...On what we agree is a most trying occasion for you Jeremy....You can partake of a glass of....Ahem....Water."

Reginald smiles and nods.

"Water?......Water Jeremy?."

The penny suddenly drops. The Curate, enthusiastically, nods his head as Reginald emphasises his strategy.

"I am sure that the....Water....Will help to calm you....Make you more relaxed and enable you to deliver your text in the manner I am certain you are most capable of."

Jeremy's face breaks into a beaming smile. Although he is not quite as confident as to the guaranteed benefits of the tactics on offer as Reginald appears to be, he is, nevertheless, fully cognisant and more than prepared to give it a go.

* * *

The Morning Service has gone exceptionally well. The larger than usual congregation are singing the last line of a hymn which ends with 'Amen'. There is some noise caused by people shuffling around as they sit back on their wooden pews. Silence descends. Reginald smiles and nods to the Curate. Jeremy makes his way across the area in front of the altar towards the raised pulpit. He climbs the steps to place his notes upon the desk top on the open pulpit. He stares down at the assembled congregation, who are gazing back at him in several levels of anticipation. Jeremy appears to be suffering from another attack of nerves as he opens his Bible and notes with a rectified, yet noticeable, fumble.

The congregation are receptive, most are smiling up at him awaiting the delivery of his words of wisdom. He swiftly scans his notes before he glances across the altar to where the Vicar is seated. Reginald smiles at Jeremy in an encouraging fashion urging him to carry on. The Curate looks back at the congregation and pours himself a glass of the water (Vodka).

The sermon starts off very well. Even Reginald is pleasantly surprised with Jeremy's commitment and forcefulness. Unfortunately, as gets further into his sermon, he continues to top up his glass from the decanter. By the time Jeremy, sways, looking flushed with a silly smirk on his face, concludes.

"And here endeth the lesson."

The whole congregation, to a person, appear to be stunned into a state of shock. Jeremy makes a meal out of gathering up his notes and his Bible. The organist, realising that something was amiss, starts playing the introduction to the final hymn. There is no disguising the level of trauma being experienced by most of the congregation as

Jeremy stumbles from the pulpit. There is a loud gasp as he slips on one of the steps, almost falling. He manages to steady himself. He gulps in a deep breath as he stares, aggressively, across the altar, at the door leading into the Vestry/Office. He physically pulls himself together to make a determined dash. Just before he reaches the Vestry/Office doorway, he trips and disappears, accompanied by a number of bangs and thuds. The congregation are still in a deep state of shock as they rise, haphazardly, to their feet for the singing of the hymn.

The Vicar, rising to his feet with as much dignity as he can muster, stares across at the pulpit to see, to his distress, the empty decanter bottle sitting on the shelf. After pausing for a minute or two, allowing the singing to settle down, sounding fairly normal, he, quietly, slips through the Vestry/Office door closing it behind him.

The bleary eyed Curate has managed to crawl across the floor to haul himself into the chair, opposite to the Vicar's chair, across the desk. He smiles in a silly, inane, way, jerking his head, as he becomes aware of Reginald's presence in the room. His speech is slurred as he enquires.

"Now I want you to be honest Reginald….How do you think it went?."

He sits back, grinning, as Reginald takes his seat. The Vicar is acutely aware of the part he has played in the eventual delivery of the sermon and also in the disastrous results.

Reginald chooses his words very carefully, the muted sound of the voices singing can be heard as a background effect.

"Well Jeremy….For your very first sermon….And also bearing in mind the state of apprehension you had got yourself into before the commencement of it….I think you acquitted yourself rather well…Er…In places that is….You certainly delivered your text with conviction and commendable passion."

Reginald's whistling is getting louder and louder as he speaks. Jeremy starts to sway, even though he is sitting down in the chair. He is making foolish little laughing noises. Reginald, coughs as he changes the style of his approach.

"But....Now listen carefully Jeremy....I really must point out one or two things to you by way of constructive criticism...First of all.... And I feel sure you will never need to be reminded of this fact ever... Ever again...There were only ten commandments..."

The Curate is trying desperately hard to hold himself together, listening intently to what his Vicar has to say. He has started to dribble slightly out of the corner of his mouth and he cannot stop himself from giggling.

"Definitely not fifteen as you said...Yes....I fear you did Jeremy... On more than one occasion...And of course we all know that there were twelve disciples....Not a couple of dozen of them..."

The smile is slowly disappearing from Jeremy's face. Reginald is doing his best to be as gentle as he can possibly be.

"I'm sure it was just a slip of the tongue."

Jeremy is now feeling nauseous, struggling to pay his full attention to Reginald. Reginald leans forward to stress the added importance of his next observation.

"And...And....Thirdly....And I really must stress this point Jeremy....Most important of all....The strictest interpretation of the written word is absolutely essential here I fear...."

The Curate is staring into the Vicar's face with his mouth wide open. Reginald takes a very deep breath.

"David slew Goliath....He did not knock his...Ahem...Bleeding head off."

The full implications of what Reginald is relating begin to, very slowly but surely, sink into Jeremy's befuddled mind.

After a few moments he manages to focus his eyes on Reginald's face. He stares at him in a disbelieving, appealing way. The Vicar merely nods his head slowly and clearly indicating in a very positive fashion that he has given a true account of what has been said by Jeremy from the pulpit.

The Curate, horrified, strains to consider all the relevant facts once again but, in doing so, he slides down the chair onto the floor. With obvious concern Reginald leaps to his feet to go to Jeremy's assistance.

The Vicar looks upwards and mumbles a prayer under his breath as he realises that the Curate, still giggling slightly, has now passed out.

* * *

"We always insist on things being done in the traditional way."

Whilst Sunday Morning Worship has been taking place at the Parish Church of 'All Souls', the Clubroom at the Lapley Vale Bowling and Social Club has been a hive of frantic activity.

Alice McCabe and Mavis Green are still working in the kitchen preparing sandwiches. They are surround by a vast array of delicious looking cakes, pies and other party treats. Denise, the Barmaid, joins them carrying a large, heavy, basket fully laden with flowers. She calls out to the two Ladies in a cheery fashion.

"I'm not sure where you want me to put these Ladies....Ricky has just dropped them off...He said he'll be back later...He looks a bit under the weather to me....Probably all the strain of today's events together with a lack of sleep due to head wetting duties...With a few others I could mention."

Mavis, nods, smiling. Alice, who is buttering bread, puts her knife down to stand back to admire the beautiful flowers. Mavis replies.

"Oh aren't the lovely?....Yes....Thank you Denise...Ricky has probably gone back to the house to collect to collect the christening cake and the trifles and what have you...I think it's best if we leave the flowers until we have the tables set up properly...What do you think Alice?..."

Whereas Mavis is a good organiser, a willing and able helper, she is always very careful not to give anyone the impression that she is too domineering to others.

Alice smiles, making some room on the large kitchen table for Denise to put the basket down. She replies chirpily.

"Oh yes I agree Mavis....I reckon we can leave those until the last....There's no point in us doing the flowers until we have the run of the Clubroom....I hope Alf manages to chase the regulars out on time for a pleasant change....He said he would...There's still lots to do yet....The last thing I want is for us to be late at the Church...That would be unforgivable on such a special day....So we all need to get stuck in as soon as possible."

She turns to Denise.

"Thanks Denise love....Just leave them for now....I hope our Ricky manages to pull himself together before we get to the Church...I don't know what's been bothering him lately but I'm his Mother and I can tell he's worrying or sickening for something..."

Denise glances at her wristwatch.

"Hecky thump....It's ten to one....What else can I do to help Ladies?..."

They look at each other, smiling and shaking their heads. Mavis speaks.

"Bless you Denise love....I can't think of anything outstanding at this moment in time....The butties are about done and all the other bits and pieces are well under control...Ricky's on schedule....What do you say Alice?."

Alice thinks for a moment before she shakes her head. Mavis continues.

"What we could really do with is getting all those tables set up so we can transfer the bulk of this stuff into the Clubroom...See if you can use your influence to make sure that Alf hasn't forgotten that time is of the essence today."

Denise nods, she is delighted to be included in the preparation and is really looking forward to the celebrations. Mavis adds, with acquired foresight.

"There's no point in putting any food out there just yet....Those hungry devils at the bar would easily demolish everything in their sight before we arrive back from the Church if we did."

They chuckle. Denise agrees.

"You're right there Mavis....Still no problems today because I'm going to stay on the premises after Alf kicks them all out...So you can rest assured that I'll be keeping a close watch on everything...It's no trouble to me....Honestly....I'd like to go up to the Church but it's been so long since I graced the inside of a Church I'd feel completely out of place...Not to mention there would probably be an unexpected streak of lightening through the stained glass windows if I dared to show my face."

They enjoy a good laugh as Denise continues.

"Anyways it's a sure way of putting all your minds at ease and I'm delighted I'm able to be useful for a change....I know how much Alf is looking forward to the ceremony...I've volunteered only on one condition though...I get to have a little cuddle of Amy when you all get back here....I'll make sure I'm available when the time comes for my turn even though I do realise that we will be very busy behind that bar serving all the drinks this afternoon."

Smiling, from ear to ear, Ralph, the Chairman, walks into the kitchen. He manages to give Denise a crafty little pinch on her bottom as he nods to greet the other Ladies. Denise emits a little scream and playfully pushes Ralph away from her. Ralph immediately realises that he was rather foolish to 'Goose' Denise with other Ladies present. To cover any embarrassment he quickly relates some good news to them.

"Oh there you are Ladies....I've got a couple of the Lads outside.... We wondered if it would help if we put the table up...Just say the word and you wish shall be granted...In a flash."

Although slightly shocked by Ralph's indiscretion with Denise the two Ladies are delighted at his thoughtfulness. Mavis responds positively.

"Well thank you kindly Mr Chairman....We were just discussing that very same subject...You must be a mind reader...Yes thank you very much."

Mavis turns to Alice before she adds.

"Would you like to show them where you want the tables putting Alice dear."

Wiping her hands on the sides of her apron, Alice is happy to react instantly.

"Yes...Thank you Ralph love....How thoughtful."

She walks towards the door as she addresses Denise.

"Denise love....Can you help Mavis with the tablecloths please....I just hope we've got enough to cover all the tables we are going to need today."

As Alice is leaving the kitchen she is met by her son Eric. Eric, looking under extreme pressure, is carrying a large cardboard box. He dashes straight into the kitchen where Mavis swiftly lifts the basket of flowers off the table so he can put the box down. Eric gently places the box on the table and stands back. He takes in a deep breath and blows the air out between his clenched teeth. He wipes the sweat off his brow with the sleeve of his jacket. He sounds quite exhausted.

"Bloody hell fire....I don't know what that cake is made of... Concrete by the weight of it."

Mavis chuckles, pretending to scold him.

"Now then cheeky....I'll have you know only the very finest ingredients...Made with loving care by Nan Dawes and myself....I bet you won't be complaining when your stuffing your face with it later on."

They smile as Mavis enquires.

"Have you seen Woody on your travels Ricky?."

Eric has pinched one of the sandwiches, causing him to splutter his reply through a mouthful of food.

"Yes Mavis…I think you'll find him at his usual place at the bar by now….He's just come in from the Bowling Green…They put him on first with Billy and Eddie so they could get their games over and done with early…You know….Because of the christening?."

Although she is pleased to have located her Husband, Mavis is not too happy to be told that he is at the bar. She cannot hide her concern.

"Oh dear….I hope he doesn't drink too much….We don't want to make a show of ourselves at the Church….I don't think he could be that daft….I think I'll be wise and keep a watchful eye on him just the same."

Eric leaves the kitchen, walking across to the bar where he joins Woody and Eddie. They are each downing a pint of beer with, unashamed, relish. Norman is perched on his usual stool. Woody wipes his mouth with the back of his hand before he speaks.

"By Christ I needed that….My gob's like a suede purse."

Eddie nods his agreement as he puts his glass down after a long drink. Woody glances around the room.

"Where old Billy Cockeye?."

They all look around.

"He can't be too far behind us Eddie…He was giving Arnie Brooks a right pasting when I finished my game."

Woody is taking another welcome drink as Billy and Arnie enter the room. Billy is looking pleased with himself but Arnie appears to be, somewhat, deflated. Billy shouts to Alf.

"Two pints please Alf….I'll see to these Arnie."

Arnie steps forward. He sounds determined.

"No you won't Billy….I know the rules….Loser pays."

Arnie shakes his head sadly as he remarks with a tinge of bitterness in his tone.

"Bloody hell Billy….I've never seen you play that well before…. Christ….21-4…That's the worse going over you've ever given me in all the years we been playing each other on that Green."

Alf places two frothing pints on the bar. Arnie insists on paying. Billy lifts up his pint to remark, rather arrogantly.

"I'm sorry about that Arnie....I couldn't mess about with you today....I've got a very important appointment this afternoon...The christening service of my first...."

He pauses to make sure as many people as possible can hear him say, with great pride.

"GREAT!....Get that....Great.....Great Granddaughter...So I'm sorry...But pressing priorities dictated that you had to be on the end of a cockeyed hammering...And no dilly dally on the way."

Billy glances all around to see if any person present has been impressed by his statement before he takes a long drink from his glass. Returning his glass to the bar, he turns to Arnie, now he speaks in a much lower tone.

"Incidentally Arnie....That operation you had done on your hooter....It hasn't done anything to improve your cockeyed bowling."

Arnie strokes his nose in a self conscious way as the others stifle their amusement. Billy nudges Arnie, teasing him.

"Now now Arnie no sulking....Don't be a cockeyed Baby."

Billy drains his glass. He shoves it forward as he shouts to Alf behind the bar.

"Same again Alf....If you please."

Smiling, Billy slaps Arnie on the back in a, false, friendly gesture. Although he is not enjoying the proceedings Arnie manages to drain his glass and hand it to Billy. Billy has still not finished pulling Arnie's leg.

"There you go now....We don't want to have to ask Alf to put a cockeyed dummy tit in your mouth do we?."

Alf takes hold of their empty glass. He feels that a word of warning might be necessary.

"Far be it for me to be a spoilsport Billy but don't you think you should take things a bit steady in the circumstances."

They are all momentarily stunned as Alf adds.

"I mean to say….I don't think for one minute that your Missus…. Or the rest of the crowd will be too impressed if the…GREAT!....Great Grandfather turns up at the Church pissed as a fart….Know what I mean?."

There is immediate realisation that Alf is giving out sound and sensible advice. Eric stares at his half empty glass before he pushes it away, slightly. Eddie is first to respond.

"Alf is correct….As usual….And my Missus will have my guts for garters if I don't get myself home very soon…What say you Woody?."

Although he was initially angry, Woody accepts that Alf is thinking of their general well being and not trying to spoil their enjoyment of a drink after a game on the Green. After thinking for a few seconds he nods his head before speaking.

"Aye….I'm afraid Alfred has a valid point to make there…As Eddie has already pointed out to us all….He is quite correct…We certainly don't want to give the wrong impressions of ourselves…Specially not in the House of God."

Everyone reluctantly agrees. Woody continues.

"Still no harm in taking one for the road."

He has the full backing of all his friends as he calls out to Alf.

"We all agree with you Oh Mighty Mouth…Could we please just have one for the road and then we promise we will bugger off home and put our best frocks on….Eh?."

All the glasses are shoved forward in formation style. Alf shakes his head and smiles as he starts refilling them. Alf is about half way through filling the first glass when Woody notices Mavis. She is standing in the doorway of the kitchen with her arms folded, tightly, across her chest. She looks far from impressed. His first reaction is to duck down but he realises that he cannot hide from her. He smiles, calling to her.

"Hello Mavis love…Are you nearly ready Dear?...Now do come along there's little time to waste."

A frothing pint of beer is placed on the bar in front of him. Woody spares no time raising it to his lips to take the top of it. As he is doing so he notices Mavis as she throws her head back in a haughty manner.

She turns on her heels and disappears into the kitchen, out of his sight. He is instantly alarmed.

"Oh shit!....Hell fire...Come on Boys...Bottoms up."

They are all drinking as fast as they can. Woody puts his glass down for a moment to speak.

"There's one consolation...."

He takes another long drink.

"At least we are coming back here for more of the same after the ceremony....So there's something else we have to look forward to.... Eh?."

Norman joins the conversation.

"Thank goodness I never associate myself with any of these tea total type families...Life must be rather dull and boring for them mustn't it?."

Billy nudges Eric as he finishes his pint. He nods In the direction of the door.

"You can say that again Norm....We always insist on things being done in the traditional manner....And no cockeyed messing...Now come on Ricky before I have to get nasty and frogmarch you out of this cockeyed establishment."

The happy band vacate the bar comforted in the knowledge that they will be returning, very soon, to continue where they have left off.

* * *

"Thank you............Thank you...."

The family are gathered at Eric and Jenny's home. Everyone is dressed in their best clothes. Baby Amy had been wrapped in the family christening robe as soon as she had finished her feed. Billy Dawes is sulking because he has been chastised, in front of everyone, by Nan for returning home from the Bowling Club smelling, strongly, of beer. Eric has received a more tactful caution from Jenny for the same reason.

Bert McCabe has just arrived to take Eric, Jenny and Amy up to the Church. They are ready to go but are awaiting the arrival of Alf in his car. Alf is collecting Woody and Mavis on his way to the house to pick up Billy and Nan.

Bert is feeling quite pleased with himself. He is aware that Eric and Billy have been chastised for offences against the drinking before you go to church act. He has not had the opportunity to have a pint at all and is, absolutely, cold sober. The reason for his unusual state is explained by the fact that Bert had driven over to the other side of Oldham to pick up his very elderly Aunty Ibby. Aunt Ibby is the elder statesperson of the entire McCabe family. She is now in her late eighties and has become rather frail and in need of personal attention whenever she needs to move around. She is very popular and well loved by all of those in the family circle. This is not just because she is confidently considered to be quite rich, she is also a very pleasant, kind and loving old Lady. Aunt Ibby had been left at Bert's house having a cup of tea and a chat with Alice.

Unable to prevent himself from tormenting poor Eric and Billy, Bert enjoys being blatantly hypocritical as he remarks.

"Dear me....I cannot understand how it is that some people are unable to leave the ale alone even though they are well aware that they are required to be at their best....I fear that some weaker persons are slaves to the dreaded hops....Why can't they be more responsible?....Like me?....Eh?...Eh?."

Billy, quickly, checks that he is out of Nan's hearing range before he snarls.

"Shut up Bert....It's a cockeyed miracle that you haven't managed to get yourself a pint or two....Play your cards right and they might even make you into a cockeyed Saint whilst you're up at the cockeyed Church."

Bert roars with laughter.

Before the Ladies can enquire into the source of Bert's obvious mirth, Alf pulls up outside in his Ford Cortina saloon car. A very smart looking trio emerge from the vehicle. Today is the second occasion in a very short space of time that Woody has worn a suit, shirt, collar and tie. Mavis is delightful wearing a neat and dressy two piece suit with a matching wide brimmed hat. Alf is wearing the new suit he bought to wear at the double wedding celebrations for the second time. There is a very strong smell of moth balls coming from Alf's vicinity.

Eric, who is clearly not at his best, opens the front door for them. Unbeknown to those present, Eric is not sulking because he has been warned about drinking, he is worried, near to death, about the impending prospects of Jeremy, The Curate, being in extremely close proximity to his little daughter.

Jenny comes down the stairs, fixing her small hat to her head with a large pin. She looks terrific wearing a blue and white dress with the matching feathered hat. She smiles, proudly and contentedly as she checks that Amy is fast asleep inside her carry cot. Bert rubs his hands together with a false air of urgency.

"Right...Come along now....Let's get this show on the road...All set everyone?...Eh?...Eh?."

Billy rises to his feet. He nods to Woody, who is rather subdued, having suffered the same fate as Billy and Eric when he arrived home from the Club. Alf calls out.

"Right come on then…Billy you'll have to travel in the back with girls…We might have difficulty fitting the Great Grandfather's head in but Woody and I will do our best…Eh?."

Alf smiles at Woody but he chooses to ignore him. They all move outside, Alf shouts to Bert.

"Right we'll see you in Church then."

They are chuckling as they clamber into the vehicles. Just prior to boarding Nan takes Billy to one side for a moment. She whispers something in his ear and then gives him a playful belt with her handbag. Everyone travelling in Alf's car appreciates that Billy was being warned to control any sort of flatulence inside the confined area of the car and they are grateful to Nan for that.

Bert makes sure the doors on his car are open before Eric and Jenny come out of the house. Eric locks the door and takes the carry cot from Jenny. She realises that Eric is not himself. She smiles, rubbing his cheek with her hand.

"Come on Daddy….Give your face a treat….Smile….It isn't everyday that you take your daughter to her christening you know?…. I hope you're not having a little sulk because Mummy told you off are you?."

Eric merely smiles weakly as they climb aboard Bert's car for the short journey up to the Church.

They arrive at the Church in good time. Kay Brown, Jenny's friend and other Godmother runs across to Bert's car anxious to get a glimpse of Amy in her cot before they have to enter the Church. Bert makes sure Eric, Jenny and the baby are clear before he drives off to collect Alice and Aunty Ibby.

Kay is cooing and swooning over, the still fast asleep, Amy as they are joined by her Granddad and Grandmother, Eddie Brown and his wife, and little Norman Smith. Ralph, Victor and Bernie are all present with their wives. They make a pretty picture as they stand chatting with

Alf, Billy and Nan, all dressed in the finery. Each person there appears to be enjoying every minute of the experience with the exception of Eric.

The Verger, Dave Knox, wearing a full length cassock, emerges from the Church. He is looking all around with an air of urgency evident in his demeanour. He approaches Eric and his group to make an enquiry.

"Excuse me....Has Bert arrived yet?."

Jenny replies, politely.

"Not just yet Mr Knox...He's just nipped back to the house to collect Mum and Aunty Ibby...He won't be long."

This answer does not appear to suit Dave Knox. He seems quite frustrated, anxious. He suddenly recognises Eric. He grabs hold of his arm, taking him to one side. He speaks in hushed tones.

"Hello Ricky...Listen....I don't want you to worry but there's been a slight problem....Believe me everything will be alright but the Vicar needs to have a quick word with your Dad...As he isn't here at the moment you'll have to do....Can you just pop along with me for a minute or two please Ricky?."

Eric is puzzled but he follows Dave into the Church.

Reginald Blackburn, the Vicar, is standing inside the Church entrance, which is at the opposite end to the Altar. He notices Dave with Eric and smiles, rather nervously. He shakes hands with, the now perplexed appearing, Eric.

"Look I am awfully sorry Eric....But I'm afraid the Curate has been....Well shall we say...Taken quite ill....I have had to transport him to his home and place him in his bed....But...Please...Let me assure you that everything will be fine...I will stand in for Jeremy and christen your little Amy myself...I have everything ready for you now...If you would like to summon your party to join me inside."

Reginald smiles politely but is somewhat bewildered by Eric's reactions to the enforced alteration to the arrangements. Eric is obviously elated. He finds he cannot speak but there is an enthusiastic expression written all across his face. He grabs Reginald's hand and shakes it very vigorously.

Eric, briefly, turns to look towards the Altar. He clasps his hands together, glancing up to the sky as he mutters, under his breath.

"Thank you.......Thank you."

Jenny wonders what kind of a transformation had caused her Husband's attitude to change so suddenly from being tense and detached to being almost ecstatically happy. Nevertheless, she is very thankful as she sees Eric gleefully urging all the guests to enter the Church, wearing the broadest smile she had seen on his face for a number of weeks recently.

THE END

Now you have enjoyed your first encounter with the good Folks of Lapley Vale start looking forward to treating yourself to reading the sequel to this book, entitled, *Still Swinging*. Re-join all the characters you have enjoyed meeting. Relax, forget about any worries you might have, allow them to make you laugh again. There are a few new personalities for you to meet as well.

R.T. Cain has also written a book about the, fiction based on fact adventures, experiences and the life and times of a young Police Officer from the same era. This fascinating, interesting, sometimes funny, often hilarious, chronicle of the experiences and steady progress of a young Constable who eventually rises through the ranks. Early in the story he finds himself transferred to Lapley Vale from elite 'Z' Car duties after his urgently arranged marriage. The Novel is entitled, *Boydie*. Sergeant Bert McCabe and many of the citizens you have already met from Lapley Vale appear in this story of real life policing in the 1960's.